The Unlikely Heroics of Sam Holloway

Rhys Thomas lives in Cardiff with his partner Amy (a fellow writer) and three cats – Aniseed, Sheldon and Henry VIII. *The Unlikely Heroics of Sam Holloway* is his third novel.

Praise for Rhys Thomas and his novels:

'A riveting and often moving read ... This is the best of its type that I've read in a long while. I'll be very interested to see what Thomas writes next' – John Boyne, author of *The Boy in the Striped Pyjamas*

'Rhys Thomas shakes concepts of "normality" to the core. It is a challenge indeed for an author to capture authentic teenage dialogue, and [this is] compelling subject matter' – *Independent on Sunday*

'Thomas effectively details the breakdown of established codes of behaviour and the depths of depravity to which humanity can sink ... Gripping' – *Guardian*

'*The Unlikely Heroics of Sam Holloway* is a joy to read. Rhys Thomas has managed to take everything I like about literary fiction and put it into one book: humor, humanity, action, and redemption. If I'm being 100% honest, I'm actually a little mad at the guy. I wish I'd written this one myself." – Matthew Norman, author of *We're All Damaged* and *Domestic Violets*

The Unlikely Heroics of Sam Holloway

RHYS THOMAS

WILDFIRE

First published in 2018 by
WILDFIRE
An imprint of HEADLINE PUBLISHING GROUP

First published in paperback in 2018 by
WILDFIRE
An imprint of HEADLINE PUBLISHING GROUP

1

Cataloguing in Publication Data is available from the British Library

ISBN 978 1 4722 4814 5

Typeset in 11/13.5 pt Sabon. Phantasm chapters set in 10.5/13.5 pt
Zapf Elliptical 711 BT by Jouve (UK), Milton Keynes

Printed and bound in Great Britain by CPI Group (UK) Ltd, Croydon, CR0 4YY

Headline's policy is to use papers that are natural, renewable and recyclable
products and made from wood grown in sustainable forests. The logging
and manufacturing processes are expected to conform to the environmental
regulations of the country of origin.

HEADLINE PUBLISHING GROUP
An Hachette UK Company
Carmelite House
50 Victoria Embankment
London EC4Y 0DZ

www.headline.co.uk
www.hachette.co.uk

for Amy

Ⓟ

The Phantasm #001

A New Threat

Only in darkness can a hero be born. An ordinary street, late at night, the land dyed orange by street light. The first cold of winter puts a bite in the air. Litter swept by wind, shuttered shops and a silent crossroads, parked cars already condensing a veneer of frost. Overhead billions of years' worth of stars shine on.

A movement of the shadows across the bushes near the entrance to the train station. Yet not a shadow: a man, unseen by the world, a guardian watching the streets. In silence he waits. If crime never takes a day off then neither does he. A mask covers his head and the top half of his face. Body armour protects his thorax and shoulders. The utility belt strapped to an assault vest houses all the equipment any superhero might need.

A mist has spread. It's too cold for most, but hidden in the bushes he lies in wait. His uniform is a camouflage; he fuses with the shadows to become imperceptible. His breathing low, he squints into the middle distance. A train pulls into the station, passengers climb off, scurry away to their safe homes. From his utility belt he takes a Toffee Crisp. It tastes good and he washes it down with some delicious Cherry Coke. Two of his favourites. There used to be a chocolate bar called Spira that he enjoyed with Cherry Coke but low sales ensured its demise. What this dark hero would give for Cadbury to resurrect their masterpiece. Loss is often a hole.

The train pulls away into the night. He can feel its rumble through his body and adjusts his position to get a clear view of the station entrance.

A superhero in the twenty-first century must be patient. Old-fashioned crime is rarer than it was, but it still happens. Rumours are the scent a hero must catch. Hoodlums hanging around the station, throwing stones at passing trains, abusing passengers. He'd heard about it at the grocery store; all those patrons going about their weekly shop unaware they were in the presence of a silent guardian. Bag up your brown rice, old lady, don't forget your change now. Safe journey. And thanks for the intel.

And here he is now, waiting for his prey. Why do people do this? Why throw rocks at a train? Countless people could be killed. These punks lost their shot at mercy the minute they decided to operate outside the laws of the land. Whatever retribution is dealt to them from the slamming fist of justice they must accept with no quarrel. If the hand wavers, the kingdom falls. What these punks need is a shock, a jolt to guide them back on to the right tracks.

Broken homes, ADHD, the Internet, domestic abuse, poverty, the death of community; people are still responsible for their actions.

Ah, here they come.

Six of them. No, seven. Aged fourteen to sixteen at a guess. They're wiry, though given substance by voluminous tracksuits and anoraks. Their tracksuit trousers have elasticated bottoms; they look ridiculous.

Our hero in the dark waits. Waits and watches. The youths saunter down to the entrance of the station and the guardian checks the view on the video camera. It's switched to night vision and is recording everything.

The boys lean against the fence. One of them spits. So far they are within the law and safe. But it won't be long. He knows this, just as he knows the sun will rise in the east. He used to

2

get this fact confused, mixed up east and west, but now there is no such doubt. He is completely clear on the fact, just as he is clear that if he waits here he will see these youths transgress the societal contract.

Maybe a part of him wishes they would do it. There is a rage burning inside him like a coal seam on fire; a thousand-year-old furnace. This is his release.

In the distance the sound of an approaching train, a freight train hauling the stuff of industry; our lone saviour knows no passenger services are due until ten forty-seven. The youths snap their heads round in the direction of the sound. Meerkats. An unspoken organisation becomes apparent.

They gather rocks from the pile of rubble left at the side of the road by some unsuspecting construction worker. Then the boys move silently into the station and ascend the footbridge until they are directly over the tracks.

The avenger moves from his hiding place. To the boys he would appear as just a shadow shifting over the land. If they saw him. They won't see him. Until it's too late.

Now he must make a decision: does he act before they throw the rocks? Right at this moment an innocent train driver, a man keeping the economic cogs of the world turning, is heading blindly into a trap. Why should he have to go through this? The rocks will be thrown; they are already in miscreant hands. And so there really is no decision. He must act.

He enters the station, silent as a rock passing through the infinity of deep space. He can hear the excited chatter of the boys as they crouch below the level of the bridge so the driver can't see them. But in turn they are blind to the thing that hunts them. He moves up the steps and reaches into his utility belt, unclips a small glass globe of chemicals.

The train is coming closer. The sound of the boys' laughter is merging with the tumult of the engine. His heart is beating fast in its webbing and he closes his eyes. Forget the police; they've got bigger fish to fry. Sometimes the only hands into which matters can be taken are those of a champion. And he is that champion. He is a hero.

He thinks of all the good things in the world. They *are* worth defending.

He pounces.

'AAAARGH!' he shouts at the top of his voice and, without hesitation, he throws the globe of chemicals. It smashes against the ground and thick smoke billows out. The boys don't move because they can't see.

The shadow moves through them; fast, light. He is ready for attack. Now!

'THERE HAVE BEEN REPORTS OF ANTISOCIAL BEHAVIOUR IN THIS AREA. IT'S AFFECTING THE VICTIMS AND THE PEOPLE WHO LIVE NEARBY, WHO HEAR YOU SHOUTING AND SWEARING! DESIST, OR I WILL COMPILE A FILE OF EVIDENCE AND PRESENT IT TO THE AUTHORITIES! THIS IS—' He coughs. Dammit. There's more smoke than he expected. This won't help his asthma. Would they understand him if he was wearing a gas mask, though? He wipes his eyes. 'THIS IS . . . your last warning!'

And then, just a mountain breeze through a gully, he is gone. He coughs and his eyes are streaming as he tumbles down the steps. The boys are not following him. He slips and falls.

'What *is* that?'

He spies through blurry eyes one of the boys gazing down at him from the top of the steps. He must be strong now. He leaps to his feet in an athletic thrust.

'Know me!' he manages. 'I am . . . the PHANTASM!'

And then, through the smoke, justice served for another night, the freight train moving safely into the distance, he is running, running into the shadows, the lanes, the alleys, the places we don't see, heading courageously for his next exciting adventure.

Chapter One

The October sunlight slicing through the windows behind the sink, that season-change vigour in the air, he stood in his beautifully finished kitchen and thought to himself, this is OK. I can live like this quite happily for ever.

The house was desperately quiet, but Sam never noticed the despair.

Two slices of hand-cut wholemeal toast covered in scrambled eggs topped with baked beans. He was a big believer in not rushing beans. When preparing a meal he always put them on first, brought them to the boil and let them simmer on a low heat while he cooked everything else. That way the beans went soft and the tomato sauce thick. People rushed beans, just got them hot and ate them. But there is an art to everything in life, even beans.

On the first morning of a week-long stretch of annual leave Sam liked to do nothing more than spend a few moments just enjoying his house. It was a lovely house and it made him feel exceptionally comfortable. As the beans softened he took in the neatness of the kitchen, the clutter-free surfaces, the breakfast bar and the oak table and chairs, the matching toaster and kettle, the shiny chrome microwave, the spotlights set into the plasterwork of the ceiling. Everything nice and simple. *Simplicity is the fuel of the soul*, his father once said.

Sam lived alone in a semi-detached house on a housing

estate less than ten years old. His front garden had a small, well-kept square of lawn, some shrubs growing in a border along one side, and a pristine black driveway. It didn't look like the house of a 26-year-old man.

In the living room he had his CDs and DVDs and Blu-rays in order, had his entertainment system comprising an HD TV, Blu-ray player, Xbox, Chromecast, hi-fi and even a video player, all the wires neatly hidden away.

He went to work at a job with a low level of responsibility, which he could put at the back of his mind at the end of each day, saved a little money each month, had two spare rooms for an office and a library, a conservatory for reading and relaxing, and a spacious back garden with a pond at the far end. And of course he pulled on the mask and costume of the Phantasm and diligently fought crime three nights a week. That these things made him contented because they papered over the cataclysmic vortex of loneliness that threatened to pull him apart in the darkest stretches of the night was nei-ther here nor there.

He stared at the beans and listened to the unique silence a house makes on a nondescript Monday morning when the rest of the world has gone to work.

The sea. The open fetch, the roll and swell. Sam loved the ocean, and on the first day of his annual leave routine he always drove out to the coast. There was a little café he liked, hun-kered down into the cliff with big windows, where he could empty his mind completely, sit and stare out at the water for an hour or two with a steaming pot of tea and a custard slice.

But before that he needed to pick up some supplies, so he stopped off on the high street of his little hometown for some chocolate and a bottle of Cherry Coke. His phone buzzed in his pocket. A sick dread crashed through him, thinking it might be work asking him to come in. But it wasn't. It was a message from his friend, Tango.

Pub tomorrow?

Sam pocketed the phone and felt annoyed at having his routine disturbed. He didn't want to go to the pub. He stood on the pavement for a moment and let the cold air press into his face.

'Give me some money.'

Standing in front of him suddenly was a female homeless person. She was short and a little dumpy, shoulders slumped forward, probably late-forties with thick, frizzy black hair.

'I'm sorry?' said Sam.

She fixed him with a stare of extraordinary power.

'Give me some money.' The aggressive demand was tempered by the softness of her voice, the quiet pitch of it, the gentle lilt of an Irish accent.

'Erm,' he said, fishing in his pocket and landing on a fifty-pence piece. 'Here you go.'

The female homeless person stared at the coin, took it, and shoved it into the pocket of her coat, the hem of which was caked in dry mud.

'Buy me a sandwich,' she said.

'Excuse me?'

'Buy me a sandwich there.'

'I just gave you fifty pee.' Sam already donated plenty of money to various charities and felt a little affronted at what he thought were slightly excessive demands. 'Can't you just ask someone else? If you get a few more fifty pees you can get a sandwich.'

'Buy me a sandwich.'

'No.'

'Yes.'

'No.'

'Please.'

'No,' he said, finally.

'Come on. Just there,' and she nodded towards a bakery a few doors down. Her voice was so gentle, like a breeze blowing through the canopies of a thousand-year-old cedar forest in a Nepalese valley, and Sam suddenly found himself walking down the street with her. Well, there but for the grace of God go I, he consoled himself. I'm being kind, not mugged.

'So what's your name?' he said, glancing across at her.

She walked with purpose towards the bakery, hands thrust in her pockets, her gaze fixed steadfastly straight ahead.

'Gloria,' she said. 'You?'

'Sam.'

'I like Samuel as a name,' she said, distractedly, her voice coming in and out on the wind.

'My name's Samson actually. It was my great-grandfather's name. Where are you from?'

'Cork.'

'I like Ireland,' he said.

'It's shit,' she said.

They reached the bakery and Sam held open the door for Gloria, who moved past him hungrily, heading not for the bank of sandwiches but the drinks. She put her hand on a can of Sanpellegrino.

Those are quite expensive, Sam thought to himself. It was those pieces of foil on the top. But then Gloria's hand drifted away to the Cokes, which were more reasonably priced. That's better, he thought. Not that he'd agreed to buy a drink, not that he'd even given verbal consent that he would buy her a sandwich. At the last moment her hand swept away from the Cokes and up to the fresh smoothies shelf, where she selected orange and mango. This was priced at £2.65.

Beverage chosen, she moved on to the next stand.

'Have they got any soup?' she wondered aloud.

'I don't think they do soup.'

'Ah,' she said, forlorn. 'I guess I'll just have a sandwich then,' before lifting from the shelf not a sandwich but a large baguette. Turning, and not looking at Sam, Gloria made her way to the counter.

'My husband died a year ago,' she said. 'Fell down of a heart attack.'

The words drifted into Sam and amplified the sense of sorrow that had grown in him towards her.

'I'm really sorry to hear that,' he said.

The immediate thoughts of his own experiences of life tugged at him. He quickly went into default mode and cleared them away with little fuss, the cool numbness releasing itself into his body.

Gloria veered to the centre of the shop, where a small island with bags of miniature pasties stood, and she helped herself to one. Sam tried to tot up how much this was all going to cost as Gloria then grabbed a packet of cheese and onion crisps.

The shop assistant smiled at her.

'Are you eating in or taking away?' she said.

Sam noticed a couple of chairs and tables against the wall. They charged extra for . . .

'Eating in,' Gloria announced.

Detecting that she was a homeless person and that Sam was her patron, the assistant glanced across to him.

'Eating in,' he echoed.

'And I'll have a coffee please, love. Americano. Black,' Gloria said.

Again the assistant looked at Sam. Gloria surveyed the doughnuts in the glass-fronted cake display on the counter.

'Anything she wants!' he said. 'Get her anything she wants!'

'Small, regular or large?' the assistant asked.

Sam grimaced but Gloria suddenly conceded. 'I'll just have a regular,' she said, and wandered off to the little shelf next to the counter where they kept the sugars, leaving Sam to pay.

'You sure you're OK with this?' the assistant said.

Gloria was stuffing sugar sachets into her pockets.

'Yeah. Stick a couple of doughnuts in there too,' he said.

The assistant shrugged and Sam paid.

'OK, well, I'm going to go now,' Sam called to Gloria, who was pouring copious amounts of sugar into her coffee.

She didn't even look up.

'It was nice to meet you,' he said.

But Gloria was no longer interested in him.

He turned to leave and almost bumped into a girl behind him. 'Oops, sorry,' he said.

The girl smiled. She had dyed red hair and glasses and had clearly been listening to the exchange, because she gave him a big smile.

His heart thumped with the shock of her prettiness, his face turned beetroot, and he left the shop.

The Phantasm #002

A Hero Acts

This is *the* moment he has trained for. For many months he has patrolled the night and, at last, his vigilance has paid off. This is the real deal, the big cahoney. He is watching a burglary in progress. The house alarm alerted him to the crime, and now, from the eaves of a grand old oak tree, the hero records the event in crisp HD.

The pair of thugs at the back of the house act fast. A window has been smashed and one man, wearing a bobble hat, is outside, while his friend inside, shaved head, passes through a laptop before clambering out.

They hightail it over the back fence, passing the laptop again like a baton in a relay race, and sprint off down the street.

The hero follows. He jumps fifteen feet from his elevated position to the communal lawn below, bends his knees on impact, and manoeuvres into an Olympic-standard roly-poly. And he's off.

His bicycle is propped up against the tree trunk and he's on it within seconds, powering down the street after the targets in perfect silence. He can't believe this is happening, but it is.

Just as a fish swims calmly along in the warm ocean, unaware of the circling shark, so Bobble Hat and Shaved reach their car and calmly put the laptop on the back seat.

The hero stops. First and foremost, get the registration

number. It's a beat-up piece of scrap that makes a loud noise as the key is turned, and though they might get away this evening, they will be paid a visit by the boys in blue tomorrow. The camera is still recording.

The Phantasm watches the car pull into the road, his work done. But then he thinks: the laptop. What if they offload it before morning? The poor people will have lost their computer, probably along with many irreplaceable photos and files. Yes, among the doughnuts and coffee the police do fantastic work, but how often do they actually get stolen goods returned?

He kicks off down the street, making a quick decision, and is in hot pursuit of the car. It's late, the roads are empty, their tail lights are easy to follow up the main street of town. His bike is no match for the power of a car, but perhaps the nation's traffic lights will lend a hand.

They do. Rounding a bend, he sees the car is waiting, exhaust fumes spewing into the cold night. Legs moving like pistons, he hammers towards the car. He's not exactly sure what he's about to do.

The lights are changing.

Amber.

He speeds up, the car revs.

Green!

The car pulls away, but now the hero is alongside it. Shaved glances out the window and looks away. Then looks back again. Yes, you saw right, my good man, a superhero is here to bring you to justice. The car accelerates and is about to get away. In an instant the Phantasm veers the bicycle towards the metal beast and, using all his force, boots the driver's door as hard as he can, putting a dent in it. He wobbles under the force of the blow but somehow – possibly through some preternatural balance superpower hitherto unknown – he rights himself.

The car screeches to a halt.

Uh-oh.

The driver's door swings open hard and Shaved is on the street. And he is exceptionally angry. He is shouting. The Phantasm puts some distance between him and the car. Bobble Hat is out now too.

'Give me the laptop,' demands the gladiator of the night.

'You're gonna fucking pay for my car, you little prick.'

'OK, OK,' he says, dismounting the bicycle and laying it on the blacktop. 'How much do you want?'

'Why the fuck you dressed like that?'

The anger seems to have lessened momentarily, overtaken by bewilderment.

'I have damaged your car. It is only fair that I reimburse you. How much?'

'Hundred quid.'

'Seems pricey, but I accept.'

He goes into his utility belt. Bobble Hat joins Shaved and they both lean in to see the thing the superhero is withdrawing from his belt. But it is not money. It is just the middle finger of his glove, which he holds aloft before them. There is a moment, as they comprehend this display of bravado, before they pounce. The hero steps back, quick as a flash, swivels on his right foot, bringing his left leg round in a pirouetting 360 – he has attempted a high-angle karate kick. He misses them both, his standing leg slips, and he falls to the pavement.

In the distance the sound of the burglar alarm rings on.

'Come on, man, let's just go,' he hears Bobble Hat plead. 'The cops will be here any second.'

But Shaved is not interested. He has grabbed the Phantasm's foot, but the avenger kicks at Shaved's hands repeatedly and gets free. He jumps to his feet but Shaved lunges at him. He is tall and skinny, with an intense, wiry strength.

'I'm gonna fuck you up,' he whispers.

Bobble Hat is coming round to the front and is lining up to

kick him in the face. He ducks his head down as the stamp arrives but he feels nothing, for his mask is also a protection, especially at the top of the skull.

The hero grabs Bobble Hat's ankle and yanks. The icy road is slippery enough for Bobble Hat to lose his footing and he falls on top of them, a three-man pile-up. The hero manages to scramble loose. He jumps to his feet just as the sound of approaching sirens drifts across on the air.

He's been turned around but sometimes fortune favours the brave and, somehow, the Phantasm has ended up back at the car. Bobble Hat and Shaved are in two minds. The flashing blue lights arrive as reflections on the walls of high office buildings a few blocks over.

But there is no hesitation in the mind of a hero and he is reaching into the back seat of the car. He retrieves the laptop and climbs on his bike. The thieves must now decide whether to go for their car and escape, or for the laptop and their nemesis. The force of justice takes a moment to watch the men from his position, a wry smile on his face, pleasure at their fury.

'Thanks for the merch,' the dark defender calls over his shoulder as he cycles away, waving the laptop in the air with one hand, before they slam their doors shut. He knows they are watching him, and he knows they can't chase him, because they've got their own worries now. His mood ebullient, he rises up on to his back wheel in triumph, and wheelies off into the infinite night.

Chapter Two

Sam had been a superhero for around five months. The reasons for anyone doing anything are myriad and diffuse but Sam considered his own destiny as a superhero in twenty-first-century Britain a kind of inevitability. All the rivers of his life had led him to it.

He was an only child, born to two parents who were also only children, and so he found himself alone for great swathes of time in his early childhood. This loneliness was felt most keenly in the long summer holidays when his father was at work and his mother, a teacher, spent lots of time earning extra cash marking exam papers. It was on one of those long, lazy summer afternoons that his life changed for ever, when his mother gave him a beaten-up copy of the first *Harry Potter* book. Having no idea what was about to happen to him, Sam took the book, went upstairs to his room, and started reading. The only reason he came back down later on was because he was too hungry not to.

For Sam the magic of stories went far deeper than mere entertainment – they wove an alternate reality in which he could feel less alone. When Harry and his friends went to Diagon Alley for sweets or wands or broomsticks, he was right there with them. He loved the world the author built, felt himself sliding off his bed and into the pages of the book, into another universe. This transporting experience, where he could be with other people, was immensely powerful, and it was in books he found his first real friends.

When he was around nine or ten, his father took him to see a matinee of *Jurassic Park* and afterwards they went for ice cream, sat in a plaza watching people going about their exciting city lives. Perhaps it was more than mere coincidence that, on that perfect day, a second huge change occurred in Sam's life. They called into WHSmith and his father bought him his very first *Batman* comic. Outside the shop, in the brilliant sunshine of the city's high street, the gleaming buildings all around him and all the people whirling past, Sam held the comic in both his hands and stared at it, blinking out the brightness of the sun.

When he got home he lay on his bed and flicked through the pages and his mind was opened up. Here was something he felt he shouldn't be reading. Did his father know the stories were this violent? Cops were being shot, acid was a weapon of choice, and the protagonist was not an innocent but an angry anti-hero, taking the law into his own hands.

But more than this, it was real. Bruce Wayne was a normal human being, flesh and blood. Sam was hooked. Like it was the most natural thing in the world, he started pretending he was Batman, cycling around the back alleys of his small housing estate in the hope of discovering a crime scene that needed investigation, though there never was.

He started exploring the large woods on the edge of town. The trees were big and old; there were hills and deep valleys and sheer cliff faces, something primal about its danger.

One winter day he discovered a weird basin filled with fallen leaves and there, on the far side, he saw a dark opening beneath the roots of a tree. Clambering up, he found himself inside. The ceiling was made up of hovering tree roots, and as he looked out across the autumn-leaved basin he had no idea just how important this place would become to him. He had found his Batcave. He didn't know it at the time, but in the coming years that cave would become a place of great solace.

Because Sam remained a child late. A distance was growing between him and the other kids in his school. He wasn't being invited to the parties at which boys and girls were experiencing their first kisses. He was smaller than most of the other kids. He didn't excel at sports and, though certainly not stupid, he was nowhere near the top of his classes. At twelve he was given his first pair of glasses, at thirteen he got braces. He knew he was ugly but was powerless to do anything about it. He'd smile in the mirror and his braces looked like insects in his mouth. So he stopped smiling in public, and this created a greater degree of separation, like he was cut adrift.

He'd go to his Batcave regularly, crawling into his space, sitting there for hours on end reading his comics, even during winter when the land was brutal and cold. In summer he would scan the latticework of branches overhead, the vivid green leaves swaying in the breeze. He would gaze at the forest floor below, at the ferns and bushes, at the way a forest moves when nobody is there. Sometimes he felt like he might disappear entirely from the world, fall through some strange membrane and out of known existence.

He never once solved a crime, or prevented one, but he felt sure that, one day, his time to shine would come.

Sam's local pub was traditional, with wooden chairs and tables, a flagstone floor and log fire.

'So everybody's still on for Friday,' said Blotchy, a five o'clock shadow spread across the lower half of his large face and double chin, the small lenses of his round glasses reflecting the low light so you couldn't see his eyes. His brow was bejewelled with droplets of sweat and his long hair, tied into a ponytail, looked lank. 'I just need to let the guys know,' he said, taking a pull of his cider.

Sam's right leg was shaking, as it often did. The room was warm, he was feeling proud about returning the stolen laptop to its owner, he had a fizzy beer in his hands, and he was with his two best friends discussing plans for an upcoming astronomy project.

'We're meeting here at seven but some people are coming for food at six if you fancy it.'

'Will you be eating food?' Tango said.

'I shall.'

They laughed.

Blotchy leaned in and raised his hands. 'The. Food. Here. Is. Nice.'

'I'm not being horrible but you've got to get fit,' said Tango.

'I will, I will,' Blotchy said defensively. 'I'm just stressed out at the minute.'

Blotchy got his nickname from the fact his face would often break out with red marks, and today they were particularly bad. At twenty-six, on bad days he looked ten years older.

'Some of us have to work and don't have time to go running every day.'

'I do work,' said Tango.

'Writing novels is not work, unless you get paid.'

'I work at Colin's Books.'

'You get paid three pounds an hour!'

'So?'

'It's not even legal.'

Sam had known Tango for ever. His real name was Alan, or Al, and their parents had been friends. Whenever Sam spent time with kids outside of school as a toddler, Tango would always be there, and so now the foundations of their friendship ran so deep it was something they didn't even think about. Blotchy they'd met in comprehensive school and had slowly accommodated him into their group because, over the years, they'd found themselves in the same lower section of the social hierarchy, not exactly popular but not strange enough to attract bullies. Ghosts, really; just numbers in the great mass of a school's population. They liked the same films and television programmes, shared a curiosity for the supernatural, for conspiracy theories, for what Freud called the Uncanny.

It was Sam's turn to buy the drinks, but before going to the bar he went over to the jukebox. He wondered if the police had caught up with the burglars he'd reported. It was one of those jukeboxes connected to the Internet, and Sam typed into the search 'What's So Funny 'Bout Peace, Love and Understanding'.

His mum had introduced him to Elvis Costello and it was this song, also his mother's favourite, that Sam had fallen in love with. The music came on and he closed his eyes for a second, saw her standing in the sunbeams on the mountainside, and then he was ready to go to the bar.

As he waited his eyes drifted up to the mirror behind the spirits, and he noticed a bright flash of colour behind him. When he turned to see, he was greeted by the sight of a girl with red hair, red like dark blood, with black streaks underneath. The cogs of recognition clicked into place. It was the girl he'd seen in the bakery, when he'd bought Gloria a meal.

She was small, even shorter than Sam, and she wore a black T-shirt with a picture of a robot on it, a short tartan skirt and a pair of cool-looking ankle boots. Her hair was cut into an austere bob; at the front, two scimitars curled around either side of her face. A small nose and mouth, a clear complexion and two big eyes hidden behind a pair of thick-rimmed glasses.

'Hi,' she said to him, and she smiled.

All at once his heart started going crazy. Was she talking to him?

'How's it going?' she said, and stepped closer to Sam.

'I'm good, thanks,' he said.

'Yes, mate?' The barman, in a short-sleeved shirt and tie, adopted an expectant look.

Sam found it hard to focus. 'Two Red Stripes and a Strongbow, please,' he said, recovering. 'One of the lagers with a dash of lemonade. And two packs of cheese and onion crisps.'

He felt her eyes on him.

'Who has the dash?' she said.

'Me.'

The lager came out of the tap interminably slowly. He wanted to get back to the safety of his friends.

'I like your T-shirt,' she said.

His T-shirt was grey with the word InGen stencilled on the front.

'It's from—'

'*Jurassic Park*, I know.'

His heart lurched into another gear. This girl was wonderful.

'Creation is an act of sheer will,' she quoted. The expression on her face was unchanged. He tried to take a mental photograph of her and wondered how old she was. Maybe twenty-two or twenty-three.

'Ten pounds twenty, please, mate.'

The drinks stood on the soggy beer mat with their bubbles rising.

'This is my favourite song,' she said, pointing at the air above her. The music swirled. 'That was a nice thing you did yesterday. In the bakery.'

Oh Jeez, he thought, I'm going red. He suddenly felt very hot.

'It was nothing,' he said, trying to laugh, before panicking, tucking the crisps under his arm, and collecting up all three pints with his small hands, not without some frenzied spillage, nodding his goodbye, and rushing back to his friends. Setting the drinks awkwardly on the table, he turned back towards the bar but the girl with blood-red hair wasn't looking. She had her arms flat on the bar and was rising up and down on her toes, talking to the barman.

'How many do you reckon we'll see on Friday?' said Blotchy, but Sam wasn't concentrating. The wonderful chemicals of excitement released through his blood, even though he'd been a complete idiot. He'd forgotten how they felt.

'Sam?'

He should go back and talk to her. This was her favourite song, and it was his too. How often did the universe throw such a coincidence at two people? And what were the odds of her seeing him in the bakery? It had to be a sign.

'Huh?'

'How many meteors do you think we'll see Friday night? The guys are running a sweepstake.'

The girl collected her drink and Sam was surprised to see her carrying a pint of Guinness back to her table. She was tucked away in the alcove in the corner of the pub, next to the fireplace. She picked up a book, the title of which was obscured in the low light.

'Sam?'

He turned to his friends and sat down. 'Friday night,' he said. Now he was wondering if the girl with red hair was looking at him. He needed to act cool, which meant not speaking too much. 'I don't know,' he said, and leaned back in his chair, 'how can you run a sweepstake on something like that?'

The way the firelight hit the lager made it look like magma. Sam gulped down a third of his pint and it made him feel better. He wondered what she was reading. The book looked second-hand, with yellowing pages and a crumpled cover. Was she struggling to concentrate on the words, just as he was struggling to follow the thread of the conversation? He considered where she lived and why he'd never seen her wandering around town before. Perhaps she had just moved here and that was why she was trying to talk to him; to find friends. He should go over and ask her to join them. But would she really want to be privy to a conversation about a weird trip to the country on Friday night to look for meteors when most people his age were in the city getting wasted?

'What are you writing at the moment?' said Blotchy to Tango.

Across the table, his face a thin rectangle, his short brown hair wiry, Tango said, 'I've got this idea in my head of a spaceship, and the crew on it start falling deeply asleep at night, all at the same time. And after a while they realise the ship isn't working so great, and one of the engineers finds that parts are being removed and replaced while they sleep. But they notice that, no matter how good the copies replacing the originals, they're never good enough to allow the ship to run smoothly.'

Sam listened, consciously pretending to forget the girl with red-and-black hair.

'But then the crew start getting nosebleeds. And then they get sick.' He stopped and opened the cheese and onion crisps, ripping the pack along its seam to open it out fully, as if on a plate. 'The ship's doctor examines the crew and they discover that it's not just the ship that's being replaced, it's them too. Their organs are not their own but perfect copies inserted into their bodies when they sleep by some strange force. But despite their perfection, there's something too complex about the way things work in the universe, and the new bodies are failing.'

Perhaps it was the effect of the girl, but the thought of being replaced sent a shiver through Sam. *If I was replaced, piece by piece, would I still be me?*

'So what's it all about?' said Blotchy, quietly.

Sam turned in his chair and thought about going home tonight and checking his voicemail on his other mobile phone, which he kept in the drawer of his bedside table, just as he did every single night. He could feel the heat coming from the fire across the room, an uneven, unpleasant sensation now. He turned around further in his chair to see her, the girl with red hair, in the seat in the stone alcove, but she wasn't there. All that remained was a half-finished pint of murky black Guinness, the foam making strange shapes on the sides, as he heard Tango say, '. . . slow invasion.'

Ⓟ

The Phantasm #003

The Tragedy of Mr Ho

The rain falls in drenching sheets. A small child out in this weather? Why? At a guess the child is twelve, thirteen, maybe eleven. It is hard to tell these days, when children grow up so fast, are taught the World so early.

The child is spying on a bus shelter, looking down on it from the top of a grassy slope. All of this is seen through the light-giving magic of night-vision goggles. Our masked crusader is hiding in a tree again. An old lady is in the shelter, which is lit by a single bulb. A classic set-up: the predator, the prey, the protector.

One thing is for sure: this punk is up to no good. The Phantasm can feel it in his bones. Innocent until proven guilty might be all well and good in the comfort of the courtroom, but when you're out in the jungle you get a sixth sense for danger. And you act on the agent, or the agent acts upon you.

Sure enough, it happens. The boy picks up a stone and lobs it at the shelter. In the night vision its arc is like tracer fire. The rain hammers down. The missile misses the roof by inches and the little old lady with her old-person shopping bag on wheels continues her wait for the bus without knowing she is under attack. But somebody knows. A man in a tree with night-vision goggles knows.

Only in darkness can a hero be born, and tonight it is very dark. In his heart he sings an elegy for the loss of respect.

Coming up the hill now is a new saviour. The number 49 bus. It glows in the night like a beacon of hope as it splits the rainstorm in two, its windows bright yellow rectangles of light, the streaks of rain slanting like arrows in the headlights. It hisses to a stop and the elderly lady gets on, to be conveyed to some safer destination.

Game on.

He is out of the tree before the bus is in second gear. Over the road he goes. The rain hits him hard and is cold, but this is no ordinary person. There will be no umbrellas here. He lifts his arm towards the child and points the finger of justice.

'You!' he calls.

He hopes the child will run in fear, but he does not. Instead, he spies the champion of the night and brings himself to full height, which isn't very tall. The distance from the bus shelter to the top of the grassy slope is little more than ten feet. Such bravado in one so young.

'Fuck off!' the child calls.

'Charming! You kiss your mother with that mouth?'

'I kiss your mother with this mouth,' he says.

This kid has got some moxie. There's a bin next to the boy and he's found something. From the dark cavern of the bin's maw he produces what looks like a discarded bag of chips. He throws one at the Phantasm but the masked warrior is too fast and ducks inside the shelter. The chip impacts the Perspex wall with a dull thud and slides down.

The hero pokes his head out.

'What are you doing?'

The boy throws another chip. Twenty-first-century thugs often require a twenty-first-century solution. The hero takes his Phantfone from his utility belt and makes a show of taking a photo of the child. But his hood is up and there's a scarf covering the lower part of his face.

'Taking photos of little kids, are you, paedo?'

'I'm not a paedo!'

'Yeah you are.'

Another chip, which flies past the Phantasm's head. Instinct kicks in and he throws out an arm. The chip is caught. The avenger swings 360 and hurls the chip back at the kid. It hits him on the chest. But doesn't knock him over. Not that a chip would. Incredibly impressive though what just happened was, Newtonian mechanics alter for no man.

Now the boy has come back with a pot of curry sauce.

'Stop right there!' shouts the hero. 'You throw that and I'll—'

SPLAT!

He can taste it. It's still warm. Hmm. He knows this curry sauce. Golden Boat Chinese Restaurant. Mr Ho would be devastated to know his fine produce has been weaponised like this. He wipes the sauce from his eyes and fixes his gaze on the boy.

Yes, you sense it too. I. Am. Pissed.

He chases the kid up the hill. The boy throws the whole bag of chips but the Phantasm knocks them away as if they're nothing. Suddenly, the child stops and turns. He's shorter than he first appeared, and younger. What the heck is a kid his age doing out so late?

'You going to assault me? Fuck off,' says the kid.

His eyes are fierce, there is a terrific anger here. His whole tragic future pans out in the Phantasm's mind. And then a puddle pans out before him, which the hoodlum has kicked up off the street in an almost impossible sweep, drenching the dark guardian.

'Right.' He stares the boy down.

'Delete the photo,' the kid says.

'What?' He is sopping wet.

'The photo,' the kid says. 'That you took of me. Delete it or I'm telling the police.'

'You threw curry sauce at me!'

'So? You're a freak dressed up like a gimp – whose side they gonna be on?'

The masked avenger narrows his eyes.

Under his breath he grumbles and shows the screen of the phone to the child. His gloves are touch-screen sensitive, future gloves, and he presses the symbol of the little bin on the screen and the photo is vaporised in the myriad streams of the Information Superhighway.

'There. Happy?'

The kid nods begrudgingly but doesn't go to move away.

'What are you doing out in the rain, son?' says the hero.

The boy shrugs.

'Come on.'

They move into a shop doorway.

'Look at you, you're soaking,' the Phantasm says. In his back-pack he has a foil blanket, which he wraps around the boy.

'Are you naughty in school?'

The boy shrugs and the Phantasm is aware that they are now on a level playing field.

'Let me ask you something. Do you like sports cars?'

'What?'

'And big houses?'

'I guess.'

The Phantasm puts his hands on the boy's shoulders.

'Everybody wants to do well in life. You can have those things. No matter what anyone tells you. You've got a quick mind, kid. But you need to focus it. I'm telling you this. I don't know you but if your teachers are mean, or even if your parents are mean, you need to believe in yourself, OK? You can do anything you want. But nothing comes from nothing – you have to work for it. And that starts with school. You know what an astronaut from NASA once said to me? He came to my school, when I was around your age. He told me the secret of achieving anything you want. And it's easy. Wanna know what it is?'

The kid looks up at the avenger. And nods.

'It's way simpler than you think. He said you need to read for thirty minutes every day. Doesn't matter what. But you need to do it. No music, no TV, no phones. You read for thirty minutes. Then you spend five minutes thinking back about what you've read, and if you can't remember something you go back and check it. You do this, every day, and by the time you're an adult everyone will think you're a genius. And, here's the thing: you will be. Your brain will be a finely tuned machine. You believe me?'

The kid has fixed him with a stare. He nods again, quickly.

'You don't even need to tell anyone you're doing it. Nobody needs to know you're reading.' He smiles. 'Hey, I see a Spar across the road there. You hungry? What's your favourite chocolate bar?'

'Dunno.'

'Come on, you gotta have a favourite chocolate bar.'

'I like Twirls.'

The Phantasm nods.

'Good choice. Twirls are great. There used to be something called a Spira. Ever heard of them? They had two fingers too. But they had this hole through the middle so you could use them as a straw. They were pretty great. Right.' He takes a ten-pound note from his utility belt. 'Let's do a deal. You promise me you're gonna try better in school, and I'll shout you a Twirl and a Cherry Coke.'

The boy thinks. 'OK,' he says.

The Phantasm hands over the money. 'Get me a Cherry Coke too. And a Wispa.'

'Serious?'

'Serious.'

The kid runs across the road to the Spar and the masked avenger waits in the shop doorway. He has no idea if the kid will come back, but he waits and watches. After a few minutes, the boy emerges into the night. He could make good his escape now if he so wished. The hero will not pursue him. There is a moment's pause. And then the Phantasm smiles to himself, as the boy trots back across the street towards him.

Chapter Three

The creation of the costume and the utility belt is of the utmost importance to a superhero. The costume is the main barrier between him (or her) and the world. It is the costume that sets a hero apart and is often the one thing that can save his life.

Sam had purchased most of his equipment online, ordering everything over a period of six weeks from different sites to avoid suspicion. He'd bought a tactical assault vest from Amazon. Black, with lots of pouches for holding magazine clips, it brought with its wearing a sense of enormous security and strength. Light and well ventilated, it allowed full mobility. He kept the vest light, using the pouches to hold nothing but a few chocolate bars, small bottles of water or Cherry Coke, and a coffee flask for when it got cold. He wore it on top of an Odlo Ninja Shirt, a thin thermal layer with a hood to pull over your head, designed originally to keep biting wind from a cyclist's face but which doubled superbly as a base layer for twenty-first-century heroes. It also utilised Silver Ions to reduce body odour. A simple pair of men's running tights, with small shin pads beneath, and a pair of New Balance 507 trainers made up his lower half, with a cricket box in his underwear. To cover his eyes he wore a black sleeping mask with holes cut out and he painted the exposed flesh around his eyelids with dark eyeliner. A black scrum cap to protect his skull, all-weather cycling gloves with touch-sensitive fingertips for his hands, lightweight Kevlar elbow pads (not only for protection but also to hit enemies, instead of punching with his fists – not that he'd ever hit anyone in his life), a shoulder, chest and biceps protection complex (worn over his Ninja Shirt and beneath the assault vest). Sam had purchased everything for less than a week's wages. It was all about striking a balance between safety and mobility, and Sam was happy with the trade-off he'd chosen.

The utility belt was the favourite part of his costume. The belt itself had come from eBay, was padded for comfort, and could clip on to his assault vest as well as around his waist. It had seven pouches for, as the product description said: pistol, double pistol, magazine clips, baton and handcuffs. Instead, Sam had: length of twine, smoke bombs, compass, notepad and pen, hand warmer, tape measure, laser pointer, £100 cash, cat treats, torch, asthma pump, rape alarm. To the clips of his belt he attached more expensive equipment: binoculars, night-vision goggles (these were a late addition and actually not as expensive as one might think, though he'd broken his first set) and a small digital camera for not only photograph-ing crimes but videoing them in HD as well. Sometimes the expensive things would go in the backpack, sometimes they stayed at home altogether. The Phantfone he'd bought anony-mously for cash – it was sturdy and practical and had £50 of credit on it. He never took his personal phone out patrolling. And that was his kit. He had toyed with the idea of wearing a cape, and had bought a waterproof one online, but he never wore it. When it came to it, a cape would be grabbed by an enemy and thrown over his head, ice hockey-style, leaving Sam blind and exposed. Moreover, a cape in real life simply does not look as good as they do in comic books, and so it remained folded neatly at the bottom of the locked fireproof chest in his wardrobe. Other things left in the chest: £5,000, $1,000 and €1,000 in cash, passport, birth certificate,

National Insurance card, emergency overnight bag, twelve cans of baked beans with sausages, and a big pack with a tent and other survival gear inside.

Before having the designs put on his costume, he wore it up to the forestry and went for several long runs to be sure he could comfortably carry everything, utility belt included, for long periods and distances. It was hard work at first but as his core strength improved it got easier.

The logo had arrived in his head at the exact same time as the idea to become a superhero. It was just there, the insignia, simple and true, and so clean he knew it was right.

He drew it on a computer, sent it to a large embroidery firm who would never remember it, and when the results came back he held the patch in his hand and knew that what he was doing had become something inevitable. When something is right it becomes immutable. He stitched the insignia to the assault vest, and then he was standing in front of his bedroom mirror, just looking and looking at the masked fig ure before him, the April sunlight coming through the window, the sound of a lawnmower somewhere down the street. There, in the middle of this perfect, pristine suburbia, a new force in the world was born.

It had been a feeling of despair mixed with elation. The costume was amazing and awful; it was insane. There in the spring evening something was badly wrong with the grand plan that had been his life. How ridiculous it was, and yet the elation – the feeling of being cocooned in another person – was intoxicating and, more than this, it was easy. It felt easy. Since donning the mask he had finally achieved an inner peace. Insane or not, it was what he needed to do. This was his calling, his Special Purpose. Whatever others might think of a twenty-something man doing this, the Phantasm was Sam's answer to the Event that had slammed into his life like a freight train all those years ago. And it was the only answer he could find.

Now his discarded costume lay on the floor. He stared at it from his bed, one arm dangling over the edge. It was Thursday already and he pondered how a week off work can slip by so quickly.

He drove to a café on the edge of town and ordered a full English breakfast. He liked this place because the furniture was solid, the tables always clean, and the breakfast was in perfect proportion: two eggs, two sausages, two rashers of bacon, two hash browns, a slice of black pudding, beans, tomatoes and toast.

Sam took a week off work once every twelve weeks. Entitled to five weeks' annual leave, he liked to split the year by quarters, saving that extra week for emergencies. And each segment of time off would follow roughly the same routine. On day one he went to the coast, on day two he liked to drive around the lanes of the countryside, stopping off at a pub for lunch. Day three was a tour of the local industrial estates that he used to cycle around as a teenager. Sam liked industrial estates. He liked the neat grass verges and simple roads with well-made kerbs. He liked the brooks that often ran under small bridges and the signs at the entrance with little maps showing what business could be located where, everything nice and simple and organised. He would just park up and walk around, an anonymous human in an anonymous space.

At home in the evenings he would buy all his favourite types of takeaway food on separate nights of the week and watch a favourite film. Monday had been pizza and *The Matrix*, Tuesday sausage, beans and chips and *Pacific Rim*. Wednesday: doner kebab and *The Prestige*. By keeping things regimented and ordered Sam was able to create a stable state for his soul.

Travel was something he had often considered, but he was scared of flying and found just the sheer effort and the thought of going into unknown environments daunting. He knew and loved his hometown, so why leave it?

Day four was a day of pilgrimage. After his full English, he would drive up to the nearby forestry and take a long walk through the pines to a small pond fed by a natural spring inside the mountain. This was a place of deep-burned memory and had become something sacred to him; if he didn't go back at regular intervals, he knew something inside him would break, and he would die.

As Sam made inroads into his breakfast, creating various combinations of tasty mouthfuls on his fork, his mind suddenly blipped and he felt his skin prickle. The image of the girl with red hair sprang into his mind.

'Sam?'

He looked across to the next table.

'How are you, Sam?'

His mind searched. Sitting at the table in a business suit was a man with greying temples. He was with a woman, also in a business suit. Then he remembered. It was his bank manager, from all those years ago, and his appetite fell away.

'I'm fine,' he said.

'Great. That's great.'

They stared at each other for a long moment and Sam resented the pity that had painted itself across the bank manager's face. 'You moved house, didn't you?'

'Yeah,' said Sam, his throat suddenly croaky.

'To the new builds on the edge of town?'

Sam nodded. The woman had obviously detected how loaded with unspoken information this exchange was, and stared down at her phone.

'That's right.'

'You don't bank with us any more, do you?'

Sam shook his head, and the manager saw he was unable to speak.

'I understand. I hope everything's working out for you OK.'

Sam tried to smile but grimaced. 'It's all fine,' he said, placing his knife and fork together on his plate.

The stillness in the air between them was heavy with the shared past experience. This man had been so kind to him. But Sam needed to get out of there. He couldn't tell if it was the bank manager or the girl with red hair, but suddenly the soft cocoon of safety he'd diligently created over many years had cracked.

The air in the forestry was cold but the sky was blue. The leaves on the trees were orange and drifting, and cold sunlight cut bright lines between the pines. Halfway up, a gravel track for the forestry trucks curled around the mountain and from here he could see right the way across his hometown. Apart from his two years at university, he could see all the places of his life in this one panorama. He paused there a while, feeling the ebb and flow of the world against his face, trying to synch his heartbeat with that of the planet, and when the moment was ready to end he continued his climb.

He was so far from the road by now that the only sound was that of the wind moving through the great pines. He thought of things – his past, his present, his future – but knew it was best not to linger on bad things, and here he was thankful for the numbness he'd developed as a teenager and which had served him so well later in life.

The small pond, fed by the natural spring that bubbled up from underground, wasn't far. Baby Christmas trees poked out from the jut of bedrock on the far side. His parents had brought him here once and told him how the water had healing properties. Sam had stared into the pool that day and spied a shiny penny at the bottom. Thick slants of sunlight came through the trees and shone across his mum and dad and now, when he thought of them, that image was the one that came to him most often; here on this mountain in better times. Now he took his own penny from his pocket and tossed it into the water. For the old gods. But he didn't make a wish. He'd given up on those things long ago.

When he was thirteen years old, Sam was invited to one of the house parties the other kids went to most weekends. Though completely normal for them, to Sam it meant a great deal, even if when he thought of it the nerves almost made him throw up.

A few days before, in the schoolyard, the boys were standing in one group, the girls in another, and messengers were being dispatched between the two, until one of the boys returned with a sheepish look on his face. He was reluctant to say what had happened but the others coaxed him until, at last, he caved and said, 'The girls said they were going to make out with every boy in the party.' A frisson rippled along the circle. But then the boy looked at Sam, with his glasses and braces and acne, and added, 'Everyone except Sam.'

It was a kind of numbness that descended on him that day in the schoolyard. Not an explosion of humiliation, not a wave of anger, but a cool mist that made him numb. He absorbed the news as a sponge absorbs water; quietly and without fanfare. The words made a slow percolation and came to a stop in his middle. All he thought was, that's not very nice. In the years to come this would become his default reaction to most things.

Although there was no tumultuous outburst of emotion, the effect of what had been said hurt him tremendously over the next few days. He lay on his bed and stared at the ceiling with that numb density sitting inside him. He ran simulations of the party in his head; all the others paired off while he sat alone on a sofa with nothing to do. He went to his wardrobe several times and looked at the smart new sweater his father had bought for him especially for the party. His parents were as excited as he was that he would finally take part in a social event outside of school.

The night came and he went downstairs in his new clothes, where his parents were watching TV. They turned their faces towards him and gave great smiles of happiness. 'You look great!' said his mum. 'Very smart.'

He remembered taking off his glasses and cleaning a smudge from them with the sleeve of his new sweater. They warned him off drink and drugs and sent him on his way. Sam left the house and collected the hidden backpack from the hedge in the front garden and, instead of making his way to the party, he went to his Batcave in the woods. He'd brought a blanket, a torch and a hot-water bottle and in the darkness of winter he took out his Batman comics and read by torchlight, read for hours in the cold of the night, a tiny sphere of light emanating from the roots of the hanging tree, until at last it was time to go home.

When he returned from the party, his parents asked how it had gone and he said, fine. And the truth was, it was fine. He'd enjoyed himself in his Batcave. He'd lost himself in that other world of superheroes, where people needn't worry about social hierarchy and girls and teenage cruelty, because they were too busy being good people.

Comics for Sam became not just a love affair but a crutch. Slowly but surely he accrued a collection. He discovered the extended universe of *Batman*, and also the *Detective Comics*, which predominantly featured the Caped Crusader. He watched and re-watched the two Tim Burton *Batman* films, and the greatest day of his life was when he read, aged fourteen, a letter he himself had penned to the *Batman* letters column.

He collected other comics too but nothing ever compared to the *Batman*. *The Flash* was entertaining but light, *Superman* a little too conventional, *Green Lantern* was excellent but lacked the realism Sam now craved, and he didn't get on at all with anything in the Marvel universe. Nothing had the dark power of *Batman*, and the discovery of adult comics like *Watchmen*, *Sandman* and *Preacher* were still years away. Slowly, the world of comics and the world of reality merged into one. And so, for Sam, comics became things with their very own superpowers, chiefly the ability to deflect the gaze of the world away from him.

Ⓟ

The Phantasm #004

And Man Might Fly

All quiet on the Western Front. A night like any other. Save for the movement of shadow in some anonymous alleyway. The railroad station lies empty tonight. A crack of light appears in the alleyway, which widens to throw an angle of illumination on the wet lane. He moves quickly, from the shadows, sleek, catlike, the only sound the clicking of gears on his bicycle. His bicycle is painted black so even that looks like a shadow. The man emerging from the doorway jolts with shock as our hero approaches, as if appearing directly in front of him from some unknown dimension.

The Phantasm takes the merchandise. 'You do good work,' he says, before one-eightying his bike and sprinting head-long down the alleyway. All he hears is his contact calling after him, 'Be careful.' And then, 'You really should be wearing a helmet.'

He cycles through a maze of backstreets until he is in the secluded lane behind his house. Here he dismounts and takes the merchandise to the Black Phantom, puts said merchandise in the boot, and drives away. The mask of his costume he pulls off. Appearing normal will draw the least attention. Into the city he goes, the deep dark city of a million secrets and twice as many broken hearts. He knows the streets well, could drive these roads blindfolded if he wasn't a law-abiding citizen. But tonight he needs to travel just one path. He parks up in a dangerous area of town. People don't come here. Tramp Alley, they call it, a hive of dropouts and ne'er-do-wells. Crime, it is assumed, originates right at the bottom.

Cowl back on, our hero stalks forward with the merchandise. The bums don't even notice as he glides past. He is the night, the night is him. Ahead, a wooden table with halogen lamps on top, an urn of bubbling soup, bearded charity workers and church-aid helpers.

The phantom is running now, the merchandise slung across his back. All together, the charity workers turn their heads and regard this vision of justice thundering pell-mell towards them. Their mouths fall open as the Phantasm holds aloft the merchandise and hurls it with both arms towards a man of perhaps forty-five, who sees the parcel in the air and dives clear. The merchandise impacts the ground and half a dozen sandwiches spill on to the dirty floor.

'It's from your friends in high places,' our hero tells the freezing charity workers.

'Greggs?' says a woman, inspecting one of the strewn sandwiches.

'From the rich,' and our hero indicates the skyscrapers blazing over the city like giant gods, 'to the poor.' He swings his arm around to encompass in his arc the collection of down-and-outs.

'Are you donating this?'

'Yes,' he says.

'Why are you dressed like that?' says someone else, an elderly lady.

What a triumph of philosophical thought, this question, but there is no time to explain the answer.

'Nourish these men,' our hero demands, turning on his heel and scaling the five-foot wall opposite the charity table.

On the other side is perhaps a thirty-foot drop, something he wasn't expecting. But it's too late now. To turn back would not be becoming of a twenty-first-century hero. The top of an enormous conifer tree is ten feet away and, without a thought for safety, our man leaps for it. But ten feet is an awfully long way and he finds himself, for a moment, flying. He is weightless and without fear. The wind whistles about his face as he plummets but his forward momentum carries him, at last, into the welcoming branches of the tree, which tear and claw at his uniform, and are surprisingly painful against the body.

He comes to rest about halfway up and glances out of the foliage to the charity workers looking over the edge of the wall.

'Are you OK?' says one.

'Yup. I'm fine.' He waves his hand in reassurance.

'Are you stuck?'

He pauses. 'Should be able to find a way down.'

'Do you want an ambulance?'

The scent of the tree is strong. Sap has found its way under his mask and is sticky. He gets himself upright. Inside the tree there are hundreds of tiny dead twigs that fall into his collar. But this is no normal man and with great effort he pushes the soles of his boots against the tree and slowly descends. The charity workers are on their way, and he must free himself before they reach him. He picks up his speed of descent until he believes he is safe to jump.

He takes a deep breath and propels himself from the tree. The branches are weaker than he expected and he is unable to generate much thrust. He is upended and falling head first. With one last gasp he grasps the dense branches in his gloved hands and, just as his grip fails, he is feet first again. He slams into the ground and buckles. His bottom teeth hit his top, and even he is shocked by the force. He glances back up at the tree. He's made a hell of a mess. There's a big gash cut out of it where he snapped the branches with his feet, but he can't worry about that now for he must make good his escape. On bended knee he surveys his surroundings. He is in a churchyard, hemmed in by a tall brick wall. Voices are coming from the entrance. But our man is a shadow, and when they reach the tree into which he leapt they will find no sign of anyone at all. The Black Phantom is not far away, and within seconds he has gained it, and is speeding off into the dark night.

Chapter Four

When he checked the mirror it was worse than he'd thought. An enormous America-shaped bruise had consumed the left side of his ribcage all the way down to his kidney. The tree had cut him along his side, despite the padded top. Little scabs had formed in inch-long lines. His left ankle was sprained from where he hit the ground, and he could hardly walk.

He drew himself a bath and lit a cinnamon-scented candle. Once submerged in the weightlessness of the tub his injuries didn't feel so bad. He imagined the soothing properties of the hot water working on his muscles, the untangling of frayed sinew networks.

Jumping off the wall had been a stupid idea. It was the suit's fault, and the false sense of invincibility it gave him. When he pulled on the simple black mask everything else – his life, his job, his bills, responsibilities, stresses, fears, the effect of a crushing loneliness – fell away. To don the mask, to be removed just for a few hours from normal life to the safe places he had found between the pages of his books and comics, was to experience true freedom. In a way he was more himself when dressed as the Phantasm than he was as Sam Holloway. But everyone wears a mask, he told himself, to a greater or lesser extent.

When he left for the pub that night the cold hurt his bones. He loaded his stuff into the boot of the car and looked up at the sky. It was a crescent moon with crisp stars. He liked this time of year; the changing of the seasons from summer to autumn. The coming of the dark nights put in his head the promise of cosy evenings hunkering down in his living room with a large mug of hot chocolate topped with marshmallows and squirty cream, and a scary book – perhaps his beautiful leather-bound edition of H. P. Lovecraft's horror stories.

When he got to the pub his friends were near the back, in the little snug between the toilets and the back door. The kit for the evening – sleeping bags, folding chairs, backpacks, aluminium flasks plus, of course, all the astronomy gear – was strewn about the floor. Sitting at another table, the long wide one next to the fireplace, were the rest of the expedition. They were older than Sam and his friends, ranging in age from mid-thirties to mid-fifties. Graham, with his big beard and bottle-green fleece, was leaning over, saying something conspiratorial to the enraptured group about the adventure on which they were about to embark.

Tango was dressed in full orienteering get-up: salopettes, sturdy boots, a skin-tight latex top. His coat hung over the back of the chair.

'What time are we leaving?' said Sam.

Blotchy finished his lasagne and said, 'After the drinks are gone. The meteors won't enter the atmosphere until later.'

As he made this statement, Tango's gaze slipped away from Sam to something moving behind him. He felt a tug at his arm. Turning, Sam's eyes fell on the girl with red hair, and his heart leapt.

'Hey,' she said.

'Oh,' said Sam, suddenly conscious of the beady eyes of his friends. 'Hi.'

She was wrapped in a thick winter coat with her book sticking out of the pocket. 'How's it going?'

'I'm fine,' said Sam. He tried to focus his attention on his racing heart, trying by pure concentration to slow its rhythm. 'Yeah, good. It's cold out though.'

'Yeah, yeah. Freezing.'

Be zen. He took a breath. She nodded at the heap of bags under and around the table.

'Are you going camping?'

'We're going up to the mountains,' he said, turning from his friends to face her, glad they were too socially awkward to make fun of him.

'Why?'

At this point Sam wished he wasn't quite so tremendously nerdy. It would have been so much easier if he and his friends were going somewhere normal.

'It's stupid, really.'

He wished he could be one of those people who found social interaction easy. At university, before he'd dropped out, he'd been more confident. He felt his friends eavesdropping so he took a step back from the table.

'What's your name?' he said.

'Sarah. I'm Sarah.'

'I'm Sam.'

'Hi, Sam.'

'I'm really sorry but . . . do we know each other?'

'I met you the other night? At the bar?'

'Right, right. Yeah. I mean from before.'

'You think I'm weird. Sorry, I'm not being forward, it's just I only just moved here, you know, and I don't really know anyone. I recognised you from the bakery that day, then you played that song, and I thought – it's a bit weird, isn't it? Nobody goes to pubs any more trying to meet people. It's sad, really.'

'It's not sad at all.'

In the low gleam of the firelight her hair looked more amber than red.

'You don't mind me talking to you, do you?'

'No!' he blurted, losing control of his voice modulation for a second. 'No,' he said again. And then, in a moment of openness, 'It's great.'

He wanted to offer her a drink but faltered. What was the correct protocol for this sort of thing? He didn't even know any more.

'So,' she said.

He tried to smile, but his face malfunctioned and he felt his features slip into something more like a grimace. Would he look back on this moment years from now and think, that was the day I took the initiative? The night before their wedding, would Sam think back on this tiny speck of history as the defining moment of his life?

'Why are you going to the mountains?'

He thought for a moment about how to answer that question.

'Well.' He looked at her. She was so pretty. 'Did you know Earth is passing through the debris of Halley's Comet at the moment?'

'No.'

'We go through it every year in October. And May, actually. We pass through that patch of space.' He shrugged.

'So is that a telescope?' she said, nodding to the pack thrown over his shoulder.

'Yeah. I mean, it's not very powerful or anything.' Oh God, I'm grimacing again, he thought. 'We're going to the mountains where it's nice and dark. Hopefully we'll get to see some meteors.'

'So do you like astronomy and space and things, then?'

'I guess so. Yes. I do like it,' he said, trying to gauge her reaction.

He smiled, and realised something. He was having a conversation, and it was OK. Admittedly, he felt retarded but overall, it was OK.

'I like that stuff too,' she said. 'I'm not an expert or anything but, you know, it's really interesting. I work in the science library at the university.'

'Really?'

'Uh-huh.'

'Wow. I'd love to do something like that.'

'That's why I moved here.'

A silence fell in. He didn't want this to end.

'So you're looking for shooting stars,' Sarah said.

'We are.'

She fixed him with a look of such solidity he thought he might turn to stone. Something slipped inside him. She tilted her head to one side and said, 'Can I come?'

Chapter Five

Sam's relationship to girls over the past few years was all but non-existent. Small, short and though not ugly certainly not a knockout, he drew little attention from the opposite sex. Moreover, in circles where girls were present – i.e. work – he was well liked by them but because of his size and his tremendous niceness he posed none of the sexual threat that seemed, to Sam, a prerequisite for the kind of kinetic firestorm type of love he so dearly longed to inspire. Girls came to Sam as a friend, to unload their problems, not create new ones. Dreaded phrases like 'just a friend' and 'nice guy' and 'just don't think of you like that' had become common to his ear at university when he still pursued girls. There were hits – he'd had sex with two students – but the ratio to misses was dismal. Not that simply bedding a girl was the end goal for Sam, far from it; it was just that the act of sex as achievement was so all-pervasive in university culture, it was hard to escape. But that was before. These days he didn't bother trying. It was safer to leave it for now and pretend he'd pick up that thread later in life.

And yet here she was, the girl with red hair and glasses, sitting next to him.

The wide road became a lane just big enough to get a car through when they reached the mountains and the lack of street lights gave Sam an opportunity to use his full beams, something he always enjoyed; how the night reveals itself in white light.

'What's your job?' she said.

'I work for a Japanese electronic components wholesaler.'

'Oh.'

'We sell screws and nuts and bolts – things that go in TVs and cars and things.'

'You work in a Japanese screw factory.'

Sam thought. 'I guess I do.'

Not strictly true. Electronica Diablique (they'd changed their name from their traditional Japanese one to sound more 'European') didn't manufacture anything, so really it was more of a warehouse.

'Is it fun?'

'I like it. It's hard work sometimes but the pay's pretty good. It's definitely not fun, though. I wouldn't do it if I wasn't getting paid.'

'Have you ever been to Japan?'

'They did want me to go, and go to China too, but it didn't work out.'

He didn't tell her how much he disliked flying.

'Oh man, you should have gone. Have you seen those mega-factories they've got in China that are like cities?'

He slowed around a bend. Reps from such factories had visited his offices. The one to which he'd been invited had its own hospital, library, school and ping-pong outhouse.

'Have you heard about this superhero guy in the city who's going around in a mask and cape?'

This not from Sarah but from Tango in the back seat. The boys had been talking among themselves the whole way, in the kind of voice people use when they want to be overheard, but Sam had zoned them out, until this sudden sentence rose from nowhere to everywhere. *Superhero.*

'I saw it on the news. Some guy going around dressed as a superhero.'

He eyed Tango in the rear-view mirror and felt the moisture in his throat evaporate.

'I've heard of those in America.' Blotchy adjusted himself in his seat. 'They go around trying to help people out. Carrying shopping bags and things.'

Out the corner of his eye, Sam saw Sarah moving a strand of hair from her face.

'I read an article in *The New Yorker*,' she said.

He could only catch snippets of what Tango was saying. Was the report on the BBC? Could he catch it on iPlayer before it went into the void?

'About this factory in Shenzhen – is that right? – where ten thousand people live.'

He tuned back into the boys but as quickly as it had come so the conversation had gone, moving on to a discussion of some documentary about a Nazi occultist called Otto Rahn.

'So do you think we'll see many shooting stars tonight?' Sarah said.

He tried to clear his mind. 'Who knows? If the sky stays clear we should definitely see a few.'

'What sort of wish will you make?'

When she said this he was thumped by a sad thought. He knew exactly what wish he would make, and who that wish would involve, just as surely as he knew that it would never come true, no matter how many meteors he saw.

It was a long trek up the mountain to the lake – according to Graham, the darkest point in the region. There were probably fifteen people in their party, each shining a torchlight before them.

Sam's light played over Graham's back. Graham lived a rustic life; he enjoyed fine ales, was a keen angler, foraged herbs and mushrooms in the dawn wilds. He had a wide breadth of knowledge on many things in which Sam was interested: UFOs, ancient secret societies, conspiracy theories, computer hacking. Sam imagined Graham on February mornings hunting the meadows for hares.

'You OK there, youngster?' came his voice, without turning back.

'I'm good.' His breath was heavy.

'You believe in magic, Sam?' Graham's words were gently slurred under the persuasion of Bishop's Assault, the strong local ale. 'There are forgotten parts of this world. There's still magic around. Just depends if you're willing to see it.'

They came, at last, to where the land flattened out. The air was freezing and, so far away from civilisation, completely devoid of ambient white noise. There were no car engines, no humming of heating systems, no trace of anything human. The torches shone out now over an expanse of water, illuminating a thin spider's web of mist on its surface. The water was black as pitch, impenetrable to the eye. Sarah came up beside him and he was acutely aware of her breath crystallising on the air. The stars here were so much brighter, the white smudge of the Milky Way making the galaxy seem backlit.

'It's lovely up here,' she said.

'It's one of Britain's dark areas, where you can see the stars properly.'

Sam set down his backpack and pulled out a collapsible chair.

Her head was facing directly upwards. 'They're so bright.'

Sam wrestled the chair into formation and set it into the wet grass.

'There,' he said, offering it to Sarah.

'Where are you going to sit?'

It was easy to see in the starlight and he found a round, flat boulder and put the chair next to it. Pulling a thick blanket from his pack, he draped it over Sarah.

'I'm not an invalid.'

'Sorry.' Though he wasn't sorry; he liked chivalry, even if it was unfashionable.

'I've got a friend who lives on a farm,' she said. 'The stars are like this there.'

Sam started unpacking his amateur telescope. It was an average telescope that didn't cost much but had been recommended to him by Graham because it was lightweight, came with a tripod, had a good altazimuth (which Sam later learned was a tripod mount that was smoother than most, meaning he could move it around easily) and had three eyepieces of varying strengths. What Sam liked most about it though was the neat back pack that came with it, with little pouches for all the different parts.

'Do you do this often?'

He clipped the telescope on to the tripod. 'Not really. This is the third time I've used my telescope. I tried it in my back garden but there's too much light pollution to get a decent view. There's a lamp post in the alleyway behind my back fence.' Sam peered into the eyepiece. 'We probably won't need the telescopes to see the meteors. If you want to make sure you definitely see one, you're better off just looking up.'

'So why bring them?'

'Well, it's quite nice looking at the stars.'

Sarah was silent for a moment. Sam pointed the telescope and brought an object into focus.

'Do you want to see something cool?' he said.

When he turned she was already standing right next to him. He jolted, her face inches from his. His heart made a solid thump, like a jump-start.

'Wow,' she said, peering into the eyepiece.

'That's Jupiter,' he said, trying to recover.

'Really?'

'Uh-huh. You'd be able to see it much better later on, but up here it's so dark you can see it now.'

'It's incredible,' she said.

Through the eyepiece Sarah was seeing the planet as a small circle.

'The light bits and dark bands you can just about see are the atmosphere,' said Sam. 'Caused by rising and falling air.'

Sarah didn't say anything for a second.

'How far away is it?'

'I don't know.'

'It feels weird looking at it. Up there in space. It's so beautiful.'

Neither of them said anything. As the moonbeams sketched the landscape he watched the others set up their kit. Graham had the biggest telescope, capable of seeing distant nebulae. Many of the other guys had clips for their phones and iPads so they could take pictures and videos of the cosmos. Blotchy and Tango were already set up and had started pitching stones into the lake. They were trying to skim them but their limited athleticism ensured the stones sank beneath the surface at first impact.

'Do you believe in God?' she said, all of a sudden.

'Jeez. I don't know.'

'Sorry, weird question.'

'No, it's not.' A breeze came across the lake. 'It's hard not to think of things like that when you see the planets.'

Sarah brought her eye away from the scope and turned to him.

'It's hard to believe in things, these days. I mean, there's a lot of bad feeling out there.'

'I think people are still basically good,' he said, thinking suddenly of his costume at home. 'You look around here,' he nodded to his friends, a group of people who'd come all the way out here with little tubes of mirrors to look up at the stars, 'and you can see that maybe.'

He looked over to the lake. A middle-aged woman in a velvet cloak had hurried over to Blotchy and Tango. 'Stop that. You're disturbing the energies.'

'That's Donna Mae,' Sam told Sarah. 'She's a witch.'

Donna Mae's round face glowed chalky in the moonbeams.

He was getting cold without his blanket and his recent injuries were starting to hurt.

'This is a very interesting group of people,' Sarah said.

'Sorry,' said Sam.

Sarah's mouth fell open. 'Don't say sorry. I didn't mean it like that. It's awesome. I'm sorry, I'm not a nice person sometimes.'

'You two want a cup of tea?' A man in full army survival gear approached them, a scarf covering the lower half of his face. Fingerless gloves held out two polystyrene cups of tea. 'We forgot the sugar.'

'That's OK,' said Sarah, reaching out to take one of the cups.

'We also forgot the milk.'

'Oh well, at least it'll keep us warm.'

Donna Mae was arranging some crystals on a small trestle table and lighting candles inside glass jars.

'We'll get a fire going and make some hot dogs later,' said the man, who Sam had recognised as Gary, the council's local handyman, as he wandered back over to the main group.

A contented silence fell in. Sam looked over at Sarah and felt warm in his belly. He thought about what Graham had said to him on the way up the mountain, about magic. There was something in his psyche, a little grain that triggered a pleasant feeling when he thought of something not quite in the realm of the everyday, something *other*, something at play behind the workaday world.

'Can I ask you something?' he said.

'Uh-huh.'

'Weren't you scared? Coming up here with a bunch of strangers.'

She shrugged. 'What's the worst that could have happened? You don't hear of astronomy club members murdering people that often.'

'You're a spontaneous person.'

'Not really, actually. Not any more. I'm trying to say yes to things more often.'

'I wish I could do that.'

There was a pause. 'Do you live with these guys?' she said, nodding towards Blotchy and Tango.

'Nope. I live on my own.'

'How old are you?' she said.

'Twenty-six. How about you?'

'Twenty-three.'

'Ah, OK.'

'It's a weird age, this, isn't it?' she said. 'Too old to be young and too young to be old. Do you know what I mean?'

'I guess.' He didn't.

'What I mean is, where are we supposed to be along the line at our age? The expectations of the world – you should be doing this by this age, be at this point in your career, visited this many countries, slept with this many people, earning this much money – I don't know. Sometimes I feel like I should be further along the line.'

Something behind her words, a sad weight, told of a lot more life experience than he had, a tapestry of complex personal history – something he did not possess, and which he found quietly intimidating. To think of how much life was being lived out there while he was in his safe home watching the special features on his deluxe, extended edition of the *Lord of the Rings* trilogy was vertigo-inducing.

'So you were looking to move further along the line by moving here?'

'New job, new life. More money. I'm trying to be a grown-up. Shitty ex-boyfriend.'

He turned his head too quickly towards her when she said the last part.

'I shouldn't have said that. I mean, ultimately, it was for the job. I've been in Lincoln for a year, working in a public library, but it wasn't what I wanted. They're more like nurseries than libraries. The job at the university came up and I went for it. I think you have to take the leap sometimes, you know?'

The smell of hot dogs wafted, steam rose from the polysty-rene cups. Gary was over by the trestle table now, an upturned bottle of Daddies tomato ketchup in his hand, Donna Mae holding her hot dog up to the mouth of it, him battering the sauce bottle, her readjusting the altitude of the hotdog with each whack so it didn't go over her flowing robes.

'Hey,' Sarah said suddenly. 'I think I saw one! Over there.' Excitedly, she pointed to a third of the way up the western sky. 'That was amazing!' She hopped into the air. 'Unless it was just a trick of the mind. I think I saw it though. Wah!'

'Whoa,' came a voice from over by the lake. Tango had seen a second one.

'I saw it too. That was a biggie,' said Blotchy.

Sam smiled at Sarah. Her eyes darted across the sky, searching for another meteor. The sky was completely differ-ent up in these dark regions, the stars so rich and bright. To be here, in this moment, with this sudden new person, was making him feel more alive than he had in a very long time. He could feel it running along his veins.

And then he saw it. A bright white streak across the pitch black. A tiny object that had been cruising through the emp-tiness of space for aeons colliding with the planet and lighting up the sky to put a bolt of joy in his soul. It was there and gone in a second, a blazing fireball. Everyone gasped at its brightness. His heart jolted as he felt her hand close around his wrist. She turned towards him and looked up. Oh my God, he thought. I feel so happy.

'Quick,' she said. He could see the crescent moon reflected in the lenses of her glasses as she beamed at him. 'Make a wish.'

On the drive home the car fell into an insulated silence. Moonlight on the fields, over the low hedgerows, made the world feel uncanny, altered. Sarah had fallen asleep, her face turned away from him, thin neck exposed. Blotchy and Tango were both snoring.

Sometimes Sam considered the various levels of thought in the human mind. First there is the simple pursuit of food and shelter; the base, outer layer into which everything else feeds. The second layer is where you live most of your life; working, thinking about work, your plans for the evening, choosing your dinner; the everyday functions. Further in is where thought gets a little deeper and you consider things such as your own personal future, what you hope for on a superficial level; a nice car, house, holidays, pensions, savings. The fourth layer formulates moral codes; what you believe to be right and wrong in the world, how you think a society should operate; at what point personal responsibility should kick in for a person's actions. Then there are two more levels; a dense outer layer around a core. In the fifth you might consider your place in the universe as you stand drunkenly under winter stars just before Christmas, or maybe wonder if magic still exists, or aliens, or secret government organisations. It is a whimsical level of belief, something separate from the true belief that resides in the core of your being, in the sixth layer of thought, right in the centre of the brain onion where everything you are becomes distilled and you must decide where you stand on the meaning of life.

He dropped Tango and Blotchy off first, bringing the car quietly into the sleeping housing estates where their parents lived, estates built within the last two decades, red-brick houses decorated with small features – yellow quoins, little porticos over the front doors, or the occasional white wood finial – and neat gardens, narrow roads with fresh tarmac that didn't bump the car. There was a neat sheen to the little estates where in the summer grew daisies and manufactured hedgerows, and each garden was well kept by people who were proud of their small patch of the planet they'd worked so hard for. Blotchy mumbled something under his breath as he collected his bag and telescope from the boot. But when they reached Tango's house, his friend nodded across to the sleeping Sarah and raised his eyebrows.

Tango smiled to Sam. 'Great stuff,' he whispered, and put his hand on Sam's shoulder.

It made Sam feel foolish but he also appreciated it.

That central core, the sixth layer of thought, usually stirs on nights when sleep is far off but you're lying in bed anyway, worrying about work the next day, how many hours of sleep you can get, deep thoughts crawling out of dark caves. We are all animals and alone, the universe is infinite, there is no such thing as a future because everything will crumble to dust in the end. Or so it went for Sam, who stayed well clear of the sixth layer as often as he could, listening to the radio before sleeping, always planning evenings well in advance so that boredom couldn't creep in; he didn't want his mind wandering down pathways he'd rather avoid, didn't want to face the existential crisis in the middle of him.

Sarah's place was in a not-so-great part of town, her flat above a boarded-up shop. The little sash windows looked dark and depressing. He woke her up and offered to see her to the door.

'I'm sorry I fell asleep,' she said. A red imprint of the seat belt was on her cheek. 'Too much talking.' She rubbed her eyes with the crook of her wrist, pushing her glasses up her forehead.

'Did you have a nice time?'

She nodded. 'I really did.'

A fluttering in his chest again.

It was freezing, frost crystallising on the pavement, the air sharp as needles.

'Thanks again,' she said. The lights had come on in the car from where she'd opened the door. 'Seriously, I've had a really, really nice time.'

In his mind the shooting star flashed and he wondered if he should try and kiss her.

'Me too,' he said.

She closed the car door behind her and he watched her let herself into her flat before taking a deep breath.

*

57

At home the house was cold. He changed into his pyjamas, pulled the duvet over him and checked Facebook on his tablet. He was so tired but he lay in bed, in the dark, scrolling down the ever so bright screen. Most of his friends were people he went to school or university with, though he no longer had real-world contact with any of them.

Facebook late at night put in him a catastrophic form of loneliness, staring at the lives being lived out there, those dutifully filed online for people like Sam to marvel over – days out with babies in country parks, the selection of wedding venues, ice cream sundaes in nice-looking restaurants, arm in arm with a lover before the Eiffel Tower. His friends lambasted social media, citing invasion of privacy, tax evasion, the addicting properties of the Internet, the unmitigated disaster of the echo chamber, but they all used it. Sam knew it wasn't good, that something deeply sinister and depressing was at play beneath the pixels, but its pull was enormously strong, way too strong for him to resist.

It had been so long since he'd taken a genuine interest in a girl, he found it hard to know how he felt. The happiness he'd felt on the mountain was already beginning to warp as all the memories of his life came pouring back in. The bubble in which he'd spent the evening had burst, so he scrolled and scrolled and tried to fight off the darkness. Why couldn't he just be normal?

At last he sensed he could fall asleep, so he quickly listened to his voicemails before setting the sleep timer alarm on his radio, listening to a debate on the coming apocalypse when antibiotics will no longer work, hearing how people will die from a common infection, how governments are burying their head in the sand and we're all doomed. But it was OK because even listening to this was better than facing the total horror of his sixth layer of thought.

Chapter Six

A real-life superhero came to the aid of over a hundred vulnerable people on Thursday night, community workers report.

The incident took place late on Duke Street, where volunteers run a soup kitchen and food bank for the city's homeless. Nicholas Bush, 47, one of the volunteers said, 'It was just a normal night when all of a sudden we saw this dark figure running towards us, dressed in fancy dress. We all thought it was a drunk guy on a stag party until he threw a big bag of sandwiches and pasties at us.'

The sandwiches are thought to have originated from popular baking chain Greggs, who were unavailable for comment.

Sharon Claymore, 54, another volunteer, commended the masked vigilante. 'In all my years I've never seen anything like it. I don't know about the costume but the sandwiches were much needed and appreciated.'

This is not the first time people have taken to the streets of Britain dressed as masked crusaders . . .

He skipped this part.

A police spokesperson said, 'No law has been broken, no crime committed, so if somebody wants to help people, even dressed as a superhero, it's up to them, though we wouldn't recommend it. Vigilantism itself is a crime and so if this man has any

Sitting at his breakfast table the next morning with a warm croissant and cup of coffee, Sam scrolled through the Google results. The story was posted on his local paper's website under the headline *Superhero Loose On City Streets*, and the story had been syndicated on a few other sites, as well as being shared on Facebook and Twitter, where it had gained the hashtag #RealLifeSuperhero.

Stunned, Sam reached for his breakfast marmalade and spread it on the croissant. He didn't know what he expected, hadn't even considered the possibility of his alter ego being reported in the press. That others might be interested in his dressing up was, in retrospect, completely obvious now. He took a bite of his croissant.

He needed to be more careful, lurk in the shadows, cut the number of days he patrolled. What would Sarah think of all this? Oh. That thought didn't feel nice. Yesterday, being the Phantasm was one thing. Suddenly today, it was another.

'You're a sensitive boy,' his mother had once told him, and she was right. He sensed the feelings of others keenly, and frequently put himself second if it meant making somebody else feel good. His friends labelled this a weakness (and sometimes pious) – and maybe it was – but Sam couldn't help himself. He took pleasure in seeing others happy – that's what made *him* happy – but being in a new relationship (not that he assumed a relationship was a foregone conclusion but it was surely a possibility) meant losing out on the safe and comfortable life he had built around himself, over which he exercised so much control. He took another bite of his croissant.

All the odd routines, like the way he took time to appreciate the lovely carpet in the boot of his car, would be gone, or at least diminished, because showing Sarah how he liked to stare into the boot for minutes at a time, at the clean, empty space, might distance himself from her. He liked his routines, they brought him tremendous calm. To lose them would be to lose a large part of who he was, and erode the dam built between him and the raging chaos that swirled at the edges of his mind.

But if he was so scared and worried at the prospect of his life changing, why did he get butterflies whenever he remembered Sarah's face in the moonlight? And as each successive memory arrived, he sensed the distant collapse of rocks somewhere in the kingdom.

Sometimes Sam would just gravitate to the place where he grew up. He sat in his parked car opposite his parents' old house and felt the enveloping warmth of being there. He knew this street so well, had cycled up and down it so many times he knew every crack on the pavement, every lip of every kerb. It still felt like home. He looked at the house, at the bedroom windows behind which they'd all slept, the front door he'd posed before on his first day of school, for a photograph.

Pushing the car door open, the cold air hitting his face, Sam walked down the street. It was so quiet, just as it had always been. Put up in the seventies – pebble-dashed walls, stone cladding beneath the ground-floor windows – it now housed mostly retirees who had never moved. Memories hatched in that quick way where they merge to form a feeling, an essence of his life then, how it had been.

When he reached the end of the street he turned left into the alleyway, which led to a small gravel track near the river, a little path between two tall fences, away from the estate and on to the horse paddocks and then across the river bridge to the woods. Halfway along the steel bridge Sam stopped to watch the water move beneath him.

The Phantasm had to endure. He would just be more careful. He'd pulled on the mask to help people, and even if only by a tiny amount, he knew he had made the world a better place with some of the things he'd done.

He crossed the river and came to the woods, turning left, heading north, wintry branches hanging still in the dead air, the sky pearlescent beyond. The air was still and so cold it carried sound easily – the caw of crows, the rush of the river. Tree roots snaked from the hard ground, fallen autumn leaves drifted against ridges of jutting rock. He'd been here hundreds of times as a kid but it never lost its magic.

He checked his phone, but nothing from Sarah. There was a text from Tango, though. *What are you doing tomorrow night?* Sam ignored it. He thought of Sarah. Try as he might, he couldn't *stop* thinking about her.

Shafts of sunlight gave the water of a tributary stream a strange white translucence, a fairy-tale effect, and then he came to a ridge, and continued over it into a small valley where he had once spent a dark winter night reading comic books by torchlight. Up the far slope a tricky clamber away stood the old tree with its overhanging roots, the cleft in the rock where the tree had split the cave open.

He didn't think he would ever come back again but here he was, scrambling up the slope, her face repeating in his mind, making him feel in turns alive and afraid, the thump of his heart at once pleasant and unpleasant. After all those years, through everything, he was back at the one place he used to come to feel safe.

Hand over fist he clambered towards the tree, breathless, leaves and rocks sliding out from under him. It was harder than he remembered, and his ribs ached, but at last he got a hold of the cliff face and sidled along under the tree roots to the cave, his Batcave, the place of ultimate safety. He thought it might open him up, give him a kind of perspective, tell him what to do, but it did none of these things. Whatever spiritual link had existed between him and this place was absent now. He looked down into the small leaf-strewn basin, at the tree trunks growing at strange angles, the black remains of a bonfire, a grey squirrel scuttling along a branch. Suddenly, he felt like crying. Turning into the cave, he found the hidden alcove at the back and reached inside, hoping to find something he'd missed last time he was here – a magnifying glass, a pencil, a comic, some message from the past – but there was nothing there save dusty rock.

It was such a familiar voice, yet so long since he'd heard it.

'Sam?'

'Oh,' he said.

The woman in the doorway of the house, not his parents' but the one next door, looked so much older now. Her face had thinned and crumpled, she was ever so slightly hunched, her hair less full. But there she was. Guilt, built over time, welled up inside him. Seeing her now, he realised the scale of his betrayal.

'God look at you.'

When he was growing up, Sam would go to Moira's house to play with the dog and eat biscuits before his parents got home from work. Being part of the old gentry, she would take him for day trips to local farms, hidden pockets of the country you wouldn't even know existed, or the country houses and huge manors on the brink of bankruptcy as the old ways died. He'd go and watch detective dramas on her huge television; would, on occasion, be taken to the cinema to watch a film she wanted to see (widowed and childless, with her family miles away, she wanted a companion and Sam was fine with that – he liked her). Moira had been a huge part of his childhood, and he hadn't seen her in years.

'What are you doing here?'

'I was just passing, thought I'd come see the old place.'

'I hope you were going to knock my door.'

'I was in a bit of a rush,' he blurted.

'You should come and see me, dear.'

She was a thin woman, but tall; even with the hunch she looked down on him as he went to the edge of her garden.

'I know. I'm just, you know, so busy.'

'Don't give me that.'

Her brazen manner was only a shell for her kindness. Sam tapped the end of his key with his little finger.

'I'm sorry. It's just . . .'

'I know. Come in, the kettle's on.'

He wanted to go in. More than anything he wanted to go in. She'd have the log fire burning in there, that special kind of heat. He could listen to her stories about her nieces and nephews – and, possibly, their kids now – what meals she had planned for the week ahead, her TV schedule. He wondered if the portrait of her old racehorse, Thunder, was still on the wall, the holiday knick-knacks still cramming every inch of every shelf.

'I really do have to go,' he said.

She stood with one hand on her front door, using it as a support, and there was the sudden sense of the crushing effects of time.

'I'll come back, I promise, but I have to go. I have to . . . go.'

She stared at him. Her eyes bored a hole through his skin, loosing so many memories, and in that moment he could tell she could see past his clothes and skin and organs, past even the years he'd put between the Event and now, right into the black scribble of his heart.

The Phantasm #005

Man's Best Friend

It's Malcolm. He's sure it's Malcolm. He checks his Phantfone and, using his 4G, finds the news article. Malcolm has been missing for five months and the campaign to find him had become so widespread it had been picked up in the news. After she lost her husband, Malcolm was all Josephine Grabham had left. But Malcolm could not get over the grief of losing Private Andrew Grabham of the British Army and, when he went missing, the story touched the nation. It had spread like wildfire across all social media, there were coordinated teams out looking for him on weekends. The Phantasm looks at the photograph of Malcolm, his sad adolescent face, and compares it to the one looking at him from between the bins in the deserted lane. Whenever Private Grabham returned from a tour of the Middle East, Malcolm was the first to greet him, running across the tarmac of the barracks and jumping up at him, welcoming him home, licking his face wildly. Malcolm is a dog.

A lovely border collie with one green eye and one blue eye and a distinctive black-and-white pelt.

When the dark hero calls his name, the dog's head tilts inquisitively to one side. It's him. Slowly, the Phantasm moves in. He reaches out his arms and pictures the joyous face of Josephine when he returns her lost love. But it's not going to be so simple. Malcolm bolts. He dashes past the masked champion of the night, who lunges but misses, and off he sprints up the lane. Immediately the Phantasm is after him.

But boy is he fast. He wishes he'd brought his bike, because Malcolm is getting away. Out into the main street the dog is up ahead, dodging traffic, and the hero's heart leaps into his mouth. Between the headlights of the cars the dog is making a beeline right up the centre of the road. There is no choice. Into the traffic he goes, following the animal. Horns blare, people wind down their windows, then wind them right back up again when they see the masked spectre hurtling towards them.

The dog is tiring and the guardian is almost within reach but, just before he can make a lunge, Malcolm darts to the left, into an oncoming Vauxhall Corsa. The driver can't see the canine, for he is below the level of the bonnet, and without a thought for his own safety the Phantasm leaps out in front of the car, hoping the driver will spy him and slam on the brakes. This doesn't happen. The front of the car misses Malcolm by a hair's breadth. Quick as a flash, the Phantasm leaps into the air. Now the brakes screech, but it's too late. He turns his body and his buttocks impact the front third of the car's bonnet, sending him into a spin where he loses all sense of up and down. The sound as he bounces sideways across the steel is extremely loud, but he rolls off the other side before the windshield reaches him.

Picking himself up, he notices a huge dent in the Corsa. Not good. The vehicle is a shocking pink, emblazoned with the logo *Shaniqua's Nails and Brows*. Shaniqua stares at the masked man before her, mouth open, the glow of her mobile phone underlighting her ample chin. An anonymous cash donation will arrive at Shaniqua's boutique tomorrow. But his main priority is Malcolm, who's hightailing it past the butcher's. No time for sausages today. The dog looks over his shoulder, his tongue lolling with exertion. Yes, the Phantasm is still on you, my good man. His upper-body protection has seen him unharmed by the puny automobile.

'Malcolm, no!' he calls.

The dog has found a gap under the fence into the train station and is on the empty platform when the hero joins him. His head is low and he looks up with puppy-dog eyes. There is a space between them of perhaps twenty feet. *Nineteen. Eighteen.*

'It's OK, Malcolm, I'm going to take you home.'

The dog seems to trust him. Or perhaps it is more akin to respect.

'Ooh, you're a handsome gentleman, yes you are,' says the costumed crusader. *Thirteen.* 'What a lovely, lovely boy you are, Malcolm. A true gent.'

The dog stares at him.

'You're such a well-behaved young man.'

Eight.

There is a rumbling behind him, which comes on fast. Malcolm's ears prick up. Before him, the Phantasm's shadow lengthens. It's the London train. Fast, long, too busy to stop at a little station like this. Malcolm leaps up.

'*No!*'

The dog jumps on to the line, which screeches electrically. Somehow he avoids stepping on the tracks.

The hero freezes for a second. The ground is shaking. And then he is in the air, dropping down. The sound wave of the train's frenzied horn clatters through him. He's misjudged this. He's not going to make it. He throws his arms around Malcolm's midriff and they tumble. With every last inch of strength the Phantasm leg-thrusts towards the far side just as the train whistles past, the sensation of its turbulence tearing at his clothes as it tries to suck him back on to the tracks. He manages to dig his free hand into the rocks between the opposite tracks and hold on, smothering Malcolm as the train screeches by. And when it is over, and the world stops shaking, he gets to his feet, a true hero, Malcolm spread across his arms like a baby, frenziedly licking the Phantasm's face.

Chapter Seven

In work he kept his desk perfectly clear: a stacked in, out and 'long-term' paper tray and, on the top, his collection of large stationery that wouldn't fit neatly in his drawers – paper punch, stapler, 30cm ruler, calculator. Everyone else in the office had normal hardware but Sam had bought a sleek, wireless keyboard and mouse. Wires made everything so complicated. He hated it when the surface of his desk wasn't perfectly clutter-free, but when he got back after his week off the plain white surface was a horrible mess of folders and letters and faxed orders.

Rebecca from Accounts had called him OCD. Sam had laughed but didn't agree. He'd seen many programmes about people who couldn't leave the house, who cleaned eighteen hours a day, who went through scrubbing brushes and whole bottles of toilet cleaner, bleach and antibacterial spray on a daily basis, whose lives had been ruined by the compulsion to clean. He wasn't *that* bad. Sam's house was spotless, every-thing organised, he had a cupboard full of cleaning products and a monthly cleaning schedule, he liked things like coasters and TV remotes to be symmetrical, but he was by no means a sufferer of OCD. True he couldn't quite relax if everything wasn't in perfect order – if he suspected the sheets of his bed upstairs weren't quite wrinkle-free, for example – but it didn't impact his life. He read road signs twice, from beginning to end, blinked in even numbers, counted off in his head every figure on his speedometer twice – 10 20 30 40 50 60 70 80 90 100 110 120 130 140 mph kph, 10 20 30 40 50 60 70 80 90 100 110 120 130 140 mph kph – but he only did these things when alone. If he was with others he was fine and didn't think about it at all. All of this notwithstanding, he definitely had to clear his desk as quickly as possible.

In no particular order he stacked the papers into a neat pile, just to get the Formica surface into view. His inbox was just as bad. His email was organised into neat folders by client, supplier and internal mail. He liked his inbox to be completely empty so when he logged on and found it four pages long – the horrible bold lettering of the unread – he knew this was going to be a long day.

At eleven o'clock he bought a sausage, egg and cheese muffin from the sandwich van that swung by every morning.

'Have you got any Cherry Coke?' he asked the driver.

'I've got Dr Pepper.'

And yet the two were nothing alike. On the way back he thought about the night before, buying a lead, tying Malcolm to the front gatepost and knocking on the door before retreating into the shadows, Mrs Grabham coming into the night, younger than Sam and widowed, seeing Malcolm, breaking down right there in the street as she fell to her knees and threw her arms around the dog's neck. True, he'd been reckless, but it had been worth it. While it was clear that Sarah was having a battering effect on Sam Holloway, she was emboldening the Phantasm, amplifying the feeling of invincibility the mask brought. He'd been hit by a car and almost hit by a train.

He printed off the picking lists for the next day's deliveries – lists of parts and where in the warehouse to find them. He took them through to Mark, the warehouse guy, a teetotal motorcycle enthusiast who worked the doors of nightclubs at weekends. He was a talented artist as well, having shown Sam some of his work when Sam mentioned he was interested in comic books. Today he found Mark sitting at his beaten-up, oil-stained desk browsing one of his many back issues of *Bizarre* magazine.

'You know we've got Romanians working here now?' he said, not looking up.

'What's that?'

'In the utility room. Ten of them. We had a reject part from Ford, so we need to sort through ten million of them in three months. They're in there already, doing it right now. The girls are absolutely incredible.'

'Ten million?'

'They're pushing them through cardboard slots Mr Okamatsu made.'

Mr Okamatsu being the UK General Manager.

'That's insane.'

'He's only just got back from China.'

'What?'

'Went on Friday night. Bought some suitcases in the airport, got a taxi to the factory, filled the suitcases with the new parts, came back. Just put them through as baggage.'

'You're kidding.'

Mark's face filled with enthusiasm. 'He did it!'

'What if he'd been caught?'

Mark shrugged. 'He had the commercial invoices with him. And Ford were on the verge of shutdown.'

Shutting down a line cost hundreds of thousands of pounds an hour, and if a supplier was responsible they'd not only lose the contract but face a court case.

'He's nuts,' Mark said.

This was certainly true. Last May, during Japanese Golden Week when factories close down, Mr Okamatsu had called Sam at home and told him to come into the office as a matter of extreme importance. An urgent order had come in and they needed it ready for delivery by three. They prepared the parts, but when it came to raising the warehouse shutters to get them out, the chains came off the pulley. At this, Mr Okamatsu made Sam get on the forklift and lift him, on the forks, the thirty feet to examine the problem. Sam had never driven a forklift truck before, let alone held a licence, but Mr Okamatsu, with his austere face and eyes surveying everything from behind his light-sensitive glasses, insisted, 'Easy, easy.' So there he was, suspended thirty feet above the hard concrete floor, wobbling on the forks as Sam tried to raise him up as slowly as possible. When he reached the chains, Mr Okamatsu leaned across, lost his footing, and swung out across the warehouse, gripping the chains Tarzan-like, fully suited with shiny leather brogues, legs kicking, body twirling as he swung his way back on to the forks, while Sam watched in horror. Upon his safe return, Mr Okamatsu was completely unfazed.

Sam's phone buzzed in his pocket. Without thinking, he pulled it out and his heart jolted. It was from Sarah.

Heya, sorry for the late reply, been away and couldn't get signal. Yeah (in reply to a text Sam had sent her on Sunday) *really enjoyed Fri. Do you wanna meet up one day this week?*

'Everything OK?' said Mark.

'Yeah, yeah, fine.'

Blood rushing, Sam tried to focus. He checked the time: 1:48. If he returned the text later that evening, say 8:30, it would give him nearly seven hours of contemplation.

What did she want to do? Was it a date? Should he buy condoms? No. That was presumptuous. He didn't even want to have sex with someone he'd just met. Is that what she wants? Don't be silly, Sam, you're not attractive. You do not have sexual magnetism.

He went back to his desk and continued his work. He hardly thought about Sarah and the text, as the calm simplicity of numbers and figures enveloped him in a kindly tide and washed him away from reality. The office numbers dwindled with the daylight as the British staff clocked out, but Sam ploughed on, processing orders, checking stock, replying to Quality Departments all over the country (better to do it himself than pass the work on to Linda, who was not great at her job) with all the information they needed on certain parts – technical drawings, chemical breakdowns, safety test results – using the efficient catalogue of parts he had created when Linda had given up.

Dark now outside, through the little barred window above his desk he watched the silver clouds edged with blue traverse the moon. A hand fell on his shoulder. He turned, and the tall figure of Mr Okamatsu, with his light-sensitive glasses and gelled hair, loomed over him.

'Sam,' he said with his short, quick pronunciation. 'You have returned.'

'Mr Okamatsu.'

A curt nod. And nothing more. Good man for working late, was what the gesture meant. Nice to have you back. Mr Okamatsu backed slowly away, pivoted on his heels, and returned to his desk.

His father said, *You can always tell a gentleman if he carries a freshly pressed handkerchief.* And it made perfect sense. Of course a true gentleman carries a freshly pressed handkerchief, and Sam was diligent in obeying the maxim. Tonight was handkerchief-ironing night. He kept his used hankies in a small white basket lined with linen, and washed them when the basket was full. After finishing the last one, enjoying the satisfying hiss of the metal meeting the cloth, he folded it up and placed it with the others on the shelf in his wardrobe and picked up his phone. It was time to reply.

Hiya, sorry, it was crazy in work today. I've got a busy week this week. What did you have planned?

He threw the phone down on to his bed, as if it were an insect. He put away the ironing board and looked out the window at the neat back garden glowing white in the moonlight.

The little pond in the top right corner, set amidst a rockery decorated with heathers, was icing over. Sparkles of frost glimmered on the rocks. The phone buzzed.

Ah no probs. Just thought it would be nice to see you.

He saw her, clear as day. The pretty face and glasses, a pint of Guinness in her hand, her red-and-black hair the shape of two scimitars. It's time to move on, the higher Sam said. He stood frozen on his carpet, staring at the phone as it balanced on his open palm. He flicked it with his thumb and it spun, and he asked himself, simply, OK, do you want to spend time with her or not? His heart was racing and he was sweating. This isn't normal, he told himself. Just a few hours in the pub, nothing deeper. Eyes closed, he thought of his parents, standing at the side of the wishing pond on the mountainside, the sunlight swallowing them.

He brought the phone up and watched the blank space of a new message, the little cursor blinking on and off.

Chapter Eight

He did this sometimes, stood in front of his collection of Blu-rays. He found the way the boxes were all the same size and feel, all lined up neatly on the high-quality, half-height oak bookcase, very soothing. There was a knock at the front door and he came back to reality. Sam went into the hallway and found Tango holding his laptop under his arm.

'I want you to read something,' he said, bustling past Sam and back into the kitchen. He set up his computer on the breakfast bar. Sidling round to see, Sam watched Tango bring up the familiar old Microsoft Word XP program that he hadn't updated since school because it would be bad luck.

'You could have called.'

'I've texted you like five times.'

Tango never emailed his writing, always insisting people read it in situ. He'd seen a DVD extra where the film director Christopher Nolan does the same thing with scripts; takes them to the actor's house where they read them while he waits in another room before taking the script away with him.

'I'm kinda busy tonight,' Sam said.

'It's only short. You have to read it because I want to enter it into a competition and I need feedback.'

He was always so jerky in his movements, the way he jabbed the keys, the way he leaned down to peer at the screen at zero degrees, even the way his pupils darted around. He'd been like this since infancy.

'So who was that girl?' he said, casually, not taking his eyes off the screen.

'What girl?'

'From Friday.'

He pulled up the file and slid the laptop across to Sam. 'Here you go,' he said, not waiting for Sam's answer.

'*Perpetual Motion*,' said Sam.

'Yup.'

'Good title.'

He listened to Tango's breath of relief. He didn't understand why Tango put so much stock in his opinions. Sam stood up and carried the laptop over to the armchair at the entrance of the conservatory.

'I'm going to make a cup of tea,' said Tango.

'No.'

'But I just want to see where you are.'

'No. Go to the living room and wait for me there. You know the rules.'

Disappointed, Tango followed the order.

Sam set the laptop on his knee and read the first line:

The devil is a code that runs through us all.

The story was, in fact, not short at all and it took Sam the best part of an hour to read it. Like most of Tango's stories it was exceedingly dense, about a man living inside a perpetual-motion machine he'd invented. There were long, detailed passages about drawing energy from other dimensions in the quantum world and replenishing it with the machine's by-products, and layered treatises on the nature of immortality.

As he neared the end of the story, he noticed a movement in the conservatory window.

'I thought I told you to wait in the living room.'

Tango's reflection started.

'I was just wondering how you're getting on,' he said, nervously.

Sam closed the laptop and turned to Tango with a sad look on his face.

'I loved it!' he said.

'Great! Cup of tea?'

A small but pleasant ritual the two had established was that, before discussing whatever Tango had written, they'd make tea in a pot and bring it into the living room on a tray along with the other parts of the tea set Sam had purchased for a lot of money from Fortnum & Mason as a special treat on a day trip to London.

'So you're saying she just started talking to you?'

He liked watching the splash sugar cubes made when dropped into tea.

'Yup.'

'This is great news, Sam.'

'Is it?'

Tango fixed him with a stare. 'Yes. It is.'

An unspoken message passed between them. Sam leaned back in his chair with cup and saucer in his left hand. He remembered Tango as he had been as a child – tall, with trousers not reaching his ankles, big glasses, greasy hair – back when he was known by his real name, Alan.

'We might be going out tomorrow night,' he said.

Tango smiled. 'I'm really happy for you,' he said, in a rare and striking display of affection that peeled off the years and put both of them them back into that childhood friendship. Then he poured his tea. 'OK, enough about you. Can we talk about my story now?'

So what's the plan? x Sarah texted him the next day, on his lunch break.

Sam replied, *Shall I pick you up at your place?*

Within seconds she replied, *Cool. What time? Xx*

And he wrote, *7? x*, a small kiss that made his body tingle.

Across the table in the tiny staffroom Mark flicked through his *Bizarre* magazine, his left hand feeling blindly for his open lunch box and the cold sausage bap squashed in the corner. Sam figured seven o'clock would be OK.

Sounds good x

And that was that. Behind the thin walls he could hear the Romanians in the small utility room, sifting through the millions of parts, one deep voice saying something loudly followed by a chorus of laughter, then silence. He sat there a moment, feeling sweat rise from his skin, and imagined a tiny green shoot growing on barren wastes.

When he got back to work after lunch, there was a state of agitation in the office, people looking through files, making calls. Mr Okamatsu sat calmly behind his desk scanning the Japanese newspaper.

Rebecca walked over to Sam, a half-run-half-walk kind of walk.

'One of the ships has gone down in the Suez Canal.'

There was a manic fire in her eyes as she flapped a wad of faxes.

'Gone down?'

'Sunk.'

Sam had seen cargo ships on a business trip to Rotterdam, seen the shocking nature of their enormous size. Huge chunks of metal, skyscrapers laid sideways, drifting calmly. That one of those things might sink – even in open sea, let alone in a canal – seemed impossible.

'They're sending through the waybills and packing sheets,' said Rebecca.

Others in the office were talking on phones, readjusting figures, pulling files, but it was always Rebecca who took the lead. He set to work checking his own accounts, entering the lost stock into the system to see the new forecasts and trying to calculate how much he would have to ship by air, which was very expensive. To not have stock arrive on time would be a huge dishonour to Electronica Diablique, not to mention the cataclysm of shutting down production lines all over the country.

The work kept Sam's mind off his impending date. He spent a lot of time emailing his clients, asking how much stock they had in reserve and how long they could manage without their parts. In the world of electronics manufacturing this was about as exciting as it got. He found something thrilling in writing the words, *One of our ships has gone down in the Suez Canal.* On the Internet it said all men aboard had been recovered safely, apart from one worker, still missing, last seen heading towards the engine room, which had flooded and caused the disaster. A life at sea comes with known risks, Sam reasoned. It is something a seaman accepts. But as he sat there with his databases and spreadsheets, the thought of that man, a humble sailor trying to save his ship, kept scratching at the window of his mind. He tried to remember how to create an Excel pivot table but found it impossible as suddenly, just like the engine room, his mind flooded and all he could think about was the act of drowning, the terror coming in the minutes leading up to death when you realise that it's going to happen and there's nothing you can do.

And the old storm clouds drifted in.

He hadn't felt this way in years, this awful desperation, hovering over the edge of a panic attack. Suddenly the raging turmoil was back, as if it had never been away, setting in motion the foggy tumult of depression. Why is this happening? He sat at his desk and printed out some sheets and tried to staple them, but he couldn't get the edges to align perfectly and he was overcome by the sudden impulse to smash the stapler through the barred window above his desk. He was sweating. That poor man, trapped down there with the water coming in, trying to save the ship. And why? Sarah's face appeared in his mind's eye. The containers that moved around the world and kept the man in a job so he could provide food and shelter for his family, the containers that were dispatched to production lines all over the world, millions of people standing over conveyer belts moving pieces of metal from one place to another and if they didn't exist the man wouldn't have been on the ship in the first place and so wouldn't have had to try to save them and would still be alive. By this far-reaching, irrefutable logic, Sam was responsible for the man's death. Through the complex web of modern-world connections he was directly linked to that drowning sailor trapped in the depths of a hulking cargo chip.

He remembered his breathing techniques and closed his eyes. He imagined a lovely beige carpet cut into a freshly painted skirting board, a bare room with minimalist furniture. Simple. Simplicity. Sitting down to a nice cup of coffee. And yet we go about our lives without ever thinking of the people working whole lifetimes on coffee plantations, living awful hand-to-mouth existences in the hope things will be better for their kids, but they never are, and all so that we may enjoy sugar-free gingerbread one-shot skinny decaf lattes with a sprinkling of cinnamon in lovely coffee shops who falsely proclaim ethical perfection. Or how we are able to afford enormous televisions with pixels so dense they're too crisp for the human eye to fully decode, all thanks to Chinese workers toiling in city-sized factories under whose roofs they work, live, breed, ail and die. Our clothes stitched by slave hands, our food drawn from land so decimated by over-farming and chemicals that it will eventually lift and blow into the sea. Businesses competing hard and, instead of it being healthy, it's become a driving down of human standards, a race to the bottom with those already there so pulverised they become the sort of men who will head *down* into a sinking ship instead of up. These were the tumbling thoughts in Sam's mind. We're just tiny organisms scuttling across the surface of a small planet, existing for a mere flicker of time, and yet we spend so much of that time in a state of struggle. There were Romanians within fifty feet of him he'd never seen and who would spend a month of their precious lives – a whole month – slotting tubes of metal through cardboard slits because a safety inspector had to make stricter and stricter regulations so he could get paid more money, the ultimate effect being tighter deadlines, things being rushed, not safer, corners cut, ships sinking, lower pay for the lower workers because people still want their motor-cars to be affordable.

He feared he might start crying, and it wasn't all because of the state of the world. The voice of reason was now telling him he hadn't recovered from the Event at all, he had just hidden everything away and become a stupid, childish super-hero instead. But if he was going to meet Sarah and make progress, why did he feel so awful? He checked the clock. Ten to five. He wasn't staying late tonight. He packed up his things, washed his face in the Gents, and left.

On the way home he called into a florist's and bought a large bunch of colourful flowers. He found the colours of their petals unspeakably lovely in their innocence. But they weren't for Sarah. It was dark now and ornate Narnian lamp posts lighted the way through the graveyard. Sam couldn't remember the last time he'd been here.

Small pellets of rain were tossed on the wind as he placed the flowers on his parents' grave. He'd spent years as a vir-tual recluse, had made no new friends since the Event, had felt a rage in him so deep and powerful it surely couldn't exist in other people. It weighed so heavily on him something vital had snapped to drive him to the person he now was, a lonely man in his mid-twenties dressing up as a superhero.

He was so far from normal the idea of something normal befalling him, something like a girlfriend, was terrifying.

Staring at the grave, he felt the numbness in which he had submerged himself all those years calling to him. He could happily curl up on the gravestone and stay there for ever. But it was impossible because Sam had to go home, go home and get ready, get ready for the future. Whatever that was.

He showered, shaved, and stood in front of his clothes, which were laid neatly on the bed. He checked the time. Outside, rain clicked at the windows. Nerves. He pulled on his clothes and imagined Sarah sitting in her flat above the abandoned shop, waiting for him.

He remembered the feeling, all those months ago, when he'd stood in front of the mirror in his costume, how insane he'd felt. What would she think when she found out about the Phantasm? The possibility of burning everything crossed his mind, and yet he knew he could do no such thing. It was too much a part of him now. He'd kept it secret from the world this long; one more person wouldn't hurt.

'What are you doing?' he said out loud to his reflection.

His heart raced. In front of the mirror he painted around his eyes with eyeliner and went back to the bed, where he pulled on his vest, clipped on his belt and donned the mask. In the mirror, he nodded, and pictured Sarah again, staring at her watch, expecting him any second, and how she was going to feel when he didn't arrive. The Phantasm stared back at him from beyond the mirror and smiled. And then left the house.

Ⓟ

The Phantasm #006

The Lonely Traveller

A great man once said, 'Never judge a person by how they treat their friends – being nice to friends is easy – judge them by how they treat strangers.' Good advice. Sometimes one must make the ultimate decision: have courage, and step out of the shadows.

Or cycle out of the shadows on a lightweight, sprayed-black-as-night bicycle if that is the preferred mode of transport for the evening. Which, on this night, it is. All thoughts of the man behind the mask are gone; the only thing that matters is the mission. And this is good. The mask removes all complications.

The registration plate on the huge artic lorry is Polish, with the letters PL set beneath the circle of yellow stars on a blue background that denotes the European Union. The lorry driver, obese, moustachioed, lost, is standing outside his truck, his faithful steed, consulting a road map in the light of the orange street lamp. A cigarette hangs loosely from his lips.

Little does he know that a phantom of justice watches from the shadows, eagle-eyed. Time to roll out. Setting his right foot on the. pedal, the mountain bike wheels from the darkness and towards the stricken traveller. St Christopher would be proud.

The lorry driver glances up casually, sees the dark entity cycling towards him, then looks back at his map. Then he looks up again quickly and the cigarette falls out of his mouth on to the map. Orange sparks go everywhere, like fireflies, and the cigarette rolls on to his ample belly, making him panic, as he swipes it off into the bushes at the side of the road.

'Friend!' says the Phantasm, braking. He puts a hand on his chest and says, gently, 'Friend.'

The driver stares at him for a moment and then says something in a foreign language. Hmm.

'English?' he says.

The driver shakes his head.

The Phantasm smiles kindly and holds out his hands, nodding at the map. 'Lost? Are. You. Lost?'

He steps slowly towards the driver, as a veterinarian might approach a frightened dog. The man has bags under his eyes and is clearly exhausted. He seems confused by the costume.

'I. Help. You,' says the avenging force, very slowly, holding his hands out further again towards the map. Poor old-timer's probably never heard of sat nav.

This time, the man of the road comprehends and starts nodding. The Phantasm nods back, enthusiastically, making the Polish man nod even more enthusiastically again. This is a superb coup for international relations!

The driver goes into his pocket and, with genuine glee on his face, pulls out a scrap of paper. On it is an address. The masked hero takes the scrap in his glove and reads it, and nods once more. The glow of a newly formed friendship warms the air.

'You,' he says, pointing. 'Follow. Me.' And he jabs his thumb back at himself, miming the motion of cycling to demonstrate his intention of leading the gentleman to his destination, which just so happens to be a factory less than a mile away.

The Pole holds out his hand and they shake on it. He is smiling, his face an expression of joy and relief.

The hero turns the bicycle around so that it is facing downhill, and he looks over his shoulder as the lorry driver climbs aboard his mighty vehicle.

The Phantasm holds an arm aloft, readying himself. The engine roars to life behind him, he is lit up by a set of powerful headlights, he drops his arm and, together, they speed off into the night. Carried away in the moment the wind sings against his face as he descends the hill.

The black bike zips under the old railway bridge and round the corner. He should have the driver to the factory in less than ten minutes. He pictures the scene: a tiny bicycle leading a huge articulated eight-wheeler to safety, just as a little tugboat might steer a colossal cargo tanker through a treacherous harbour.

He can hear the tyres of his bike grip the blacktop. Strange. Where's the rumble of the engine?

He glances over his shoulder. The truck is not there. Tracking back on himself, the Phantasm investigates. Then he realises something. Isn't the old railway bridge a low bridge? Consulting his memory, he is sure there are black-and-yellow hazard markings on it . . .

Yes, it is a low bridge. The Phantasm tries to imagine the scene in his mind. The driver, alone in his cab late at night. A friendly face come to help. He follows. A low bridge. But what happened next? He must have panicked and made a disastrous error of judgement because, as the Phantasm comes back around the bend, he sees the main body of the truck is well and truly wedged under the bridge. Cars are building up in the area, from both directions. The road is blocked: the truck's cab has veered into the opposite lane, making both ways impassable. Many, many car horns are tooting. And there he is, the traveller from a far-off land, his head popping out the window, his arms waving.

'Hey!' the driver calls.

The hero's eyes meet those of the traveller. He is very, very angry. The scene is chaos. There are too many people around. Sometimes you must lose the battle to win the war. With this thought in mind, the masked vigilante turns the bicycle around, hoping the driver won't mind too much. He imagines the view from the cab, of the hero who almost saved him but who is now undertaking a U-turn in the open road and heading in the opposite direction, around the corner, out of sight.

He retrieves his phone from his utility belt. The least he can do is call 999.

Chapter Nine

When he was fifteen years old, Sam's parents announced his mother's new pregnancy. A little brother or sister would be arriving, and how did he feel about that? Sam was overjoyed. The prospect of a new sibling he could take on adventures and hang around the house with was one that filled him with excitement. He helped his parents decorate the spare room, went shopping on weekends for baby clothes and even managed to find his first part-time job, at the local video shop, which he absolutely loved. With his wages he opened a Post Office savings account for the new arrival, depositing one pound of his wages each week, which wasn't much, but because Sam intended the fund to mature on his brother or sister's seventh birthday he could present them with a cheque for the huge amount of £364 plus interest.

He needn't have worried about it being a boy or a girl because, as it transpired, he got one of each. The twins were born one chilly December morning: Steven Paul (after his grandfathers) and Sally Jean (after her grandmothers). There was something odd at first about calling a small baby Steve but it soon became natural.

The babies were a delight. They were born at the perfect time, nearing the end of school's Michaelmas term, affording Sam a great deal of time to spend with them over the Christmas holidays. With their arrival came a new type of warmth to the family home, which Sam enjoyed immensely – for, apart from his small group of friends, school was still proving difficult.

Around that time he was immersing himself in comic lore. His new job in the video shop gave him money to buy expensive graphic novels that he had hitherto been unable to afford. He started off with *Batman* cycles and discovered darker writers like Grant Morrison and Frank Miller, but it was following the discovery of the *Preacher* comics that he really became aware of the power graphic novels can impart. Here was a story of fallen angels and the destruction of Heaven, blended with the adventures of humans trying to make their way in the world. And it was very, very violent. Its quality was so high that, when he finished, he craved more. And that was when he discovered Neil Gaiman's *Sandman*, arguably the greatest set of comics ever written, a series that encapsulated almost every conceivable human emotion and behaviour. He found it hard to believe that stories could operate at such high levels with hardly anyone seeming to know about them.

At the same time he loved watching the personalities emerge in Steve and Sally and would sit with them for hours in the evenings, giving his parents some downtime. They were a lot older than when they had Sam, nearing their forties, and bringing up twins at any age is always difficult. Because of the age gap he couldn't help but wonder if the twins were an accident, and this led him to a much more awful thought. Maybe *he* was the mistake and they had the twins because the time was finally right. Had he ruined their lives?

School was better when he got to sixth form. Most of the jocks and tougher kids had left for the nearby college, leaving space for Sam to grow into. He got contacts for his eyes, and when his braces came off he became more confident, he started smiling again, and this made him happier. He talked more to girls, though mainly in the capacity of friend rather than potential lover. He fell in love with a girl named Alexi

Richardson, but his feelings were desperately unrequited. He started going to the pub, where underage drinking was more or less permitted, and though he spent most of his time in a dark corner with Tango and Blotchy, he did on one drunken occasion, with the wind in his sails, kiss a girl in the alleyway where they kept the bins.

The twins learned to crawl, walk and talk. Big Steve, as Sam's friends called him, because he had grown more quickly than Sally, was boisterous, a big character who would have overwhelmed Sally were it not for her being, like her older brother, naturally introverted. When Sam was studying for his 'A' Levels Sally was old enough and quiet enough to accompany him to his room, where she would sit silently flicking through books with cardboard pages.

Hormonally, acne notwithstanding, Sam was relatively unaffected by late adolescence. His love for Alexi Richardson was powerful, but not so powerful as to throw him off his schoolwork, as it did with Tango, who fell head over heels for a girl two years his junior. During those months leading up to their final exams, Tango complained of not being able to revise because his heart was too full, even though he and Eliza had not exchanged a single word. As a result of this he got a C, an E and a U in Sociology, English and Computer Science, respectively. But Sam, even through the fog of love, managed A, B, C and was accepted to read Geography at Warwick University. His life was writing itself. Soon, he would move away from everything he loved, and take a step into the big wide world.

When he got home he checked his phone. There were two missed calls and two texts from Sarah. The texts just asked where he was, nothing more. The last one was at 8:15. They weren't angry, and the lack of anger just made Sam feel worse. He pictured her dressed up and ready to go, her coat on, checking her watch, and the terrible familiarity of regret crunched into him. Usually, after getting back from a patrol, the adrenaline buzz would keep him buoyant but this time all that lift was gone as soon as he climbed out of the costume.

Before going to bed he grabbed his spare phone, checked his voicemails, and closed his eyes in desperation at the sound of distant human voices.

He dreams of a shiny grey runway cut into a lush rainforest. A beautiful day. The sun, just past noon, draws short shadows; crisp, fluffy white clouds drift. On the ground, in the shade, the air is moist and cool. The forest breathes. He dreams a bright white plane on the runway, sleek and futuristic. He and his family climb aboard and the plane speeds down the runway and lifts over the canopy.

The forest from the sky looks like an expanse of broccoli florets. The family sit together and his sister turns to him, a spoke of sunlight turning through the cabin.

Thumbs up. *This is great.*

He wakes and remembers, and his sheets are drenched in sweat.

In the deep dark of night, pre-dawn still a few turns of the planet away, he fetched his wooden rod and opened the hatchway to the attic. Popping his head over the precipice, he pulled the cord and the strip lights clicked to life. Not high enough to stand, just a crawl space between the low wooden shelves bowed in the middle under the weight of all the comics, he dragged himself on his elbows past the enormous collection. He pulled off one shelf a copy of *Sandman Volume I: Preludes and Nocturnes* and pushed it along before him, the shelves and stories and memories of all the panels closing in around him. An embrace of stories.

He couldn't stop picturing Sarah at home, waiting for him, and couldn't understand why this image was making him feel so unhinged.

He made this maze, just wide enough to fit a human on his belly, when his library overspilled. After the Event he'd gathered these comics to him as a source of comfort. He'd never read them all, but it didn't matter. Just the sheer volume of stories made him feel safe. Back in those days, when he was still in his parents' house, he would feel the numbness start its slow saturation, and open the pages just to stare at the pictures. The narratives were of no consequence at that point; nothing mattered. On rare occasions, simply staring at the images helped.

He rounded the first corner of his comics maze, the wooden shelves just three storeys high, and came to a fork in the road. The further into the warren he went, the safer he felt. Unable to see behind him, he imagined the shelves sealing shut, feeling himself entombed by stories, sealed on the other side of reality. Life was so much easier when he hid away. Shifting right and right again, he came at last to a small opening, the centre of the labyrinth, where the space became wide enough to house a low Japanese table you could put your tea on. A travel kettle, a mini-fridge, a sugar pot, an RNLI teaspoon that had belonged to his mother, a milk jug, a cup and saucer. The only other thing on the table was a framed photograph of his family, his dad's arm around Sam's shoulder, his mum's gentle smile, the twins in the front. He couldn't remember the day it was taken. Sam lay down and turned out the lights and, tucked safely away from the world, he wrapped his arms around the *Sandman* comic, tried to clear away the thoughts of the girl with red hair, and hoped that Dream might come for him.

Chapter Ten

The cursor on his screen flashed. It was dark outside the little barred window above his desk. Strong winds made the roof of the office moan and sigh. Everyone had gone home, apart from Mr Okamatsu, who was at the printer station near Sam.

A bond existed between Sam and Okamatsu that wasn't there with the rest of the British staff, who clocked out at five on the dot and spent a lot of the day on Facebook or surfing holiday sites, yet complained the work conditions were too severe.

'Mr Okamatsu, can I ask you something?' he said.

Mr Okamatsu looked up from the printer.

'The ship that sank. Do you ever think why the man who went down with it did it? I mean, would you do that? Give your life just to save some stock?'

Mr Okamatsu paused, the papers from the printer hanging gently in his hands.

'He was doing his job,' he said. 'It is sad, but maybe, if everyone was like him, the boat would not have sunk in the first place.' He stacked the papers neatly and then said, mysteriously, 'There are always long consequences to action.'

It was misty out. Rain was close, headlights like young suns in early galactic clouds.

He churned through thoughts and emotions, inhaling, digesting, expelling as he ran.

Chemicals streamed along his veins.

That summer holiday before he went to university was the happiest of his life. Sam had learned to drive and he'd take Tango and Blotchy on regular excursions to the coast or the country or the city in his mum's car. Sam had wangled some extra shifts at the video shop, giving him considerably more disposable income, part of which he saved, part of which he spent on alcohol and comics, and part of which he used to buy presents for the twins.

When he finally arrived at Warwick he missed home terribly, but was determined to embrace the student experience. He could be anyone he wanted, and this gave him a new kind of freedom. He found himself creating an alternative Sam, pushing down the things he disliked about himself (his lack of confidence, his wish to be alone more than most people, his nervousness) and bringing to the fore the things he did like (he could occasionally be funny, he was kind, he could even be *outgoing* at a push and with a little drink). And this slight alteration of the dials paid dividends. In the Student Union bar he found himself being able to talk to girls quite easily and even put the moves on some of them, with varying degrees of success.

He dispensed with his virginity in the sunny days following his first year-end exams, bedding a girl called Amelia after the student ball. The whole thing was a bit of a mess and, in his mind, at the moment of penetration, this strange thought: There we are then, I'm in, this is what all the fuss is about. It was an awkward session and though she made the right noises he couldn't shake the feeling of there being an element of theatre at work. They had sex a few more times before summer break, but Sam soon discovered that having his alone time was more important to him than he'd ever realised. Amelia wanted to be with him all the time, and the feeling was oppressive. Fortunately for him, she Facebooked Sam in the summer to inform him she'd found someone else (a seventeen-year-old from her hometown).

Halfway through the final term of his second year, his parents visited and said they were going on a family holiday to South America. Images of the Amazon, Mayan ruins, of the Nazca Lines and Machu Picchu raced through his mind, but Sam was unable to go because he had signed up for a field trip to the Brecon Beacons in Wales, the results of which would make up the backbone of his dissertation. His parents said they'd postpone but Sam would have none of it. He knew it was their dream holiday and, being the new, well-adjusted young man he'd invented, he insisted they go.

It was incredible to observe the development of the twins. They were changing all the time. Steve was fully conversant by this point and had developed an adult neurosis, insisting on placing a clean handkerchief beneath his dining plate or bowl at mealtimes. And Sally was even more impressive, having mastered the basics of reading.

Just before they left that day Sam's father took him to one side and told him, 'You're doing really well, kiddo. Me and your mum are so proud of you.'

It was odd. Despite his semi-sarcastic maxims, his father wasn't one for speeches and it meant a lot to Sam. In the golden sunlight the warmth in his bones came from more than a burning star. Sam watched them drive away at dusk that day, down the hill, with the twins in the back seat turning round and waving through the window to him. Down the hill they went, between the blocks of student high-rises, disappearing around a corner, a deep-red sky beyond them.

Showered and changed into his pyjamas, Sam went to the conservatory with his tablet but couldn't concentrate on anything. As he sat there, staring out the window into the blackness, he felt his leg shaking. Something was starting to become clear. If there was to be any future with Sarah the time would come when he would have to tell her about the Event, about what had happened. He would have to speak about it. Out loud, to another person. He wasn't sure he could do it. It wasn't fear, or guilt for moving on, it was more the unwillingness to face what had happened. God, why did the gravity of others have to have such an unbalancing effect on his own orbit?

He lifted the tablet and reflexively scrolled through the news stories on BBC.

His phone buzzed, making him start.

Hey, how are you? Everything OK? x

He froze, then sat up in his chair, leaning over the phone. Something was happening, he sensed it; some deep undercurrent taking place in the universe. Just as she texted he'd noticed a weird story on the right hand side column of his tablet. He zoomed in on it, understanding instantly the connection between that story of the sinking ship and the girl who'd come into his life. He tapped the link and then looked back to his phone screen. It buzzed again, a vibration in his hands.

What are you doing tonight? X

He read the headline on the tablet again. Was this right? He imagined an image of a rope being thrown over the side of a ship. A lifeline.

Missing Sailor Found Drifting On Red Sea In Stolen Lifeboat.

Chapter Eleven

Sarah was in the corner, where she'd been sitting the night he met her, drinking Guinness and reading her book. She looked up and saw him and reflexively he raised an arm to wave. She sat up and pushed her glasses up her nose. Her hair was tied back into a short ponytail, her fringe parted at the side, right-angling over the rim of her glasses like a waterfall. The black streaks showed darker than the red. What on earth was someone like her doing asking someone like him to the pub, especially after last night?

'Hi.'

'Hey.' She smiled, her whole face.

The fire crackled and spat orange embers on to the rug before the hearth.

'I'm so sorry about yesterday,' he said, straight away, and as soon as he said it, he felt a lightness in his head.

'Forget it.'

'No, I'm really sorry. I feel terrible.' He set his coat over the back of the chair as she reached across the table. Sam thought this was odd but took her hand and shook it.

'Oh,' she said. 'I was just going for my drink.'

'Right, yeah,' he said, spying the near-empty Guinness next to his hand. 'Here.' He slid the glass one inch towards her.

'Thanks,' she said, with a laugh.

No problem, just pretend those last eight seconds never occurred.

'So what happened?' she said.

'I . . . uh.' He'd thought of a thousand excuses – late meeting, car broken down, tree fallen through kitchen window – but this seemed the best. A nice, simple lie. Whatever you do, don't tell her the truth, it's too weird. For all the good he did as the Phantasm, for all the good it did for him, the sense of dread about her knowing was a constant thrum at the base of him. 'I was just so tired I fell asleep.' He winced. 'I'm sorry.'

'Oh, yeah, I know what that's like.'

He knew she knew he was lying.

'Well, you're here now.'

'Yeah. Um, can I get you a drink?' he asked.

'How about we go in rounds?'

'Sure. What do you want? Guinness?'

She looked small in her seat. Looking down on her, the shape of her face was a strawberry.

'Yes please. With a dash.'

Sam pondered this. 'Lemonade?'

Sarah stared at him. 'I'm shitting you, Sam. I'll just have a Guinness.'

'Oh, ha ha ha!' The laugh came out super loud, and then they made eye contact and a sudden *Zap!* of chemicals rushed through him. Whoa. It felt nice. Quickly, he went to the bar, trying to be calm, trying to stop the buzz making his body feel like it was having a sugar high. He bought the drinks and felt good about it. It was a normal thing to do, the whole thing felt normal.

'Cheers,' she said. 'I've got a lot of drinking to do tonight.' She winked at him.

Sam was a little startled by this. He wasn't used to girls being funny around him. He wasn't used to being around girls at all, not outside of work.

'Sure, yeah.' He took a big swig of his lager dash.

'So how come you have lemonade in your beer?'

He shrugged. 'Beer's disgusting, isn't it?'

'I like Guinness.'

'It tastes different in Ireland. Apparently.'

'Have you ever been there?'

'Uh-huh. I went to a place called Wicklow once, with my parents. Down on the harbour there we watched the fishing boats come in and all the families were waiting for the fishermen and they all stayed on the wharf thing and played tug o' war.'

'That sounds nice.'

He remembered the way the sky had been so massive. That was the last holiday before the twins. He took another large pull on his drink and was already halfway down.

'It was one of the loveliest things I've ever seen. You don't think things like that happen these days, but they do. They do still happen. I also saw a woman call a guy the C word because he almost ran her over. "You C," she said. "I hope you die of an F-ing heart attack." But in a really quiet, Irish voice.'

She laughed. 'Swings and roundabouts, I guess. Hey, did you know that after the smoking ban in Ireland people kept getting run over because they were standing out the front of pubs in the road?'

'That's not true.'

'It is too. Look it up.'

He laughed. This was OK. This was not bad at all.

'So I had a really great time last week, with the shooting stars,' she said.

'Great!'

The pint glass in her hand looked massive.

'Did any of your wishes come true?'

He stopped himself saying something cheesy.

'Not yet,' he said, his eyes falling away.

Am I already in love with you? He finished his drink and the chemicals of alcohol glistened and sparked in his blood.

'Easy,' she said, looking at her nearly full pint. 'Same again?'

'I can wait.'

'It's fine,' she said, and went to the bar.

He looked into the fire and tried to find patterns. It was going well. He hadn't said anything too stupid, and there was no sign of any darkness in his mind.

She came back with a lager for him and a cider for her, then leaned back. She was wearing a long-sleeved T-shirt with white torso and blue arms, and the number 85 in American sports font on the front, sleeves rolled to the elbows.

'I don't normally do this,' he blurted.

A pause and a space where they flowed into a connection. He looked at her for a second.

'Me neither. But it's hard moving to a new place where you don't know anyone.'

'So you want to be a librarian for your career?'

'I guess so. I just wish you got paid more. But it's nice being around those sorts of people, academics and students, and it's nice finding books for people who are making a difference.'

'Did you go to uni?'

She shook her head. 'I thought about it but my folks weren't well off and I wouldn't really have been able to move out, even with the loan and a job. Well, I could have afforded it but the debt . . .'

'Yeah.'

'It's too scary. I didn't do that great in school, either. Kind of lost it for a bit.'

She shook her head and there was a pause. He twirled his glass on the table.

'Hey, are you any good at pub quizzes?' she said.

'Um, I'm OK at them. I'm not great. I'm not thick or anything but I'm not that clever either?' He could sense her looking at him in a kind of 'What is he talking about?' way. 'I mean, I don't know anything real or useful. Do you know what I mean?'

'Sam. Would you like to come to a pub quiz with me?'

His pint glass wobbled in his hand.

'I'm sorry. You're probably doing something—'

'No. I'd like to go.'

As soon as he said this, he felt something uncouple from something else.

'I said I'd go, but it's with people from work and it's all a bit new to me and, you know, it'd be nice to go with someone I know.'

'Sure.' A silence fell in. 'It's funny, you seem like such a confident person.'

Her eyes slipped to the table. 'I'm not. I mean, I sometimes am.' Tiny droplets of sweat dappled her forehead.

He picked up his glass and stopped, put it back on the table. He found himself wanting to be in the moment.

'I'm having a nice time,' he said.

'Me too.' She smiled. Her mouth was small, her lips thin. It was such a neat face, each feature separate from the next. Boy, it was so hot in here. The fire was stifling. He pulled off his sweater.

'Did you go to uni?' she asked.

He held up two fingers, the peace sign, as he sipped his drink to cool down. 'Two years.'

'What did you do?'

'Geography.'

'Town planning.'

'Climate change, actually. Well, climatology mostly. But geomorphology, geology. Rivers. Glaciers. Reconstructing Quaternary environments.'

'So what do you think about climate change? Are we all doomed?'

'Ha. Depends if people are willing to change. You know, we'd have to drop our living standards. Are people willing to do that?'

It was a depressing thought.

'Why'd you drop out?'

He sighed. 'You don't wanna know about that.'

'Try me.'

He waved his hand. 'It's a long story.'

Here her face lost all of its tension and, in what seemed like slow motion, she said, 'I've got time.'

He looked at her and she looked at him.

'How well can you see without your glasses?' he said, sabotaging the moment.

Sarah's head moved, just a fraction from right to left, a tiny jerk from one space to another, and in that movement the momentum was lost.

'Hardly at all,' she said.

Part of Sam felt relief, that front part of him where everything was easier. But an older, deeper part of him felt incredibly sad and let down by what he'd just done.

'Here.'

She gave him her glasses and he lowered the lenses over his eyes. Across the table she turned into a blur of colours.

'I can't even make out your face,' he said.

'Yup. I'm pretty blind.'

The sadness in the deeper part of him started to spread. His throat went dry.

Her eyes were smaller than they looked with the glasses on, a pale blue near the pupil strengthening to navy, almost black, at the edge of her irises. She put her glasses back on and she caught his eye and their gaze held for a second. The pub dog lumbered over to the fire and lay down on the rug.

'Let's go and put some music on,' she said. 'You can show me how to work the jukebox.'

'I had a really nice time.'

'Me too,' he said.

The air froze frost on the roads, the moon so bright you could see its craters. The idling of a taxi engine. *Kiss her!* yelled the audience of his life, though he knew he wouldn't.

'Don't forget you're coming to that quiz with me,' she said. 'No "falling asleep".'

'OK.'

Sarah smiled and stepped forward quickly and hugged him gently, only for a second, a quick thing, there and gone.

'See you later then.'

She opened the taxi door and looked back at him. He wished he was braver, a braver person.

'Goodnight,' he said.

They looked into each other's eyes and he smiled, and despite every part of him telling him to do something, he couldn't. Time halted, just for a moment, before she climbed into the cab. The red tail lights in the dark, and she was gone and he was alone.

There was a bright object beneath the moon that he knew was Venus. He pictured it traversing the surface of the sun. The transit of Venus, they called it, a black dot moving across the impossible, ferocious heat of a star inching its way towards complete death with every reaction. It was strange to think that, whatever happened, whatever anyone did in the world, everything would ultimately end up being swallowed by the sun as it bloomed outwards at the end of its life.

Chapter Twelve

The costume. He stared at it on its hanger in the bright moonlight. He couldn't patrol tonight because he'd been drinking, but some weird nether-sense made him long to become the Phantasm. He remembered a moment in one of his early patrols. An old lady had been struggling down the street in the dark with bags of heavy shopping. It had been his first interaction with another person, dressed in the costume, though she seemed curiously unperturbed by his appearance. He carried her bags for her, she didn't live far, and had helped her put the shopping into the cupboards of her old-fashioned kitchen.

He explained what he was trying to do, to help, and she'd said, 'I grew up in the Second World War and I've never felt more afraid than I do today.'

The words had hit him like a thunderbolt. Until that point his dressing up had been about him, about dealing with the Event and its aftermath; there had been an element of selfishness in it. But suddenly, there in that poky little kitchen, with that poor woman feeling hard the danger of the modern world, all of that went out the window. In that moment the Phantasm became something more.

He closed his eyes. Wasn't he supposed to be happy now? Hadn't he just had a great night?

He went downstairs. The light on the oven had turned

orange so he slid a ham and pineapple deep-pan pizza in and set the timer. He'd tried lots of post-pub snacks but this was the best. The thick crust absorbed the alcohol, the ham hit all the flavour targets, and the pineapple was like a refreshing sorbet against the drunkenness. Opening the fridge and feeling the cool on his face, Sam grabbed a can of Coke and waited before opening it. He brought the ring pull to his ear to enjoy the snap and pressure-release sound. Ah. He took a big slurp and went back upstairs.

The costume called to him. *Put me on. Feel safe.* He stepped towards it.

The room was dark, the light coming from the landing, and in the mirror he looked like nothing more than a shadow. In the completely silent house the costume clacked and rubbed. He took the wooden reaching stick that opened the hatch into the attic and ascended the retractable ladder. He'd never been up here before in his costume but it felt absolutely awesome.

'Just like a bat in the belfry,' he said, his voice sounding loud.

He started crawling towards the centre. He imagined Sarah at the same moment. She was probably safely tucked up in bed. He pictured her glasses sitting on a bedside table next to a lamp, on top of a book. Would she think it was weird that at the exact same moment Sam was not in bed but dressed up as a superhero, crawling through his attic? Could Sarah in his life and the Phantasm coexist? No, she would think it was crazy. And yet here he was, after a lovely evening with her, dressed up anyway.

He didn't even know why he'd come up here. Reaching the low table at the centre he lay down, propping himself up on one elbow as he waited for the travel kettle to boil. He picked up the picture of his family and stared at it blankly. He had looked at it so many times that it had almost totally lost its meaning. Why couldn't he remember the day it was taken? It was warm up here with the costume on. He took the phone he'd brought from his bedroom and put it to his ear, and, suddenly exhausted at the effort of the evening, he drifted off to sleep.

There was a siren going off in his nightmare. And an overriding sense of claustrophobia. It took a while to realise that, in fact, it was not a nightmare but real life. The light from the desk lamp on the low Japanese table looked like a proto sun in an early solar system, interplanetary dust swirling before it. Sam blinked. His throat hurt. Slowly, the facts of the situation dawned on him.

'Oh wow,' he said.

There was smoke everywhere. Remembering how people caught up in 9/11 had felt the heat in the floor he pulled off his glove and pressed his hand to the rug. It wasn't warm. Sam coughed. He tried to figure out what was happening as he turned himself around and started crawling for the entrance. The smoke stung his eyes and the sensation of burning in his throat worsened as fear hit him. He coughed again. He couldn't really see. The smoke thickened near the hatchway leading to the ladder.

He went as fast as he could and got down the ladder. The top floor was thick with smoke. It was just past dawn and there was a dim grey light coming from the windows. The smoke alarms blared. He put his arm to his mouth as if it would make a filter. There was no way he could make it downstairs. He stumbled down the corridor into the spare room and pulled open the wardrobe where he kept his stuff. Thank God he'd practised doing this in the dark. He found the oxygen mask he'd bought after the debacle with the smoke bombs in the railway station and pulled it to his mouth. The breath was deep and long. He fell back and sat against the spare bed for a second.

The pizza. The deep-pan ham and pineapple pizza was still in the oven. He grabbed his asthma pump and went down the stairs on his belly, keeping low where the air was clearest, and crawled into the kitchen. He grabbed a tea towel and pulled the oven door open, diving backwards as he did so – expecting it to explode in flames, which it didn't. Moving quickly from room to room, he opened all the windows. In the living room he looked out on the dark street. All the curtains were still shut, so he guessed his neighbours wouldn't see the smoke. He'd give it half an hour, then close the ones at the front and leave the ones at the back open. A nagging disappointment pulled at him that he hadn't got to eat the pizza and it would go to waste. Still, at least he hadn't burned his house down.

Back in the kitchen, he approached the oven slowly. The pizza was a black circular crisp inside. There were brown burn marks all over the front of the oven. He switched everything off, pulled on his oven mitt and removed the pizza. The burnt bits of pineapple and ham and strands of cheese were still discernible, like fossils. He stared at it for a moment and a sudden shock shuddered through him. He'd almost burned his house down, and yet he was normally so cautious. He took the pizza into the back garden. Beyond the back fence an orange line of dawn light cut across the sky beneath a steel cloud bank. He blinked his stinging eyes through the thick smoke. The air was freezing as he moved down the garden and he suddenly realised he was outside in his costume. He reached the back fence and stood there, looking at the frozen pond. Then he faced the sky and launched the pizza like a frisbee over the fence. It caught the air perfectly and glided elegantly into the distance, a black disc against the dawn laser light, like a flying saucer departing the atmosphere. It seemed to go on for ever, the image so strange he felt it burning hard into his memory in the moment. The sound of the smoke alarms stopped.

'I need to go for a run,' he said.

*

His running shoes eating up the streets, Sam let the chemicals wash away the stress of last night with Sarah. The sun made the frost on the lawns and trees a brilliant white and the road curled between winter bushes in the front gardens of the pretty little estates. Sam came at last to a children's park, which he circled and slingshotted off, just as a rocket might use the gravity of Jupiter to catapult off into interstellar space, towards the main road.

He pictured his phone sitting on the breakfast bar, its screen illuminating with a text from Sarah. He leaned into the hill, the road passing beneath an avenue of huge chestnut trees, leaves and split shells all over the pavement crunching beneath his feet. He always thought of his family at this point in the run. Not a solid thought, a memory or image; just the *idea* of them. Up and up, he could feel the juices of effort secreting into his thighs, but he always kept going.

She hadn't texted.

Even after showering, his phone was latent. He sat in the living room with the TV off. The smoke had gone but the house smelled weird. The heating had just come on and he could hear the clicking of the boiler rattle through the walls, pipes expanding in their networks, and he was struck then by the quiet of the place. All this house with just one person moving around it.

He spent the next seven hours cleaning the smoke stains, and as he inhaled the various antibacterial sprays and bleaches he felt the cleansing properties of the chemicals disinfect his soul so that it could start afresh.

Sometimes Sam would think back to a happy day in his past. At the end of the Easter holidays in his second year of university, the day before the journey back to campus, they went for lunch in the nearby Frankie & Benny's. It was one of those spring days where warmth comes back for the first time, blue skies with cartoon white clouds.

Sam loved his relationship with the twins at that time. His

absence while at university, and the age gap, meant that when they saw him the delight on their four-year-old faces was multiplied. They lavished him with attention and looked for approval all the time. That Easter holiday had been amazing. Steve had started telling rudimentary jokes ('What's my favourite food? Snot.') while Sally, like her father and older brother, had become fascinated with dinosaurs.

'Watch this,' Sam's dad had whispered to him the first night Sam got back from uni, before turning to Sally. 'Sal? Want to do the alphabet for your brother?'

She looked up from the TV, stood up, walked the three feet to the sofa and sat down again.

'A,' said Sam's dad.

'Apatosaurus!'

'Whoa,' said Sam.

'Yup,' his dad nodded. 'Listen. B.'

'Brachiosaurus!'

Then she went all the way through to Zigongosaurus without hesitation.

'Sally, that's amazing,' he said, stunned. Staring at her looking up at him, he'd tried to imagine what impact this little person was going to have on the world.

In Frankie & Benny's the twins were given balloons and the family ordered their food. There was an outside seating area to the rear of the building, fenced in by wooden boxes with vivid green conifers growing out of them. Steve and Sally persuaded Sam to join them. They found a table and the twins climbed up into the seats and sat down in what, to Sam, seemed a very civilised manner.

'Well, isn't this a lovely day,' said Sally.

'It is,' Sam agreed.

Across the table Steve tilted his head. His fine brown hair, parted messily to the side, was getting long.

'Don't you wish it could stay like this for ever and ever?' he said.

Sam looked at Steve when he said this. This moment would replay itself countless times over the coming years.

'I do,' he said, quietly.

After Frankie & Benny's they took ice creams to the park and sat on the grass together.

'Can I have the present?' said Steve to his mother.

She looked down on the top of his head and tidied his hair.

'It's in the bag.'

Steve went to the bag on his knees and fetched a sheet of paper, and turned to Sam with an expectant smile on his face.

'Here,' he said, holding out a hand-drawn card. On the front was a picture of two small people and a big one in the middle. Sally, Steve and Sam. The figures were drawn in the way kids draw people, with a circle for a face, and the arms and legs coming directly out of the face instead of a body. The three heads were the same size; the thing that made Sam bigger was a pair of extraordinarily long legs that terminated in a pair of circular shoes. The three of them were holding hands at the end of long spaghetti arms. Scratchings of coloured pencil were scribbled randomly across the page. Inside was a handwritten note, the writing slanting diagonally downwards from left to right, but the words were clear.

> To Sam, Have a nice time in uni.
> We will miss you. Sally, Steve xxx

He sat on the grass and felt the warmth of the sun move into his bones. He imagined them sitting at the kitchen table, steadily writing the card with his mum, their faces pictures of pure concentration.

'Thanks, you two,' he said.

Sally just shrugged. 'No problem.'

The sun on the white card hurt his eyes. This was the most precious gift he'd ever received.

He caught the eight o'clock train back to uni and they waved him off on the platform. As the train pulled away, he adjusted himself in his seat and was conflicted by how much he was looking forward to getting back to his new life and how much he missed being at home. Wasn't there a term for that? Seagulls wheeled against the pink sunset. He saw the ghost of his reflection in the window and started to look forward to the end of the summer holidays when his family would get back from South America and he'd be able to spend more time with them. He remembered the term now. Feeling two things that should be mutually exclusive. He mouthed the words under his breath. Cognitive dissonance.

'OK. Now you're sure you know what you're doing?'

Blotchy mimicked moving the gearstick into first and flicking the indicator switch. He made a hoop with his mouth and expelled a short blast of air. Nerves made his skin particularly blotchy today.

'I think so,' he said.

'OK. Let's do it.'

Blotchy looked like a giant at the wheel of the little car. Sam had put him on the insurance as a favour, because Blotchy's mother had refused to take him out for driving practice any more. The engine revved loudly on the deserted industrial estate.

'Hold on a sec,' said Sam, calmly, above the noise, already realising this was a bad idea.

Blotchy took his foot off the pedal and looked at Sam with fear in his eyes.

'OK, what did you do wrong?'

Silence.

'You forgot to put the car into gear, didn't you?'

'Right. Yeah.'

'How many lessons have you had again?' came Tango's voice from the back seat.

'You said you wouldn't talk!' Blotchy's voice betrayed his hysteria.

'Calm down,' said Sam. 'Let's start again. Now, you know the route? You're going to pull out, turn left, go round the roundabout at the end and then pull over on the side of the road.'

'Got it. Easy-peasy.'

Tango scoffed.

'Do you want to get out?' said Blotchy, looking in the mirror.

'Ignore him,' said Sam.

Blotchy composed himself. He was a loud breather generally but he was almost snoring now.

'There is no spoon,' he said quietly, slid the car into gear, revved the engine, released the handbrake and shot forward.

Sam braced with one arm pressed into the roof, the other on the dash, and he said very quickly, 'OK-slow-down-immediately.'

Blotchy panicked and yanked the wheel around the turn in the road, mounting the curb. He was going to hit the lamp post. Sam reached across and pulled the wheel back into the road and they whizzed across to the wrong side, up the other curb, and on to the muddy grass bank, where they finally came to a stop.

Blotchy hit the wheel and turned to Tango in the back.

'It's your fucking fault!' he yelled. 'I can hear you sniggering.'

Tango, whose eyes were wide, said, 'Fair play, that was awful driving.'

'Better than you can do,' said Blotchy.

'Guys,' said Sam. 'Let's just get this sorted.'

He and Blotchy got out of the car to swap seats and as they passed each other at the back of the car Blotchy said, 'Sorry about that.'

The grass underfoot was squelchy and as Sam climbed back into the car he almost slipped. The air was tense now and nobody said a thing as Sam tried to get off the grass verge, with no effect. They were stuck.

'Time to get out and push,' he said, looking across to Blotchy. 'Go on then,' he said, 'out you get. You too, Alan.'

Blotchy was staring at him through his small, round-rimmed glasses.

'What?'

'I can't get out and push,' he said.

'Say again.'

Blotchy awkwardly lifted his left foot out of the footwell, revealing his shiny white, new Air Jordans.

'I can't get these muddy,' he said.

'Are you taking the piss?'

He shook his head. 'Not going to happen,' he said. 'My mum will kill me if I get them dirty. They're brand new.'

'You're twenty-fucking-six!'

Blotchy just shook his stupid, fat head with his ponytail swinging from side to side. Rather than finding this ridiculous refusal to help amusing, as he might have, Sam was very angry. Blotchy shrugged and looked out the windscreen.

Sam stared at him incredulously. 'Fine.'

Blotchy climbed back into the driver's seat and opened the window while Tango and Sam went to the rear of the car.

'Now you're sure you know what you're doing?' Sam called.

Out of the window appeared Blotchy's stubby hand, forming the 'OK' sign with his thumb and forefinger.

'Just put the brake on as soon as you get on to the road.'

But Blotchy revved ahead of time, and immediately Sam and Tango were sprayed by a powerful wave of mud spewing up from the wheels.

'Argh!' said Tango, leaping clear.

Sam leaned into the car, just wanting to get it over, his face completely covered in seconds, and the car slowly moved up the verge and back out into the road. But instead of slowing down, Sam watched in horror as Blotchy hit the accelerator instead of the brake and sped out along the road, swerving back and fore, until he reached the roundabout and went up on to the centre of it, through a low bush, and straight into the metal advertising sign in the middle.

Sam stood there for a second, covered in mud, as Tango rejoined him.

'Probably best if you hadn't let him do that,' he said.

Chapter Thirteen

He wondered if you could call a pub a chocolate-box pub. It was in one of the cooler suburbs of the city, on the corner of a crossroads, and had brass light fixings above the arched windows, spilling circles of cream light on the red Victorian brickwork. In the dark night it was like a pair of open arms. Her friends from work were there, but that was no problem. He could drink because his car was still in the garage and Sarah had said she'd give him a lift home. Riding the bus in the city at night made him feel cool and street smart. Statistically, the chance of getting stabbed was actually pretty low, and hard data always helped Sam when his more irrational side started to stir. His heart was beating very fast as he pushed the door too hard and it slammed into the wall, but the inside of the pub was loud with chatter and good cheer and nobody seemed to notice.

If you included the first time he saw her in the bakery, which he did, this was the fifth meeting with Sarah.

The pub was furnished in a cool, modernised Victorian shabbiness with beat-up wooden chairs and tables and old leather wing-back chairs in the corners. Green-shaded banker's lamps illuminated dark wooden booths. It was a bit like a cross between Dickens and Urban Outfitters. It was excessively hot though and he immediately started sweating. Sidling through the crowds he found a place at the bar where he was quickly served by a young Australian with curly hair.

'A pint of lager with a dash, and half a pint of tap water please,' he said, quickly.

He immediately downed the water in an attempt to stop sweating and took a slug of the lager in an attempt to calm his nerves. Then he went to the bathroom, where he took off his sweater and inspected himself in the mirror. He felt a bit better.

In the centre of the pub was a spiral staircase that led to the first floor. At the base of the staircase he stopped for a moment and closed his eyes to compose himself.

There was more shabby leather furniture upstairs, low-slung sofas and mismatched armchairs. He found Sarah and her friends in a far corner, grouped around a low coffee table with a few tea lights in ceramic pots. She had her back to him so he tapped her on the shoulder.

'Hi,' he said.

'Oh, hey,' said Sarah, turning to him. She was wearing a floral shirt and a neckerchief and looked amazing, like someone from Paris. He tried to gauge how happy she was to see him, but his mind was doing somersaults.

'This is Sam,' she said to the other people sitting around the table. She pointed to each of them and told Sam their names, and he nodded and smiled to them, feeling not at all cool in his brand-new T-shirt he'd just bought from Tesco and smart straight-cut jeans, saying hi to Charlotte and Felicity and Emily. The guys were Gareth, Charlie and then, sitting next to Sarah, a dark, handsome person.

'. . . and Francis.'

Francis was exceptionally handsome, in fact. His hair was black and wavy and looked impossibly cool. The collar of his shirt was all wrinkled and the sleeves were rolled up past his elbows. Great forearms; lithe, lean, with an easy, muscular grace.

'Hey,' he said to Sam, smiling.

The introductions over, Sam stood there for a moment with them all looking at him. He needed to do something. And it had to be cool. He made a shiver gesture and said, 'Brrrr! It's cold out!'

Charlotte nodded and smiled.

'It is,' she said.

Sam stood there for a second and then realised he had nothing more to add so sat in the low tub chair next to Sarah. There was a slight pause, and when the others realised that Sam was done they went back to talking.

'You OK?' said Sarah, quietly to him.

'Uh-huh,' he nodded.

He took a sip of his drink. She had a glass bottle of Coke with a curly straw coming out its neck.

'It's nice to see you,' he said.

'And it's nice to see you too.'

A hand tapped her arm and Francis's face peered over her shoulder. He was sitting in a higher chair than Sam so was looking down on him.

'So how do you know Sarah?' he said.

'Oh, well, I don't really.'

Something flickered on her face.

'I mean. We met in the pub.'

Francis nodded and stared at Sam for a second too long. 'So what do you do for a living?'

'I work for a Japanese electronics wholesaler.'

'Cool.'

'I'm in admin.'

'Right. Good for you, man,' said Francis, which made Sam feel about an inch tall.

'Francis works in the library with me.'

Francis was drinking a tumbler of whisky.

'Yeah. Part-time,' he said. 'I'm doing a PhD in English Literature.'

'Oh, great,' said Sam. 'Sarah likes literature. Books.'

'Well, books and literature are not necessarily the same thing,' said Francis, with a chuckle.

'Definitely,' Sam said.

'Francis is what you might call a literary snob,' said Sarah.

'You will only read a certain number of words in a lifetime,' said Francis. 'You might as well have them in the right order.'

'Francis is writing a novel about Easter Island,' Sarah continued.

'It's going to cover a thousand years but will be minimalist as well,' he said. 'Three hundred pages max.'

'Sounds good,' said Sam.

'Easter Island is where they have those giant stone heads.'

'Yeah, we all know that,' Sarah said.

Francis looked at her and smiled, like it was just the two of them. 'They call them moai,' he said. 'Easter Island is thousands of miles away from the nearest continent. That's a long way. What were those people doing out there building those stone heads?'

Sam turned away and looked around the table. The others were huddled around the sheet for the picture round.

'For me,' he heard Francis say, 'Easter Island is a delicate miniature of all human civilisation. We come, we build wonderful things, we destroy, we go again.'

The annoying thing was that he didn't sound stupid. It sounded interesting. It was frustrating how he could say obnoxious things but still come across as cool just because he was good-looking.

'I'd love to read it,' said Sam, aware that he was butting in.

Francis's eyes flicked to him uninterestedly. 'It's a long way off, and I never show anyone my work before it's ready.'

Just then a sound came from the speakers, the voice of the quizmaster telling everyone to settle down. Sam drank more of his beer. The first question was, Which president was involved with the Watergate scandal?

Francis leaned forward enthusiastically to give Charlotte the answer, which she was already writing. Sam was disappointed by this. He was always disappointed when he found out people were really competitive. But at least Sarah would see the same thing in Francis – even though, as Francis leaned across her, she didn't pull away.

All of a sudden Sam felt like a spare wheel. He picked up the picture round and took a sip of his drink.

Francis started explaining to Sarah what books she should read over the course of the next year.

'Have you ever heard of Don DeLillo?'

'Yes,' she said.

'He wrote this amazing book called *Underworld*. *TIME Magazine* listed it as number two in the greatest books written in the second half of the twentieth century. It starts off with this *incredible* scene at a classic baseball match that takes place at the same time as the Russians are conducting their first nuclear bomb test. The winning home run is struck at the exact same moment the bomb goes off. It's an amazing juxtaposition. He does it amazingly.'

'Yeah. I've read it.'

'Did you get how the book follows what happened to that baseball from the moment it was caught in the crowd right up to the end of the twentieth century? It's genius. Of course, nobody knew that 9/11 was just around the corner.'

Francis's intense talking was like a hairdryer to Sam. He looked at his beer and wondered if he should just get hammered. But just as it had the other night, something stopped him and it was clearer now, a recognition of how important this time was.

The next question was, What was the name of the geological time period during which the dinosaurs existed?

Perfect!

But Francis was leaning forward again.

'Jurassic,' he whispered to Charlotte.

'No, wait,' said Sam, deciding to also lean forward. 'It's the Mesozoic.'

Francis looked at him and smiled. 'I don't think so,' he whispered. He tapped Sam on the knee and used his other hand to point at the answer sheet.

'Put it down. Jurassic.'

Charlotte looked around the table for help but nobody said anything.

'Trust me,' said Francis. 'If I'm wrong, I'll buy a communal bag of peanuts.'

They all laughed.

'Oh, Mr Generous,' said Gareth, over in the corner.

Sam was sure he was right. The Mesozoic was the dinosaur period, made up of the Triassic, Jurassic and Cretaceous periods. He didn't know what to do and before he knew it, the next question was being asked and Francis was nodding insistently at Charlotte until she eventually scribbled the answer down.

Though closer to them than Sam, Sarah was still a bit of an outsider. He found the way she leaned forward to speak, as if guilty for interrupting, endearing; the side of her face so smooth, a tiny glistening of anxious sweat at her temple, the shape of her seashell ear.

These people were far more articulate than him and his friends, and it felt to Sam as if a second level to the world had suddenly revealed itself, a level where different people existed, and he felt a little disappointed that this wasn't his life when, perhaps, in another offshoot of the multiverse, it might have been.

At half time there was a thirty-minute break and Sam listened quietly to them talking about their weekend plans. There was a vintage market taking place and afterwards they were going to a new place that sold cronuts.

'What's a cronut?' said Sam.

'It's like a mix between a donut and a croissant. You should come,' said Charlotte, smiling.

'Oh, thanks. I'm already doing something with my friends on Saturday,' he lied, making a mental note that he would definitely go and eat a cronut on his own soon.

'OK, switch papers everyone, in a few minutes we're going to have some answers,' the quizmaster announced.

'I'm just going to nip to the loo,' said Sam.

'OK, cool,' said Sarah.

He was keenly aware of Francis listening. Sam smiled a little too long, and went to the top of the staircase. By the time he turned back to the table Francis had already engaged Sarah again.

He locked himself in the toilet. Fucking Francis. Was this really worth it? He could just bolt, get a taxi and disappear. The others were all upstairs, they'd have no idea, and he could go home, cook a pizza in his new oven and watch *Inception*. But then he thought of Francis, and Francis talking to Sarah, leaning close so she could smell his sophisticated aftershave, Francis with his superb looks and encyclopaedic knowledge and, no doubt, his worldly experience. He stared at himself in the mirror and felt very strongly that he was at a crossroads. If he went home now, then . . .

He found himself at the bar ordering another drink, and a Coke for Sarah. He looked at the shelf of spirits on the wall behind the barman, all the beautiful bottles lined up. Something had happened in that bathroom, like the crossing of a threshold, a moment of rare bravery where he'd made a decision to do something for himself, and he felt good.

He collected his drinks and went back upstairs, just as the quizmaster said that the time of the dinosaurs was known as the Mesozoic.

'So who's that Francis guy?'

'What do you mean?'

The thin road was silvered at the edges with frost in the headlights.

'I mean, you seemed to know him from before. Turn left up here.'

'No. He went to uni in Edinburgh so we were talking about that.'

'I thought you didn't go to uni.'

'No, but I lived there. I told you that?'

'Did you?' She'd lived in Lincoln but definitely hadn't said anything about Edinburgh, because he remembered everything she said to him.

'That's where I worked. In Edinburgh, before Lincoln.'

'You're not Scottish though are you?'

'No. My old boyfriend was.'

'Oh, OK.'

'It's a long story.'

A strange feeling fluttered through him that was something like envy, a set of beating wings against his organs.

'I can't believe I didn't know you lived in Edinburgh.'

The road here was dark without street lights and the cones of headlights were mesmerising.

'I know hardly anything about y—' He lost his breath for a second. 'You.'

'You're so drunk!'

Leaning his head against the cold window, he said, 'I'm not that drunk.' And it was true. He was a little tipsy but the reason he'd lost his speech was because his heart was beating too fast.

'Francis is a bit of a mansplainer though don't you think?' he said.

'Francis?'

'Did you hear him telling you about that writer, with the baseball match?'

'He's OK,' she said. 'But he does like to offer advice. He's a bit of an advice raper.'

'Oh wow.'

Sarah laughed. 'That was funny. You're really funny.'

'Am I?'

'Yeah.'

'Why?'

'Because you're such a dork.'

Oh. He didn't know what to say to that.

'In a good way.'

He was hoping she'd agree with him about Francis, and the fact she didn't was frustrating. Why couldn't she see he was annoying? The car came into Sam's village and the orange balls of light from the lamp posts brought normality rushing back.

'I'm sorry you had to drive.'

'Hey, it's the weekend. You should be allowed to drink.'

'It's Thursday.'

'That still counts.'

'You're funny . . .' he paused to let his thoughts catch up to his mouth. 'You're funny too.'

'Thanks, but you don't have to say that just because I said it.'

'I mean it!' he blurted. 'You're super funny. You're great, Sarah. I think you're awesome.' The click of indicators at a junction.

He watched the line of houses through the window as they threaded down the neat black roads of his estate. The rate of his heartbeat crept up again as the journey neared its end.

His friends, as ill-informed on the subject of the opposite sex as they were, insisted that being friend-zoned was a real thing, but Sam genuinely believed true love must find itself in friendship just as much as in passion. True love, for him, was not like in the films, all lust and sweat; it was warmer and more solid, sinking itself deep into the heart so as to make it unshakeable. People like Abraham Lincoln had true love, not Justin Bieber. That one might have no chance with a girl because of a pre-existing friendship was an incredibly depressing thought to him, and one he refused to believe.

The car stopped and he unclipped his seat belt. The

quantum vibrations that she was detonating sang through his body.

'Thanks for the lift.'

She looked so gorgeous.

'Can't I come in for tea?'

His mind rushed into his house, upstairs, to the hidden chest where he kept his superhero things.

'Tea? Yeah, sure, sure. I've got loads of tea.'

They went up the driveway, he leading her, heart rate chugging.

She didn't even mention the wooden partitioned tea box as she chose English Breakfast. He left the Fortnum & Mason tea set in the cupboard – that would be overkill.

In the living room she checked out his CD collection.

'You've got a lot of Queen albums.'

'Don't judge. Have you ever heard *A Night at the Opera* all the way through?'

She shook her head and Sam felt a gust of confidence as he crossed the room and took it from the shelf, with Sarah close to him, and pushed it into the player. She didn't move away. He skipped it to a song called ''39'.

'I love this song. It's about time travel. Brian May has a doctorate in astrophysics.'

Sarah smiled, and there was a pause.

'You're cute,' she said.

The two of them stood in the living room and he saw the surprise on her face when the perfect Queen electric guitar riffs didn't come on, but instead earthy acoustic guitar started up, hopping simply along a major scale. She nodded her head and smiled.

He thought he might be in Heaven. It was almost as though he was in a new reality, as though he was on a quantum wave, a blister on the skein of time, and this world he found himself in had peeled off the real one, a double, and soon it would pop and he would never have really spoken to Sarah that first night and everything he'd done since would dissolve as he woke up in his bed and everything was just the way it had always been.

But she was here, looking around the room, at his entertainment system, his music and film collections, the prints of comic-book artwork.

'You must have a good job,' she said.

'It's OK. It's not as hard to get a mortgage as people think. It's just the deposit.'

She looked somewhat forlorn now, as she gazed around the perfect coving and handsome plasterwork.

'It's nicer than my flat.'

They sat on the sofa, one knee up, facing each other, and all of a sudden he felt like a bit of a cheeseball, like a businessman trying to impress a date with his spicy flat in a marina with a little metal balcony outside some French windows.

'I only have this because I'm boring and I want security.'

'Everyone wants a home, though, even if they don't realise it.'

They looked at each other for a long moment and then she said, 'What?'

'What?' he repeated.

'Why are you looking at me?'

'You're pretty.'

He just said it, a trapdoor falling open under him, a flash across her face.

Make the move! the little people in his heart called out in unison. He remembered his resolve in the bathroom of the pub. Where was that courage now?

'What's your favourite film?' he blurted.

'Maybe *Totoro. My Neighbor Totoro*? The Japanese cartoon?'

'I haven't seen that.'

Her eyes widened. 'What?! You should come over to mine one night and we'll watch it.'

'I'd like that.'

She sipped her tea and the song ended.

'We could do it next week, if you're not busy. I could do my speciality Thai green curry. Do you like it?'

'I love it,' he said. 'Spar do these amazing Thai green curry sandwiches.'

'Thursday?'

'Thursday.' This was too fast again, but this time he didn't feel the compulsion to rally against the chaos. 'Yeah, great.'

She nodded.

'So,' she said.

'So.' He smiled.

Sarah got up and went over to his Blu-ray collection. 'That's funny. I thought you'd have them in alphabetical order.'

'They are in a rough order. Genre, I guess, then by year.'

She ran her fingers along them.

'Why don't you like talking about yourself?' he said.

Her fingers stopped.

'You changed the subject in the car when we were talking about Edinburgh.'

She carried on looking at his Blu-rays.

'You noticed that, huh?' She turned to him and smiled. 'Let's leave it for another day.'

'Yeah, of course. I didn't mean . . .'

'It's fine,' she said. 'I broke up with my boyfriend because he was a dick, but it's OK now. I'm normal. Hey, you know what? I'm really tired. You don't mind if I go, do you? I'm suddenly shattered.'

Oh, he thought.

'Of course not. Sorry, I'm keeping you.'

'No, not at all, it's just all of a sudden, you know?' She yawned.

He cursed himself for being such an idiot. He took her tea and led her to the door. The air outside was arctic.

'So I'll see you Thursday?' Her glasses reflected the porch light.

'Yeah, should be good.'

He felt deflated by her sudden U-turn.

'Listen. I didn't mean anything b—'

She stepped towards him and he thought, oh my God. But she didn't kiss him. She put her arms around him and they hugged and he found himself gripping her tighter than he meant to, her tiny frame, and pulling her closer for a second. He was sure he felt her bones relax into him, and he thought from some far-off corner of his mind, there are few more special things in the whole human canon than a hug. He wanted to kiss her but he just couldn't. His mind rationalised his cowardice by trying to persuade him that kissing her would spoil this moment. She pulled away and looked at him. The end of her nose was red.

Be brave, his father had said. *The two most important things in life are to be brave and to be good.*

But at the exact same time the thought that had been haunting him from the start reared its head: if you keep this up, you will have to tell her about your family.

'You'd better go. It's freezing,' he said, his voice quick.

Her eyes fell away from him. 'Yeah,' she said. 'Yeah you're right.'

He felt so stupid now. His heart and mind were see-sawing; he thought he could feel a piece of his soul falling apart. And yet, like always, he did nothing.

Chapter Fourteen

Monday morning. A beautiful, chill October morning with a deep-blue sky. What a lift in the body the hatching of love can bring. How it makes the world appear benign. How it brings up a screen between problems that, before, seemed so massive. Left to his own devices in the office that morning, Sam spent a pleasant few hours clearing a huge wedge of work, even finding time to water and prune the bonsai tree on his desk. The food guy had Cherry Coke on his van, Mr Okamatsu was on a business trip and, all the while, rather than dread the coming Thursday – his date at Sarah's house – he looked forward to it with eager anticipation. If anything, his brush with death had galvanised in him the will to live.

At lunch in Tesco he had chicken nuggets, chips and beans before heading into the store, wandering the aisles, alighting in the men's health area. He wasn't expecting anything, but he felt it only responsible for him to take care of himself.

Such a selection these days: thin feel, comfort, ribbed and dotted, extended pleasure, mutual climax, tickle me. It all felt a bit sordid. He only wanted something simple; to pull out a pink raspberry-flavour double-ribbed would almost certainly be a blunder. He picked up a box of ultra-safe and thanked God for the self-service checkouts. Entombed as his condoms were in a sturdy Perspex security box, he dreaded the checkout supervisor coming over to take off the security toggle. But the gods had answered him because as he scanned them the checkout island didn't call for assistance. That the toggle was still on, and the box was still surrounding the condoms, was not a problem – he'd smash the box open with a hammer in the privacy of his back garden. He left quickly and almost had a heart attack when he triggered the theft alarms. An error had occurred. Think! Rather than be accosted by Security, his mind worked at preternatural speed. He turned quickly and made a beeline for Customer Services, surreptitiously producing the condoms in the Perspex box. The woman, fifty, large, short hair dyed plum, her name badge reading *Theresa*, observed Sam above the horizons of her half-moon glasses.

'I think these set off the machine. When I scanned them, nothing happened.'

They both stared at the offending article on the counter. Condoms. CONDOMS.

'Have you got your receipt?'

He didn't, of course.

'I've left it at the till,' he said, ashamed.

We'll just go over to the till and find the receipt and I'll be on my way, he thought. No need to take the condoms with us; let's just leave them here and collect them later. But Theresa did feel the need, lifting them up, resting them on her ham-joint forearm, as Sam followed her to the till, at which a pretty young mother was purchasing a fruit salad.

'Sorry, love,' said Theresa, as she rifled through the raft of abandoned receipts, the box of condoms placed proudly on the top of the machine, the young mother looking at them, looking at Sam. Sam smiled at her but then worried that it might come across as a very creepy smile, so he stopped and went beetroot.

Why this? he thought. Why did it not happen with a Blu-ray? I buy lots of Blu-rays.

At last Theresa found the receipt and waddled on back to Customer Services, with Sam in tow.

He felt he had to say something. 'I'm so sorry about this.'

'Don't be silly,' she said, loudly. 'You got nothing to be sorry about. You've got nothing to apologise for. It's good you're buying them.'

A clever quip on how he should not continue his line in the gene pool? Hard to tell.

He stowed the emancipated condoms safely in the boot of his car to prevent further humiliation, and headed back to work.

He spent some time emailing his clients about the parts that had gone down in the Suez Canal with the stricken tanker, and which they still hadn't got back to him about, because everybody was avoiding the discussion about who was going to pay for air shipping.

At three o'clock Sam went into the warehouse to check the deliveries going out that day. At the far end he noticed a group of girls sitting on pallets eating sandwiches. The Romanians. It was the first time he'd seen them. Even from this distance their beauty was clear. Just the way they sat, long backs curving over their food, legs crossed. They had long, healthy hair the colour of sunset on the trunk of an oak tree, and they ate silently, po-faced, staring at nothing. There was a skylight in the ceiling and a shaft of sunlight illuminated them.

'You OK, Sam?' Mark, standing next to him with a clipboard.

'The Romanians?' he said, quietly, nodding up at the angels.

'Their last day.'

'They've finished sorting?'

'Yup. Ten million parts.'

'Jeez.'

Sam and Mark stared at the girls for a long moment until Mark hit him on the shoulder with the clipboard.

'Come on, let's do this,' he said, indicating the pallets of orders that needed double-checking.

*

He knocked on the door and waited. He was nervous but there was no dread. Through a small blurred-glass window in the front door he saw the hallway light come on and a shape moving down the stairs.

'Hi,' she said.

For a second he got caught between heartbeats.

She led him up a narrow flight of stairs with woodchip wallpaper, bubbling at the skirting. At the top of the stairs they came to a long landing with two doors on the left. It was dark, but an orange street light outside the window at the front of the house illuminated a swirly-patterned carpet. And it also illuminated a strange architectural feature. At the end of the landing, with the doors on one side and a banister on the other, was an open space the size of a room, as if a room had been meant to go there but they hadn't put the wall up. The square of carpeted space had a comfy-looking chair on it, a tall lamp for reading, a small side table and a crammed bookcase.

'That's an unusual space,' said Sam.

'It's weird, isn't it?' She paused at the second door, her small hand on the handle. She was wearing a baggy American sports T-shirt and a pair of skinny jeans, and as the dim light painted her she tilted her head to one side. 'But the window gives good light for reading. And you can look down on the street.'

She led him into the living area with a kitchenette in one corner. It was neat, but the furniture was old and mismatched. She had a pink portable TV on a small rickety coffee table, with a DVD player propped up on a phonebook underneath.

'Not quite the same as your place, but it's OK while I save money. It's cheap.'

More bookcases on one wall, chock-full of old-looking paperbacks, the shelves sagging under their weight. There were, on closer inspection, an enormous number of books, stacked up at the side of the bookcases and scattered in piles around the room. It reminded him of the comics in his attic.

'Have you read all these?'

'Mostly. I have trouble getting rid of things. Sad isn't it? I had to hire a van to get them here.'

'How long does it take you to read a book?'

'I read like three a week, maybe. But I just pick them up in charity shops.'

He couldn't perceive how it was possible to read so fast.

'I don't watch much TV,' she added.

He sank into the cushion-laden sofa. There were pictures on the walls, watercolour landscapes and black-and-white photos of New York that must have been here pre-Sarah. A tasselled lampshade threw warm light and dark shadows. She sat next to him. Her hair was tied back, and he noticed how the red was fading out, dark-brown roots emerging.

'How was your day?'

'It was . . . great,' he said.

They looked at each for a moment and both smiled awkwardly, lost in a moment, and then she sprang to her feet. Over at the kitchenette she chopped vegetables and sliced chicken and chatted happily to Sam about an event on the bus to work earlier that day, when an elderly man had told her about his wartime experiences in the tropics. As she spoke Sam listened and flicked through an orange-spined paperback with yellowing pages. *À Rebours*, by J. K. Huysmans. There was the faint scent of paper degrading.

Across the room Sarah smiled at him. Despite the nerves, it felt good being hidden away in a bedsit above a boarded-up shop, where nobody knew he was, apart from the girl cooking dinner in the corner. He'd never had a girl cook for him before, and it felt . . . nice. He felt like a frog that had hopped off a sinking lily pad to a safe new one.

They ate at a small table with a folding flap so it could be stored against a wall when not in use. The Thai green curry was delicious – she'd put sweet potato and sliced mangoes in it – and they drank cheap rosé wine and she did most of the talking. She couldn't tell exactly what it was that had made her want to be a librarian but had loved books since early childhood when she had discovered, just as Sam had, *Harry Potter*. She said box sets and Netflix were replacing the novel at the moment but books will always come back – all people care about is stories, doesn't matter what format. She'd travelled a little bit – Peru and Australia – but not much. It was almost exhausting, being bombarded with all this information, though there was something strange about it all, as though she were telling him everything without actually telling him anything.

'Life's funny, though, isn't it?' she said.

The wine had made his vision hyper-real.

'Yeah.'

'A friend of mine used to have this idea of life being like a rocket tree.'

'A rocket tree?'

His wine glass had pictures of cactuses on it.

'So when you're young, everyone you know is dangling from the branches of this big tree that's safely stuck in the ground by its roots, but as you get older and life gets going the tree suddenly blasts off, like a rocket ship, into space and you're all heading for the stars together.'

'Uh-huh.'

'At the start it's easy to hold on. Everyone you know is on there, and it's not too bumpy. But then the wear and tear of blasting off gets to the tree and it starts shaking. A few people fall away and you watch them drop through the clouds. And, you know, it's quite shocking when it first starts happening. But anyway, you keep going, and more and more people can't hold on, right? You look at their faces; they want to keep their grip, but it's too hard and they just can't. Their hands aren't strong enough and away they slip, back from the stars and down into the real world, you know?'

'I guess so.'

'I guess he was talking about giving up. Resignation. When you get into your twenties, people start giving up and accepting their lot. Well, maybe giving up isn't the right way to put it. But that's when they fall off the tree. Even so, you still try and hang in there and hope things will get better before you have to take an easy option. This is your world, you know, your one chance at life, how you want it to be. The universe is doing everything it can to shake you out, but you've got to hang on.'

Sam looked into his glass. He'd let go of the tree years ago.

'And it's lonely, you know? And you start wondering if maybe you really should have fallen off, like everyone else. But then,' she said, 'out there in space you see the other tree, and that's only got one person in it too. And the next one. And the next one.' Sarah sat back. 'You just gotta hold on long enough.'

He stared at her and found his soul opening up and wanting to pour out his heart.

'Maybe, even though the person has fallen out of the tree, they can still feel it,' he said. 'When they close their eyes, maybe they're still there.'

Sarah smiled wanly at him and it made Sam want to ask about what had happened in her past that had made her move across the country for a job with such low pay.

'That's a nice thought,' she said, finishing her glass. 'Shall we watch *Totoro*?'

They stacked their plates next to the sink and he sat on the sofa as she went down on her knees in front of the TV and slotted in the disc. When she came back, she was closer to him.

Watching the film, about two children moving to the Japanese countryside, thrust him back to memories of his own childhood. He remembered the Batcave in the woods of his youth, how he'd watch the glimpses of blue sky through the green leaves high above. He remembered the simple happiness of lying in a field or running along the compacted soil of a forest path. He remembered the wonderment when he first saw the tall buildings of the city, the way sunlight and sky were in their windows, just like in America. The thrilling danger of rivers, the nervous beating heart when he went further into the woods than ever before. That sensation, the way his body trembled, the deep shudderthump of the heart, the feeling of doing something for the first time, was in him now, in this room.

'Sarah,' he said, turning his head to her.

The screen reflected in her glasses, a huge tree on a summer's day. Was he really going to do this?

'I need to tell you something,' he said.

Chapter Fifteen

He watched them drive away at dusk that day, down the hill, with the twins in the back turning to wave goodbye.

That summer, when he thought about it after all these years, had passed without the formation of any real memories. He recalled hardly anything from it. The geography research trip to the Brecon Beacons was a blur, the memories malformed, half formed, and not like memories at all but something more akin to a person being aware of experiences that took place in a previous life.

The first time he became aware of a plane crash was when his professor came to get him for the phone call, though even this was unclear.

The plane was flying from Rio de Janeiro to Manaus and had come down in the rainforest. A remote voice from the ether was telling him – directly, one to one – that 150 souls had been lost. There were just four British nationals on board and all belonged to Sam's family: his mother, father, Steven and Sally.

It was an impossible thing, hearing this, impossible to grasp the information in the message. He remembered more emotions than events, sitting with the phone at his ear, a physical kind of shock, electric, as though a surge of power had flashed through him, then a feeling of disbelief, the familiar numbing, then panic, horror, anger; all hustling to get front and centre. All these feelings would revisit him later, and for longer periods, but he felt them all in those first few moments, a carcinogenic bubbling tumescence before disbelief won out; they weren't really on the flight, they had bailed out and were safe in the rainforest, there had been an awful mistake, it was mistaken identity, it was an elaborate prank.

But none of these were the case. They were on the flight and they had all perished. The plane had entered a zone of turbulence and was struck by lightning, igniting a fuel tank, blowing a wing off, and causing catastrophic failure across the whole vessel. It fell seven miles to Earth. Sam had read the reports because his capacity for hope, back then, was undiminished. He devoured article after article, looking for clues as to his family's survival. Many of the bodies were unidentifiable and some completely vaporised by the fires. And if this was the case, and a true body count was impossible, then surely some people might conceivably have survived and walked away. There were rare cases where people had survived mid-air plane crashes by simply falling out of the thing before it hit the ground. It was rare but it *was* possible.

The local press took a melancholic angle on the story, focusing on Sam, lonely Sam Holloway who had lost his whole family. Cut adrift. He didn't reply to any of the offers for an interview. It was all pointless anyway; his family would eventually return.

Even after the funerals he couldn't bring himself to believe it was true, that they were truly and eternally gone. He pictured them trekking through the Amazon jungle, his mother identifying the plants and animals, Sally quietly digesting the information, Big Steve feeling the texture of waxy leaves between his thumb and forefinger, his father foraging for their meals, a real Swiss Family Robinson adventure. They were easy thoughts, benevolent, a kindly offering from his mind to his soul. It couldn't be true that they'd burnt to death in a falling aeroplane.

The reaction of his hometown was kind. His parents' friends

visited with cards and offers of help, and it was during these visits that Sam was thankful for the internal numbness acting as a great wall, deflecting everything the world threw at him.

At night though, when the phone calls stopped and the visitors left, the numbness would crack open and the fingers of truth grasped at him through the slits. A great hand was tugging at his centre. His entire family were gone and he was alone. Alone in the house, he watched his mother walk across the carpets, Big Steve sitting in the corners, Sally smiling at him, his father reading newspapers. The visions became so vivid, it was as if the images he superimposed on reality were actually happening.

Time after time he asked the same question: How could this happen? And the cruel, uncomplicated answer kept coming back: Because it just has. In one awful moment everyone he loved had been wiped off the face of the earth.

As he told her all this, Sarah said nothing. She put her hand over her mouth, and though tears lensed her eyes they didn't break.

'Sam,' she said at last. 'I'm so sorry. God . . . I – I don't know what to say.'

He shrugged and reached for his wine glass on the table, but when he tried to lift it he realised he was shaking.

'Are you OK?'

He couldn't look at her all of a sudden.

'Yeah I ju—' He stopped himself. His voice had caught. 'I've never told anyone this before. Sorry.'

'Hey, don't say sorry.' Her voice a soft song.

She put her hand on the top of his arm, and he started. The wine sloshed over the top of his glass on to the table. Sarah jumped up.

'Don't worry,' she said. 'I'll get a cloth.'

'Shit, sorry,' he said, upset. 'I'm gonna just . . . Can I use the bathroom?'

'Sure,' she said.

He swung his head around and caught a glimpse of her and the two tears that had run down her cheeks, which she wiped away with the back of her hand.

In the bathroom he pulled on the light cord and took a massive breath. There was a tiny wood-framed window with a little spider living in a web in the corner. His breathing was erratic. He thought he could just tell her and it would be fine. It had felt right. He hadn't expected for it to be like this. He thought he'd be able to handle it but he couldn't. His mind was swimming.

In the weeks and months after the accident Sam had isolated himself. The house was making him sick but he couldn't bring himself to leave it. Offers of counselling were rejected and after a time Sam had grown weary of people's offerings of help. In his mind he was readying himself for dealing with what had happened, but he wanted to do it the same way he wanted to do everything: alone. He'd unplugged the landline and refused to answer the door. He'd switched off his mobile and didn't use the Internet.

His friends had found it hard. Socially awkward, emotionally immature, they could not engage with his family's death head-on. They showed their support by taking him to the pub, the cinema, board-game nights in the local community centre. But this just made him feel guilty, guilty for going on living when his family could not. And he hated how quiet he was, how unable to participate, as though his energy core had lost its fuel, and how he was nothing but a burden, a bore.

In those few weeks, with the latticework skeleton of family gone, everything else in his life fell apart. And now, having spoken about it out loud for the first time, everything felt weird. He felt untethered, but not in a good way. He splashed cold water on his face and inspected himself in the mirror. What would they make of him? His parents. How disappointed would they be by the coward staring back from the mirror?

Back in the living room Sarah had brought the bottle of wine over and refilled the glasses.

'Hey,' she said, looking at him over the back of the sofa.

'Hey,' he said. 'Listen. I'm sorry. I shouldn't have told you all that. I don't know why I did it.'

'Sam, don't be silly.'

'I think I'm gonna go.'

'I've just poured you a new glass of wine,' she said.

He smiled but didn't move, and there was a long silence. He really couldn't handle this. He reached for a way but there was nothing.

'OK,' she said, at last.

The whole thing seemed staged, somehow. The room shook with the passing of a train, and he thought of that day in his past when they'd waved to him from the back of the car as they'd driven away. Steve and Sally smiling, two little kids with so much love in their hearts. It had been the last time he'd ever seen them. Before his world broke in half.

℗

The Phantasm #007

Vulpes Vulpes

Another cold night, frost on the blacktop like glitter. A truck rumbles down the high street and the masked hero smiles. The economy turns, the world of man endures. He pushes recent events on the other side of the mask away – this is what a true champion of the people must do. This is the sacrifice.

Perhaps the driver is heading to one of the nation's mighty industrial complexes, like Telford, delivering the nuts and bolts and cogs to the myriad factories so machines can be made, brought forth from the countless assembly lines, into the world. And it is all done in darkness, at the aprons.

From his perch atop the flat roof of the public library he reaches into his pack, past the night-vision goggles and HD digital camera, the rope and the handcuffs, until he finds what he's looking for. A nice flask of coffee. Army issue. He pours himself a cup and drinks. Ah. Not much action tonight. A cat ambles up the empty street, finds a bush and disappears.

There is a moment of satisfaction. Life in the costume is a form of uncomplicated bliss.

Somewhere behind him he hears a noise. A whimpering sound. Behind the library he spies a stack of cardboard boxes. With the stealth of a professional gymnast he slides down the drainpipe to the gravel. His breath is a fog, his shoes crunch the frost as he approaches the boxes. From his utility belt he withdraws a flashlight and the frost in its beam glistens like quartz in a rock face. The whimpering continues. Something in distress. He shines the light across to the boxes. A scratching starts now too. The nervous sense of adventure tingles, and he steps on a branch. It snaps.

Suddenly, all is silence.

The boxes have been stacked in such a way there is a dark alley into the centre. The champion of the night halts. A black line runs down into the alley. Under the light the line turns a brilliant red. The immediacy of the blood puts a thump in his heartbeat. Slowly, he unpacks the boxes in the way a god might undo a world.

Flashlight clenched between his teeth, when his breath is caught in the photons it billows and swirls. One box left until he will see into the heart of the cardboard alleyway. The line of blood shines with freshness. He leans in. Holds his breath. Takes the final box.

And stasis.

If the whole world spins around a central point, to our hero it is this moment.

A pair of dark, almond-shaped eyes stare up at him. It is a baby fox, frozen in the flashlight's beam, wrapped into a ball but in a strange, unnatural way. He guesses its size: twelve inches from the tip of its black nose to the tip of its white cloud tail. Its head is the size of a squash ball, its snout tiny but perfectly formed, its little triangular ears like sailboat sails covered in a soft orange fur. Two small front paws are splayed in front of it.

A vision of woods, the fox asleep on a soft bed of moss.

Two creatures living in two worlds, the wild and the civil, in a chance encounter. He hears his own voice: 'It's a baby fox.'

It twists its body away from the light to reveal a puddle of blood, and its wound. A deep gash at the top of the hind leg. Beneath the brightness of the blood, a line of white bone. Our defender notices a small pool of vomit and considers the act of mercy killing. But it is a sacred thing, to save a life. He thinks of the Event that is his origin story.

'You will not die today,' he whispers to his fallen friend.

He unhooks his backpack and finds his sweater, lays it inside one of the boxes and scoops the little fox as gently as he can on to its new bed. It's too sick to struggle. But just before he releases it, he is swept by a wave of emotion and he brings the creature up. And kisses it on the head.

Time now is of the essence. His automobile, the Black Phantom, is nearly a mile away. That's six minutes. His digital watch beeps as he starts the stopwatch. He modulates his run to make it as smooth as he possibly can for the stricken creature. He reaches the car in good time, fires up the engine and cruises smoothly along the blacktop towards his secret lair, the baby fox in its box on the passenger seat. Autumn leaves spiral in his wake.

He depresses the automatic garage door opener and sails into safety. Out the car, into the house and up the stairs, to the hidden chest in the closet. Secret compartment. Currency from many countries, but he needs good old-fashioned GBP. Vet's bills don't come cheap, he knows. £1,000 ought to do it. Back into the Black Phantom, satnav glows and the voice soothes.

He wipes away a single tear. 'I'm going to save you.'

In the blink of an eye he reaches the twenty-four-hour veterinary practice. Good people doing good things. He parks away from the building; can't be too careful with CCTV. The night is freezing and he almost slips. He sets the box down in front of the door and opens the lid. Scribbles a note.

Please help this little tyke. £1,000 enclosed for fees.
Send to RSPCA when better.
£500 donation to RSPCA in progress.

He places the envelope of cash in the box, presses the buzzer, and is away into the embracing arms of the night. He finds his way back to the Black Phantom and cruises through the dark, in silence, hands clenched on the wheel, fighting away the tears, the horror of his life, fighting away the darkness of his origin.

Chapter Sixteen

The house was quiet when he got back. In silence he stowed his costume away and tried to slow his mind. He'd known it would be hard to tell Sarah about the plane crash but this felt physical, like he'd undergone some terrible trauma. As he'd spoken to her it was like he was back there, and now, after creating that initial crack, the whole thing had split open . . .

It was an Indian summer, the year of the crash. Long hot days ran into one another and Sam found himself more often than not in the haven of his Batcave, looking down on the quiet, secluded basin before opening his comic books and staring. He didn't read them, couldn't focus to that level, but he would stare at the simple coloured panels where everything was clear. Life was simpler in comic books, people drawn clearly; their trousers and shirts didn't have shades of colour; the sky was blue and trees were green, everything as it should be.

There is nothing more certain than the passage of time, his father used to say, and as time went on his concentration slowly returned and he found himself able to do simple things like watch the news, but still, every few minutes the shock of what had happened stabbed him and he'd lose the next few moments to grief.

From the upstairs bedrooms at the back of the house he could look down the line of back gardens. Next door, on the right-hand side, weeds and grass grew between the paving slabs in the garden of his elderly neighbour, who'd died some months before and whose kids had yet to put the house on the market. Tendrils from the bushes snaked along gravel, and the swimming pool – the type that stands above ground level, constructed of a circle of vertical wooden slats – was empty. Cats gathered there, lying in the sun.

Slowly, official-looking letters arrived, phone messages came from solicitors, but Sam ignored them all. Across the playing fields behind the house he watched cars speed past on the busy road, people out in the continuing world with continuing lives.

The only contact he had was with his neighbour, Moira. She had taken to knocking on his window a few times a week to check how he was doing. Sometimes he would go into her house for tea and custard tarts, and she would offer advice on being strong and thinking about what his family would have wanted for him.

The letters to his parents kept arriving but he never opened them, not even the ones marked as 'urgent', or 'final notice'.

One morning, he got changed and went into the back garden. The day was cool with a crisp blue sky and puffy clouds, glacier white. The green of the trees swayed in a light breeze and Sam climbed the fence into the deserted garden on the other side.

Cats looked at him, plant seeds floated. The zone was somehow cleansed by having had no human contact. He sat on a wooden bench with flaking paint and opened his backpack to fetch a comic. It was the first *Sandman* collection, *Preludes and Nocturnes*, and he turned to the last of the eight stories, entitled 'The Sound of Her Wings'. In it, the Sandman, maker of all the world's dreams, meets up with his sister, Death. They walk together as she collects the souls of people and tells them their time is up. For that person, her visit is heralded by the sound of beating wings and then the person looks up, sees her, and she tells them it's going to be OK. Sam found this version of death extraordinarily comforting, so much more beautiful than anything offered by religion or science. Why could it not happen like that? Or the way the band My Chemical Romance suggested: death coming to welcome you in the form of your most cherished memory. It didn't matter, the truth. A great choice exists in life: truth or happiness?

Sam scanned the pages of the story, Death and Dream sitting side by side on the steps of Washington Square Park, and then, all of a sudden, the light breeze flickering the corners of the pages, something happened that hadn't happened in a long time. He began reading. He began reading the words on the pages, bubbles emerging from mouths, and as he did this there came a sensation of warm fluid flowing though him. He was reading again, as the perfect white clouds drifted across the dome and the wind moved serenely through the trees of the garden. The idea that his parents and brother and sister might not have died in horror but been welcomed by a kindly force into the void brought him tremendous comfort in that deserted garden. When he finished the story, he went back to the start of the comic. He read for hours and this time, when the pangs of loss hit him, they didn't hold in their mass quite the same power.

He started opening his parents' letters. Most were unpaid bills. He needed to call all the companies and tell them what had happened, which he duly did over the course of the next week, and when he imparted the information his voice held together surprisingly well.

The meeting with the bank was the most difficult. The manager took Sam into a small glass-fronted meeting cubicle and offered his most sincere condolences but there was still the small matter of the mortgage repayments, and did Sam know if his parents had life insurance? Sam did not know so the manager with a wave of his hand said not to worry as he would personally contact the Association of British Insurers, who would be able to find any policy that might exist, and in less than two weeks a cheque for an extraordinary amount of money arrived from a life insurance company Sam had never even known existed.

So it was the world that forced his hand, not any inner strength. He took the cheque to the bank, and the manager placed a reassuring hand on his shoulder, a manly act. All the money in the world wouldn't have made any difference to him but every cog in the economic machine must keep moving, every mortgage repaid, every bill settled; the machine never, ever stops. The feeling was the worst he'd ever had, even worse than when he'd been told about the plane crash, because here was a slip of paper that told him, categorically, 'You've got to move on now. It's over.'

In work the various production lines that had been relying on the ship that sank in the Suez Canal were running low on parts, and panicking. Sam had warned them this would happen but hardly any of his clients had sent him the figures for what would be needed and when, even after several emails explaining the urgency and stating their liability for expensive air shipping costs – everything was in writing. But now the time had come, he was getting it's-not-*our*-fault-the-ship-sank messages. But it wasn't Sam's fault either. If they'd done what he'd said, this could all have been easily avoided.

It wasn't Sarah's fault, what had happened.

'Sam, honey,' said Linda from Quality, whose desk was opposite him, though they couldn't see each other because there was a blue felt-upholstered partition between them.

He popped his head over the partition.

'You're shaking your leg again, babes.'

Sam was in a crouched position, standing just high enough to see her.

'Was I?'

He was very glad of the partition – her desk was such a mess he probably wouldn't be able to handle seeing it all day.

'Sorry,' she said. 'It makes me feel seasick.'

'I'll stop.'

He sat back down and concentrated on keeping his leg still. On the windowsill he noticed the corpse of a spider, upside down, its legs folded. He took some pincers from his desk, lifted it up and buried it in the soil of his bonsai tree.

He thought back to the text Sarah had sent him the next evening and winced. He still hadn't replied. There was a kind of paralysis towards her.

I'm sorry it ended badly but I had a nice time last night. I know it was a huge deal for you and I want you to know that I'm here x

He'd tried to reply probably a hundred times but had deleted every attempt. Instead, he simply said nothing.

There was too much dust between the keys of his futuristic wireless keyboard. He remembered the great day he'd spent in the city, buying it and the matching mouse. From the top drawer of his desk he took out his USB desktop vacuum cleaner, plugged it into the computer and sucked up the dust on the keyboard.

'Sam!' came Linda's voice.

'Sorry.'

He took out a wet wipe and cleaned the surface of his desk, and then used some antibacterial gel to cleanse his hands. Outside the barred window next to his desk grey clouds had moved in. The time of day was approaching for the daily fax to Japan; all the order and delivery documents collected into one. When the fax arrived at HQ in Tokyo, all the parts would be sourced from the vast network of suppliers scattered across the Far East. If Sam's clients wanted their parts air shipped on time, the documents had to be included in today's fax, but nobody had signed the authorisation sheet accepting the costs.

Nevertheless, Sam diligently printed out every air shipping

request, because he knew the only other option was for their lines to shut down.

'There's a lot of these.'

Sam looked up to see Rebecca standing over him with the huge sheaf of air shipping requests.

'It's this or line stop. I did tell them – it's not my fault they're idiots.'

Rebecca blinked with the shock of hearing Sam say something like this, a series of butterfly-wing flutters, something he'd seen her do before with the less efficient members of staff, but she'd never done it to him.

'Have they confirmed they're going to pay?'

'Well, I've put it in the emails that they're responsible.'

'But have you got it in writing that they'll pay? Have they signed the authorisation forms?'

This was the tone she took when his colleagues answered her questions in vague, wishy-washy terms; a type of energy in her voice that said, Look, I'm trying to get a black-and-white answer here so we don't have to get legal down the line.

'I haven't got it in writing. But I've sent emails saying I've organised the shipments and will fax the documents by five o'clock, and if they don't reply I'll assume they accept responsibility for the costs. That's what I've written.'

'Sam.'

'It's fine, Rebecca.'

In a perfect world all excess costs from the ship sinking would have been collected in a neat insurance claim, but the world is not perfect and though the goods were insured, nobody was going to pay to have replacements shipped expensively by air.

'Make sure you get the forms signed,' she said. 'Do *not* send these without written authorisation.'

He found the way she spoke to him uncharacteristically patronising, and when she was gone he had to close his eyes to compose himself. He envisioned a scene where he got up and flipped his desk into the wall. Almost shaking, he went into the warehouse to check the day's deliveries.

He looked at Sarah's message again. She hadn't sent anything else, and probably too much time had elapsed for him to reply. He found Mark sitting at his desk, flicking through the pages of a porno magazine as if it was nothing.

'Heard about the new company policy in Nihon?' he said, dabbing the end of his finger with his tongue and turning the page as if he were a delicate old lady flicking through a copy of *Reader's Digest*.

'Should I?'

'They're turning off the power in the building at ten every night to make sure people go home.'

'Ah shit, they haven't had another suicide, have they?'

'Yup,' said Mark, not looking up from the magazine.

It was strange to think how an office like that must work, day to day. Three people had thrown themselves from the sixteenth-floor roof garden in the last eighteen months. How could the others just turn up for work the next day and go about their business, knowing what had happened?

'I'm going back into the office for a second,' he said.

At his desk Sam collected up the air shipping documents. He'd sent the emails saying that his clients assumed responsibility for the costs if they didn't reply by 5 p.m. It was almost that time now and nobody had replied. Rebecca wasn't at her desk, so Sam put his air requests in with the Japanese fax documents and called out to the office.

'Any more faxes for Japan? I'm sending now.'

His voice sounded all over the place, and he cleared his throat.

He put the papers into the sorting tray on top of the machine, pressed the button to bring up the number for Japan. The green light flashed, calling to him to send the documents. Well, this was the only thing to do to avoid line stoppage and, anyway, Sam was in complete control of his thoughts and emotions. He was just being a good professional. It was so important to be a good professional. He looked at the flashing green button.

Another suicide in Japan. He sometimes wondered about depression and anxiety and how people called them mental illness. It made no sense. How could somebody look out at the wide world and *not* have an anxious or depressed reaction? Surely it was those people who were suffering from mental illness.

Everything's going to be fine, he told himself. And he pressed the button.

(P)

The Phantasm #008

Dark Night, Dark City

City lights pierce the night. Workers hurry home, cutting through backstreets, shoes clicking. Quiet down these side streets; quiet and lonely. Even parts of a city can feel unloved. And yet the eyes of an unseen guardian watch on.

This is the first time he has done this, come to patrol at street level in a place as big as the city. There is more than criminal danger now. Here he is exposed. He sits in a dark, thin alley between two buildings, but when he moves he will move into a city with all its rumble and flux.

A hero thinks more of society than he does himself. Personal problems? Forget about them. People are in danger, and there aren't enough police. Even now, at this young hour of the night – nine o'clock – there is drunken shouting. A gang of young rich kids in skinny jeans and ragged T-shirts are larking around, ignorant of the fact that a pair of eyes surveys them from the shadows.

Behind him he hears a movement in the alley. He turns. Just a cat in the garbage. Beyond the cat our hero spies a fire-escape ladder, not dissimilar to the ones we see in the great cities of America. Is it legal to climb such a thing? Is it trespassing? Doesn't matter; he's going up.

It is exhilarating, climbing up, hand over hand, the steel frame wobbling under his weight. The roof is covered with gravel. There are ventilation pipes amassed in ranks and an old Victorian chimney stack from the building's heyday. A colourful cuboid protrusion near the middle of the roof; the fire exit from which people would emerge in the event of a catastrophe. The roof is hemmed by chest-high wire fencing.

The satisfying crunch of gravel under his shoes. He stands at the cusp of the building, the wind in his face, a true hero regarding his city. The view is good. He can see all the way down the main drinking street, the writhing den of squalor and excess; like Nero's Rome but with worse haircuts. A girl vomits in the street, one of her stilettos in her hand, the other strapped to her foot but hanging sideways. Her friends watch, bored. Thursday night: Student Night. Education is important, yes, but at the expense of civil dignity?

The rooftops. He sees them all from this perspective. A giant could leap from one to the next like stepping stones. The rooftops. Where heroes come to rest. He closes his eyes and feels cold air on his face.

'Hey.'

Eyes open. A security guard stands silhouetted in the rectangle of light that is the open fire-exit door.

'What are you doing?'

He's overweight, too many burgers and bad coffee on the graveyard shift. The Phantasm moves forward.

'Wait there!' Urgency in the voice. Fear. A good man should fear nothing.

'It's OK,' our dark hero reassures.

'Don't fucking move, OK.' He speaks low into his radio.

Reinforcements on the way. Time to take flight. The ladder lies on the other side of the guard at 45°. In cricketing terms, if the guard is the batsman we're looking at deep third man.

He runs.

The security guard runs.

The Phantasm arcs around the guard and is thankful for his excellent physical fitness. What he lacks in genuine pace he makes up for in determination. The hope is that the obese guard will not be able to run very fast. It pays off – he can't. He is extremely slow, in fact. He imagines the scene from overhead: a form tracing the bend of a circle, with a central locus drifting towards the form.

There's a lot of wheezing from the guard. 'He's going down the fire ladder,' he says into his radio. And then, 'He's just a little guy.'

A crackly, indecipherable voice responds.

The Phantasm gains the ladder and descends quickly but bears health and safety in mind the whole time; he can't afford a slip. Halfway down he looks up. The obese guard has not given chase but his head peers over the lip of the building.

'You have nothing to fear,' calls the Phantasm. 'I'm one of the good guys.'

Back on terra firma adrenaline fires a chaos through him. His way is blocked now by a second guard, this one a lot fitter looking. Torchlight blinds.

'Police are on their way,' the guard warns, his gait that of a stuffed bear on its hind legs in attack formation.

Our hero runs down the alleyway in the opposite direction. Block out the fear. A wooden fence. Dead end. But a drainpipe and a wheelie bin; he uses one to climb the other. Over the fence and a small drop down to a deserted car park. On impact pain shoots through his bad ankle. Ignore it. Move on, dark avenger.

He hobbles across the car park and sees the security guards are not following. He's outside their jurisdiction now. He runs off the pain in his ankle and emerges suddenly on to the main drinking street, in full view of the revellers, as well as the network of CCTV cameras.

The drag is all bars and clubs, a wide pedestrianised avenue between. Look up at the Victorian splendour of yesteryear gazing sadly down on the horror of modernity.

Halfway across the avenue two packs of lads shout rowdy taunts. Escalation. A doner kebab is launched across no-man's-land, impacting the muscular chest of what has become an extremely angry young man. What a waste of good food. The virile youngster steps into the battlefield, towards the other group of boys.

Our hero stands and watches. Engagement is imminent. Those of the call centre generation and the student masses are drawn towards the fracas, but their gazes slip from the two gangs to the shadowy figure standing close by, a masked man, a crusader of justice: a superhero.

The victim of the kebab attack sports a purple/pink T-shirt cut tight to emphasise his muscles, stonewashed skinny jeans turned up at the bottom and a pair of white Converse plimsolls with no socks. His hair is shaved at the back and sides, with a permed clump of black atop. And he has grabbed in his fist the shirt of the kebab launcher. The two sets of gangs have closed the gap. It's all kicking off!

Foul, foul language.

Faces redden, fists clench.

And here, now, a hero surveys the scene and must make a decision. Fight-or-flight chemicals rage. He narrows his eyes . . . and moves forward unto the fray.

The eyes of the gathering crowd are on him.

'What the hell *is* that guy?' calls an Americanised voice, though British.

Halfway to the tumult the first punch is thrown. A short, stocky man rages, 'Come fucking on then, you cunts!' and launches himself at a back-wheeling opponent. This is now a fully fledged fight. Blood has been shed; it stains Hollister muscle vests. He cannot turn away. If a hero is not needed here, he is not needed anywhere. He can do this.

He is a shadow.

He is a phantom.

He is the Phantasm!

'Gentlemen!' He clenches his fists. 'I'm placing you all under citizen's arrest!'

Someone spins towards him and lamps him in the side of the head with extraordinary force. He hears the watching crowd gasp as he wheels across the concrete on jelly legs before hitting the deck. He raises himself on all fours and tries to straighten his mind, remember the martial arts training from the Internet. A feeling of recklessness sweeps through him. Abandonment. A great sinkhole opens beneath him, into which tumbles his fear, inhibition, sense. It is glorious, this feeling.

He charges, head down, into the squall.

'Stop fighting!' he shouts.

He is buried within a mass of human movement, all motion and hustle. He is struck again, on the top of his head, and again in his injured ribs, sending a snap of pain into the kernel of his mind. Someone throws their arms around him in a bear hug and the crowd murmurs the word, *Superhero*. The Phantasm releases a mighty roar and envisions pushing his arms out, creating a wave of energy that sends the fighters outwards in all directions. A bomb detonating. He tenses his muscles, grits his teeth, closes his eyes and . . . *HEAVES!*

But it has no effect on the bear hug. Close-quarter combat is not his forte and, to make matters worse, his rape alarm has been set off. It causes a momentary pause in the action. The crowd is now large and they cover their ears as the siren scream of the alarm sounds along the street.

'What the hell is that?'

The muscle-bound fighters are forced to cover their own ears. The noise is awful. The bear hug ceases and our hero stands. He realises something. The fight is over. A quick nod. He is satisfied. But bobbing through the crowds now, the helmets of Her Majesty's Constabulary.

Work done, time to disappear.

He reaches into his utility belt, finds a smoke bomb, and smashes it into the street. A hiss, a mist, and the time for freedom is opportune. He turns to run but is thwarted by a lunging officer of the law, who bundles him to the blacktop.

A second officer steps in and smacks a thunderbolt into our hero's thigh with his truncheon.

The crowd has shifted; the ones who were fighting are now part of the masses. All focus has fallen on the stricken crusader.

'I stopped the fight,' he appeals to deaf ears.

The police talk hurriedly into radios, he hears one of them ask his name, and suddenly our hero realises they think he is a demented gunman because of his outfit.

'I am the Phantasm,' he grunts, 'Let me go.'

They pat him down, slap the cuffs on, put a knee in his back. He hears five awful words: *Get his mask off him*. A hand reaches towards the mask and fingers curl under it.

His secret identity.

'Please . . . don't.'

Lots of shouting, the city wheeling, why now, not now, the fingers clenching, the mask lifting . . .

Chapter Seventeen

He thinks of that day, when he was younger, sitting outside on a beautiful spring day. The sky was so blue, the trees surrounding him so green.

One of those days when the warmth comes back into the world after winter.

The little voice had said, *Don't you wish it could stay like this for ever and ever?*

The moment Sam realised fully what was happening was around three seconds after the police bundled him to the ground. He was in handcuffs, wearing army gear, having just exploded a smoke bomb. They were rough with him, rougher than he would have expected – did they think he was a terrorist?

His mind was scrambled. The punch to the head had left a pulsing behind his eyes. Noise everywhere, drunken laughing, faces peering in. Yet at the centre of him, down in the sixth layer of thought, the deep machines worked calmly. This thought: What have I done? Not the getting into a fight, not even being floored by the police; more far-reaching. Faced by the world of upside-down neon nightclub signs and litter-strewn streets, he remembered the quiet spring afternoon, staring into the mirror at his costume. And then he thought of Sarah.

'What's your name?'

His powerlessness under the brute force of the policeman made him feel how he'd felt in school: weak and pathetic and small. He heard himself say he was called the Phantasm.

'Get his mask off him.'

He panicked. All the faces staring at him as he tried to wriggle out, his cheek scraping the pavement. The two cops tightened their grip on him and one reached down to his mask and hooked his fingers under it.

The life fell out of him.

'Please . . . don't.'

He lay there and felt all the energy of the Phantasm dissipate. The fingers tightened on the mask and he closed his eyes. 'No.' Tears welled now but not in a dramatic way, rather in a slow, steady grieving. He willed the protective numbness to come and save him, but it did not. The mask came up and a cold wind whipped across the street and into his face. He turned away; as the mask came off, there was the sound of cheering.

'What's your name?'

This time the voice was kinder, obviously because Sam was crying now.

'Sam,' he heard his own voice say.

He hated it, being cleft open like this.

'OK, Sam,' said the voice into his ear, the whole world condensing down to just one square foot. 'We're going to lift you up and search you, OK?'

Head down, he nodded.

The two cops dragged him to his feet. Another cheer. The flashes of camera phones. He put his chin to his chest so they couldn't see and tasted the make-up running from his eyes.

'Have you got any needles on you?'

He shook his head. They went through his things but so weird were the contents of his utility belt and assault vest, they couldn't decide if they were weapons or not. The thought of people finding out about this was unbearable and the great hand of loneliness, of having to deal with this alone, was even worse.

'I'm sorry,' he said. 'I'm so sorry.'

The two policemen glanced at each other.

'Have you got anyone we can call for you?' said the kind one.

He shook his head again. He felt so tiny among these giant men.

'Wait,' said the other one. 'Let's get him in the van.'

He hadn't even seen the riot van, with its blue lights spinning silently. The back door swung open and he went into the brilliant light. He caught a glimpse of himself in a strip of steel. The running eyeliner made his face look like a Rorschach test. The last thing he saw of the street were the faces of people leaning in, like sunflowers in the breeze, before the doors slammed shut.

'No family or friends?'

He shook his head.

'What's your name?'

'Sam.'

'Your full name.'

'Samson Holloway.'

A pause.

'Your address, Sam?'

In the comics it didn't happen like this. In comic books they would do anything, go to any length to protect their identities. In the comic books everything always ended up OK.

He gave them his address and one of the officers left the van to check his details. Grainy voices crackled from the other cop's radio. Sam's breath was loud and the song of sleep drifted into his mind.

When the second cop came back he said, 'OK, Sam. We're going to arrest you for a Section Five Public Order offence, OK?'

Each word after the word *arrest* was like a thunderbolt. Nerves fired sugars down his bloodlines and made him feel dizzy.

'We're taking you to a custody suite, OK?'

Why did they keep phrasing it like a question? Like there was an option. When he didn't respond they started reading him his rights, and this couldn't be happening, he hadn't done anything wrong. Street lights through the tiny window making spokes on the floor of the moving van, swaying round corners, and the thrum of rubber on tarmac.

'What were you doing out there?'

'I . . . don't know.'

Down corridors, through doors. They took him to a cell and he lay down on the uncomfortable bunk and tried to block out the sound of heavy doors clanking shut, tried to block out his thoughts, all the thoughts.

Do you have someone to call?

No.

I'll never do this again, he told himself, almost in chastisement. The Phantasm is over. It's over. And yet this idea was instantly more disturbing than he thought. It was, in fact, breaking his heart.

During the long summer following the plane crash Sam visited the empty swimming pool in next door's garden a lot. He paid attention during those days to the nature of loneliness and its impact on the mind. Being alone was making him sick, and he could feel it, like a cloud unfurling at the edges, pulling apart.

He needed something to propel him back to the real world and, over the slow days, when the leaves browned and fell and became brittle, he tried to think of an alternative to the plan hatching in his mind.

Putting the house on the market felt like a catastrophic betrayal, a grand turning away from the memory of his family, but the idea of moving into a brand-new house seemed so obvious. A crisp, fresh house where no one had ever lived, with pristine carpets, newly plastered and painted walls, bright lights set unobtrusively into the ceiling, everything finished to a high standard; a house with no baggage or memories or ghosts.

It wasn't long before the call came from the estate agent with a serious offer on the family home, and as soon as it ended Sam went to the back of the house and opened the door. As he lay in the deserted swimming pool a cat popped its head over the rim and jumped in. It was grey-and-black striped, with paws the white of virgin snowfields, and it came over to Sam and nuzzled its head against his arm. Sam could hardly control the tears as he lay on his back looking at the sky, with the cat sitting on his chest, thinking, *I'm going away from the only place I feel safe.*

Finally, the removal company came and took the contents of the house. Everything was loaded up. Everything. All the furniture, electronics, kitchen equipment, the letters, all the presents he'd ever bought and received, everything his little brother and sister owned, their toys and colourful chairs, their books, their tiny clothes, to be taken anywhere, he didn't care, he just needed for it to go. Be scrapped or sold – whatever the removal company wanted to do with it.

At dusk on that last day he collected up the small box with family memories he'd saved, things like cards and photos and some heirlooms, and stood in the living room with a blood-red sky beyond the window. For everything he loved – this was the centre.

And he left the house. He left the woods and the swimming pool and the cats, and he moved to his new house with his new car and new furniture and new entertainment system and new life, and he felt, at last, like he was ready to get better. At least, that's what he'd told himself.

*

An unfathomable stretch of time concertinaed and then the heavy door of the cell opened and a doctor came in with a couple more officers, bringing him back to reality.

'Sam, isn't it?' said the doctor.

Sam stared at him.

'It's OK, I just want to talk.'

They took him down some corridors to a small, comfortable room with a sofa, two tub chairs and a low coffee table. A Van Gogh print hung in a cheap frame. A bookshelf with leather-bound books was against one wall, a TV played BBC *News 24* in silence.

'You can leave us,' said the doctor to the officer, the one who'd spoken in a kind voice to Sam before arresting him.

'Am I going to get into a lot of trouble?' he said.

The doctor, a good-looking man with tremendous confidence, said, 'No, not at all. They're going to release you without charge.'

Sam didn't say a word.

'Listen, Sam, they wanted me to talk to you.'

It was nice in this room, surprisingly cosy for a police station. Surely not every station had a room like this. The Van Goch print was of rain falling over rolling fields. The carpet was light grey in colour, a nice tight weave.

'The officer who brought you in recognised your name.'

It wasn't the sort of carpet you could have in a home, too formal, too efficient, but it was a good carpet. It seemed new, still had a little fuzz, and was cut beautifully into the wall.

'He remembered what happened – he lives in your village? – and he wanted me to speak to you.'

The carpet was blurring. *Jeez, will you just stop crying?*

'Why are you dressed like that Sam?'

Sam knitted his fingers together. On the TV they were replaying a helicopter shot of the stricken tanker in the Suez

Canal from a couple of weeks ago. Mostly submerged, its stern was still just about poking up above the water.

'Are you dressed up as a superhero?'

His throat felt hot, his eyes stung.

'I'm not a psychiatrist,' said the doctor, lowering his head and trying to look up into Sam's eyes, 'but people react to tragedies in a whole host of ways. Some are healthy and some are . . . less so. But look,' he placed a sheet of paper on the coffee table, 'this is the number of a counselling service. Did you have counselling?'

Sam stared at the sheet of crisp white paper and shook his head. He felt so stupid, sitting there in his costume.

'You should. It really helps. And it's completely confidential of course. This service,' the doctor tapped the paper with the end of a Montblanc pen, 'it's free to use. Just give them a call. You can talk on the phone or arrange a face-to-face meeting. They can help you.'

Sam took the paper. He hated the idea of counselling, hated the idea of going to a place and just moaning to some poor soul for an hour and being a complete buzzkill.

'Thank you.'

'Things like this,' said the doctor, indicating Sam's Ninja shirt and trousers with luminous strips stitched down the legs. 'You're trying to do a good thing, but the most important thing is you getting better, OK?'

'So the policeman brought me here because he wanted to help me?'

The doctor nodded.

'So I can go home?'

The doctor sat back in the comfortable chair. 'You can go home, but you should think about what I've said. You should know, too, this sort of thing attracts attention. Papers, TV. Maybe you need to think about that too, what you're trying to achieve.'

But Sam didn't fully know what he was trying to achieve. This really was a lovely room. They didn't show rooms like this on cop shows. Now he knew he could go home, he'd stopped listening to the doctor, who was still talking. On the TV screen the stricken tanker had shed its shipping containers, some of which were drifting like Lego bricks across a puddle.

Chapter Eighteen

It was still dark when they released him unceremoniously from the police station. His vest, utility belt and mask were stowed in a clear plastic bag. Using the money from his utility belt he got a taxi but only as far as the edge of his town, so the driver didn't know where he lived. The high street was completely deserted as he walked home. He'd walked through his home town thousands of times but all the familiar things – the shop fronts, the churches, the bridge over the railway line – seemed now unfamiliar through the filter of his state of mind. He felt like a stranger. When he got back to his house he didn't even turn the lights on. He went straight up to the attic and curled up in the centre of his comics maze, where he fell instantly asleep.

There was a month of rain and Sam hadn't heard from Sarah. It swept across the land and stripped the trees of what leaves they had left and then turned the ground to mud.

As the days flicked by, the distance from Sarah did little to ease the feeling of discomfort in Sam. He returned to his old routines. In the rain he ran around the forestry on weekends and through the streets on weeknights. On Saturday nights he got takeaway and watched movies he'd seen countless times before. He cleaned for hours on end. And as he did these things, he quietly went about the business of packing away the memories that had been unleashed by Sarah. But what had once made him feel safe now made him feel lonely.

The only thing that made him feel any better was patrolling. When he pulled on the costume, all his stress fell away. In the aftermath of the arrest he'd not donned the mask for a week but the pull was overpowering and, in the end, he'd relented. The conflict he'd been feeling between the Phantasm and Sarah dissipated. At least without her he got to keep the mask.

In the diner on the beach the windows shuddered in the frames as powerful winds swept in off the sea. Huge waves crashed against the shore and the world was trying to get at him, but that small seaside building kept everything out. Slowly, things were getting back to normal.

The problem was, normal didn't feel so good any more.

Sam landed on Trafalgar Square.

'Oh *well*,' said Blotchy. 'Well, well, well. Would you like fresh towels?'

It was very frustrating. Sam had hotels on Mayfair and Park Lane, as well as on some of the lower-value properties, but Blotchy had them on all the reds, as well as the yellows and oranges, and Sam kept landing on them. This roll of the dice meant he had to downgrade his hotels on Euston Road and Angel Islington to afford Blotchy's bill.

Blotchy took Sam's money and folded it into the personalised money clip he always used when he played Monopoly and which was a constant source of annoyance to both Sam and Tango. Tango, who was safe on his own Bond Street, rolled the dice and passed Sam's hotels unharmed.

Wind pushed against the windows of Blotchy's parents' conservatory and tossed leaves against the glass. No matter how frustrating Blotchy's tactics, Sam was grateful to be here, with his old friends.

'I can't believe how unlucky I am,' he said.

'Nothing to do with luck,' said Blotchy. 'It's all about playing the statistics.' He reached his big bear hand into his bag of toffee popcorn and tossed some morsels into his little mouth.

'So what are your plans for the week?' said Tango.

'Nothing much,' said Sam.

'What about you, Blotch?'

'My business is my own.' He rolled the dice and glided past some of Sam's properties on to the Electric Company, which he owned.

'Any news from the dating site you signed up for?' said Sam, trying not to sound too sarcastic. He and Tango were both surprised that Blotchy had done this. Not that he'd signed up, but that he'd told them about it.

'Oh, listen to Mr Experience over there,' said Blotchy. 'Now he's got a girlfriend he thinks he's cock of the walk.'

'I haven't got a girlfriend.'

'I don't know why you're trying to hide it from us.'

'I'm not trying to hide anything. I haven't heard from her in a month.'

'Oh,' said Blotchy, stumbling. 'Well, you're better off without women. They're trouble. And expensive. Especially the pretty ones.'

'Blotchy is subscribing to the school of meninism,' said Tango, leaning sideways to Sam.

'Not at all,' said Blotchy. 'I just think feminism is going too far.'

'Let's stop talking about this before you lose whatever dignity you have left,' said Tango.

'Pretty?' said Sam.

Blotchy's cheeks reddened when he realised Sam had latched on to the word, and in the air of the moment Sam felt the satisfying shift in power back to him.

'I meant . . . well, she was pretty, wasn't she?'

'She's not dead!'

'No, I know that but . . .' His whole body went loose and he sagged. Slowly, he reached sheepishly for more popcorn.

'Plenty more fish in the sea, eh?' said Tango. He put his hand on Sam's shoulder and said solemnly, 'Would you like me to sign you up to Blotchy's dating site?'

'You're OK, thanks. I'll let Blotchy blaze that trail.'

'You're about as funny as the thing I'm about to deposit in the toilet,' said Blotchy, standing up. 'Now if you'll excuse me.'

He took his Monopoly money and put it in his pocket, then took the dice and put them in his pocket too. He then took a photo of the board.

'Just in case you get any ideas' he said. 'I may be some time.'

And, with that, he left the room.

Tango waited until he heard Blotchy climbing the stairs.

'You OK?' he said.

'Yeah.'

'What happened?'

Sam felt Tango's eyes on him as he considered this.

'It just . . . kind of fizzled out.'

There was a long pause after this. Sam ordered his money into neat piles.

'She seemed nice,' said Tango.

Sam felt his face flush.

'Did you want it to . . . fizzle out?'

Sam cleared his throat. His Monopoly piece glinted in the light. 'I don't know,' he said. 'Probably not.'

Tango nodded. 'Well, you know, is there anything you can do?'

Sam didn't answer this.

'You don't need to take my advice,' said Tango. 'You know I'm useless at this sort of thing, but I'll just say this. If there is anything you can do . . . you should just do it. Be brave.'

Sam looked up at him when he said those two words, at

his old friend, just as the flush sounded upstairs and the floorboards creaked under Blotchy's weight.

When he got home, there was a brown package on the doormat in the hallway. He picked it up, along with the rest of the mail, and went into the kitchen to make himself an apple and elderflower tea. He sat at the breakfast bar and hooked his finger under the perforated strip of the parcel. He loved opening that perforated strip. He looked inside and the strength fell out of him.

Inside the brown envelope was a first edition of a short story collection by Raymond Carver called *Cathedral*. Sarah had said it was one of her favourite books, so he'd ordered it weeks ago from a seller of rare books in America. It was going to be her Christmas present, and he'd forgotten all about it. The pages inside were yellow and old. Closing the book again, he set it down on the table and looked around the empty kitchen, at how neat and clean it was.

He could hear the silence of the house, and the image of her face smiling at him flashed across that silence.

He sipped his tea and noticed his leg was shaking.

Chapter Nineteen

The fisherman cast his line out, far across the stretch of water. Even from this distance Sam heard the heavy weight plop through the surface. The brittle reeds that had turned brown with the changing of the season chittered on the shoreline. The angler, just a stick man on the far side of the lake, set his rod on a rest and sat down.

Unable to sleep, Sam had come here before work. It was peaceful. Sometimes, in the summer, he'd bring his lunch to this lake. It was hardly light yet there he was, the fisherman, out for an early catch. To his left, a heron was standing perfectly still in the shallows.

In his hand, Sam held the copy of *Cathedral*. The air was freezing, but Sam barely noticed. He was remembering being in the bathroom at the pub quiz, on the verge of going home, and the feeling that had come over him of needing to stay – to hold on. It made him think of Sarah's Rocket Tree. The one he'd let go of so many years ago. She'd said that after a while, when you think you're all alone, you suddenly look out and that's when you see it. The other tree, with the other person in it.

He nodded. It had taken weeks to get here but he was ready. He took out his phone . . .

Hi Sarah, was just wondering how you were. Sorry I haven't been in touch. Hope all is OK.

. . . and exhaled.

*

Across the way Linda was talking loudly to a customer. Sam picked up the phone from his desk but Sarah still hadn't replied. He warmed his hands on his cup of tea. Mr Oka-matsu was staring out of the window near the entrance of the office, his back to the room, with his hands on his hips and legs apart. He was swaying gently. The second hand on the clock on the wall didn't seem to be moving fast enough and it was impossible to concentrate as the slow realisation that he'd blown it sank in.

At lunch he drove as far as he could for half an hour, before turning the car round and driving back. When he parked up he checked his phone again, but there was still nothing. He sat at his desk and stared at his monitor. He watched a money spider lower itself on a spun thread from the eaves of his bon-sai tree and it was when the spider touched the soil that the phone finally buzzed.

Sam froze. His heart rate started up and his skin went clammy. At last he summoned the courage to look.

Hi Sam! Nice to hear from you! Yes, all good here. We should meet up for coffee sometime x

He stared at the message. All this time . . .

Definitely. When? He scrubbed out the last part. It was too desperate. *Definitely. We should go to that place near your work you told me about, with the comfy chairs.*

She was typing and his skin prickled with the thought of her.

Fo sho. When's good for you? I miss speaking to you x

Whoa. That was a good message. He sat there for a second.

Great! How about tomorrow maybe? Do you still finish at half 5? I could be there at 6. I miss speaking to you too.

He deleted the last sentence, thought for a moment, and then retyped it. At the other end she was typing. Then she would stop, and then restart. Stop, restart. Sam waited, tap-ping his foot on the floor, heart thumping.

Awesome. See you there x

Was that it? All that worry. The phone felt warm in his

hands. He started typing but then noticed she was typing again, so he stopped. She stopped. He waited, and she started typing again so he let her finish. At last, her message came through.

I'm so glad you messaged me. Can't wait ☺ *x*

The coffee house was in a Victorian building, where the plaster had been ripped off to reveal the original brickwork. There were fake stags' heads and floating shelves crammed with old books and retro teapots. There were metal advertising signs from the fifties and old movie posters. The tables were upturned crates and the mismatched leather chairs were low and so comfy he might have fallen asleep if he wasn't so nervous.

'Sam!'

She sidled her way through the chairs, a vision in a red dress with a black collar and black buttons down the front. His heart lurched. It felt like when you pull your foot out of wet, sticky mud. And in that instant he knew he'd done the right thing.

He got up out of the chair and they hugged and she fitted perfectly.

'Hey, let me get you a drink,' he said.

'It's OK, I've got money,' she said. 'You wait here and guard my stuff.' She threw her bag and coat down messily and disappeared to the counter.

Sam took a seat and dried his sweaty palms on his trousers. She came back with a coffee and a slice of cake.

'What's that?'

'Chocolate and chilli and lavender.'

'Oh. I wonder if that works.'

'And I've gone here for a gingerbread latte,' she said, sweeping her hand across her coffee, with a cinnamon-dusted surface. 'I've been Jonesing for this.'

'It smells like Christmas.'

'It *does* smell like Christmas,' she said, opening her eyes wide. There was a pause and Sam tried to fight back the sudden surge of thoughts piling into his mind: the arrest, his not getting back to her.

'It was really nice to get that text from you,' she said.

The fact that this was the first time they'd spoken since he told her about his family's death ballooned around the moment.

She looked at her cake and cut off the front corner with her fork and popped it in her mouth. 'How come you sent it?'

How to answer that question?

'I just thought about you,' he said.

'Aw. That's nice.'

A man passed them and Sam noticed him checking Sarah out.

'Thanks for seeing me,' he said.

'Oh, no problemo.'

'No, I mean . . . you know. Last time.'

'Yeah, I know.'

She made a half smile. He went to pick up his teapot but it was heavier than he thought and he dropped it back to the table with a bang.

'Yeah, that thing's made of iron,' she said.

Sam nodded. 'I'm really sorry about not being in touch, though.'

They both drank.

'I heard somebody order a lager with a dash the other day,' said Sarah, skipping over the subject like it was nothing. 'And do you know what they said?'

Sam shook his head.

'They said, "Pop a drop of pop in the top." Isn't that lovely? You should say that. I thought of you when they said it.'

Sam smiled sadly and felt forlorn. In a way he was glad she didn't want to linger on his absence but in another, there was a sense they should at least talk about it. 'I should.' He dropped a sugar cube into his tea. 'So how have you been?'

Sarah tried to hurry the swallowing of her cake and made

a circling motion with her fork before saying, 'Everything's good. I'm going to a Christmas fayre on the weekend, with Francis.'

Sam's heart froze. Francis. He'd forgotten about Francis.

'On a date?'

'Uh-uh,' she shook her head. 'At least, I don't *think* it's a date. We've been out a few times, but only as friends. I mean, Francis is OK, obviously he's super hot, but . . . I don't know. I'm not sure what it is.'

The jealousy shook Sam hard. 'I'll come,' he blurted.

'To the fayre?'

'Sure. Why not?' He already half regretted saying it, as he imagined how incredibly awkward this was going to be. But only half.

Sarah thought for a second and shrugged. 'OK,' she said. 'Cool.'

He stirred his tea, trying to be calm. But this was tough, because Francis was so much better looking than him. 'So what are your plans for Christmas?' he said, steering the conversation away. 'Are you going home?'

'I am home.'

'To your family, I mean.'

'Nope. I'm going to stay with a friend at his country house.' She spooned some foam off the top of her coffee and ate it. 'How about you?'

He decided not to say anything about how she diverted him away from the subject of her family again. 'Staying local,' he said.

'What do you normally do on Christmas Day?'

'Oh, you know, just the usual.' If not seeing a single person on Christmas Day could be considered usual. There was a pause. 'So what else have you been up to?' he said.

She shrugged and ate some more cake. 'Been going to a lot of literary things. Readings. Francis knows lots of local writers. They're really good. You should come.'

The thought of Francis was making him feel very anxious. Why did she keep coming back to him?

'How about you?' she said.

Oh, just sending myself crazy about you, thinking of you every ten seconds, getting arrested because you've made me insane because you're amazing.

'Just the usual.'

'It's good to see you, Sam. I've missed this. Talking to you.'

'Yeah,' he said. 'Me too.'

Behind her, a girl was preparing a cappuccino, raining chocolate sprinkles down through the flame of a blowtorch, igniting them, backlighting Sarah with tiny fireworks. An uneasy feeling settled over him. He might, in some small way, have overcome his demons by sending that text at the side of the fishing lake, but now there was a bigger, badder demon. And its name was Francis.

Chapter Twenty

It was a nearby boarding school that was holding the Christmas fayre. The school hosted international students, not only from the local American air base but also extremely gifted kids from all over the world. These kids stood at the gate now, freezing in their hi-vis vests and wellington boots, tall scrawny things ushering the cars up a long, tree-lined track.

'It's like Hogwarts,' said Sarah, staring out the window at the tall tower of an old castle, the focal point of the grounds. Francis said something that Sam couldn't hear in the back seat, and the jealousy when they both started laughing, and then when she casually put her hand on his forearm, was like being stabbed.

The place was old with its sturdy grey bricks, arched doorways and stone mullioned windows. Francis pulled the car into a parking space, ushered in by a couple of enthusiastic pupils.

'Hi,' said one girl, when they got out. She was very tall, in a pair of red jeans and hair tied in pigtails. 'It's this way to get in.' She indicated a wide, arched entranceway with an iron portcullis suspended above it. On the other side they came to a courtyard of lawn. Skywards, turrets with small leaded windows and stone balconies looked down. Opalescent skies beyond and a creeping mist made a magic in the air. A brass band played 'Good King Wenceslas' in some unseen hall.

Fudge sellers spun cellophane bags airtight, wooden reindeer carvers adjusted displays, mulled wine vendors dispensed, wreaths smelled of cinnamon, soaps of lavender.

At one of the craft tables a couple of women were selling snow globes with intricate Victorian dioramas inside. He watched Sarah lift one from the table and bring it up close, lifting her glasses off her face and squinting to see. He watched the smile emerge as she studied the tiny street of houses and shops and the little figures of people dressed in their hats and scarves.

She turned to Francis and held it up to him. 'I love it,' she said.

Francis glanced at the snow globe and nodded. 'It's pretty awesome,' he said. 'Let me get it for you.'

'Oh, it's OK,' she said, 'I didn't mean that.'

'No, I want to,' he said, rifling around his cool-looking duffel coat for his wallet.

Now Sam really started feeling like a third wheel. Sarah was funny, clever and completely gorgeous. He was none of these things, and with a pang of sadness it became suddenly obvious how she'd be better off with someone like Francis.

'Here,' said Sarah, quickly fishing a ten-pound note out of her pocket and handing it across to one of the women before Francis could pay. She glanced up at him, and Sam had to watch as they shared a smile.

They found a room with a bar and tables and chairs, filled with revellers. A glass-fronted addition to the stone building looked out across long, terraced lawns to a wide, grey lake. Empty paper cups and plates lay strewn across a spare table, at which they sat with their mulled wine and mince pies. Outside was a stall selling freshly grilled lamb burgers.

'What an amazing place,' Sam said.

Francis looked around at the architecture. 'Sixteenth century,' he stated firmly.

'I disagree,' said Sarah, winking at Sam, reversing something and making him confused.

'No, no, you can tell by the windows. Stone mullions and quite small. See? Unless it was a Victorian revivalist effort, but I'm not feeling that.'

'And the turrets,' said Sarah. 'Because it's a castle.'

Francis ignored her and looked out the window in a way that Sam thought was a bit arrogant.

'Who wants lamb burgers?' Francis said. 'I'm buying.'

'I'll have one,' said Sarah.

'Sam?' he offered, begrudgingly.

'I'm OK. Thanks, though.'

'Whatever, your loss,' he said, almost with a bit of barb now, before heading out.

'I think he's on the spectrum,' said Sarah. 'But I'm teaching him.'

Sam wished he could just ask her outright what her feelings were for Francis. One second they were sharing intimate smiles, the next she was poking fun at him. Across the other side of the room, where the new glass met the old stonework, he noticed an elderly gentleman wearing thick-gauge tan corduroy trousers, a smart cotton shirt and a red sweater beneath a smart green wax jacket. Before him he had a slice of Christmas cake and a steaming polystyrene cup. He picked up the cake and broke it in two, shook the crumbs off, and bit into one half, a rolling motion to his chew as he took a sip of his tea.

'Have you ever noticed,' said Sam, 'those old couples who have lunch in Tesco? They sit there and eat and don't say anything to each other.'

'That's sad.'

'No it isn't. They've said everything they need to say but they're still together. They just want to be around each other. They don't need words any more.'

Sarah smiled. She didn't get what he was trying to say but that was OK.

'Hey, have you heard about this superhero guy around here?'

He sat perfectly still. 'Hmm?'

'I saw this article about a real-life superhero who got arrested in the city centre a few weeks ago. Do you remember your friends were talking about him in the car when we went to that lake?'

The table was a bit wobbly so he pushed his knee into its underside to steady it.

'That sounds pretty . . . cool?'

Sarah shrugged. 'I thought you might be interested because of your comics. It sounds nuts to me.'

'Yeah, it does a bit, doesn't it?'

'Why would someone do that? There must be something bad in there somewhere.'

'Bad?'

'Fucked up. Something tragic. I mean, it's not normal, is it?'

A string quartet were setting up at the glass doors before the lawns. Outside, Francis was slowly making his way towards the front of the queue.

'I don't know,' said Sam. 'Maybe he's just trying to do something good.'

Her fingers twirled a piece of paper into a roll. 'So volunteer for a food bank or something, you know. It's a bit egotistical, don't you think? Hey, what's that?'

'What?'

She reached across and grabbed his hand, which sent a surge of chemistry up his arm.

'You're bruised.'

She pulled up the sleeve of his sweater to reveal a long, dark bruise on his forearm.

'Oh, it's nothing,' he said, pulling away and covering his arm. 'I hit it at work.'

He had, in fact, done it falling off the roof of the library when he lost his grip on the drainpipe, smacking into a railing, not that – he now realised – he could ever tell her this after what she'd just said.

'Looks painful.'

'It's fine. I bruise easily, it's nothing.'

She laughed. 'You bruise easily?'

'Well, you know, I . . .' He didn't know what else to say.

Sarah turned and looked over her shoulder. 'Where's Francis?'

Sam swallowed. 'You said you've been to some literary events with him or something?'

'Yeah, a few. They're fun.'

'You'd think someone like him would have a girlfriend.'

'He's just finished with someone after, like, six years or something.'

'Wow.'

'He's pretty messed up about it. I think she cheated on him.'

'Oh jeez.'

Sam didn't usually like mulled wine, but in this situation it was good.

'So have you done all your Christmas shopping yet?' she said, deliberately changing the subject, whatever that meant.

'I guess so. I don't really do Christmas shopping.'

'No?'

'We do the Secret Santa in work and I got Rebecca. It's a ten-pound budget and she likes to have cash so . . .'

'Sam. What are you doing on Christmas Day?'

'Um. You know, the usual. Christmas dinner. All that.'

'With who?'

'What's that?'

She put her hands around her mulled wine to warm them. 'Are you going to be on your own?'

He couldn't meet her eye.

'Oh my God. OK. You're coming with me.'

'What?'

'You're coming with me to my friend's house. He won't

mind. There's plenty of room up there. You will absolutely love it. It's like Wayne Manor.'

'What friend?'

'My friend I told you about. He's got this old country manor. He has people stay over and they throw a bit of cash his way and bring food. There'll be a load of us. You've got to come. It'll be fantastic. Ah, I'm excited now. I can't wait for you to meet everyone.'

'Who are they?'

'I met Kabe, he's the one who owns Arcadia—'

'Arcadia?'

'Like a poet's paradise? I met him in Edinburgh. He's a really, really nice guy. American. Tell me you're gonna come. It's three days. We'll get the train. We'll take a train ride through the English winter countryside. There's a lake there, and a wood, and a walled garden with apple trees, and a forest of rhododendrons—'

Outside he saw Francis heading back across the lawn. It was like an opening on a battlefield.

'Yeah, OK,' he said, quickly, darting through.

'Really?'

'Sure,' he said.

'No being weird and flaking out last minute?'

'Nope,' he said. He looked at her and couldn't suppress a smile.

'Great!' She leaned across and wrapped her arms around his neck.

'All right, all right,' he said, pulling away, laughing. 'It's not a big deal.'

Though, of course, it was a massive deal.

Francis came back with the lamb burgers wrapped in paper napkins. 'What are you guys talking about?' he said.

'Sam's coming to Arcadia for Christmas too.'

Francis stopped, and there was a quick friction.

'Oh. Cool.' He took a bite of his food, pretending not care, though Sam had seen the prickle that had flashed across his face.

The string quartet started playing 'Winter Wonderland'. The old man with the cake had gone and the table was empty. At their table, an awkward silence had descended. Sarah inspected the Victorian snow globe she'd bought. She turned it upside down and let the snow circle, drift and fall.

Chapter Twenty-One

Okamatsu-san walked with a kind of sashaying gait, his expensive yet thin trousers rippling with each stride, a shock-wave moving from the hem to his iron buttocks with each footfall. He wore shiny leather slip-ons with tassels and the turquoise worker's jacket given to everyone but worn only by Sam and the Japanese staff. He could have at least made an effort for this and got changed.

It was the first office Christmas party Sam had ever been to. Francis or no, after what he'd been through he felt buoyed by the idea of spending three days with Sarah over Christmas, and now here he was in a blaring karaoke bar packed with other office workers, feeling merry.

Ten of them were seated at a long table with tall chairs. Mr Okamatsu came away from the bar with a tray full of drinks. The colourful disco lights reflected off his glasses. A British colleague who had spent five years in Japan had once said to Sam the difference between the Japanese and the British was that Japanese people think of the whole instead of the individual. But then he added, 'All Japanese men live lives of quiet desperation.' There must be some truth in this, because of the suicide problem at HQ, but Mr Okamatsu seemed like a man in complete control of his life.

He took his seat at the head of the table, with Sam as his

right-hand man, and the drinks were passed along. Everybody sat in silence.

Okamatsu raised his beer and said, '*Kanpai!*'

The table loved this and raised their glasses. As soon as it happened, the mood lightened and some of the awkward tension fell away. Little conversations sprang up around the table, leaving just Sam and Okamatsu on their own.

The music was blasting, a woman massacring a version of 'Please Release Me'.

There was a bang at the front door and a drunken crowd of people tumbled into the club, Christmas hats on heads, one guy clutching the hips of a large woman, conga-style. Mr Okamatsu's small eyes behind the light-sensitive glasses seemed to absorb everything in their wake, eyes that sucked wisdom from the world.

'Mr Okamatsu, do you celebrate Christmas in Japan?'

Sam had to lean in as Mr Okamatsu spoke because he was conceding nothing to the loud music.

'We do. More than when I was a child.' When he was talking like this, his voice appropriated a tender smoothness. 'We go to KFC. You know KFC? And maybe we go to the cinema. We spend time with family. I will FaceTime my family this Christmas.'

Sam said, 'Do you look forward to going home?'

Mr Okamatsu replied, matter-of-factly, 'I miss my family. That is worst part of my job here.'

Sam looked at him and felt a moment of empathy for this man who'd been sent to Britain, away from his family, to work in a thankless job. Sam knew Okamatsu had two children, both still in school, and it didn't seem fair. A father shouldn't be away from his kids because of work. He wanted to put his hand on his forearm, but that would be a bridge too far.

One of the drunken revellers banged into the back of Sam's chair. 'Wheeey!' he shouted, dancing towards the bar, shimmying, shaking imaginary maracas.

'OK, up next,' said the guy running the karaoke, 'we have Okamatsu and Sam.'

Sam froze. The heads of the people around the table turned towards him in shock. When Sam looked at Mr Okamatsu he was already standing, tucking his shirt neatly into his trousers.

'Mr Okamatsu?'

'I put our names down,' he said, like it was the most normal thing in the world.

Sam's guts turned to mush and his heart was throbbing. He didn't want to do karaoke. Mr Okamatsu was halfway across the dance floor as the opening bars of the song started up. A piano. Oh God, the song was the romantic power ballad 'Up Where We Belong'.

'Go on, Sambo!' Mark nudged him, laughing.

Okamatsu had the mic in his hand. 'Sam,' he called unashamedly across the dance floor.

Lights flashed and his head was woozy. Mark tilted his chair so Sam slid off it.

'Go on, Sam!' Linda screeched.

But he didn't want to sing. He couldn't sing. His voice was awful. The music stopped and there was silence as the karaoke guy had to start the song over. The other revellers were aware of the coaxing going on at Sam's table and were craning to see. Mark pushed him in the small of the back and Sam edged on to the dance floor. Everyone cheered and the music started again. Sam turned back to the table and downed the double whisky in front of Mark, and everyone cheered again.

He felt Mr Okamatsu's eyes staring at him hopefully. Everyone at the table was laughing and clapping, but Sam was thinking about Okamatsu missing his family on Christmas Day.

'Fuck it,' he said, under his breath, and set out across the dance floor. The place erupted now and it felt like the climax to a film – apart from, instead of Sam walking towards a beautiful woman, it was Mr Okamatsu.

He started singing just as Sam reached the first of the three steps leading to the stage. Mr Okamatsu's voice was surprisingly pretty, a mid-range syrupy easiness to it. He had taken the female role.

Sam vaguely knew the song but not who should sing which part. Fortunately, the lyrics on the screen at his feet were divided into pink and blue but, unfortunately, it was his turn to sing. He couldn't hold a note to save his life, and he was well aware of how awful his voice was as he practically whispered the lyrics into the mic that the karaoke man had thrust under his nose.

'Louder,' someone shouted.

When he sang louder, everybody started half groaning, half laughing. Sam turned beetroot as they reached the chorus and Okamatsu joined in with him. The big man was shimmying from side to side as he harmonised with the main melody.

The second verse came and Sam watched Okamatsu sing. His eyes were closed. He was absolutely loving it, and yet everyone in the room was laughing at him, and so when it came to Sam's turn he made the quick decision to go for it. He belted out his lines, and even he felt the pain in his ears as his voice mutilated the melody. But then something happened he didn't expect. Sensing the effort he was putting in, the crowd got on board with the performance. They started cheering and clapping. Some couples grabbed each other and started dancing, including two large, older men, much to the delight of their colleagues. It felt good. No, with the alcohol and the sudden upswing washing across the crowd, it felt great. The second chorus approached and Sam felt Okamatsu put his arm around him.

Sam took a deep breath and, together, they belted it out as loud as they could, Mr Okamatsu's pretty birdsong against Sam's bludgeoning drone. The crowd loved it. Mr Okamatsu turned to Sam, relinquished his grip and gave him a satisfied nod before returning his attention to his audience. He thrust his left arm into the air for the repeat of the chorus and, all of a sudden, it wasn't just Sam and Okamatsu singing but everyone in the room.

Everyone was so happy, happy that Christmas was coming, happy that things were looking up. The atmosphere was something wonderful and as Sam watched a drunken man wobble across the dance floor, pointing towards one of his female colleagues, he thought of Sarah, and of the trip.

At last, the song came to an end. Sam was dripping with sweat and physically shaking with adrenaline, but the place erupted. And he knew that, if this were a film, the scene would freeze-frame now, Okamatsu and Sam jubilant in triumph, the credits would roll, and the lights would come up. But, of course, Sam knew this wasn't the end of his story.

The Phantasm #009

In the Presents of Goodness

Christmas time. Mistletoe and wine. The present. Night. A church.

The Black Phantom coasts through the graveyard, lights killed, night-vision goggles guiding the dark defender between the headstones. He parks up out back. The sound of carols emanates from the old building, the stained-glass windows emit colourful light. He knows the concert is on, which means there will be people at the church. He will leave the presents at the side entrance towards the rear, a vestry door, and then leave a series of chalk arrows drawn in the concrete to lead the congregation to them after the service.

He pops the boot. The Black Phantom is completely stuffed full of large boxes. He removes the first package and places it quietly on the step outside the door. The singing is wonderful. The hero stands and listens for a moment.

'I know you.'

'Aaargh!'

He places his hand on his heart. The vicar is standing in the light spilling from one of the windows. She is female. She has short hair and glasses and is smiling as she approaches him.

'I come bearing gifts,' the hero says.

'I read about you in the paper.'

'That wasn't me.'

Another step forward. 'Can't be too many superheroes around here.'

He is silent.

The vicar spies the Black Phantom full to the brim with presents. 'This is far too generous,' she says.

'I give what I can.'

She smiles and her serenity is contagious. 'Thank you,' she says.

He unloads the vehicle while the priest opens the door to the vestry and takes the gifts into the warm. The sound of singing is louder now. It is children. A children's choir singing 'The Holly And The Ivy'. He deposits the last box and brings himself upright. And is standing face-to-face with the priest.

'Come inside,' she says.

He shakes his head.

'Just in here. Nobody has to see you. You've given us all this, the least you can do is come in to hear a song and have a mince pie.'

Well, one mince pie won't hurt. Inside it is warmer. She hands him a plate and with his gloved hand he takes a pie. Beyond the door into the church, which is open a crack, he can see the congregation watching the line of children. They are singing 'Silent Night' now, and even this serious man must admit it is lovely.

'This is very kind of you,' she says, over his shoulder. 'You know, we have children from Syria in there.'

The hero's head shifts towards her a fraction.

'The council have accepted fifty refugees. But they won't tell the media because they're afraid of the backlash. Isn't that awful? Just fifty people. And the public will be angry. Two of the kids are orphans.'

He closes his eyes. 'Will you make sure they get a present?' he says.

Her hand falls on his shoulder. 'Of course.'

'I mean, I know Muslims don't celebrate Christmas but—'

'Jesus was an important prophet of Islam. They can have a present.'

The Phantasm nods and takes a long, deep breath. 'I must go now.' In the cramped space the avenger of the night shuffles awkwardly past the vicar. 'You won't tell anyone I did this, will you?'

'Why don't you want people to know?'

He considers this for a moment but has no real answer.

'You know,' she says, and he turns just as he's ducking under the archway of the door. 'You're always welcome here. With or without the mask.'

She smiles a smile that rushes through him like a wind. It's strong enough to take his breath away as he closes the door gently and allows the night to wrap itself around him.

Chapter Twenty-Two

Since the plane crash Christmas had been a solitary time. Sam had always hunkered down at home, shutting himself away from the world for a few days. All the ingredients for his Christmas dinner fitted into a small bag at Tesco and looked depressing – a turkey crown, a small pack of Brussels sprouts, a single carrot, a single parsnip and some potatoes for roasting, a jar of cranberry sauce, Tesco Finest stuffing, and a bag of frozen peas that would last him the entire year. He'd take a trip to Marks & Spencer for fresh gravy and a tin of shortbread with a picture of a stag in a misty meadow on the front. The preparation of Christmas dinner with his Johnny Mathis CD (his mother loved Johnny Mathis) playing in the background was nice but the sitting down to eat, with Cherry Coke in a wine glass, pulling a cracker with one end wedged beneath his foot (the same box of luxury crackers had been on the go for years) was depressing. Not unbearably, but depressing in a comedic way. With a paper crown on his head, the humour of how pathetic he was being was not lost on him. All of this notwithstanding, this was the day he missed his family most, and after his long Christmas Day run, which blew away a lot of the badness, he would sit in front of the TV and watch BBC One, even if he didn't enjoy it – because in some way it made him feel connected to others, other families gathered around the TV with their loved ones, watching the same thing as him. But this year would be different. He felt ready and prepared, and there wasn't even a hint of guilt.

The sheep in the freezing winter fields and the ploughed lands with frosted furrows as they whizzed by on the train, the bleak winter trees and a black river curling down a wide, flat valley made him think of old English ghost stories. They'd managed to get a table seat opposite each other to look out the window, and it felt weird that this was Christmas Eve.

Sam had brought his Settlers of Catan dice game but Sarah had lost interest after a few goes, so now they were sitting enjoying the view. She'd brought a headphone splitter and said she wanted him to hear her favourite album, called *For Emma, Forever Ago*, by someone called Bon Iver.

'He split up with his girlfriend and went off to a cabin in the woods in the middle of America and recorded this album,' she said.

Sam put in the headphones and lost himself for the next half hour in the sound of lush but strange harmonies, quite unlike anything he'd ever heard, a kind of rich, woody, soulful sound, and the type of voice that only a broken heart can make. Occasionally he'd steal a glance across the table, at Sarah staring at the rushing landscape. The music and the harshness of the cold countryside were a perfect combination. It was wonderful. This was wonderful. His heart started vibrating at the exact same frequency as the whole universe. The last song was one of the most beautiful things he'd ever heard.

'Isn't it amazing?' she said, taking her headphones out.

'You love music, don't you?'

Her face tilted towards the window, making her skin look golden in the morning light.

'It's like, when I have my headphones in, I'm safe and the music blanks everything else out. All my troubles and stress;

the music puts a wall up between them and me. Just for as long as a song.'

'That's a sad thing to say.'

And it made him aware again of how little he really knew about her.

'Walter Pater said all art aspires to the condition of music, like music is the art form that creates the biggest response in people. I don't know if that's true for everyone but it's like, for me, if a song gets me at the exact right moment, I get these . . .' she thought for a second and shrugged '. . . little quakes of the heart.'

Sam imagined telling her he loved her. The rhythm of the train traversing the tracks made a chugging in the cabin and he couldn't tell if that was creating the effect in his own heart, those same quakes, or if it was something else. Something he never thought he would have. Because what else, if not Sarah, would have got him on this train?

The taxi took them through a maze of tall hedgerows. Between farm gates he saw forestry conifers spiking the horizon, or cow-grazed fields, or wild meadows with cold, colour-bleached winter grasses. Sometimes they passed through small stretches of ancient woodland where the tree trunks had grown thick and distorted with deep fissures, gnarled branches and dense beards of moss. The road curved around, and on the right a steep slope ran down to a rushing stream curling between banks of bracken.

'Beautiful, isn't it?'

He glanced across to Sarah, wearing a checked lumberjack shirt over a hoodie, the light as the trees passed between them and the sun strobing gold and dark across her face.

'This is it,' she told the driver.

They took a sharp left between two grey boulders and came to a set of ancient-looking iron gates that led them up a steep gravel path, with views out across fields for miles and miles, until it became long lines of trees that stole the view and leaned over the lane to form an archway. A cathedral of trees and the sense of deep magic.

'What is this place?'

'Isn't it awesome?' she said.

The lane snaked and the trees grew denser. Even without summer leaves the branches made a near-impenetrable, knotted canopy, giving the impression of hundreds of snakes inter-tangled. Glimpses of deep-green moss carpets punctuated by brilliant red toadstools, a fairy-tale world.

Ahead, the trees relented and the lane became more of a sweep, the colour of the gravel ochre. A stone fountain covered in lichen patterns and then, beyond it, a house: Arcadia. Maybe three times the size of Sam's own house, two sets of bay windows protruded either side of a small portico held aloft by grand columns. Three storeys and a small slate roof with a few red-and-yellow-bricked chimney stacks, the stonework stained dark by dirty rain. Dead vines crawled around the windows.

The front door swung open and a tall, lean person came out, skipping down the low steps and hurrying towards the car.

'You made it!'

The American accent was recognisable right away, though it was soft and generic.

'You must be Sam,' he said, shaking his hand and smiling, revealing a perfect set of pearly whites. 'I'm Kabe.'

There was an energy to him, but not a fast one, a solidity to his essence; a presence. He was cool-looking, if not quite as handsome as Francis, with a well-formed nose and big, brown, alert eyes behind long lashes; vaguely androgynous. He was wearing a pair of ragged cords and a striped, woollen sweater that looked hand-knitted; he had the kind of skeleton that all clothes look good on. Sam guessed he was a few years older than him, around thirty maybe, but it was hard to tell.

Overhead, a V of geese crossed the opal sky and there was a hushed silence.

'Come on, let's get you guys inside,' said Kabe. 'It's freezing. Lunch is almost ready.'

He led them into the house, from the bright, winter-slanted light to a dark atrium with peeling wallpaper and damp patches. Aware that decaying decadence was in vogue, Sam nevertheless thought it a great shame a lovely house like this was in such a state of disrepair. How could someone Kabe's age even afford a place like this?

They came to an old kitchen where a blonde girl stood guard over a bubbling pot of gravy on a 1970s hob.

'Kristen, look who's here.'

The girl turned. 'Hey, you,' she beamed to Sarah.

The two hugged and, over Sarah's shoulder, the girl smiled at Sam. Her hair was very blonde, cut messily at her shoulders. As he stood there he felt a sensation fizzle up. Welcome. It was the feeling of being welcome.

In the open area of the kitchen a farmhouse table was laid with steaming food; a rustic meal of potatoes and vegetables and a big orange pie in the middle.

'Sweet potato, pumpkin and butternut squash,' said Kristen when she saw Sam eyeing it. 'Hope you're hungry.'

Two men entered the room from a side door and sat at the table. Both older than Sam, they smiled and nodded to him. Then a woman came in, mid-forties, with unkempt greying hair but a pretty face; French-looking. Quite who these people were Sam had no idea and Sarah didn't introduce them. They took their seats at the corner of the table and Sarah spooned some cauliflower on to her plate. More people came in and the room flooded quickly with conversation, streams criss-crossing.

Kabe sat next to Sam and poured himself a glass of wine, lifting the bottle with long, elegant fingers.

'Thanks for having me,' said Sam.

'Absolutely no problem at all,' he said. 'I've heard a lot about you, man, and you're welcome here.'

This surprised him. Sarah had told people about him?

'I've got you a present.' He went into his bag and handed Kabe a wrapped parcel. 'To say thanks.'

'There's no need to—'

'It's only small,' said Sam, thrusting it towards him.

Kabe took the parcel. 'Should I open it now?'

'You can open it now.'

Kabe's eyes glanced across to Sarah and a smile fell on his lips. He unwrapped the present.

'It's the best,' said Sam. 'It's from Marks & Spencer.'

'Oh man, I love shortbread,' said Kabe, examining the picture of a mother and son stag standing in a misty Scottish glen. 'Thanks, Sam. This is really cool.'

Sam beamed. 'That's OK.'

He turned to Sarah and found her smiling at him.

'What?'

'You're so funny.'

'No, I'm not.'

She laughed. 'Eat,' she ordered.

Sam looked at all the food on the table.

'So, Sam, you work in a Japanese screw factory, Sarah said.'

'I do.'

'Japanese screw factory. Love it! Do you like it?'

Kabe grabbed the pumpkin pie and used his free hand to expertly shift a slice on to Sam's plate.

'Thanks. It's OK. It's different from working in a British office.'

'I bet, yeah.'

Despite Kabe's friendliness Sam felt self-conscious about how normal his life must appear to someone who lived in a place like this, how unimpressive.

'They're a mysterious people,' he said, trying to compensate, though he knew as soon as he said it that it must have come across as racist.

'Its land too,' nodded Kabe, surprisingly. 'They've got all those sacred islands and sacred mountains. And their art. It's, like, so in tune with more . . . elemental things. Makes you think they know something deeper than us.'

'Listen to you two,' said Sarah.

Kabe turned to her. 'Ignore her, Sam. Sarah believes the days of the polymath are over.' He put a small slice of pie on his plate and nudged Sam. 'This is the best pie in the world,' he whispered.

He was so friendly! Sam felt a little overwhelmed by how well he was being treated. So unused to this, he didn't know how to respond.

'So what do you think of the house?' said Kabe.

'It's amazing.'

'It was made grand like this by a coal magnate in the nineteenth century. There are two hundred species of trees here, apparently, from all over the world.'

Someone else joined them at the table, sitting next to Sarah, so she had to shuffle up and press into Sam.

'I'm glad you've come,' said Kabe, quietly.

Sam wondered just how much Sarah had said about him. Did he know what had happened to his family? Was that why he was being so nice?

'We're gonna have an awesome Christmas,' Kabe said.

Sarah pressed into him a little more.

In the last hour of daylight a lane running alongside the house took them down a hill to a line of overgrown cottages with roofs half collapsed and brambles in the smashed windows and, after these, on the left, to two stone gateposts with no gate.

'Does he own all this?'

'Uh-huh. Come on.'

'How?'

'He won the lottery.'

'Seriously?'

'Yup. He won eight million pounds, bought this place, sold off lots of the farmland to farmers who always used to rent as his concession to social justice, and now lives off the interest on his winnings.'

Sam thought about this.

The gateposts gave to a steep path matted in leaf mulch. Steps cut into the path carried them down a dark curve beneath thickly knotted branches, so dense the light of the late afternoon was gone. The suggestion here of deep age.

'These are rhododendrons. You should see them in spring. They're so beautiful.'

Slow and the world will reveal itself, his father had once said during a walk in the woods, explaining how chaotic and fast things had become, how the world is harder to understand because it operates at a speed non-conducive to humanity and how in hectic moments the act of slowing down, closing your eyes, taking a breath, offers a fresh perspective. Here in the dark forest of giant rhododendrons the natural pace of the world dominated. He felt the strange connection you sometimes make with nature when you suddenly fit perfectly into it. They stopped, and in the gloom he could hardly make out her face.

'Thank you,' he said. 'For bringing me here.'

There was the briefest of pauses, like they were about to kiss, but instead she smiled and punched him on the shoulder, quite hard.

'Come on,' she said. 'The lake's not far.'

At the bottom of the steps they came to a small clearing where it was brighter again, with stacked logs and a paddock of horses. Tall trees hemmed the horizon, and the soft sound of running water was nearby.

Sarah looked somehow smaller among nature. The white rims of her Converse boots were muddy and her winter coat engulfed her.

'Come and look at this,' she said, and dragged him to a stand of brush.

A stone staircase led down to a pond. A wall next to the staircase was inscribed with scripture from Genesis. In the centre of it a tiny archway leaked spring water.

'You can drink it,' she said.

The pond released a gentle mist to its surface. Sam loved how a place like this just . . . existed . . . while the world happened around it.

She slipped her hand into his and he said nothing when this happened, like it was nothing, as if a lightning bolt hadn't just shot through his body.

They found themselves wandering down a path between beech trees, a brook from the pond running alongside. The mist thickened around their feet and through the trees he caught glimpses of open water on the right. From the main track they found a narrow walkway, a spit of land, and at the end of it rose the white steps of a stone bridge. Water to the right and left, they were at the waist of a figure-eight-shaped lake. Mist swirled. Up the steps on to the bridge, Sam breathed what felt like the cleanest air he'd ever tasted.

'There's no need to thank me,' she said, leaning against the stone balustrade. 'I wanted you to come. You do know that, don't you?'

Her cheeks were white in the dying light as she stared out across the glassine water, this perfect space.

'I'm really glad you're here,' she said.

The fire was roaring in the stone fireplace of the drawing room. There were lots of old sofas and chairs, and Sam and Sarah found themselves tucked away in a warm corner. Kristen came over and refilled their glasses with some of Kabe's home-made cider. It was very strong so Sam made sure to only take small sips.

'How long have you been together?' Kristen said, her head tilting on its neck and her fringe flopping out from behind her ear.

'Oh, we're not a couple,' Sam got in first before Sarah was embarrassed.

'Oh,' said Kristen. 'Sorry, I thought . . .'

'I haven't got my talons into him yet,' Sarah said, reaching across and trying to squeeze his cheek.

He pulled away and some of his cider sploshed over the top of his glass.

'Shoot.'

Kristen laughed and took the cider to the next group along.

Sam watched the particles in his drink drift, having to squint to focus because, despite his best efforts, the cider was going to his head.

'You know,' said Sarah, 'you always dress very smartly.'

He was wearing a pair of navy cords and a tucked-in gingham shirt.

'Have you ever seen when Mormons go door to door?' he said. 'They always wear very simple clothes but good quality, and very smart.'

'You're going for Mormon chic?'

Sam smiled. 'Yes! I don't know. I just think . . . clothes like this. They help you disappear into the background, don't they?'

Sarah sipped some of her cider and grimaced. 'This is fucking awful,' she said, holding the glass up and staring at the contents. 'You know, you might be ahead of your time. I read the next evolutionary step for hipsters is going to be norm core. Which is wearing smart clothes, like you.'

'That's cool,' he said. 'So how come you're here for Christmas? Don't you want to visit your folks?'

She shook her head, seemingly not noticing his segue. 'Nope.'

'I still don't really know much about you.'

'Sure you do.'

'I don't, though.'

She drank some more cider. 'Look, I was in a relationship and it ended badly.'

Sensing it might be OK to push a little, he said, 'But how does that affect your family?'

She went to say something but stopped.

'Can I ask you something?' he said. 'Ages ago you said you didn't like yourself. Do you remember? You said you weren't a nice person. When we were looking for shooting stars.'

She put both her hands around her glass.

'Did I? I didn't mean it. Not really. I mean, I used to not like myself, but I'm better now. I'm not the same person I was then, when I was in Edinburgh.'

'You're awesome though.' He looked down, hoping she didn't realise he'd just said that.

Sarah was silent for a moment, thinking something over.

'Look.' She paused, thought again, and lowered her voice. 'My old boyfriend used to deal drugs.'

'That's not that bad,' said Sam, quickly, though he hadn't expected her to say that.

'It is bad, Sam. He wasn't a good person. And I was complicit in his happiness, and I don't like that. I shouldn't have done what I did and it's always going to haunt me. I mean, I thought I loved him, he was so much fun and things, but . . . he did ruin people's lives, you know?'

Sam nodded.

'You don't wanna hear this.'

'Sure I do.' Though he was getting the same twisted feeling in his stomach he got whenever Francis was around.

The low chatter of the other guests cocooned them. She drank more cider and smiled at him. 'Let's talk about something else,' she said.

'He cheated on you.'

'No, not that. Look, I don't want to talk about it, OK?

Can we just have a nice time? Who cares about the past? Everyone has a past, right? We've all done stupid things.'

'Let the past inform your future, but not define it,' he said, quoting another of his father's maxims.

'That's good,' she said, yet again changing the subject from whatever it was that had happened to her in the past. 'I like that.'

He woke up freezing and hard of breath. Reaching over to the bedside table, he took a deep pull from his asthma pump. Checking his watch, he saw it was already Christmas Day. It was Christmas Day and there was no sense of crushing despair. Instead, he felt excited with anticipation.

He was in a tiny room with an iron-framed bed, like something from the 1950s. He curled his legs over the edge and pulled his blanket around his shoulders. At the window he gazed at the silver hoarfrost encrusting the grounds in the dawn light and could feel the tremendous cold coming through and off the glass, an encroaching force. He stared at the beauty of the landscape, out over the silvered terraces at the back of the house and the rhododendrons, up the other side of the valley. A fox appeared on the lowermost lawn and padded across it with its wiry strength, leaving dark paw prints in its wake.

He'd once heard an expert on the radio say a sign of depression was the inability to imagine a future, and this was something Sam had suffered for years. He could never imagine being fifty, couldn't imagine having children, leading a balanced, normal life. It was impossible to see himself as a seventy-year-old going out the front door to fetch a pint of milk. Sometimes, late at night, he would wonder how long he'd be dead in his house before anyone noticed. But now . . .

It almost felt as if the universe was giving him a chance.

He was startled by somebody knocking on his door. He

opened it to find Sarah standing on the other side, in white pyjamas patterned with green Tyrannosaurus rexes in red Christmas hats.

'Hey,' she said, quietly. 'Let me in.'

She pushed past and a wave of awesomeness swept over him. He was in a gothic country manor on Christmas morning with a girl he was crazy about.

'Happy Christmas,' he said.

'Come here,' she said, and gave him a hug.

He was still tired and wasn't fully aware of what was going on, but he knew it was suddenly making his blood course.

'What's this?' she said.

For an awful moment he thought she meant the bulge in his shorts, but then he saw she'd spied the wrapped present on his bedside table.

'Oh. It's your Christmas present,' he said, sitting on the edge of his bed, pulling his T-shirt down.

'You got me a present?'

She was sitting over the other side, her knee hitched up. There was a red crease mark on her cheek that for some reason set off a chain reaction, the lust falling away and remoulding itself as he realised, fully, how deeply he now cared for her.

'I know I shouldn't have, but it was something I thought you might li—'

'I got you one too!' And she took from behind her back a small box.

'Oh,' he said.

His first Christmas present in years.

'Heads up.'

She tossed the present and as he tried to catch it, it hit the tops of his fingers and dropped to the bed.

'Butterfingers,' he said.

'Let's open them together,' she said, wide-eyed.

They pulled off the wrapping and, seeing their respective presents, fell into a pause.

She opened her copy of *Cathedral*. 'A first edition? Oh my God.'

But he didn't respond. The sensation of profound affection bloomed. He was holding in his hands a small replica of the Batmobile from the Tim Burton films. It was so shiny and beautiful. He didn't recall ever mentioning it, but they were his favourite Batman films. He looked up from the toy and was struck by the face of happiness staring at the book.

'I can't believe you got me this,' she said. 'Sam, this is the best present I've ever had.' She looked at him. 'It's so thoughtful.'

In turn, he couldn't comprehend that she'd bought him such an amazing present, and he wondered then if maybe it was possible for two people to know more about one another than they did about themselves. Deep down.

Her bare forearm was angled towards the window and through her top he could make out the curve of her breast. He shifted across the bed to get closer to her, his heart going crazy. She tilted her head inquisitively to one side and a line of light ran along the arm of her glasses. Her gaze danced across him. The world held its breath . . .

And the bedroom door swung open and Kabe waltzed in.

'Come on, you guys!' he shouted. 'I thought I'd find you in here. Everyone's downstairs already. It's Christmas Day!'

He needed to make the move. He knew that now. All he needed was to get her on her own. The time would come, later that afternoon, or that night. You can do this, he told himself. There was a hubbub of activity in the kitchen as they got ready for Christmas lunch but his mind kept running back to the bedroom. What he would give to see inside her brain now, to know her thoughts.

'You do it like this,' she said, her face turned towards him, leaning over the pan and tossing the onions, garlic and bacon bits on the hob, acting like nothing had happened. 'It's all in the wrist. OK, how long have the sprouts been on?'

Maybe it was normal to play it cool and he was just being overkeen. He checked the stopwatch app on his phone. 'Two minutes forty.'

The onions sizzled. Next to them Kristen removed a huge baking tray from the oven and the smell of mustard tingled in Sam's nostrils. The ends of the parsnips were charred and hard and perfect.

'OK, strain!' said Sarah.

Sam took the sprouts off the hob and poured them into a colander. The bacon in Sarah's pan was browning nicely. He tipped the sprouts on top and Sarah mixed them in with the bacon and onions using a wooden spoon.

'These are gonna be aces,' she said. 'You can hardly taste the sprouts at all.'

Kabe thrust a long knife into the enormous turkey and when he removed it he placed it to his wrist, inspecting the pain of the heat.

'It's done,' he announced.

The French couple, Claude and Eloise, prepared the gravy, pouring in measures of cornflour with scientific precision, stirring and tasting as the other food was brought to the table. There were honeyed carrots and parsnips, Sarah's sprouts, red cabbage braised with cider and apples, a Welsh mashed potato with leeks and cheese, a vegetable Wellington for Claude and Eloise and the other vegetarians, potatoes roasted in local goose fat, spiced apricot and sausage-meat stuffing, cranberry sauce from a nearby farmer's market.

Sarah was crammed in next to Sam. Their legs were touching and she made no effort to move away. Sam beheld the feast with a sense of joy. He was joyous. It drizzled through him, a sensation almost physical.

When everybody was sitting down Kabe clinked his cracked wine glass with a fork.

'OK, OK, OK,' he said, as the others stopped talking. 'I'm not big on speeches—'

There was a collective groan.

'OK, maybe I am big on speeches, but listen. I just want to say thanks to you all for coming.'

As Kabe spoke Sam noticed Sarah's hand on her thigh. His heart thumped. He lifted his own hand and touched her little finger and, for whatever reason, she curled it around his.

'It's really awesome how people keep coming to spend Christmas here and I just want you to know that, whatever happens, everybody will always be welcome, and I mean that.'

Looking around the table, Sam watched the rapt faces.

'I know the world's a bit shitty at the moment but just remember this place, and today. All of you guys are nice people and, in the end, that's what will matter. I think we all feel better when we're doing something good instead of doing something bad and, you know, I think it's easy to forget that sometimes. But it's easy to see, if you look hard enough. Just look around this room.'

Sarah tightened her little finger around Sam's.

'You know, it's hard for me sometimes, not having my family near. It can get lonely. But sometimes, you realise family can mean lots of different things . . .' Kabe trailed off and Sam felt his throat go dry.

'Let's eat!' someone shouted, making the others laugh.

Sam surreptitiously wiped the corners of his eyes and picked up his cutlery.

'Yes!' said Kabe. 'But seriously. I really appreciate it.'

A sensation of warmth blazed around the table.

So the sudden disturbance in the room knocked the atmosphere weirdly off-kilter. People were turning, there was a gust of cold air in the kitchen, and a person was standing over the table.

'Sarah,' he said. 'I'm sorry. I had to come.'

Sam felt her finger unhook from his in a jerky motion. He looked up at the face and everything he'd just been feeling melted away to nothing.

It was Francis.

Chapter Twenty-Three

He helped with the dishes. The others still chatted happily, as if nothing was wrong. They didn't seem to pick up on the extreme awkwardness that had crunched across the room with Francis's arrival.

He felt sick. In a way he blamed himself. He'd had countless chances and he'd been too scared to do anything about it. Kabe handed him a soapy pan, which he dried off with a towel and set on the countertop.

'You OK, man?'

'Yeah, I'm good,' he said, adding nothing more.

Kabe went back to the dishes.

Were they kissing right now? Out there on the terrace, Francis's perfect hair blowing in the breeze, the collar of his winter coat flapping as he tenderly touched the side of his face? He was telling her he loved her and he'd travelled across half the country to get to her. How could Sam compete with a gesture like that? He simply wasn't the type of person who was capable of making those sweeping demonstrations of love, and he knew that was why she'd be better off with Francis. She was way too good for him and he reminded himself that she'd only invited him here because she felt sorry for him.

'We'll have fun later on,' Kabe said to him. 'Trust me.' And he handed him another pan.

The back door opened. Sam didn't turn, he didn't need to.

He could feel their combined presence coming up the corridor into the kitchen.

I'm so stupid, he told himself. *I'm just so stupid.*

A gathering of starlings preparing to roost covered a quarter of the sky, moving in quantum patterns, their caws colliding and shattering into the woods below where Kabe and the others entered the rhododendron forest. It was mid-afternoon but the wood stole the light from the day.

'There's something special about this place,' Kabe said to Sam, as he fell into step with him. 'Something happens when you come here, when you spend time. It feels like, I don't know, something gets restored. Can you feel it?'

He'd felt it before, but he couldn't feel it now. The sickness of dread was all he could feel now. It seemed strange that Kabe was talking so mystically when he was wheeling a BMX at his side, but then they'd all been drinking steadily since lunch.

Directly in front of them Sarah walked with Francis; he was talking in a hushed voice Sam couldn't hear. He'd been here for over an hour now and Sam still hadn't managed to pluck up the courage to speak to them – and they hadn't come to him, either.

They picked their way along the stream that led towards the lake. The water leapt in rainbow shapes over the rocks. Sam just wanted to know what was happening. Why couldn't he just say something?

Along the nearside shore of the lake was a smooth, straight path. Geese made shock waves in the air as they hissed on to the surface of the water. At the water's edge the path split and one fork led down to a large log that looked out over the lake.

'This place is amazing in the summer,' said Sarah, looking over her shoulder. 'We should come back.'

His shoe hit a stone embedded in the path when she said

this, and he almost tripped. He just caught Francis's eyes before they snapped away.

There were about ten of them who'd come down to the lake. Kabe stopped and the others gathered around him. They were at the edge of a small cliff, overlooking the water about ten feet below. 'I thought of this the other day,' he said to them. 'It should work.'

He adjusted the saddle of the bike, ratcheting it upwards, climbed on the BMX and, to everyone's surprise, started pedalling along the track, back towards the water. Kabe had a strong, lithe body and got up a head of steam quickly.

'Where's he going?' said the man in front of Sam.

Swaying from side to side with each thrust, the sound of tyres zipping over the ground was loud in the cold air. As he came to the water's edge Kabe turned sharply towards the log. The bike went down into the hollow, struck the log, which was elevated around five feet above the surface of the lake, and the mechanics of the situation saw Kabe propelled over the handlebars. He yelled something mid-air, arms swinging, body twisting as he slapped into the water with a loud and inelegant crash.

Everyone burst into laughter and spontaneous applause as Kabe rose to the surface. In front of him Francis was doing a completely over-the-top clap.

'It's fucking freezing!' Kabe cried, as he climbed on to dry land and trotted back up the path with the BMX. 'OK, who's next?'

He had the type of personality that enthused people around him, a contagious, endearing, childlike recklessness that made him magnetic.

'I'll do it,' said Francis.

'Good for you, Francis,' said Kabe as the others started clapping.

He pushed forward through the crowd to get to the bike but slipped in the mud, bumping into Sarah. Sam watched in slow motion as she stumbled and fell towards the cliff. She reached out to grab Francis and he lost his balance again, instinctively yanking his arm away and sending Sarah over the edge. Sam moved without thinking. Her body was already out over the water, at forty-five degrees, as Sam reached out and hooked his arm under her back, taking her whole weight. 'Whoops,' he found himself saying, apologetically. His core activated, his free arm grabbed an overhanging branch for support, and he stopped her mid-air, easily pulling her up and away from the edge.

He set her down gently and could see the shock on her face at his strength. He felt like Clark Kent.

'Sam, that was fucking awesome,' someone said, breaking the weird silence of the moment.

He could physically feel the perception of him changing across the group, just as he could feel her eyes on him. He met them, but she broke away and looked at the ground.

'Did you see that?' someone else said.

Sam's heart pumped hard, the blood thumping through him a drumbeat. His own strength had shocked him, but it shouldn't have. He'd trained for this.

After a beat, Francis turned to Kabe. 'OK, here we go,' he said, taking the BMX, trying to deflect attention away from what had happened, as if it was nothing.

Francis climbed on to the bike, pushed his perfect hair away from his eyes, and stared at the log in the distance. Sam wondered if Sarah realised how Francis had pulled away from her. He sped off down the path. Kabe went into his pack and brought out a bottle of whisky, which he handed to Sam.

'You deserve this,' he said.

Sam took a sip, hoping it might calm his adrenaline.

Francis hit the log hard but as he went over the top his knees caught the handlebars and he was dragged straight down, head first into the lake.

'Whoa!'

There was a collective groaning sound and Sam couldn't figure out why everyone was then falling about in hysterics.

Standing next to him, Sarah was silent.

'I'm OK!' said Francis, resurfacing and clambering out.

'Er, I don't think I want to have a go at doing that,' said Sam, trying to make light of the situation, looking down at his smart new Tesco clothes.

She snapped out of her trance and smiled at him. 'Sure you do,' she said, grabbing the whisky off Kabe and taking a large slug. 'You just need a bit of Dutch courage.'

Over by the log someone took the BMX from Francis as he sat at the edge of the lake.

'Sarah,' said Sam. 'What's happening?'

A robin landed on a branch above her head.

She sighed. 'He's reckons he's in love with me.'

'Oh.' His throat turned to sand. 'He said that?'

Sarah shrugged.

Next up for the BMX was Kristen.

'Be careful,' Eloise warned her.

'So what are you thinking?' said Sam, wishing he could be a more confident person.

'I don't know.'

'Well, you've been going on these nights out with him, so maybe he thought . . .'

'I wasn't trying to lead him on.'

'No, of course not. So . . . you don't like him?'

'What do you think, Sam?' she said, suddenly testy. She stared at him for a bit too long, and when Sam didn't reply, she said, 'Sure.'

He watched the disappointment on her face.

'Of course.' She changed her tone. 'He's nice. He's a good person.'

There was the sound of splashing and everyone laughing again as Kristen went over the log.

'He's made a big effort to get here,' she said.

He wished he knew what to do, what to say. But he did. He knew exactly. So why couldn't he just do it?

'Sam.'

Kabe was smiling at him. Somehow, the BMX was already back.

'You having a go, bud?'

'I think I'll leave it for a second,' he said, his mind clouding.

'Give it here,' said Sarah. 'Hold this.' And she passed Sam her phone.

'You sure?' he said, quietly to her.

'Yes, Mum,' she said, climbing on the BMX and holding her arm out. 'Whisky,' she demanded. She took a slug and set off down the track.

Why was he always so pathetic? Why couldn't he ever say what he was really thinking?

Sarah got up a surprising speed. Something about her small frame on the BMX reminded him of how Kermit the Frog rides a bike.

'Go on, Sarah!' someone shouted.

She veered off the track and Sam's heart leapt into his mouth as she hit the log and flew over the handlebars into the air. Everyone gasped as, mid-flight, instead of putting her arms out to cushion the blow she tucked them behind her back. It was so dangerous it shocked Sam, gave Sarah a new angle. 'My glasses!' they heard her shout at the last second – she was still wearing then. As everybody else laughed, Sam felt a stab of fear as she face-planted the water.

'She's so funny,' said Kabe, clapping Sam on the shoulder. 'She deserves a great life.'

Sam turned to Kabe. That was a weird thing to say.

'After what happened,' Kabe continued.

The reeds behind Kabe swayed in the breeze.

'What do you mean?'

Sarah resurfaced, pushing herself up, her glasses somehow

still on her face, arms in the air with her fingers extended into the peace sign, making everyone cheer.

'You know,' said Kabe. 'All that shit with Zac in Edinburgh, and everything after.'

This was too much. Her ex?

'Yeah,' said Sam, watching her climb out of the lake absolutely drenched. Next to the water he noticed Francis watching the scene without any emotion on his face.

This was of course the problem with awesome people, he was quickly understanding. Everybody else wanted to be with them too.

Sitting on the saddle, Sam concentrated on the log.

Kabe put his hand on his shoulder. 'Just let go,' he whispered into his ear.

Sam pushed off and was on his way.

'Go on, Sam!'

Sarah's voice sang into his brain. Well, they'd already seen that he was stronger than they thought; he decided to go for it. He went as fast as he could, ploughing towards the log, legs pumping, going so fast he almost lost control. He swerved off the path and towards the log.

Just let go.

The force of forward momentum was like a great hand grabbing hold of him and dragging him up, up, up into the cold winter air, the water sinking away below him. He was flying. He knew how far everyone else had gone, and he was well beyond that.

He heard the sound of cheering.

The hand. It wasn't dragging him into the air. He felt it now. It was dragging him into the future.

As they filed up the lane back to the house, freezing and shivering, it was almost dark. The windows orange with candlelight, the slate roof indigo with moonbeams. And the sound of the piano in the drawing room drifting in and out on the freezing air, sliding crystallised across the molecules of winter.

'It's Claude,' said Kabe.

The piece was melancholic and beautiful. It made a sadness with its passages of minor runs that turned and melted major, blooming into a spreading joy, unstitching the fabric of the sadness and reforming it. Sarah and Francis were together again, at the rear of the group.

It made Sam feel like, no matter what he did, he would never be happy.

'He writes them himself,' Kabe said of the music, his words barely audible.

'It's beautiful.'

'I think true beauty still has a lot to say in this world,' said Kabe. 'Or any other.'

After his shower, Sam made his way along the corridor back to his room. It was freezing, the cold making his skin burn. A door opened and Sam jumped. It was Francis.

'Oh,' said Francis. 'Sam.'

There was a moment. This was the first time they'd spoken since he'd arrived, and the tension was immediate.

'You've come here,' Sam stated.

'Listen, Sam,' Francis said, ignoring him. 'I think it's great what Sarah's doing for you but . . . you know . . . I've come all the way here, and it's cost me a shit ton of money. Do you think you could, like, give us some space?'

It felt like a little thundercloud floating above his head was rumbling. What Sarah was doing for him?

'Just a few hours. You know how I feel about her.'

What about what *I* feel for her? he thought. It was like being back at school, like he was a ghost, a side story.

'What if she wants to hang out with me?'

Francis leaned against the door frame of his room and grinned.

'Look, Sam, be real for a second. Everybody cares about you, including me. But think about other people as well, yeah?'

Sam stood there, unable to speak.

Francis shook his head. 'I've gotta get showered,' he said. 'I'm sorry to be so blunt but, you know, help a brother out.'

He patted Sam on the shoulder and sidled past him to get into the corridor. He disappeared off into the bathroom, leaving Sam in the darkness, freezing cold, feeling the size of a blade of grass.

On the last day Sam spent in his family home he stood in the empty living room, clutching the box of family heirlooms, the only thing he'd kept. Amongst them were his grandfather's MBE for services to nursing, his grandmother's writing box with her old pens and papers inside, a gilded key gifted to his great-grandfather for setting up a library on behalf of a nearby town's working people after they elected him their union representative, resulting in him taking a penny of their wages for years to create a space for books and learning and advancement. His father's England cricket cap that he'd got as a schoolboy, a crocheted flower his mother had made for him as a baby. All the family photos.

It was dusk, and it was time to go. But he didn't take the box to the car. Instead, he found himself in the deserted swimming pool again, the cats watching him from the overgrown bushes and unruly trees. The sky was a fire red, a dry wind whipped his face. He opened the box and removed his parents' wedding album. He flicked through the pages, not thinking much, pausing on one image of his mum and dad standing on the steps of the church with confetti drifting. He was in the photo too. In her belly. You couldn't see any evidence of an unborn Sam, but he was in there.

He placed the box in the centre of the pool and took out

the canister of lighter fluid, spraying it wildly and chaotically all over. He made a path of it to the far side of the pool, where he struck a match and waited, his hand protecting the flame from the wind. He closed his eyes and even from that distance felt the heat of the fire against his face as he dropped the match.

Then he took out from his back pocket the card his little brother and sister had made – the last thing they'd given him. He opened it and read the message and remembered sitting outside Frankie & Benny's, Steve opposite him, his head leaning to one side.

Don't you wish it could stay like this for ever and ever?

Sam had turned his face away from the fire and thought, I can't believe I'm doing this. But he did it anyway. He dropped the card, and everything burned.

The spindly Christmas tree with a string of coloured lights stood guard in the corner of the drawing room, behind the beaten-up grand piano, next to the French windows with black night looking in. Claude, rake thin, pale as bone, wearing an ill-fitting pair of pyjamas, played slow versions of Christmas carols to the twenty-odd people gathered on the sofas and the large threadbare rug. The huge fire in the hearth burned bright, laser sparks spinning bird migration patterns up the flume.

Francis had gone outside to make a phone call and when Sarah came in, Sam grabbed her and they found a quiet corner of the rug where the heat of the fire just about reached. A wind rattled the French windows, flames sidled, shadows bent.

'Here,' he said, pushing a glass of cider into her hands.

'You're not trying to get me drunk, are you?'

'Aren't you already drunk? I am.'

She laughed. 'Where's Francis?'

'Outside on the phone.'

They took a sip of their drinks. Claude was playing 'Winter Wonderland'.

'Hey. I just wanted you to know something. Thanks for bringing me here.'

'Sam, I told you yesterday—'

'I know, I know. But still . . . it's been a good Christmas. So thanks for looking out for me.'

'Looking out for you?'

'I just don't want to get in your way.'

'What the hell are you talking about?'

'I mean, you and Francis.'

'What about me and Francis?'

Just as she said that, he appeared at the doorway and looked around the room. He saw Sam and Sarah, but didn't come over. Instead, he went to the piano and spoke quietly to Claude, who gave up the stool for him. He started playing a piece of music and, of course, it was amazing. As Sam listened his heart sank. He had no skills, no talents, he wasn't even very good at being a superhero.

'It's his first Christmas without his girlfriend,' said Sarah.

Half his face was in shadow.

'He's very talented,' said Sam.

'He is. And he's super hot and clever and funny.'

Sam nodded.

'But I want to be here with you.' The suddenness of the words made his heart feel melted, and when he glanced up she glanced down. 'I know you're not interested in me in *that* way but—'

'Wait. What?'

'Like, you and me. And I can handle that. It's fine. Friends is fine. But I didn't ask Francis to come here.'

'Sarah, what are you talking about?'

This felt completely weird. The atmosphere had suddenly flipped.

'I mean Francis is great, he really is, and maybe another time I—'

'No, before that.'

'You and me. I get it. I tried and you . . .'

'Whoa. What?'

'All the chances you had . . .'

An awful realisation dawned. The colours in her irises seemed to be shifting, different shades swirling like the thickened atmosphere of some alien world, her pupils expanding black holes in the dim and flickering Christmas lights. He hadn't even noticed that the sound of the piano had stopped. She thought he didn't like her? An image flashed, of two hands reaching for each other in the darkness and missing.

'Sam.'

Francis loomed over him. All the dread washed right back in.

'Can I have a word with Sarah?' he said.

Sam was frozen to the spot.

'It's fine,' Sarah said, nodding to him. It was like in slow motion. 'I'll see you in a sec, OK?'

She was sending him away. Her eyes darted across Francis's body.

Despite every muscle, every impulse trying to root him to the spot, to stay and fight, Sam found himself on his feet. 'I'll—' his breath failed him. 'I'll go fetch some more drinks,' he said. And as he walked away he could feel the presence of Francis like a pulse.

He went into the kitchen. At the sink he poured himself a glass of water. He felt hot and disoriented so he went out to the terrace at the back of the house. It was misty and the disc of the moon was a large circle.

'Samson Holloway.'

Sam turned to find Kabe smiling at him. He swayed drunkenly in the night. Standing next to him was a girl of extreme beauty, the kind of beauty you'd throw away your life for, with thick, dirty-blonde hair parted right at her temple. She wore a pair of mirrored Aviators, her head tilted gently skywards, the lenses reflecting crisply the swirling mist.

'Your zen is disturbed,' said Kabe.

The girl next to him slanted her head to one side and bit her lower lip.

Kabe spoke, but this time more quietly, with a lilt in his voice. 'Do you know about Shangri-La?'

Sam could see through the windows into the drawing room, could see Francis lean in towards Sarah, creating a space that was cut adrift from everything else.

'Shangri-La?' he said.

'A mystical paradise.'

It felt now like they were entombed by the mist, and that the outside world had evaporated. He watched Francis's lips move, his hands gesturing, Sarah's eyes fixed on him.

'I know of a Holy Man who went looking for it in the high mountains of Nepal, and the villagers told him Shangri-La is not a place but a knowledge. The secret of happiness.'

Inside, they had stopped speaking now.

'And they told the Holy Man he would find it at the top of the mountain next to their village. And do you know what he found when he reached the top?'

Sam shook his head, and as he did this Sarah leaned in towards Francis and put her arms around him. He couldn't look. He was falling apart.

Kabe said, 'A mirror.'

Even through the Aviators the girl's stare burned a hole right through him.

'Everyone is looking for Shangri-La, Sam,' said Kabe. 'But they're always looking the wrong way.'

The girl stepped forward and lifted her hand. Sam felt his breath leave him as she pushed a long finger into his chest.

'It's in here,' she said.

The cold of the night pressed against his body and he remembered what his father had once said.

The two most important things in life are to be brave and to be good.

His father was not spiritual, and his maxims were said

half in jest, sarcastically, but now, when he thought about them, Sam realised they were almost all completely true. He looked at Kabe, and the girl, their breath turning to silver, and he went inside.

Claude played something like snowflakes falling on a glass roof. The music now had taken on strange properties. It was no longer a purely sensory thing but, mixed with the adrenaline, a physical one as well. It brushed against Sam and put a vibration in him with its touch, a far-reaching vibration moving inwards, a conducting force setting all the atoms that made Sam into a rhythmic beat. It snaked through him, gliding and sliding, making tingling glissades up his arms and legs.

His heart beat so hard it felt like it might break. Sarah was right there, in the hallway. Light ran across her lower lip and, behind her, the others in the room were all prone, like people sleeping in a plane that's lost its pressure and is gliding uncontrolled to Earth. Francis was there, walking towards her from behind.

Sam took her hand. 'I want you to know that I think you've saved my life,' he said.

'Sam—'

And then he leaned in and pressed his lips against hers. He just did it. He could sense her shock, then felt it slip away as she relaxed and pushed back into him. When they broke apart she fixed him with one of her stares.

Behind her, Francis had stopped.

He pulled her away, out of sight, and she kissed him again, mouths opening and joining to form a black space that was their mouths sealed tight against one another.

'I have a . . .' – he wanted to say something – '. . . very deep affection for you.'

Sarah laughed and shook her head.

'Come on,' she said, and kissed him again.

He couldn't believe this was happening. They ran upstairs

and down a long corridor to his bedroom and she kissed him again and he felt her tongue move into his mouth.

'Wait,' he said. 'What about Francis?' Then he cringed for saying it.

Sarah pulled her top off and pulled him towards her as they collapsed on the bed.

'I don't care,' she said. 'It's you.'

On the ceiling a patch of damp the shape of Africa. She moved her hand down his body and took off her glasses; long lashes, white spaces. There was no thinking now. He pushed her off and removed his top and jeans, all so easy, as if this happened all the time, no thought of folding them into a neat pile as she climbed on top of him and whatever this was turned into a great surging of emotion. He ran his hands from her hips upwards and felt his perspective heighten, as though her body went on for ever and, no matter how far he moved his hands, he would never reach the end of her. She met his eyes and kissed him again as she unhooked her bra. It didn't feel like two people but one, like they were melting into each other.

'I love you,' she said, suddenly and quietly, words like fireworks.

This couldn't be the real world. What he was feeling was not possible. Nothing in the real world could be this good, not for him. They quivered and shook, two hearts beating inches away from one another, two souls, and everything fell apart as he felt her chest against his and he was nothing but a moment, a breath, a flash in the dark, and it felt to Sam like this might never end, that time was mutable now. Had she really just said that? He closed his eyes and let the wave ride over him, as if infinity was something right there in front of him, something he could reach out and touch. It was an explosion of infinity, a fireball of hope, of possibility, and around it, all at once, the light from it illuminated the great expanse of what he knew, instantaneously, was the future.

Chapter Twenty-Four

The next morning came and when Sam woke she was still lying next to him, asleep on her back, her head turned sideways on the pillow, the palm of one hand sticking out above the covers, a vision of grace.

He reached to his bedside table and toked on his asthma pump as quietly as he could so as not to wake her.

'What are you doing?' she said.

There was a bolt of shame about his asthma. It made him feel puny. But then, just as quickly as it came, it went away.

'I've got asthma,' he said, taking another, deeper toke in front of her. 'Do I look like the Diet Coke man?'

Sarah laughed and reached her hands under the covers for him.

'What are you doing?'

'I've got major hangover horn,' she said, like it was nothing.

In the silence of the morning she rolled over and on to him and arched her back, and the frame of the bed creaked with their weight. As she rode him he looked at her face. Her eyes were closed and he was hit by the impression that she wasn't really there in the room with him, like she'd withdrawn to some other place beyond the veil, where nobody could touch her, a separate space of her own personal ecstasy. She leaned forward and kissed him deeply, grinding hard with her hips, both still a little drunk, and when it was over they lay on their backs, panting for the longest time, until at last she curled up next to him.

They lay there for a second, Sam deep in thought about how great this was, how all of a sudden they were in bed together having sex when only yesterday he felt so awful. Outside the window birds cawed. He felt her pressing closer to him and an image appeared in his mind of a white sheet hanging from a line, being blown dry by a spring breeze.

After Christmas Day they were supposed to be going home. Instead, they'd stayed for ten days. They'd taken long walks through the estate, past an old dilapidated chapel tucked away in a wooded hollow with a witch hazel sapling poking through a window, and had talked about so many things. As the days passed the number of people at Arcadia dwindled but it only made things more intimate. They found a path made of upturned champagne bottles, which the old owner of the house had made in its heyday, and it had glimmered ethereally in the twilight gloaming. They'd slept together every night, which was in some ways confusing to Sam, who couldn't understand how someone could want him that way to that degree, but he wasn't about to complain.

The day after they got back, Sarah took him to see a band called Frightened Rabbit. They went to a pub and drank cloudy cider in a dark corner until their minds were foggy and he couldn't stop thinking how awesome this was, how new and exciting, and how being out of his comfort zone wasn't even a thing now. They ran across the busy street, hand in hand, to the venue; dark night sky and bright head-lights, rain spitting sideways.

He'd never been to this kind of cramped, sweaty, grimy, ramshackle place. Metal girder columns with huge rivets blocked the view of the stage from the bar, and the mezzanine looked on the verge of collapse. He'd never seen a band like Frightened Rabbit either; amazing in an earthy, aggressive, lovely way, the singer laying himself bare, covered in sweat after a couple of songs.

Sam stood at Sarah's shoulder and at the end of each song, when the room erupted, she'd turn back to him and smile, and he was so happy it felt like his bones might liquefy. She called him sappy but he didn't care. At the front people bounced up and down, and the way so many of them knew all the words to songs he'd never even heard made him think he was being welcomed into a secret world.

His T-shirt was slick with sweat, like he was melting into the room. He put his arms around her waist and it felt like an OK thing to do. All borders had come crashing down. Sam watched the back of Sarah's neck and the side of her face. Her hair tied back, sweat glistening behind her ear, the wet skin catching the orange light from the lighting rig above the stage. He could just see her eyelashes when she blinked.

He was almost completely happy. Almost. Because now the thought of the superhero had been sparking flashes of dread across his chest. He couldn't tell her about it. When they'd been at the Christmas fayre she'd said it was messed up and over the past week, between the long stretches of happiness, that conversation had played and replayed in his head. He wished the Phantasm could enter early retirement, but that's what was producing the flashes of dread. The call of the costume was way too strong to overcome.

ⓟ

The Phantasm #010

Amongst the Tombs

The graveyard. Witching hour. Full moon. In the old times they said the veil between this world and the next thins in these places. Realities shift, and things that go bump in the night are close. But that was in the old times . . . wasn't it?

The hero is a man of reason, he worships at the altar of science. And yet at his feet is the Orange Chocolate KitKat he'd climbed over the gate to enjoy in solitude. Even heroes need time to think. But he is not alone. He dropped the chocolate bar as soon as the groaning started out among the tombstones. The stirrings of fear were immediate. The old legends suddenly don't seem so stupid now. Yes, this dark protector can defeat men of flesh and bone, but what of something *other*?

His first instinct is to run, but then, what kind of a hero would he be? Would Bruce Wayne run? Of course not. In the moonlight and low mist, the headstones look like the skyline of a city abandoned for a hundred years, great monoliths tilting this way and that with the erosion of centuries. Soil mechanics 101.

He picks up the KitKat and inspects it with his Maglite. It is too dirty to salvage. Looking out across the graveyard, he crushes the chocolate bar in his fist. Whatever that thing is out there, it has his attention.

The grass is slick from the day's rain. Need to be careful. The groaning has stopped. Cold air washes over him like ghosts, and a sixth sense warns him of a presence nearby. And yet there is nobody in sight. Was it a trick of the mind? Just the trees aching in the wind? A stray cat?

Then his blood freezes. It's behind him.

He spins round. Nothing there.

The chemicals of fear surge through him and again the call to flee is strong. There is a dark area before him, where a tall tree has blocked the light from the lamp post skirting the graveyard. He teases the Maglite over the space but it lands on nothing. Composing himself, he steps forward. The headstones here are tight together but there is a clear path through. At the end of the path he sees a missing spoke in the railing – and the safety of the street beyond.

And yet it seems a hundred miles away. And then, louder, the noise returns. Something is groaning, and he realises with horror that it is coming from under the ground. Rooted to the spot, he looks down and finds himself unable to move. The bodies. All the bodies. Then, when the groaning comes again, he starts to run. The ground is slippery and he almost falls, but he uses a headstone to stay up. He slips again but this time he can't right himself, for he has fallen, and the rules of logic dissolve: he can't stop falling. He has pierced the veil of the worlds and is plummeting downwards, into the Underworld.

For six feet.

He lands on his legs, which buckle. He tries to fall sideways but is propped up by a wall of sheer earth. A shiver runs through him. It accompanies visions of Hades and Satan. He is in pitch blackness as his mind catches up. He has fallen into an open grave.

He pauses and thinks. No need to panic.

'Geeerrrggghhhh.'

PANIC!

The thing is in there with him!

He scrambles up the side of the wall but it's too high. It's so sheer that there's no purchase. His guts in his throat, he initiates a huge star jump to get a hold of the edge but he's not tall enough and slips back down. Oh God, he thinks. Oh God oh God oh God.

The presence of the creature is so strong he presses himself up against the far side of the grave and grits his teeth. But he quickly realises he must face his adversary. It becomes apparent: this is a test, a rite of passage.

Calm as an ocean, he grips the Maglite, hoping to blind whatever beast shares this sacred space. He takes a deep breath, turns, and points the light. The sorry thing in the grave with him puts up its pale but muddied talons to block the light, as if the photons themselves are causing it pain. His first thought is, there is UV light in this torch, I have happened across a vampire and the UV is burning it. His second, more accurate, thought is, it's a drunk man who's also fallen into the grave.

The man is bald, mid-forties, overweight, and wearing nothing but an orange T-shirt and jeans. Must've been taking a short cut towards that gap in the railings.

'What on earth are you doing in here?'

His sense of control coming back, he is able to speak in his official Phantasm voice.

'Errr?' says the man. He is absolutely hammered.

The Phantasm goes into his backpack and fetches his foil blanket, drapes it over the drunk.

'Helen's left me,' he says.

Face-to-face, the Phantasm shakes his head solemnly. 'I'm sorry to hear that.' He pours a coffee into the lid of his flask. 'Here.'

The man drinks, and the caffeine revives him a little. 'Have you got any sugar?' he slurs.

The Phantasm goes into his utility belt and withdraws a sachet of white sugar, pours it into the flask lid and swirls it around before handing it back. It is only then the man

realises that the presence come to his aid is wearing a mask.
But he does not seem perturbed.

'Batman?' he says.

'I'm not Batman,' the hero whispers. 'I am the Phantasm.
And how may I address you?'

The man's head wobbles on his shoulders. 'Colin,' he
mumbles.

Colin is bereft after the loss of his Helen.

'Let's get out of here,' the guardian says, kindly.

He knows that getting Colin out of this grave is going to be
difficult. From his pack he takes a length of rope. Here, his
training is called for. With the Maglite in his mouth he makes
a lasso knot, remembering the YouTube tutorial he watched.
Then he searches his memory. There was a headstone just
outside the grave, no doubt inscribed with the name of which-
ever poor departed soul will be spending eternity in this
hallowed spot. He knows he won't be able to pull Colin up,
and so the plan will be for the big man to go first, with the
Phantasm pushing him from beneath. He tosses up the lasso
but misses with his first attempt. Stepping back to give himself space, he twirls it above his head and misses again. But
he is nothing if not persistent.

Behind him he hears the trickling of water. And a few seconds after, the sound is joined by an odd aroma.

'Colin? What the hell are you doing?'

Colin is standing behind him now, facing the opposite wall.

'I gotta have a piss, I'm busting.'

'Colin! This is a grave!'

But Colin just shakes his head, his large frame swaying.
Steam is rising from the ground. He leans his one hand on
the wall of the grave, above his head. It is unbelievable.

Success! The rope holds tight.

'OK,' he says. 'Colin? I need you to pull yourself up. I'll
help you.'

'I can't believe she's left me,' he whimpers.

'Colin, forget about Helen for a second.'

This snaps him to life. He sniffs, shakes his head and takes the rope, not even looking at his saviour.

'Can you climb up?'

Colin doesn't even need to reply. Up he goes. His mighty arms pull, hand over hand, and the Phantasm crouches beneath him. Colin's deep-tread shoes claw painfully at the avenger's back, but it's fine. He ratchets his legs up to elevate Colin, who is making constipated gasping sounds with his struggle.

It is going very well, until there is a loud groaning sound again. This time, it is not born of a living creature. The knowledge of what's happening is immediate. With the rain and the weight the headstone is subsiding.

'Colin, get down!'

The Phantasm leaps clear and Colin falls. In one smooth motion, the masked avenger loops his arms around the big man and drags him away just as the headstone topples into the grave and impacts the ground with a heavy *thunk!* On his back, the heavy man on top of him, a pool of the heavy man's urine seeping through his costume below him, he stares at the stars overhead and exhales a long breath.

'Oh man,' he says. 'I'm getting too old for this.'

Chapter Twenty-Five

The red tail lights of the cars whizzed past as blurs through the rain-soaked windows. He could see the bright neon sign of the noodle bar reflected in the puddles on the street, as people hurried past with umbrellas turned into the wind.

Sarah arrived with a gust of cold air from the open door and he waved to her from his seat. She took off her coat and laid it over the back of her chair without making sure there were no creases. The front of her hair was wet and her glasses were all steamed up. As it had so often over the fortnight, his heart skipped a beat.

She wiped her glasses in the sleeve of her sweater and moved the wet pieces of hair off her face before picking up the menu.

'I'm starving,' she said.

'They do really good noodles here.'

Sarah scanned the menu and said, 'I want something spicy.'

'How was your day?'

'It was a bit weird, actually. My old boyfriend messaged me on Facebook on New Year's Eve,' she said, not glancing up from her menu, as if it was nothing.

'Oh.'

'But I didn't see it because the app's not on my phone, so I only check it on my laptop.'

'I thought you weren't on Facebook.'

'I'm not. I've got a page but I've hidden it. I just use it for Messenger.'

He tried to make his voice sound normal. 'What did he say?'

'Nothing really. Just that he was sorry and hopes that I have a good new year.'

Sam felt suddenly cold. He wanted to be friends with her on Facebook. And what else was she keeping from him?

Sarah picked up both menus and slid them into the holder behind the condiments, out of the way. 'It must have been weighing on his mind.'

'What's weighing on his mind?' Sam noticed a stray noodle from the last customers near the condiments and swept it away with a napkin, trying to ignore the sudden out-of-depth feeling.

'You know, the drugs and everything.'

'You've never told me, though.'

'Told you what?' Her voice tightened. 'I did tell you about him. The dealing stuff. It's not a good life, all that paranoia all the time, and he feels bad for putting me through it I guess. We used to have to take different routes home to make sure we weren't followed and things. It takes a toll in the end. Kinda screwed me up.'

Sam looked around for a waiter.

'That OK with you?' she said.

'Yeah, it's just . . .'

'What?'

'There must be something else. Kabe mentioned it up at Arcadia.'

'He what?'

She was sitting up straight and there was an edge to her he hadn't seen before.

'He just said how you deserved better.'

'What exactly did he say?'

'Just that.'

Sarah picked up the menu again.

'I'm sorry,' she said, dodging. 'I think I'm hangry. I need some food.'

A waiter went to the next table and the couple sitting at it leaned forward in unison. Sam didn't know what to say so he leaned way out into the aisle to grab the waiter's attention, nodding his head and pointing at his table.

'He wasn't a bad guy, he just got mixed up. It kinda just runs away with you.'

'Maybe it was because it was New Year's Eve and he was lonely.'

'You're not jealous, are you?' she said. 'I'm telling you, aren't I?'

'I'm not jealous.' He laughed. His stomach hurt. 'OK, I am.'

Sarah winced. 'Look, Sam, don't be one of those guys. I'm with you, OK? I know this is new to you,' she said, 'but you don't want to go down that line.'

'It's not that,' he said. 'It's just, you said he was a bad person. You seem to be changing your mind.'

Her face flickered with irritation and she exhaled slowly.

'You can't keep worrying about the past,' she said. 'Eventually, you have to just accept it and make a future.'

He relented.

'I sometimes think my whole last six years was spent facing the wrong way,' he said. 'Always into the past.'

'Let the past inform your future, but not define it,' she said.

'You remembered,' said Sam, trying to smile but failing.

They were both trying to act like things were normal. Why had her ex-boyfriend started messaging her out of the blue? And who was he? The waiter arrived at their table and Sam smiled at him, feeling Sarah's eyes boring into him.

Sipping beer abjectly, Sam looked at Tango and Blotchy. They'd managed to get the best table, the one tucked away in the corner, in the alcove near the fire.

'All we're saying is,' said Tango, in the seat opposite him, 'it's great you've got a girlfriend but we're still your friends too.'

He'd been looking forward to seeing them after Christmas away, but now he wasn't sure why.

'What do you want me to say?'

'We didn't know where you were,' said Tango.

'I told you. I was away. I don't get why it's such a big deal.'

The way they were looking at him made him feel small. And more than a little confused.

'This guy,' said Blotchy sitting next to him, the pores on his cheeks wider than Sam remembered, 'up at the house. Sounds like a cult leader.'

'Are you guys jealous?'

'Pfft. Don't be so ridiculous.'

Tango reached across and put his hand on his shoulder. 'We miss you.'

Sam looked at the hand. 'And you're saying *they're* like a cult?'

'OK, let's just drop it,' said Tango.

'It's fine,' said Sam. 'I don't mind. If you guys have something to say you should say it.'

' "Guys"?' said Blotchy, face screwing up. 'Since when do you say "guys"?'

Sam rolled his eyes. Why weren't they happy for him?

'All we're saying,' said Tango, 'is that all of sudden it's Christmas time and you drop off the radar for a week. What are we supposed to think?'

'Oh, I get it. Don't worry,' he said, 'I'm not going to get lonely at Christmas and throw myself off a cliff.'

'No, it's just . . . you haven't been yourself lately. We don't want you rushing into something you're not ready for.'

'Jesus Christ, are you listening to yourself?' His voice was wavering as his frustration with them grew. 'How come you guys care so much about my *feelings* all of a sudden? You never did before.'

'You need to check yourself,' said Blotchy.

'Oh, come on. You don't own me and I don't own you. Can't you see how shit like this holds us back? All of us. We're all too scared to do anything new because we make fun of each other. Constantly. We should be happy for each other occasionally.'

Blotchy said, 'I see during his absence he's become a Professor in Sociology.'

'Very good, Blotch, but at least I'm not fat.'

'Resorting to insults.'

'Better than resorting to lasagne.'

'Sam.' Tango looked at him. 'We're not trying to hold you back – that's not what this is about. We're just looking out for you.'

'Why the hell is this table so sticky?' Sam said, trying to dislodge his beer mat from the wood.

There was an uncomfortable silence.

'Well now, gentlemen,' said Blotchy at last. 'We've said what we wanted to say and now I would like to show you one of my Christmas presents.' From his man bag he produced a small remote-controlled drone. 'This, my friends, is capable of flight.'

Sam noticed Blotchy and Tango exchange glances, and the anger he'd been feeling dialled back. The tiny craft was square, about an inch long, with small propellers at each corner. Their plan was to state their point then bring out the drone to sweeten the mood, like a cat being given a treat after taking some medicine. He imagined them plotting in their WhatsApp chat and it was almost sweet. Blotchy put the drone on the table and fiddled around with the remote.

'You can't fly it in here,' said Sam.

'Watch me,' said Blotchy, winking.

'Clear for take-off!' said Tango.

'Take-off imminent!'

Sam stared at them incredulously. Blotchy's tongue popped out, as it was wont to do when he was concentrating. The drone rose up off the table quickly and Sam jumped back.

'Oh wow,' he said.

A tiny red light blinked on and off on the undercarriage of the drone. But Blotchy's piloting skills weren't honed.

'Shoot,' he said, as the drone hit the ceiling and tumbled out of the air towards Tango, who tried to get out of the way and instinctively batted the drone away, straight into the fire.

'No!' said Blotchy, jumping up.

'Bloody hell,' said Sam, laughing.

Blotchy grabbed a brass shovel from the poker stand next to the fire and tried to dig the drone out of the logs. He turned to Sam desperately. 'I pushed it further in!'

The people on the tables nearby were looking over at him as the sparks drifted up out of the fire.

'Let it go, Blotch,' Sam said. 'It's gone.'

Tango caught Sam's eye and they looked at each other across the table and many messages tying in across the years drifted between them in a single moment of time.

A few years ago he set up a little widget on his computer so that when a new email arrived there was a whooshing sound and an American female voice said, 'You've got mail.' Sam loved it. He'd turned it right down following many complaints from Linda but refused to mute it completely. It reminded him of the nineties when the Internet was new, and it always made him feel nostalgic. He clicked the email from one of his clients and his stomach tightened.

Hi mate,

Writing about Invoice #ED0041765 dated 5th Dec. There's an air shipping bill for £3518 and then another one on Invoice #ED0041799 for £1845. Is this an error?

Cheers,
Phil

'Sam, hun,' came Linda's voice from the other side of the blue felt partition. 'Your leg's shaking and you're wobbling the floor, my love.'

Sam quickly turned his monitor off so he didn't have to look at it. He spun his chair forty-five degrees and saw Rebecca leaning over her keyboard, squinting at an Excel spreadsheet all the colours of the rainbow. Sam stood up and went to the warehouse, being sure not to glance across the office to Mr Okamatsu, whose eyes followed him all the way through the door.

That night Sarah had invited him for dinner and he'd be staying the night. He stopped off in the local Spar on the way to buy a Viennetta for dessert, and by the time he got to her place it was almost seven. She'd given him a spare key and so he let himself into the flat through the narrow front door at the base of the stairwell.

'Hello?' he called up.

There was no answer. As he neared the top of the stairs he heard voices coming from behind the living-room door. He did a quick calculation to try and remember if she'd said there would be other guests and for a second the idea that it might be Francis flickered in his mind.

Knocking on the door, he went into the living room. Standing in the corner, next to the TV, was a man with dark hair, cropped close to his head. He was wearing a grey tracksuit and a pair of white trainers. His eyes were narrow and as they met with Sam's, silence fell across the room, like the shadow of a cloud blocking the sun across a farm field.

'Sam. You're home,' said Sarah. She was standing in the middle of the kitchenette, beneath the harsh white light. There was a note of distress in her voice.

'I am.'

The silence fell back in.

'This is Zac.'

His mind searched the memory files and suddenly clicked into place.

'Hi,' he said. 'Nice to meet you.'

'You too, wee man,' he said.

He was tall and lithe and there was an edge to him. The Scottish accent was faint but there, and the 'wee man' comment was definitely filled with passive aggression because Scottish people surely don't go around calling people wee man. Zac made no move to shake hands so Sam didn't either.

'Zac's staying here for a while,' she said.

'Here?' Sam said, pointing directly at the floor.

'In town,' said Zac. 'Fresh start.' He smiled.

This was bad. The corner where Zac was standing was the one where the lamplight didn't reach and he was half in shadow. He was one of those people who put a disturbance in the atmosphere, the way a patch of ocean changes when a shark is present. It was hard to believe that Sarah would ever go out with someone like this.

'What's that?' said Sarah.

Sam held up the box in his hand and felt stupid.

'Viennetta,' he said. 'I'd better put it in the freezer.'

As he crossed the room Zac watched him.

'Sarah said you work in a factory,' he said.

'It's a wholesaler,' said Sam. 'We don't make anything.'

What was he doing here?

'Do you want to stay for dinner?' Sarah said.

Zac shifted and coins in his pocket clinked.

'Nah, you're good. I'd better be off.'

'OK, cool,' said Sarah. 'Well, it was great to see you.'

'Aye, you too. We'll go for that drink sometime, yeah?'

Sam opened the freezer and felt the cold touch his face. It was so quiet he could hear the hum of the refrigeration element. He closed the freezer and turned around. He'd been in the flat less than a minute but it felt like an hour.

'Well, I'm off,' Zac said.

He moved across the small room like a wild animal in a cage, then stood at the door, turned, and winked at Sarah before leaving.

They listened to him going downstairs, opening the front door. The sound of it closing was like a gunshot. Sarah glanced at Sam and smiled, then followed Zac out of the room. Quickly she came back again.

'I just wanted to check he'd actually gone.'

'You think he might have pretended to go?'

She leaned her back against the closed living-room door.

'No, I don't know. He seemed on edge.'

'How did he know where you live?'

'Urgh, I told him. I didn't think he'd just turn up unannounced.' She pushed herself away from the door. 'Sorry, I was just a bit taken aback. He's not a bad person. He's just a little lost.'

'Well, he is a drug dealer,' said Sam.

Sarah went into the kitchenette, where there was a pile of unchopped radishes.

'Not a real drug dealer. He just used to do a bit, you know. And it just snowballs without you realising.'

'Right. He did used to sell cocaine, though.'

'Sam, please, it's no biggie.'

She picked up the chopping knife.

'You're shaking,' he said.

She turned away from him. Her hair was tied back but a few strands were hanging over her neck. Her shoulders slumped.

Sam turned her around.

'It's OK,' he said. 'He's gone now.'

She sniffed. 'It's not that,' she said, 'I'm not scared of him. I'm just sad.'

He hugged her.

'He's not a bad person.'

'Has something happened?'

She swallowed. 'He's been to prison.' The words hung in the air for a moment. 'I know it's stupid and he's not part of my life any more and he probably deserved it, but how's he going to get on with his life?'

'He'll be fine,' said Sam, trying to soothe her.

He felt her shake her head.

'He won't. Something's gone out of him. He's changed.'

Sam didn't say any more to this. He remembered a holiday in France when he'd gone out into the sea, as deep as his neck, and the current had pulled him out. He'd been able to swim back easily enough but that moment when he tried to plant his feet on the ridges of sand and there was nothing there, angling his toes down and failing to gain traction, the sensation of a great force having control over him, was how he felt now.

'God, I'm a mess,' said Sarah, and she laughed and pulled away from him. 'I'm gonna go and clean up.'

She'd left her laptop open. On the kitchen counter the screen glowed ghostlike. The Facebook Messenger chat window was open in front of a BuzzFeed article. He knew he shouldn't do this, and he swore he would never do it again. He wouldn't even read what had been written, because that would be such a breach of trust. This wasn't to check up on her, he suspected her of nothing. All he needed was an address.

The Phantasm #011

And the Tower Blocks Wept

Every great civilisation has its own myth system. In Sumeria the gods created man to ward the animals, in Greece Zeus defeated the Titans, in Finland bears became the embodiment of the forefathers, and in Rome the boatman collected you from the banks of the Styx to take you to the next world. Stories bind civilisations, shared around the campfire, spreading like a warm blanket across the lands, bringing people together in a way nothing else can, and in the middle of the twentieth century the greatest civilisation of them all, the American West, created a new structure, of men, men and women, with incredible abilities, with masks over their eyes, working together to fight injustice. The superhero was born. The world made more sense with them in it than not. Earth was a hard, scary place; war reached terrifying new scales, there were weapons that could destroy the planet, economies collapsed, terrible things happened in secret camps and only in darkness can heroes be born. Imagination sets us free, stories make us feel safe, and now, in the darkest time of all, they are spilling into reality, falling off the pages of the books and into the real world. Men and women everywhere, with nowhere else to turn, are dressing as mythic heroes and taking matters into their own hands, hitting the streets, trying desperately to hold back the dark tide that only used to happen in stories. All over the world it is happening. Something must be wrong.

Patience is a virtue and in this part of town virtue is given short shrift.

He waits. He waits. He waits and watches.

Our hero can't help but wonder. What would his great love think of him doing this? And yet he knows it does not matter. He can no more abandon the mask than a pope might abandon his robes.

The target emerges from the stairwell at the bottom of the high-rise. Hood pulled over his head, he plunges his hands into the pockets of his puffer jacket and moves into the night. This night he has a shadow that is not his own, stalking him, watching, waiting.

Modernist bridges cross filthy culverts.

Having attained through cyber espionage the name of the estate where he resides, the hero stalked the local store for three nights in plain clothes until at last the target showed his face. Following him home was easy.

It's the same every night. The candlelit windows in the top floor of the tower block go dark and the target walks, on foot, a circuitous route, to a thin alleyway between two of the high-rises. It is a place of darkness, and though it might be true that only in darkness can heroes be born, for every yin there must be a yang, and villains too have their own origin story to tell.

There is a good peeping spot, higher up, halfway along an elevated walkway, and here our masked crusader waits, crouched, watching with his night-vision goggles through metal bars.

Sometimes the client waits on foot, sometimes he is sitting in a beat-up old jalopy, sometimes he is on a bicycle. In the four days so far it has never been a she. The exchange takes place in the centre of the alleyway, where they think nobody can see. They think wrong. Night vision can see. The lens in the camera mounted on a tripod for stability against the retinal insertion points of the night-vision goggles can see, just as cameras placed against the eye of a telescope can discern the mighty rings of Saturn. Yes. The camera never lies. The camera is a man of truth and honour.

Money changes hands. The silent vigilante shakes his head. You can't teach an old dog new tricks, but old dogs still need to eat. That's why they resort to old tricks. Come on, Rover, jump through the hoop, there's a good boy.

The target exits the alleyway while the client leaves from the far end and is on his way. On his way down a dark path, but that is of no concern to the Phantasm. He knows the best treatment here is to cauterise the wound.

This night is different. The target does not return back to his high-rise the normal way. He is going somewhere else. He steps into lanes and down side streets and the hero follows. Is there a second deal? What's going down?

What a fool this target is. He has already repaid his debt to society and now he is busy rebuilding his crime credit rating. It is so sad. Whatever happened to the self-worth drawn from a day of good work?

He zigzags through the estate until, at last, the landscape becomes familiar again and the target has returned home. The hero remembers how drug dealers take different routes to avoid pattern and suspicion. But his distraction techniques are nothing compared to the Phantasm's tracking skills. He has Bear Grylls on series link. He waits as the target disappears back up the stairwell, and he sees the light come on in the flat on the top floor. The target, unseen, relights his candles that glow in the darkness every night. It is a sad and lonely existence really. Perhaps he will give him one more chance. Perhaps when he returns to his lair he will delete the photos from his camera, as he has done the past two nights. The first night the photos were blurry, hence the tripod and hours of practice in the belfry; the second time he'd experienced a change of heart, for Samson Holloway is a better man than his alter ego.

For now his work here is done. Danger lurks everywhere. Perhaps there is another adventure to find this night. He runs down the empty street unseen, until the darkness consumes him.

Chapter Twenty-Six

There was a whooshing sound and the American woman's voice said to Sam, 'You've got mail.' Sam sat forward. This was from one of Japan's major car manufacturers, querying an air shipping bill of £4,343. They wanted to see the standard authorisation sheet for air shipping but, of course, it didn't exist because it had never been returned to Sam. He did, however, have the emails explaining how air shipping costs would be incurred following the Suez Canal incident if they didn't say no, which they didn't. He fired off the emails and tried to ignore the low fizzing of dread that was operating slowly at the base of him. He was getting lots of these emails now.

It was OK, though. He'd taken the small square pad of paper from the miniature shipping pallet on his desk and jotted down some figures. The sales revenue from his accounts per year was just north of one million pounds and the profit margin was 30%. That was a lot of profit, even after VAT and corporation tax and whatnot, and Sam's wage was minuscule in comparison. Also, he'd calculated that over the years he'd been there he'd given the company eight whole months of unpaid overtime. The air shipping costs might sound like a lot but they were nothing, really.

The next day even more querying emails appeared from other clients. 'This could be described as an avalanche,' he said aloud, under his breath, in the middle of a twenty-five-minute toilet/composure-regaining break, during which he leaned against the wall inside the cubicle and tried to stop sweating. When he got back to his desk he pinged off those original emails stating he assumed they were OK with incurring the costs because they hadn't replied. Emails that seemed very puny all of a sudden. He'd sent a few WhatsApps to Sarah from the cubicle but she hadn't replied, even though they'd arrived at her phone and she'd read them.

In the afternoon the big Japanese car manufacturer wrote back.

You've got mail had become a banshee call now and filled him with horror.

The email said that, without the signed authorisation sheet, they would not pay for the air shipments. Sam reread the message but it couldn't really be clearer. He was fucked. What if all the other clients refused to pay? Which was definitely what would happen. The slow dread that had been bubbling away started to rise through him. He thought of Zac dealing his little drugs in the middle of the night and how much easier that life seemed, and how unfair it was that Zac got to sit in his nice, cosy flat watching TV all day while honest people like Sam had to endure this.

For the rest of the afternoon he went through the old courier bills to tot up all the air shipments, and at this point the dread morphed into panic and then finally something else. Sam tried to conjure the word in his mind, and finally decided on terror. He was feeling a cataclysmic sense of *terror* as he stared at the calculator screen.

£60,057

Probably best to say nothing. Just say nothing and sit here and pretend absolutely nothing is terribly, terribly wrong. He considered some options. Selling his house was one. He could pay back a lot of the money that way. The other option was simply never to return to work. If he opted for this, could they have recourse through the courts? Was the scale of his mistake so big they could prosecute him? Much in the same way that CEOs sometimes go to jail?

He considered another twenty-five-minute toilet break, which would take him nearly up to home time, but they might get suspicious. Instead, he lifted his clipboard off the nail stuck into the side of his desk and pretended he needed to do something in the warehouse.

When he got home Sarah was already waiting outside in the car.

'You know you should really give me a key,' she said. 'I'm not going to steal anything, I promise.'

Sam laughed.

'I'll get one cut for you,' he said, though he had no intention of doing so because, of course, she might find all his Phantasm kit. Since they'd been together the flashes of dread had been growing steadily. Whenever she was over, he'd started feeling on edge. She had no problem wandering around the house, and when she headed towards the room where he kept his secret chest he became gripped with panic. He knew he needed to do something but didn't know what. With the mask on he felt invincible, and he'd achieved more in the last few months as the Phantasm than in his whole life as Sam Holloway.

As they went down the hallway to the kitchen she said, casually, 'Ugh, Zac keeps messaging me. He wants to meet up.'

This wiped out all other thoughts.

'Oh, OK. Are you going to?'

'I don't know. What do you think?'

He switched on the lights and caught sight of their reflection in the window, of the two of them, together, like they were normal people in a normal relationship.

'It's up to you,' he said.

Sarah threw her bag on the floor.

'I don't know. I feel sorry for him.'

'You moved away to get away from him,' he said, picking up her bag and putting it neatly on one of the kitchen chairs. 'If you ask me, it's kinda unfair what he's done, moving here.' Kinda unfair meaning completely fucking mental.

'Yeah, I know, but . . . I don't know. He needed to get away from his hangers-on. Maybe I should meet up with him and tell him how I feel.'

She sat at the kitchen table and picked up Sam's tablet and started flicking through it, the blue light casting weird patterns on her face. He wished he could tell her Zac was dealing drugs again. He tried to gauge her anger on a scale of one to ten if she knew he'd dressed up as the superhero and stalked her ex-boyfriend for a week. It would probably be pretty high.

'You can do whatever you want,' he said. 'Don't worry about me, I trust you. But make sure you do what *you* want, not what *he* wants.'

She looked up from the tablet.

After a simple dinner of baked potatoes with tuna mayo, red onion and chopped peppers and a salad, they went into the living room and started watching a film on Netflix with Sarah snuggled up to him. As she flicked through pages on her phone the stress of the day fell away. Her being like this towards him was still weird but less so every day. His arm was a little distended and he was getting pins and needles in it but it was fine. He stared at her face for a while – she was lost in the Internet – and when she looked at him he grinned very widely.

'Look at us two having a lovely time,' he said.

'Shut up,' she laughed, and went back to her phone.

Sam watched the TV and they fell into a silence, and over those minutes he tried to fight off the feelings coming back in, of worry about work, about her finding out about the Phantasm, and then, more strongly, about Zac.

Before bed, Sarah decided to take a shower and left Sam alone downstairs. He listened to her moving around, making sure she wasn't anywhere near the secret chest. When he heard the shower come on he picked up her phone and it came to life. He noticed she had downloaded the app and was logged into her Facebook.

He looked at the ceiling, and listened to the sound of water hissing.

Quickly, he went into her photos and scrolled down. He knew this was awful but he had to see. Then he had a better idea, and found Zac's page, and scrolled through his photos. Why was she looking at Facebook so much now when she never used to use it? The most recent photos were dated eight months previously, meaning he was no longer using Facebook, or not posting at least. It didn't take long to find pictures of her and Zac, happy together. He had longer hair then and looked much better than he had when Sam met him in her flat. There were lots of pictures of them sitting on sofas in dingy-looking living rooms, with lots of people. And they were happy. They were having a good time. Sam scrolled further down, a year and half backwards, scanning each scene, of pubs and barbecues and so many friends. They didn't look very savoury but there was no denying how much fun they were having.

He went to scroll down again and horror smashed him. He stopped. Oh God. No.

He'd liked one of the photos.

His finger had meant to scroll but had jabbed the screen too hard, right where the 'like' button was, and now it was pressed. His mind was working horrifyingly fast. Zac was going to get a notification saying Sarah had liked a photo from eighteen months ago. The photo was of them standing together with his arm around her in a fairground, both with thick winter coats and Sarah holding a stick of shocking-pink candyfloss.

In Zac's mind, Sarah would have been scrolling through very old photos and liked an old favourite, a special memory. This was bad. Instinctively Sam unliked the photo immediately. Oh no. When the original notification popped up on Zac's phone what would he think? It was obvious: Sarah was sending a hidden message – she remembered the good times. Then Sam realised that when Zac clicked on the notification Sarah's like would no longer be on there because he'd just unliked it. He threw his face upwards and closed his eyes. Then he liked the photo a second time. A second notification would arrive at Zac's phone but maybe he would think it was a glitch because it was the same photo liked twice. This was so complicated. He felt sick. Sam quickly got everything on the phone back to the point he'd started at, so that Sarah wouldn't think anything was up. It was in the lap of the gods now.

Upstairs, the shower stopped hissing.

Chapter Twenty-Seven

It was when the phrase 'sixty thousand pounds' slammed him that the nausea would return. In work the next day he awaited the emails from his clients. Nobody would phone, of course. Nobody did that any more. Having decided to mute the American woman, he sat there stewing, unable to concentrate, until the bold black letters of new emails arrived.

He clicked the first one and held his breath. Refusing to pay. And the next one. All morning they came in – all refused to pay. Sixty thousand pounds. At the same time the fear of Sarah finding out about what he'd done on Facebook got churned into the mix, which in turn set off further anxiety with the wider problem of her discovering he was the Phantasm.

It took nearly three hours and lots of trips to the toilet and the warehouse to finally get up the courage to go over to Rebecca's desk and ask if he could have a private word in the meeting room.

'Everything OK?' she said, as they took seats facing each other across the beech-effect surface.

'Yeah, great,' said Sam. 'Actually, not really.'

He spat out the information, unable to make eye contact, choosing instead to fixate on the notepad in front of Rebecca. The clock on the wall ticked, in the warehouse you could hear the forklift telescoping. When he did eventually look up

Rebecca was smiling, smiling so he could see her teeth, top and bottom rows touching. Her eyes were open in a kind of manic wideness.

'So you've got the authorisation forms,' she stated.

'No.'

Rebecca did a series of rapid blinks. 'And how much did you say the shipments came to?'

Sam scrunched up his shoulders like he was wincing. 'Sixty thousand pounds?'

'OK.'

'I sent them the emails though,' he said. 'They knew what was going to happen.'

'But their argument is going to be they didn't sign off on the shipments.' Fast blinking again.

'But they didn't stop them either. It was better to air ship than go on line stop,' Sam offered.

'Yes, but . . . Sam, you've got to get things signed. That's why we have the forms.' The tension in her chest appeared in her voice.

'It's OK. I mean, my accounts alone make three hundred thousand pounds profit a year.'

'What?'

'I've got a thirty per cent profit margin.'

'That's just the cost of the part and the shipping cost from Japan.'

'And the cost of shipping out. That's included too.'

Rebecca's eyes fluttered again.

'You can't seriously think it's as simple as that. Do you know how big our wage bill is? Our rent? Our rates? Insurance? Office costs? All the different tax bills and PAYE contributions? We're barely breaking even across the whole UK branch, Sam. We're hanging on by the skin of our teeth because the Czech branch has taken all the business.'

Sam felt cold.

'I'll have to speak to Mr Okamatsu about this.'

'Of course, yeah, absolutely.'

And his relationship with Mr Okamatsu had been going so well.

'You should have done it properly. This is so unlike you.'

He went back to his desk, about halfway down the main office. Mr Okamatsu sat in the desk at the far end, his back to the meeting-room wall, surveying his kingdom. Because Sam worked with his back to Okamatsu he could only listen as Rebecca approached him.

'Could I have a word with you please?' he heard her say, quietly.

'Yes,' he said.

'In the meeting room?'

There was the sense of everybody listening now.

'Here,' said Mr Okamatsu, shortly.

Sam felt Rebecca's hesitation. A tiny leaf dropped off his bonsai tree. Rebecca lowered her voice to an inaudible level as she told Okamatsu about the air shipments.

'Huh?' he said.

She whispered something else. And then silence. The image of a giant black hole in some distant part of the universe arrived in Sam's head, a galaxy of swirling debris slowly consuming everything in its influence. He could feel Mr Okamatsu's eyes burning laser holes in his back from behind those light-sensitive glasses and he felt paralysed. Up until now the situation had been too big to fully comprehend, but now he realised he was in huge trouble.

Mr Okamatsu appeared at Sam's desk in absolute silence.

'Follow me,' he said.

He closed the meeting-room door behind him and Sam felt like the whole world had just been closed off. Mr Okamatsu sat down and offered Sam to do the same. He was drinking black coffee from his Pebble Beach golfing mug.

'Why didn't you get the forms signed?' he said, outright.

Sam's eyes fell to the desk.

'Because they wouldn't respond to my emails and if I left it any later production lines would have stopped.'

He thought again about how what he'd done might be a criminal act in some way.

'But why didn't you get the forms signed?'

Sam was unsure how to proceed. Hadn't he just answered that question?

'You tell me,' Mr Okamatsu insisted. Suddenly, he was no longer the pantomime villain of Sam's mind but a genuinely dangerous force. He was sweating just beneath the hairline.

'I don't know,' said Sam.

'You bring me the invoices. Shipping invoices.'

Sam hated it and considered going to his car and driving off, but then he was back in the meeting room handing over the documents. Okamatsu sifted through them, a slight tremor in his right hand. Sam's fear was turning to sorrow. How was Okamatsu going to explain this to head office? His mouth went dry. Mr Okamatsu tutted, clicking his tongue against the roof of his mouth. He placed the papers gently on the table.

'You must tell me why you didn't get the forms signed.'

'Mr Okamatsu, I . . . they wouldn't sign them. It was because of the ship. In the Suez Canal. It's—'

Sam jumped with shock. Mr Okamatsu had punched the table with so much force it shook Sam's chair. The room emptied of air.

'Why did you not tell me?' he said, calmly

'Because . . .' But he couldn't say anything.

'Go away,' said Okamatsu, turning his face away.

He then raised his hand to dismiss Sam with a flick of his wrist. Sam couldn't move. Mr Okamatsu waved his hand again, more urgently this time, his signet ring glimmering in the fluorescent light. It was hard to tell if Sam had ever felt this humiliated before. A part of him hated Mr Okamatsu for being so rude but the other half was accepting of the

253

behaviour being dished out. Whatever happened to Sam, it was going to be far worse for his boss. At last, he stood.

'You must not speak of this to anyone,' said Mr Okamatsu. He removed the ring from his finger and placed it on top of the papers, then leaned forward with his head in his hands.

Sam stared at the signet ring. It was emblazoned with an insignia of a lizard.

The clock on the wall said it was 3:33.

At home he stared at the costume laid out on the bed. All he had to do was make a little bonfire and throw everything on top of it. Forget about the Phantasm, and focus completely on Sarah. But why did that idea feel so terrible, make him feel such a strong surge of emptiness?

He thought of all the times he'd been patrolling in the last few months – all the things he'd done, the good things, coupled with the awesome feeling of invincibility the mask brought. The costume made him whole. Whatever had been missing, he'd found the answer in that other person. He knew about functioning addicts and wondered if this was similar to how they feel, the dirtiness of the secret measured out against the serenity of the high.

He lifted the utility belt and held it up to the light. If he didn't go out tonight, he knew – through some *other* sense, he knew – that all the pressures piling in would crush him . . .

℗

Rivers of Asphalt

It feels good. It feels right. He nods to himself. Yes.

Revellers on a Thursday night, a small cluster of office workers staying late at the flat-roofed hostelry of the industrial estate gather in the car park. They shout and laugh, and this is acceptable to the entity that espies them from the shadowy grass bank on the far side of the road. Lying on his front, propped up on his elbows, he watches and waits unseen.

It feels better, being in the costume. It is a clarifying lens and brings with it a sense of freedom. At last he feels at home. The grand mystery of belonging is solved. In the suit he belongs. These streets are his.

And he'll be damned if someone thinks they can destroy those streets with crime. A man is being pushy with a woman at the edge of the car park. Overbearing. He's seen it a thousand times, how guys grind girls into submission. He checks the time: 01:46. He is warm in his suit. He feels invincible. Jerk is trying it on hard with Girl. She has her hands in front of her face and he is cradling each of her elbows. The great persuading tactic: begging. What is going through Girl's mind? She is perhaps twenty-four, a few pounds overweight. She is making a cawing sound: laughter. Cabs arrive from the night, a caravan of them, headlight cones carving out the darkness. Our champion ensures no innocent pedestrians are in peril and when he returns his gaze to the couple they are kissing in an appalling way. Jerk's hands wander drunkenly and brazenly.

The cabs come and the cabs go and he is alone with the night. He lies there, on the top of the grassy bank in the shadow of a tree, and it no longer seems insane to be here in the mask, because this is good.

It is so quiet. He needs to move, to find action. From down the street a large artic truck pulls out of its depot and trundles along, probably heading back towards town. Don't mind if I do. He hops on to the back as it passes.

Not like in the movies.

There is nothing to grab on to – his fingers fold at a right-angle around the back corner. The ledge he's on is only three inches wide but the truck's going too fast to jump off just yet, and it's not so hard, holding on. The truck heads to town; he can jump off when he gets there. Beats walking, and what's wrong with a little danger? It's good for the soul. The wind in his face is an elixir. But boy is this thing moving.

There's a left turn ahead, the route into town; the truck will slow and, like a cat, he will jump clear and land at a run, returning to the shadows from whence he came.

No, not a left turn but straight ahead. Towards the motorway. Should've known, really; a truck this size isn't delivering milk to Spar. Panic does not rise in our hero. There are traffic lights and roundabouts on the long road to the mayhem and certain death of the motorway; he will save himself when they slow down.

The first traffic light approaches. Safety is not far away but perhaps it won't come immediately as he sees red, then amber, then green. The truck storms past, really getting up a head of steam. A car is coming the other way down the dual carriageway. It draws close, its headlights bright, a beacon of opportunity.

'Help me!' he wails, and for a second the driver of the car – male, mid-fifties – and the masked avenger lock eyes.

The man looks away, then quickly looks back. That's right, a superhero is in peril, good citizen, hurtling as he is on the back of a truck; please help!

Though how he might help is unknown as he's already disappeared back into the night. Ah, the sweet tang of fear in the throat. The speed of the road thrashing beneath him. Terror blasting his eyes.

'Help!' he cries once more, to nobody.

At the roundabout there are no other cars and the truck hardly slows at all. Speed limits are there for a reason and this guy isn't playing ball. Only two more sets of lights now and they'll be at the motorway. The first set is green and they flash through, the speed of the lorry now truly petrifying. Our hero considers his life and its termination. Is this really all there is?

One set of traffic lights to go and, were the driver to glance in his mirror, he would see a masked vigilante peering out to check what lies ahead. Green, with a good distance to go. It will switch by the time he reaches the lights. Using every neuron of his brain, he wills the light to change. He closes his eyes and . . . yes! Amber. Just relax now and wait for the truck to . . . speed up?

The lights. They have spurred the driver into a game of cat and mouse, and the only winner here is going to be the cat. The driver. The light turns red and a law-abiding citizen would have stopped, but this driver is not interested in the law. They power towards the river of speed and steel. If the driver heads west he will have to circulate the large traffic-light-strewn roundabout. East will carry him directly to the motorway. The hero crouches. His hands are freezing, his legs are seizing, he just wants to have a nice stretch. Head west, head west, head west.

Heading east. No deceleration is picked up by his keen senses. This is it. Soon he will be hurtling at seventy miles an hour London bound. At least, the truck will be. Our hero will be thrown clear and destroyed.

Think. Quick.

No solutions present themselves. He looks at the river of rock. It is moving so, so fast.

'Aaaagh!' he war cries. And jumps. The Phantasm is airborne. For a second the wind seems to lift him and hurl him backwards but, of course, nothing is happening save for Newtonian physics – and what goes up must come down. He considers those Newtonian laws. If he pedals his legs in the air, when he lands will he be able to run to an elegant stop? The answer is no. His legs hit concrete and he face-plants the deck, his body like a toy, bouncing down the slip road, round and round like a washing machine. There is a kind of awful bliss in the chaos. He is aware of things flying from his utility belt each time he lands. Then he is rolling through long grass. His mind tells him: *You are not dead.* He braces for each impact and wonders when it will stop, and thinks that maybe he'll never stop. He spies the receding tail lights of the truck as it continues on its way, and then, at last, all is still.

Chapter Twenty-Eight

The car arrived and he saw the neon signs of the Services in the windscreen. He guessed nothing was broken, as he'd managed to crawl through the grass to the slip road, and to the payphone to make a reverse charges call, because his Phantfone was smashed to pieces all over the road.

'Sam? Is that you, my love? What's the matter?' Blotchy's mum had said in a sleepy voice.

By the time Blotchy arrived Sam had tried countless times to remove his mask but it was stuck to his face with blood, and too painful to move. Slumped against a brick wall away from the main building, Sam raised a hand to wave. A bolt of pain shot up his arm.

Blotchy came over, wearing a bathrobe on top of his pyjamas and his deerstalker hat, and the look of shock on his face was frightening.

'Sam?' he said.

Sam imagined being in Blotchy's head, seeing his friend dressed like this, hurt like this.

'Please don't tell anyone,' he said.

They stared at each other, Blotchy crouched before him.

'You're the Phantasm?'

Through one eye Sam could see the cogs of thought turning.

'I'm calling an ambulance,' he said.

'No.' Sam shook his head.

'You do know you're bleeding, right?'

Sam nodded. The sticky feeling of blood covered half his face and he could feel it sticking his clothes to his skin.

'Can you move?'

'Yeah, I'm fine.'

He groaned as he tried to lift himself. Blotchy came forward and helped him up and put him into the car. He was surprisingly tender.

The road was clear and the white lines moved under the car in a hypnotic rhythm. It was weird how quickly his friend had become good at driving.

'What were you doing?' Blotchy said, at last.

'Trying to . . . I don't know.'

Sam laid his head against the window and told Blotchy the story of the truck. When he moved there was blood all over the glass. Hands ten to two on the wheel, Blotchy considered the information.

'I meant why are you dressed like that?'

Sam put his head back against the window.

'I don't know that, either,' he said.

Back at Sam's house Blotchy took him to the bathroom and they soon realised Sam was going to have to be cut out of his tactical assault vest and mask.

'This is like one of those scenes in a film,' said Blotchy. 'But I can assure you – we are not about to start making out.'

'Don't,' said Sam, restraining a laugh. 'It hurts.'

They got him out of his top.

'You're going to need to have a shower. But I'm not going to help you with that, either,' said Blotchy. 'You're on your own.'

The water was so painful his mind fogged with white, and when it came back the sight of all the blood rinsing off was shocking. So red against the white, it didn't seem real. And there was so much of it. He thought about Sarah. This had to stop – though when he told himself this, he knew it was always going to be nothing more than an empty promise. He already wanted to get straight back out there.

When he finally managed to get out of the shower, he wiped the condensation off the mirror and paused. A huge red graze stretched from his left temple across his cheek. It seeped globules of blood and shone in the harsh light. The white of his eye was completely red. Secretly he thought he looked quite cool, but he tried to quash that thought.

It was an hour before he got out of the bathroom. Blotchy was dozing on a kitchen chair he'd brought from downstairs.

'I made you some hot chocolate but it was going cold,' he said, indicating two empty cups on the floor.

'Thanks,' said Sam.

The landing was gloomy. The light from the bathroom reflected in Blotchy's glasses as he looked up.

'Don't tell Tango about this,' said Sam.

'I won't. But you have to.'

Sam swallowed. His jaw ached.

'We're all friends, Sam, even if you don't think it as much as we do. We're all looking out for each other. Does Sarah know?'

Sam shook his head and Blotchy tried to give him a friendly smile.

'Actually,' said Sam, 'I think I do need to go to the hospital.'

'Holy shit,' said Sarah, when she saw him.

'Yeah,' he said, sheepishly, getting up from his seat in the coffee house to give her a kiss.

'How's your bike?' she said, looking him up and down.

'Hardly a scratch on it.'

She made an over-the-top sad face that made Sam feel completely pathetic, because here was this girl he was in love with, and here he was lying to her.

'And what about the hedgehog?'

Sam's eyes fell to his coffee. 'He was fine. Just waddled

off.' The ease with which he lied to her surprised him, and not in a good way, but rather in a way he didn't recognise, as though there had been another level to him hiding away all this time.

'Aw, you're a hero. But seriously Sam, you've got to be careful. Why are boys so stupid?'

'I got you a gingerbread latte,' he said, pushing her drink across the table, grateful for how warm the place was so his bones didn't hurt.

'Thanks. What did the doctor say?'

'I haven't broken or fractured anything, so that's good. Just a few stitches.'

At the hospital he'd told them he'd come off the bike while swerving to avoid a hedgehog too. Although they'd said he was fine, he swore he could feel blood in the cavities of his body from where his arteries had been crushed. The good thing was, he'd managed to get a day off work and now it was Friday night. He didn't know if Rebecca believed him when he called, but she could see the proof on Monday.

'Your face is a mess,' Sarah said.

'Hey!'

She changed the angle of her head to get a better look.

'I'm meeting up with Zac in a couple of days,' she said.

'Oh,' said Sam, a new level of anxiety pouring in immediately.

'So I guess you'll need to eat soup for a while?'

'You're changing the subject again.'

'No, I'm not. There's nothing more to say.'

Sam finished his coffee.

'Soup does sound good.'

He watched Sarah scoop up some of the froth from the top of her coffee, something carefree and innocent in the action, unaware of his eyes on her, of the thoughts chugging through his mind, the growing guilt of how she was open towards him but not the other way round, how he could just make up a lie and have her believe it, and how he was still holding back the biggest truth of all.

They lay in bed that night and watched the patterns the rain made on the window.

Sarah ran her fingers along the curve of Sam's ear.

'Do you still miss them a lot?'

He sighed. 'My family? I guess I never dealt with it properly. When I told you about them it was the first time I'd ever spoken about it, and I thought I was going insane. But if I feel like I'm missing them, it's weird, I can sort of sense them near me? I know it's not real, they're not like ghosts; just the sort of stuff they taught me about being a person. Any goodness in me comes from them. My dad used to say people will let you down. All the time they'll let you down. But you must never let *them* down. I try to stick to that in work and things, and it helps. Don't get me wrong. I'm making my parents out to be saints but it wasn't like that. They definitely weren't perfect. God, they used to argue crazily sometimes, especially when I was younger. But all that stuff falls away over time and you just remember the best parts.'

She swung her legs off the bed to get up. When it was like this, nothing else mattered. The thought of his mistake in work dissolved into meaninglessness. It was like Zac didn't exist. The only thing that still tugged was the secret.

'I like you,' she said.

'Thanks.'

The wind strengthened and whipped a pocket of raindrops against the window.

'Can I ask you something?' he said. 'How come you never talk about your family?'

She turned to face him, then leapt back on to the bed.

'Tickle monster!'

He rolled away as she grabbed at him. He hated being tickled. That's why she loved doing it.

'Tickle monster attack on scab face!'

'Scab face?'

He got his arms under her and pushed her off in a surprising display of masculinity. But she had a preternatural strength and pushed up off the mattress and with the sole of her foot kicked him in the guts, winding him.

'Scab face must die!'

He buckled over, tried to speak but couldn't, instead holding up a just-a-second finger. She laughed and her glasses ran down the bridge of her nose. He grabbed her wrists and a muscular pain shot right up the side of his body.

'Argh!'

She laughed really hard then and flopped down on her back, pulling the sheets over her.

'Why won't you talk about your family?' he said.

'We don't talk,' she said, breathless. 'It's no biggie.'

'Why not?'

'We just don't, but I don't care. We were never close, not like your family. I don't think they even like each other.'

'Have they split up?'

'Nah. They're just not happy together. They never were, not really. Not every family is close like yours. Some of us are just . . . different. It doesn't matter.'

He felt like saying how much he would kill to have his family back and how she needed to speak to them. How could she not see that?

'Do you remember when you played that Elvis Costello song in the pub?' she said.

'Yeah,' he said, still panting from the pain.

'It's weird. After what you did for that homeless woman in the bakery, I felt like I knew you. I watched you after you put that song on. You nodded your head a little bit and, I don't know, I had this whole idea of who you were. And I was pretty much right, I think. And I fancied you. You had nice arms. Do you remember you were wearing that InGen tee?'

'Yeah,' he said, looking at her and smiling.

'Oh God, he's smiling again.'

He smiled wider but was then hit by another shock of guilt about the superhero, and the smile faded.

'When I saw you again,' she said, 'the shooting star night, I'd come to the pub hoping you were there. I don't know . . . I couldn't stop thinking about you. And I sometimes think – what if you hadn't played that song?'

The rain outside stopped and the water sluicing down the windowpane made shifting ribbons on the wall.

'All of this from that one little moment. Isn't that weird?'

He was suddenly hit by the sad thought that, if they stayed together for the rest of their lives, one of them would have to die first. He watched her lying next to him, and wondered if she ever thought things like this. By that time they would have shared a large percentage of their lives together and grown into one soul. When death split that soul back into two, the one left behind would be shrivelled and dry without the other. He imagined a scene where he died first and Sarah, as an old woman, was washing up a single plate and knife and fork, and it broke his heart. He thought of her dying first and him reaching nine o'clock at night quite easily but the next few hours before bed being crushing in their loneliness, the kind of end-of-life loneliness half of all people must face. And as he thought these things and myriad other scenarios of being alone again, he considered it was maybe a blessing the way his parents died. No time to ponder or worry, they had died in their prime, before the true cruelty of life had a chance to dig in its claws.

Outside, just as abruptly as it had stopped, it started raining again.

Chapter Twenty-Nine

When Sam pulled into work on Monday morning there was no sign of Mr Okamatsu's gold Lexus, which was odd, but good. He exaggerated his limp as he went into the office and sat down.

'Bloody hell, it's the walking dead,' said Linda from Quality.

Sam reached under his desk and switched on his computer. The office was still quiet. It was 8:56 a.m. so hardly anybody had shown up yet, and Rebecca had a chance to talk to him.

'Just so you know, Mr Okamatsu is visiting clients to sort out the air shipping,' she said.

Sam looked up at her. 'Oh, OK.'

'Your face looks sore.'

'It's not too bad.'

'What happened?' said Linda, poking her head over the partition.

Sam told her about the hedgehog.

'Aw, bless,' said Linda. 'Mind, lucky you didn't go over it. It would have punctured your tyres!'

Rebecca did a manic, over-the-top laugh.

'Aren't they supposed to have those tunnels to cross roads now?'

'I don't know,' said Sam.

He spent the morning working quietly and ignoring the quips from his colleagues about the state of his face. At lunchtime he took a drive to the marshlands, back to the fishing lake, where he ate his sandwiches while watching a tall, elderly woman casting off from a wooden jetty.

When he got back to the office, something had changed. It was quiet. Usually, when Mr Okamatsu was away, the mood was more boisterous. Perhaps he was being paranoid but he thought they might have stopped talking when he opened the door. He put the slight shift in people's behaviour towards him, the way they couldn't quite meet his eyes, the spike of alarm when he addressed them from his seat, down to his air shipping error. Or the scab on his face. It was nothing more than that.

At three o'clock he went into the warehouse to check the deliveries going out that day. It was cold and he pulled on one of the thick blue Electronica Diablique worker's jackets with the warm collars.

'You OK, Sam?'

Mark was standing next to him with a clipboard and a smirk on his face.

'What?'

'Nothing.'

And he turned away from Sam, to check the boxes on the pallet.

At home he warmed some bread in the oven and soup in a pan and sat at the table with his tablet, scanning the day's Internet. He wasn't seeing Sarah tonight – she was covering a late shift at the library – and he felt bored. After letting his dinner settle, he went upstairs and changed into his running clothes, pausing on the landing beneath the hatchway to the attic. He stared up at it for a moment, and thought about what Sarah would say if he came clean, if he just sat her down and told her everything, about the superhero, about how it made him feel, about all the things he'd done. Would she understand? If he waited for the right opportunity?

He went outside. It was cold but he soon got used to it and let his mind empty as he ran. He took it easy but was surprised how the pain from his injuries wasn't too awful. He didn't go far, just a quick circuit of some of the nearby housing estates. The roads were still busy, people getting home from work, unloading groceries from their boots. One family ran from their front door into the garden, chasing an escaped puppy.

When he got back to his street the pain from his injuries was starting to get worse and as he reached the garden he saw a figure standing in the porch, a human form in the pool of light. As he came closer he saw that it was Tango.

'I've been trying to call you,' he said, as Sam came up the path.

'What's wrong?'

There was a weird look on Tango's face as he stepped forward and threw his arms around him. Sam panicked.

'Al, what's going on?'

He had a terrible thought that Sarah was dead. In the garden, the leaves on the bushes rustled and a fluffy ginger cat turned its head in Sam's direction. A second, smaller cat – black and white – followed and they bumped noses and went out into the street, side by side. Tango released him.

'Jesus, Sam.'

'What's wrong? What's happened?'

Tango gauged Sam's face.

'Come on, let's go inside.'

Sam fumbled for the key in his pocket and let them in. Tango went into the living room, found Sam's tablet, tapped in some words, and held up the screen.

At first it didn't register. Just a bad practical joke – though that would be impossible, because nobody knew the secret. So, if not a joke, it must be real. He couldn't quite bring himself to remove his eyes from the screen and point them at Tango. Thoughts bottle-necked, prickly heat stung his face. This is very bad, he thought. This is so, so bad. Tango was showing him the *Sun*'s website, naming him as the Phantasm;

alongside a better-quality image of his face was a picture taken on the night of his arrest.

'It's in the actual newspaper as well.'

The voice sounded distant, and when Sam finally looked at his old friend he was more like an idea of Tango, a hologram. Too much blood flooded his brain and he felt woozy.

'Whatever this is, whatever you've done, you've got to stop it, Sam.'

'People weren't supposed to find out,' he said, vaguely.

He flopped on to the sofa. Already he was thinking about Sarah, about what she was going to say.

'It's not about people finding out,' said Tango, sitting next to Sam. 'It's about *why* you did it, you know?'

Because he wanted to do it. Because he felt like he could do it, and he *should* do it. Because the world needed more goodness in it. Because he was addicted. Sam covered his eyes with one arm. The humiliation was awful. From the dark, her face in moonbeams.

'You could have told me. You know I'd've been there for you.'

'There're loads of people doing what I do.'

'No. They're not.'

'Yes, they are. Look it up.'

Tango inhaled deeply through his nose. 'This is different.'

'No it's not.'

He couldn't say the precise words, couldn't mention his family. Just like he hadn't been able to face it head on when it happened. Sam was on his own then, and he was on his own now. Not that he cared; he didn't need anyone.

'Look. I appreciate you coming over, but can you go? I need to think.'

'Sam—'

'I'm sorry, Al, but I want to be on my own.'

'It's being on your own that led you to this.'

Christ, he thought, it's not that bad. I'm not hurt and I'm not hurting anyone – what's the big deal? And the way Alan

269

looked at him, that maudlin sympathy, as though he were a cancer patient, compounded the humiliation.

'You're not going to be able to handle this—'

'How do you know what I can and can't handle? I've been through worse than this, *Tango*, a lot worse, and I handled it.'

'You obviously didn't. You need to sort yourself out, Sam, to get to the bottom of it and fix it. I can help you.'

'Like last time? Where were you then? No, Al, I don't need your help.' He let the words hang. 'I just want to be left alone.' *That's all I've ever wanted.* 'I dread going to the pub with you, you know that?' He closed his eyes. 'I dread it for days. I just want to come home and be on my own, but you never let me.'

'Because I'm your friend.'

'You're not, though, are you? You say you're there for me but you're not. You never were, not when it mattered.' Why was he saying this? 'We're only friends because we couldn't find anyone better. All of us. You and Blotchy hang out because you don't want to be lonely but I . . .' His voice caught. He tapped his chest and, as the reality of what this meant seeped in, tears rose in his eyes. 'I do.'

'You can't just be alone. What about Sarah?'

'What about her? You can't stand that I'm with her, not that it matters. She'll be gone after this. Doesn't matter though. I'm happier on my own.'

'Sam—'

'Just go.'

'Sam, you don't talk like this. And that means I'm getting through. I'm not going to give up on you.'

'You really have to go.'

Tango stood up awkwardly.

'This is ridiculous.'

It felt ridiculous as well, but his focus was set purely on ending this immediate humiliation. He had to get upstairs to the attic. He'd be safer up there.

Tango stepped into the garden.

'I'm going to go, but this isn't the end.'

Sam just shook his head, thoughts jamming, and closed the door. He got changed and climbed into the attic with his portable radio, but sleep was not even a speck on the horizon. Even with the radio on, the voices in his head held sway, telling him how he was broken beyond repair, a freak, too much water under the bridge to ever recover.

He thought again about the radio show he'd heard when somebody said part of depression was the inability to see a future. Everything was going to fall apart again. He hated himself for how pathetic he was, how the attic was just allowing him to live on in self-pity. But here he was anyway, hiding out yet again, with the photograph in his hands.

It was probably a year after the plane crash, safely ensconced in his brand-new house, when a bubble-wrapped package had arrived on his hallway mat. Inside was the framed photograph of his parents, his dad with his arm around Sam's shoulder and his mum smiling, her head tilted gently to one side so that a patch of golden sunlight fell on her cheek. In front of them Sally and Steve wore yellow rain macs and red wellington boots. Sam had his hand on top of Steve's head.

It arrived out of nowhere, after all that time where he'd had nothing to remember them by.

He couldn't recall the day it was taken. It was winter, maybe a Christmas holiday? They were standing in front of the family home. He remembered the twins being older and taller than the two kids in the picture. The photograph arrived with a short handwritten note, and Sam recalled that day in the hallway, rain battering the front of the house, the photograph in one hand and the note in the other, holding it up and feeling bereft. She'd seen him light the fire. An image of goodness, a glowing white hand reaching out in the darkness.

Just in case. Moira x

At his desk the next morning he kept his head down, the image of his name spelled out in a national newspaper still recurring every couple of seconds. And it wasn't just about his name, it was how they wrote it: *Vigilante street fighter.* It wasn't true and it wasn't right. But what could he do? The feeling of injustice was the same fierce temperature that had made him want to be a superhero in the first place.

The atmosphere in work was weird, even if nobody said anything. He could feel a collective desperation for someone to pluck up the courage to mention it. The phone ringing made him jump.

'Hello, is that Sam?'

It was a woman called Janice, a buyer who worked in the offices of a well-known Japanese electronics manufacturer.

'Jan?'

'Is it you in the paper? There can't be that many Sam Holloways down your neck o' the woods.'

She spoke like a seismograph registering an earthquake, up and down quickly.

He couldn't speak. He always imagined Janice on the phone pulling a line of chewing gum from between clenched teeth. He could feel his face burning. How did brazen people always make him feel so unbalanced?

'You there, Sam babes?'

'Yeah, I got . . . I don't know what you mean.'

'You was in the *Sun* yesterday and the *Express* today. I think it's cute.'

Jesus.

'You can come and save me any time,' and she let go a machine-gun laugh.

'Did you want to order something?'

'Order something? Naw, babes, I just wanted to speak to you. Not every day you find out you know a real-life super-hero, is it?'

Silence drifted down the line.

'Aw, I've embarrassed you, ain't I? I'm sorry, babes, I'll let you go, OK?'

'OK.'

'I'll see you later, Sammy. I gotta order new panels soon.'

'OK.'

He replaced the receiver very slowly and looked around the office to check if anyone had heard. He wished someone would make a joke and get it out the way. Every minute that passed he imagined the size of the separation growing, the prospect of someone asking about it getting more difficult.

He checked his phone and there was a text from Tango.

Community centre tomorrow night. Gaming all-nighter. COD. I need you there.

But still nothing from Sarah. He didn't even know if she knew about any of this.

His eyes were fighting to stay open after having only two hours' sleep the night before. The day was like a shovel being dragged across concrete. He checked the Internet and came across a story about the cargo ship that had sunk. He sat in his seat and stared at the screen. The crew member who had stolen the lifeboat, it transpired, was wanted for murder.

When he got home he noticed his landline answer machine blinking with a message. People used to call them ansaphones, now they call them voicemails, he thought. It was a journalist claiming to be from the *Daily Mirror*, requesting an interview to get Sam's side of the story, and there was a possibility of payment. He deleted it.

The thought of Kabe and the people at Arcadia came into his head. What would they think of him? He'd never met people like them before, and after this he never would again. The urge to go out running called to him but he found himself unable to move from the sanctuary of the conservatory at the back of the house. When the telephone rang, as it did several times, he didn't answer. The Facebook app on his phone registered thirty-seven notifications, so he deleted the app.

And all the while not a word from Sarah. He considered messaging her but couldn't.

He wondered if he would ever be able to go running ever again. People would laugh at him and whisper about him as if he was the village idiot. Perhaps he should move away. Or emigrate to the Pacific North-West, to one of those sleepy little towns at the bottom of a mountain where the mist rolls in off the sea every day.

Images of all the happy times he'd had with Sarah flashed through his mind and he suddenly couldn't work out why he hadn't told her. She was such a good person – she didn't deserve to be going out with such a fuck-up.

And then he realised something terrible. The night when he'd fallen off the truck. Blotchy had come to pick him up. It was suddenly obvious. Blotchy was the only person in the world who knew about the Phantasm.

He picked up his phone, deciding to message her, but at the exact same moment the phone buzzed.

It was a message from Sarah. It said, *We need to talk.*

Sure. Do you want to come over here? Everything OK? x

Can we meet in the pub? There was no kiss at the end of her text.

That was two texts with no kisses at the end. He trawled back through and pretty much every other message had an x at the end.

Sure. I'll leave now. How was your day? Xxxx

He didn't know why he was pretending to be so casual. She clearly knew. And why the pub? Why not one of their places? That she might not feel safe alone with him really hurt.

Through the window at the front of his house Sam watched a man walking his dog. He paused at a lamp post and took from his pocket an electronic cigarette. He hunched over to smoke it, feeling the cold, and Sam thought how sad the man looked, smoking his electric cigarette, having given up something he loved and not really being able to let it go, like a widower carrying around a photo of his dead wife.

As he pulled into the car park it felt like entering a trap. He had a quick flash of anger as he thought again of Blotchy's level of betrayal.

Their favourite seat, in the corner by the fire, was taken so she was sitting at one of the centre tables. Sam hated sitting here because he felt exposed – he liked to sit with his back to a wall.

'Hey,' he said.

'Hi.'

She didn't smile and the expression on her face was cold.

'Can I get you a drink?' he said, even though she had a Coke in front of her.

'No thanks.' Her voice was small and flat.

'I'm just going to get one, if that's OK.'

'You're a big boy, Sam, you can do whatever you want.'

Every word was like a sliver of some dreadful element poisoning his stomach. She wasn't giving him anything. All around him was the loud chatter of the customers, acting as if nothing was wrong, though he was sure a few of them were staring at him. He ordered his lager and went back to the table.

'You should have told me,' she said, right away.

'I know. I'm sorry.'

'Do you know how I found out?'

Sam didn't respond.

'Francis. OK? In work. Francis came over, acting all concerned, and told me all quietly and confidentially.'

Sam pictured this scene.

'Do you know how I felt? Do you know what this feels like?' she said. 'I thought we had something special. I really did.'

'We do.'

'But we don't, do we?'

She stared at him. This was worse than he could have imagined.

'You know, I'm meeting Zac tomorrow. I wanted to show him how well I'm doing, how I'm moving on and improving my life, and now I'm going to look like a fucking idiot.'

This really hurt. She was *embarrassed* by him.

'I'm sorry,' he said.

She leaned forward and rubbed her brow.

'I wanted to tell you,' he lied. 'It's just . . . you know.'

'What are the people in work going to say? Francis is bound to tell them.'

Truth be told, he thought she was being a little selfish and it put a spike in him.

'It's not such a big deal,' he said.

'Not a big deal? My job's not a big deal? My moving to a new place to start over isn't a big deal? We even talked about it. The Phantasm or whatever the fuck it is. We *had a conversation* about it. And you said nothing. How do you think that makes me feel?'

'Bad.'

'Yeah. It makes me feel bad.'

She shook her head slowly. 'I'm sorry Sam, I'm just . . . having trouble. It's not even the superhero thing . . .'

He found himself internally cringing when she said the word 'superhero'; it sounded so absurd.

'It's the fact you couldn't trust me.'

'I'm so sorry,' he said. 'I don't want to fuck up your life, your job.' He thought he might start crying. 'This isn't what I wanted.'

'What did you think was going to happen?'

'I don't know. I thought I would stop doing it. But . . . I don't know. I couldn't.'

276

Sarah sighed and piled the beer mats on the table together. 'Why do you even do it?'

Sam wiped some of the condensation off his glass. 'It's how I keep my head together,' he said, quietly and honestly. Across the table he thought he sensed a loosening in her. 'I do it because it's . . . like a bridge. To when I was last happy? When I was a kid.' His hands locked around his pint glass. 'After it happened, the . . . accident, and after I, you know, with all the photos, I had nothing linking me back to my family.' Still not able to look her in the face, he nevertheless sensed a stillness descend on her. 'Then one day I put on the costume . . . and was standing in front of the mirror . . . and everything was OK again. It just happened, and then I couldn't stop. I was doing things. I was helping people. It became something more. I just . . . I know it's ridiculous but—' He stopped. 'I'm so ashamed. I'm so happy now and,' he felt his voice shake, 'I don't know why I still feel the need to do it, but I'm really scared because really, deep down . . . I think I might be crazy.'

'What really happened to your face?' she said.

'I jumped off a lorry when it was going too fast.'

'Jesus, Sam.'

'It's not that bad,' he said.

Her body language bristled as he said this.

'You lied to me, Sam. It is *that* bad. Is there anything else you're hiding from me?'

'What? No!'

'You should tell me now.'

'Sarah, I've told you things I've never told anybody.'

'You can't put shit like that on me, Sam. It's not fair.'

She finished her Coke.

'I need to go,' she said. 'It's getting late.'

'Sure,' he said, his heart sinking. 'Let me walk you to your car.'

'No, it's OK, just stay there.'

He got up anyway.

'Sam, I said stay there. Just . . . give me some space, OK?' She pulled her coat over her shoulders and untucked her hair from the collar. 'I'll speak to you tomorrow,' she said, sweeping past him, not stopping to kiss, barely even looking at him.

Chapter Thirty

The meeting room was empty. The telephone had been brought from its usual place on the stationery cabinet to the big round table, its cable a white meandering river on the carpet. Rebecca smiled to him and closed the door, leaving him alone.

'Hello, Sam?' A woman, young-sounding. 'This is Michelle from Human Solutions, your company's HR company? Rebecca asked me to give you a quick call about how things are going.'

'They're fine,' he said.

He tried to push away the image of Francis telling Sarah about the Phantasm.

'I guess you must know why Rebecca called me.'

'No.'

He thought he might have heard the silence of a secret line, another person listening in.

'Oh, well, your . . . activities . . . outside of work. And how they might be affecting your performance . . . inside of work.'

What did his activities outside work have to do with Michelle from Human Solutions?

'You know what I mean, I'm sure. Now, just to put your mind at rest, you're not in any sort of trouble so you don't have to worry about anything like that, OK?'

'OK.'

'It's just that the job you do is high-pressured—'
Really?
'—and Rebecca and your General Manager, Mr Okamatsu, are quite concerned about you, especially given your
recent work performance.'

He imagined Mr Okamatsu's reaction to being told Sam
was a superhero and closed his eyes tight, pinching the bridge
of his nose.

'Our advice is to send you on a two-day course to get to
the bottom of things.'

'What kind of course?'

'It's a residential anger management course—'

'What?'

'It's two days in a very calming setting and, just to make
this clear, there is absolutely no mention here of it being man-
datory. This isn't a suspension. But it is highly recommended
that you go. You can take the two days as annual leave. It
could theoretically be taken as sick leave but you'd need a
doctor's note, and I think we can all agree that's a little bit
too official.'

'I don't want to use my annual leave on a stupid course.'

'OK, Sam, there's no need to use that tone with me.'

'I'm not using a tone, I'm just saying that I don't need to go
on an anger management course. It's stupid.'

'Yes, but with respect, sometimes a person needs a guiding
hand.'

'It's just,' he said, careful to stay calm, 'I don't have much
annual leave left.'

'There's also the option of unpaid leave.'

'Are you serious?'

A pause. He imagined Michelle leaning over her desk.

'We think you would benefit enormously from the course,
and your company will foot the bill – that's how much they
value you as an employee. It'll do you the world of good.'

'I don't need help. Look, I know I've done stupid things,

OK? But I've got it under control. I'll just keep working. It'll be fine.'

The secret second line seemed to impart a pressure into the exchange. And that pressure, coupled with everything else, was crushing.

'Well, Sam,' said Michelle, her voice stronger now, 'obviously, because of your personal circumstances, there are lots of things to consider. And really, everyone just wants the best for you.'

A burning up inside. It was all so stupid, typical over-the-top HR corporate procedural bullshit because nobody was capable of acting like an adult any more. Why did people have to hide behind procedures, slip into business buzzwords to disguise what they were really doing? An anger management course was completely ridiculous. He simply never felt anger.

'So it's agreed, then? You'll attend the course in a couple of weeks and see how you feel, and if you need further help your company will be happy to provide it. You really are a valued member of staff. They wouldn't have gone to all this trouble if you weren't. Well, it's been nice talking with you, Sam, and I'm glad we've been able to hammer this out together.'

He placed the phone back in the cradle and wondered exactly what he was supposed to do next. Did everyone in the office know about this? They must think he was such an idiot. In that moment he was too shocked to feel the humiliation. He fired off a quick text to Sarah.

Hey. How you doing? Something funny just happened at work xx

Then he took the side exit from the room, trying not to think of her meeting up with Zac for coffee that afternoon, emerging into the dark corridor at the back of the building that led to the fire door one way and the warehouse the other. It was almost lunchtime, so he didn't bother going back into the office and instead went out through the roller doors to his car.

When he got back, Mr Okamatsu's gold Lexus was parked up – he was back from his business trip. There was a black crow sitting on top of the Lexus and this had to be a bad omen. He checked his phone – still no reply from Sarah. As Sam got out of his car into the freezing air his tender muscles seized and all his cuts started stinging again.

'Sam,' came a disembodied voice on the wind.

Sam looked around but there was nobody there. From where he was standing he could see right down the whole length of the building, where he spotted Mr Okamatsu peeping out, beckoning him. Tracking the side of the unit, exaggerating his limp, his feet crunched in the drainage gravel. This was going to be bad.

Without even mentioning the scab on his face, without saying anything about the superhero incident, Okamatsu led him in through the fire exit and back into the empty meeting room.

'Sit.'

He felt weak. Mr Okamatsu eased himself into the chair opposite. It felt like the end of a film where the two nemeses discuss things civilly before an inevitable final battle.

'I have spent many days on the road,' he said. 'I have visited all our customers.'

Sam couldn't see his eyes at all through the light-sensitive glasses, though he felt them keenly, coring a hole through him.

'They will pay half of all fees.'

It was hard to read Mr Okamatsu's tone. He'd managed to save thirty thousand pounds. Surely this was good.

'Thank you,' said Sam, bowing his head slightly. 'Half of all the fees is good,' he said, his voice quiet. It was, in fact, the amount of profit he generated for the company each month, despite what Rebecca said.

Then Mr Okamatsu said, 'Sam, you have failed.'

He said it calmly and it felt as if, were Sam to look down, he would see Mr Okamatsu's hand covered in blood, holding a knife he had just stabbed into his stomach.

'I made a mistake. I really am sorry.'

Okamatsu raised a silencing hand.

'No,' he said. 'Gross misconduct. You know gross misconduct?'

'I do.'

Was he about to be fired? What about the anger management course? Did Okamatsu even have any idea about the anger management course? Five years he'd been at the company, his whole working life, and now he was about to be sold down the river for thirty thousand pounds.

'But it was just one mistake,' Sam said, meekly. He remembered times at home now, Sunday nights when he'd lain in his maze of comics, times when he was drowning in the sixth layer of thought, and how the prospect of going to work, of being around people, of being *normal*, was a lone beacon on the horizon.

Mr Okamatsu removed his glasses and set them on the table, revealing how difficult this was, even for him.

'Sam. People like those in there have second chances.' He gestured towards the office where his useless colleagues worked. 'They need chances. You are different. You are a better person, a good worker. Like me. We work hard to keep other people OK, and we ask for nothing in return.' He turned the signet ring on his finger. 'But you doing this, not getting the forms signed, you are not like that any more. You have stopped being one of us. We have no room for another one of *them*.' And he nodded towards the office.

Sam closed his eyes. 'I don't want to stop working here,' he said, his voice catching.

'You will not stop working here.'

Sam looked up.

'On one condition. This is agreed now. You will come to Japan and apologise in person to Mr Takahashi, the President of the company.'

The words entered his head and rippled across his mind. He felt so many things, the accretion of shit from the last few days shunting into the back of him.

'The flights are booked. We leave Thursday evening. You don't come to work tomorrow and you must leave now.'

Sam thought he could feel himself shrinking in his chair. He knew it was impossible. He couldn't fly. Just the word made him shiver. Tears grew in his throat and he felt too stunned to speak.

'You must agree, Sam,' he heard Mr Okamatsu's voice. 'You must come with me to Japan. Or you can no longer work at Electronica Diablique.'

Sarah finally replied to the text he'd sent her after work saying good luck with Zac, and how sorry he was for everything.

Her reply simply said, *Come over to my place at 7.* There was still no kiss at the end but at least she hadn't asked to meet in a public place again.

He realised he was gripping the wheel too tight. A car overtook him out of nowhere and he almost swerved off the road. There was no way he was going to Japan. He'd simply get a new job.

He was going to be earlier than expected and the idea that he would get to Sarah's flat and walk in on her and Zac in bed just wouldn't go away. When he reached her place he parked up and looked at the window that led into the strange architectural space at the front of the house, but the lights were off.

He opened the door and listened out for voices but there were none. Climbing the stairs, he noticed an open cardboard box on the top step. When he looked inside he saw some of his clothes and DVDs and the book he was reading.

He stopped. Then he looked along the corridor at the closed door that led into the living room, a heavy feeling in his gut.

She was standing over the sink doing the dishes. The TV was off – the only sound that of splashing water. He closed the door in case she hadn't heard him come in, but she had, and she still didn't turn.

'Sarah,' he said.

'I left your things on the stairs.'

'Yeah. I saw those.'

'Because we're not going out any more.'

She placed a cup calmly on the draining board, still pointedly not looking at him. He didn't know what to do so he just stood there.

'You can leave your key on the table.' The silence between sentences had its own mass. 'You never did get that key cut for me, did you?' she said. 'You never did quite trust me.'

'What are you talking about?'

Now she did turn around, leaning with her back against the counter.

'I said to you. Yesterday. To tell me if there was anything else.'

'What are you talking about?'

'You've been spying on me.'

'I've been what?'

She shook her head and the calmness dropped for a split second before she regained it. 'You were looking on my Facebook. I know, Sam. Do you know how fucking *embarrassed* I am? Having to sit there with *him* laughing at *me* liking some shitty photo from fucking years ago, and me having to pretend that I knew what he was talking about, and then having to pretend it was true because even *that* was less embarrassing than telling him my psycho boyfriend – who, by the way, dresses up as a superhero – was snooping on my Facebook. I came here for a fresh start, to have a healthy life and try to be a good person. God, I should have stayed single. I knew I didn't want a boyfriend. I was happy before, the happiest I'd been in a long time.'

'Please don't say this.'

'Don't tell me what to do,' she snapped. Her glasses caught the light coming through the window and a sick feeling sludged in his stomach.

'I like being on my own. I don't need a boyfriend to be happy. I used to be a right whore, you know that? You know how many people I've slept with?'

'Stop,' he said.

'Over twenty.'

She set her jaw tight and stared at him for a reaction.

'Why are you telling me this?'

'I just want you to know that you're not special. You think we have something special but we don't.' He could see how she almost started crying at this, but she composed herself. 'I was getting so much better before I met you and now my head's fucked again.'

'I love you,' he said.

She turned to him then, with a look of disbelief on her face. For some stupid reason he thought those words might find a critical point in her armour and cleave it open but instead she just said, 'Did you really just say that?' She closed her eyes and said quietly, 'I can't handle this. I've *never* dreamed of you, you know that? Not once. You've never been in my dreams. Don't you think that says something?'

'I don't know what I was doing,' he said. 'There's no excuse.'

'It's too late, Sam. I thought you were this . . . amazing person.'

Glimpses of their few months together zoetroped in his mind.

'Please stop.'

'Oh God, Sam, don't be such a pussy.'

'I fucked up, OK?' It came out louder than he meant but

he wasn't breathing right. 'This is all new to me, you're right. And I haven't got a clue what I'm doing. Do you have any idea what it's like being me? How hard it is for me to even get out of bed in the morning? To put on clothes every day and go to work?' He didn't know why but he was angry with her, with the way she was speaking to him. 'It's agony. But you're right. I can't handle this, either.' He tried to calm his breathing because his voice was coming out so shakily.

'Well boo fucking hoo,' she said.

'I'm just agreeing with you.'

He took out his keys and unhooked Sarah's. 'Here.' He put it down on the table.

'And just so you know, seeing as all your experiences come from films, this isn't the point in the movie where we argue and get back together later, OK?'

That really hurt. 'I don't see my life as a movie,' he said. 'I just want to go back to how it was before – because, like you say, I'm not ready. This,' he pointed down at the floor, and his mouth hung open for a second, 'is killing me.'

She stared at him and he couldn't read her reaction.

'Well maybe you should have thought about all this before you lied.'

'It's not that easy, though, is it? You don't know what it's like being me.'

'Oh please.'

'You deny your family's existence, and there's me who lost mine. You have a choice, but that was taken away from me. I don't have that choice. You have no idea how lucky you are. How do you think it makes me feel to see the way you are with your family, and you won't even tell me why. I have to live with what happened to me every day. I lived, they died.'

Sarah stared at him.

He made his mouth into an O and exhaled.

'I get it now, and I do love you,' he said. 'But it's not enough, is it?'

A car rushed past outside. Why was he doing this? The coward, the Sam who wanted a simple life, smiled from some deep, dark place inside. He swallowed and said, unable to stop himself now, 'Just because I love you, it doesn't mean I can't be happier without you.'

Chapter Thirty-One

He couldn't remember the drive home. He peered into the living room, at the stillness and neatness, and a strange sensation of nausea crept up on him. The light was harsh and the house cold. He went through to the kitchen and leaned on the counter. Taking a glass from the cupboard, he poured himself some water and gulped it down.

'I miss you,' he said to the vision of his parents in his mind, fully aware of how crazy and stupid this was.

The out-of-control feeling was back. He regulated his breath and closed his eyes and counted to ten. Then he threw the glass as hard as he could against the wall. At the breakfast bar he untucked one of the tall stools and took it into the living room. He calmly turned it on its side, legs facing the wall, and smashed it through the screen of the TV with such force the glass spat back into his face.

He remembered seeing a documentary about people living close to Chernobyl and how, on the night it happened, they sensed what felt like tiny bits of sand being fired against their skin when, in fact, it was gamma radiation.

Sam stepped back into the middle of the living room and examined the stool, two-thirds suspended in mid-air, the other third through the screen and out the back. He didn't feel any better. Making his way back to the kitchen, he unlocked the side door into the garage and took from one of the metal racks a stack of folded-up cardboard boxes and the tape gun.

Ascending the ladder to the attic, he switched on the lights. He had grown to hate this place. He filled box after box without stopping, without hesitating, for three hours straight. Inside himself there was a staccato cascading. Before taping up the final box he noticed an eight-page preview comic of *Y: The Last Man*. In the hallway he took it out and flicked through it. In the same box he found a reprint of *The Death of Superman*. There were all the *Akira* books. There were lots of *Suicide Squad* comics, *Hellboy*, *Neonomicon*, *We3*, *From Hell*, *100 Bullets*. He loved these comics so much. They had done so much for him.

He taped up the final box and when he loaded it into his car he looked at all the boxes, filling the inside to the brim, but even so it didn't seem like much. His eyes and throat stung with hidden dust, and he opened the car window on his way.

When considering his chosen superpower he used to think if things were getting too hard he could blink and everyone in his field of vision would disappear. He would love that so much – to be alone, to go back to, if not a happy life, a life he could bear.

He felt perfectly calm as he arrived at the tip. He pulled up at the paper recycling area and started unloading the boxes, untaping them, tossing the contents over, quick as he could, throwing them jerkily, as if they were covered in disease.

He suddenly remembered exactly how good the first volume of *Y: The Last Man* was. What an awesome premise for a story: the death of every creature with a Y chromosome, apart from one man and his pet monkey. He'd read it in springtime, season-change weather, the sun higher in the sky. Now his breathing faltered again and the rain, falling in sheets, was freezing. His T-shirt provided little protection from it. He started opening the remaining boxes but couldn't remember which one it was in. It was dark and he was in the shadow of one of the huge metal containers. Pulling the tape back, he felt a certain degree of panic. He'd just keep that one. But he couldn't find it. He upended a box, then another, then another, the comics spilling all over the concrete. He kicked them aside but to no avail. What if he'd already thrown it over the top and into the container? He looked up. The container was red and blistered with rust.

'Just forget it,' he said aloud.

He tried to stay calm but his lip was shaking and he put his hands to his head and grabbed two clumps of hair and started pulling as hard as he could. His eyes were pinched so tight they hurt. He threw away the few strands that had come out of his scalp and from the corner of his eye caught them drifting up and away towards the orange light. He went down on his knees to find the comic, but it wasn't there, and then started punching the sides of his head, fighting back the tears, determined not to be pathetic and cry. He could feel the last vestiges of sanity slipping into the distance as he ran at the container, brought his fist up and smashed his knuckles into the side as hard as he could. He felt the bones crunch and the pain shoot up his arm. He lay down in the soaking mud for a second. It was dark and late and nobody was around so he stayed there.

At last he sat up, and threw what was left of his beloved comics over the lip of the container. In the last box he came to the first book of *Sandman*, the book that had pulled him back into the world that day in his neighbour's deserted garden. He tilted it towards the light and turned to the last story, about Death. How many nights had he gone to sleep with this book lying next to him? He watched it flutter upwards, a broken butterfly, and time seemed to slow with the image of the book coming open, the leaves flapping, the backlight of orange halogen. Then it was gone and the rain picked up.

Shivering in the car, he sat for a moment, soaked through. His chest was tight and it felt as if fingers were at his throat. The unnatural, prickly sweating and light-headedness. And then the feeling of impending death. His mind fell back, years crumbling as his memory accessed the coping mechanisms for panic attacks. He imagined a forest glade, bright sunlight, the cool shade under the eaves of the trees at the fringe.

But the Andromeda Galaxy was on a collision course with our own Milky Way, comets from the time the universe started hurtled across space in never-ending streams, the sun was going to burn out. Eventually the whole universe will tear itself apart.

He thought of the magical pond on the mountainside. And his mum and dad. What were people going to do when they recognised him on the street as the weirdo who dressed up as a superhero? What was he going to do now that he was a freak in the only place he felt safe – his hometown? What was he going to do without Sarah?

In the night he read every road sign under his breath twice, and blinked with a little nod as he passed every lamp post.

He pulled up outside the community centre, where his friends were camping out for a *Call of Duty* video game night, and ran to the front door, pushing through it with his shoulder. In the hallway blue light glowed through the square of reinforced glass set into the double doors. Inside, banks of screens stood on a fold-out table, computerised images of war, with steel frames draped with black netting and plastic vines like camouflage around the centre of the room. There was a table of supplies: chocolate bars and kettles and milk and bottles of Coke. In the centre of it all men in sleeping bags lay on their fronts on top of camping mats, ratcheted up on their elbows, their gaming controls held up before them. Sam sidled round, found Blotchy and stood in front of him.

'Hey!'

Botchy tried to crane his neck to see around Sam's form.

'Congratulations, you got what you wanted,' said Sam, leaning over him.

'You're not covering us,' someone shouted.

Blotchy's glasses caught the reflection of the screens and the rest of his face was in near darkness, but Sam felt his eyes behind the lenses.

'Don't ever speak to me again. You hated it that I was going to be happy, and now I'm not and I just came here to say I don't need you. I never needed you, and never speak to me again.'

Sam gave a final nod from his head down to the centre of his chest, and then he made for the door.

The night outside was even colder now. He started shaking uncontrollably. He couldn't remember ever being this angry. Something had snapped.

'Sam,' a voice called from behind.

Tango. Sam reached the car and got in, slamming the door.

'What's happened?'

Tango's voice was muffled through the glass. The anger growing and growing, Sam screeched back up the ramp that led to the road. There was a flash of light and the sounding of a deep horn, the screeching of brakes and tyres squealing as a lorry swerved across to the other side of the road. Sam put his foot down, his back end fish-tailing, his heart beating so hard it shook his bones, and tore off.

He imagined the scene, Blotchy laughing to himself, emailing the newspaper, telling them about Sam and his superhero alter ego. He accelerated up the streets, blowing dead leaves into vortices as he cut through the night.

He picked up the photo on the passenger seat, of his family, and glimpsed at it whenever he passed under a street light. *They'd want you to be happy*, people had said to him when it happened, but he couldn't be happy. That path was not open to Sam. He wished it would come to him, the memory of the day, like a hidden door sliding open, but he knew it never would. The day the picture was taken was lost in the synapses, data corrupted. The past was gone for ever.

Chapter Thirty-Two

The low dread returned immediately when he woke up. He'd finally fallen asleep at four in the morning and now it was half one in the afternoon.

Many years before, when he was fourteen or fifteen, he had fallen head over heels in love with a girl at school. It happened at the end of May, those pre-summer days when languid sunsets through moist air give a soft focus to the world. Hormones firing in such floods as to be almost overwhelming, he would sit on the riverbank tossing pebbles into the gentle water and think to himself, I will never forget this. This is the most important thing in the world. He saw adults walk the world and they were serious, distracted, tired-looking, and he thought to himself, I must never be like that. I must never forget the importance of true love.

And he hadn't forgotten it. But at last he understood why love must, in the end, fade away, how difficult it makes the business of living life. He knew now why the adults of his youth had appeared as they had. Love was too hard.

He was supposed to be meeting Mr Okamatsu in a couple of hours for the trip to Japan so he needed to get out of the house until that time had passed, just in case he showed up. He pictured the little café at the seaside, his perfect hiding spot. He got showered and changed and went out into the driveway, noticing subconsciously a gold Lexus parked opposite. Sam went to open his car door when the realisation of what was happening dawned. There was the sound of footsteps clicking on the driveway, a flock of birds flew out of the tree in his garden, and a strong hand pressed itself into Sam's shoulder.

'I have come to collect you, Sam,' he said.

In the cold air, the sound of a magpie cawing from a rooftop.

'I can't go.'

'The tickets are bought. You are coming to Japan with me.'

His light-sensitive glasses were half clear in the winter light.

'I have a family, Sam,' said Mr Okamatsu, firmly. 'I cannot lose my job because of you.'

Sam stared at him, the energy in his bones singing. A family.

From the drawer of his bedside table he took the fireproof security box where he kept his passport, and also removed the spare mobile phone, locking the box and double-checking it was secure. When he came back downstairs he found Mr Okamatsu staring into the living room, at the stool he'd smashed into the TV, but he said nothing.

His hand hurt like hell, his legs felt weak and cold sweat ran down his ribs as they drove to the airport. They didn't speak but Mr Okamatsu listened to his classical music compilation album, just as he always did on the business trips Sam had taken with him in the past.

He checked his phone for messages from Sarah, hoping that maybe something had changed, but nothing came and he knew he just had to accept it.

They got to Heathrow and checked in and were ushered through to the departure lounge and it was all dreamlike, the sci-fi sweeps of the steel, the mezzanines, the walls of screens and all the people criss-crossing the atriums, like a moving photograph. His mind felt blurry, fuzzy, not quite able to accept things. He followed Mr Okamatsu, who moved gracefully between the crowds with his small suitcase on wheels. Sam thought of all these people, their lives, their destinations, and this interchange where they amassed. He should have been to more places. *They'd want you to be happy.*

Huge plate-glass windows looked out on to the runway and here was the first time Sam saw the planes and reality returned. They were so massive. They were impossible and awful. The one nearest the window, the nose so close to the glass it was almost touching, had rust on it where the bolted-on panels met.

Mr Okamatsu took a seat on a bench and Sam joined him. He swore he could feel the temperature of his blood dropping and the chemicals inside it separating out. The low burn of fear. Mr Okamatsu had lied about the flight time because he guessed Sam would try to escape, but even so their gate was soon announced and Sam had no choice but to follow his boss. He never thought he would set foot in an airport again and the fact that he was in one now made no sense. Something didn't connect. Even thinking about Sarah didn't work. No matter how hard he tried to focus on anything, the thought slipped from his mind as the irrationality of his fear swelled, as the conjoined histories replayed in his mind, over and over.

On the one side he was in London, on the other he was in an airport in Brazil, his family tugging their luggage along, the twins hopping and jumping. The two moments overlapped – Sam and his impending flight, and what was about to happen to his family. He would arrive at the door of the plane and take his seat, just in the same way they had. He would roll across a strip of concrete and the physics of flight would bear him up into the air – the plane's angle shifting so that it was no longer in line with the angle of the earth but a curve upwards into the atmosphere – just as their plane had.

'I need to go to the toilet,' he said, his voice croaky.

He locked himself into a cubicle. He could hear his own breath, as if his ears had pressurised, and he remembered something. He remembered the day outside with Steve and Sally, the spring day with blue skies and cotton white clouds. *Well, isn't this a lovely day?* she'd said. And Steve there, a red balloon on the end of a stick brilliant against the blue of the sky, his voice slow and his eyes on fire. *Don't you wish it could stay like this for ever and ever?*

But that's not how things work. He'd lost Sarah, and his future was nowhere. The trauma around which he'd cobbled together what passed for a life spread through him like a virus.

In his pocket he felt the lump of his spare mobile phone that he'd kept all these years. He switched it on. The blue screen flashed to life. He'd used this phone so many times. Before he met Sarah he used it every day. Then it was every few days, then every week and then hardly at all. It could no longer make calls but he needed it now. He needed to check his voicemail.

His mother spoke first and she said, *Hey Sam*, extending the word *hey*: heeeey, *Sam, just checking in on you.*

In the background Steve and Sally were laughing and talking but Sam had never been able to decipher what they were saying.

Our flight to Manaus is delayed so we're just calling to see if you're OK. Hope you're having a good time in the Beacons – examining your mud.

His dad's voice called, *How's the mud studies going?!*

Sam imagined them huddled around their bags in the airport with the bluster and flux of all the people rushing to be rocketed across the planet, how happy they seemed, and how this made Sam happy because they were happy there, right at the end.

The call was just as long as it was, less than a minute.

They'd been in the airport and just made a quick call to check in. To say goodbye. *Bye, honey, speak to you soon, be good*, she said. *Bye Sam*, he heard Steve shout, *Bye Sam*, called his dad, then Sally, then it became a game, and in his mind's eye each time they shouted *Bye Sam* an image of whoever shouted it appeared in his vision, each overlaying the last: his mum, Steve, Sally, his dad, Steve, Sally, his mum; *Bye Sam. Bye Sam. Bye Sam.*

He saw them, burning up, a tide of fire washing across them.

The phone was held in his left hand by his side, clutched tight, and the sound beyond of an aeroplane taking off put a frost in his blood. The sound rushed and filled, penetrating deep into his core, a sound so loud it might shake him apart, then it was cut to nothing by the door swinging and a voice.

'Sam,' it said. 'It is time to go.'

He placed the palms of his hands calmly down on each arm-rest and pushed his head back into the seat. He took a deep breath. The sound of things ramping up, the quick shudders across the structure, the sight of the enormous wing and the huge cone of the engine. How things might have been different if he'd answered that phone and spoken to them one last time.

Mr Okamatsu, sitting next to him, leaned across and did something Sam did not expect. He put his hand on his fore-arm and said, 'It's going to be OK. This is normal.'

Sam turned, but Mr Okamatsu's face was staring straight ahead.

He saw his signet ring, with the carved lizard motif.

This was happening. He was on-board and though his mouth was dry, and his fingers were digging into the arm-rests, he was, at least, on-board. He closed his eyes a moment and felt the acceleration. He'd forgotten the power of the thrust and the moment when you hold your breath, the way the world floats away beneath you, the horizon shifting as you turn, and suddenly the view from above the clouds is beautiful, dreamlike, like something special that was forgotten at some unknown moment in our history, that day we let go of the rocket tree.

Chapter Thirty-Three

Fields rolled and gave to winter woods, then flat marshlands with wide expanses of water; pylons marched back to the horizon. Sometimes the train passed along the side of highways standing on tall concrete pillars, and towns and villages on hillsides, until the Earth spun away and in the darkness orange and white lights suggested lives out there in the black.

Sam had never experienced jet lag. He'd dozed in and out of sleep on the plane and now didn't feel tired at all. The lights in the countryside became brighter as the train bore them towards Tokyo. The city was massive, stretching far, far back as the train carved its route between a hotchpotch of architecture, sixties-looking buildings with balconies stuck on here and there, buildings put up between other buildings, wide roads and thin, jagged alleyways. Sam jumped as another train passing in the opposite direction slammed past and he got a real sense of how fast they were going.

They arrived in Shibuya Station and collected their things.

'We will catch another train to our hotel but first I want to show you something,' said Mr Okamatsu.

They made their way through the throngs and Mr Okamatsu spoke over his shoulder.

'Tokyo is too busy for me. Too many people.'

Sam watched the lights flicker on the lenses of Mr Okamatsu's glasses. He led Sam out of the station on to a big plaza that he recognised from films, the Shibuya crossing, the idea of Tokyo most people carry in their heads, with the bright lights, the swarms of people, the mysterious, other-worldly glyphs on the signs, the banks of brilliant screens set into the side of buildings.

'All this,' said Mr Okamatsu, turning and leaning on the pull-out handle of his suitcase, 'is only part of Japan.'

He went over to a circular slab of concrete stuck on to the edge of the plaza, surrounded by low bushes and trees. In the centre of it was a bronze statue of a dog on top of a stone plinth. The sound of the city was deafening and Sam had to lean in to hear Mr Okamatsu.

'This is Hachikō.'

The dog was resting on its hind legs and was big, bear-like. One of its ears flopped forward.

'Hachikō's owner lived near this station. When he came home each day on the train, Hachikō would wait for him. One day his owner did not return. He had died in work. Hachikō arrived on time but his owner was not there. The next day the same. Hachikō came back every day, at the exact time the train was due, but his owner was never there. But he still came back. Every day. For nine years.'

Sam looked up at the statue of the dog and felt his throat go heavy.

'He was very loyal. He was . . . a good friend,' said Mr Okamatsu.

Wide awake in the middle of the night, Sam dived into the empty swimming pool of the hotel. As a child he would swim down to the bottom and touch his chest to the floor, kicking his legs, seeing how far he could make it without surfacing for air.

The next morning, Mr Okamatsu knocked on his door. They were both wearing suits and, though he looked smart, Sam felt absolutely terrible. He was sick with tiredness and his hand throbbed with dull pain. Outside their hotel they walked with their suitcases along a busy four-lane expressway until Mr Okamatsu took them down a quiet alleyway, a secret cut-through lined with thick-trunked, winter-bare trees that leaned over like crooked old men.

Sam looked out between the gaps of the trees at the quiet backstreets. He was struck by the telephone wires and electrical lines that criss-crossed the sky at every angle. There was a gentleness in the air; even with the bustle of the city, there was a calmness beneath it that Sam, in his state of fatigue, was able to synch with.

They came out, at last, on to another wide road with tall buildings either side. The Electronica Diablique HQ was near the big Sony building in Shinagawa and when they reached the atrium – a wide space with tiles shined to a high gloss and potted trees standing sentinel, each equidistant from the next – Mr Okamatsu turned to Sam.

'OK, we go in now. You remember what to say?'

'*Ohayou gozaimasu*,' said Sam, pronouncing each syllable slowly. It was a Japanese greeting.

Okamatsu nodded his approval.

Sam then bowed just a little and said, '*Oh-aye dic-tish-te ko-ee dis*.'

'Very good.'

Mr Okamatsu inspected Sam, and Sam detected the nervousness in the big man.

'Sam,' he said. 'Do not mention the air shipping costs at all.'

Over at the desk a woman in a smart red suit answered a telephone.

Okamatsu stepped towards Sam and said conspiratorially, 'You are here to meet Mr Takahashi. Nothing else. For all the good work you have done.'

Sam didn't understand.

'Come,' said Okamatsu, moving across to the lifts.

They were ushered into the President's office and a short, stocky man stood up from behind a huge maple desk, the grand panorama of Tokyo stretching out behind him as far as the horizon.

'Ah,' said the President, sidling round to greet them.

His face was impressively ugly, seemingly wider than it was long, and like it was made of granite. He came over to Sam, and Sam only just remembered to recite his lines.

'Yes, yes,' said Mr Takahashi, shaking Sam's hand warmly and smiling. 'I hope you don't mind if I speak English,' he said, perfectly. 'I don't get to use it much these days. When did you fly in?'

'Today,' said Sam. 'No, yesterday, sorry.'

Mr Okamatsu said a long sentence in Japanese and Mr Takahashi nodded and said, 'Ah,' several times.

'Sam,' he said, 'come and look at this.'

He took him to the side of the room where a big display cabinet stood. Inside was a collection of gleaming electrical components. Mr Takahashi took a key from his pocket, unlocked the glass doors and removed, from the lowermost shelf, a samurai sword. There was a steadiness in his every movement, an assured dignity that countered his ugliness and made him appealing.

'You know what this is?' He drew the sword from its sheath with a metallic hiss.

Sam said he did not.

'This sword belonged to Mr Yoshimoto, the founder of this company. He made it himself in his smelting shop, many hundreds of years ago. And with all the developments of the world, it is still here. In this room.'

The blade reflected silver light across Mr Takahashi's cheeks.

'It is a great treasure. Sometimes, when I am feeling a little . . . glum, I will take out this sword and hold it and remember that everything passes.'

Sam nodded.

'Mr Okamatsu tells me you are an excellent employee, a true asset to our company.'

Sam glanced across to Mr Okamatsu, who was staring out the window at the building opposite.

Was he hallucinating all this? Mr Takahashi opened one of the drawers in the cabinet, removed a black lacquer box, and presented it in both hands to Sam. Sam stared at it, then up at Takahashi, who was grinning at him expectantly. Sam remembered the etiquette, bowed and took the box.

'We do not give these to many people,' said Mr Takahashi.

Sam opened the box. Inside, on a bed of silk, was a perfect, miniaturised replica of Mr Yoshimoto's katana. Sam blinked his heavy eyelids and removed the tiny sword from the box. He took it out of its scabbard and the steel was so shiny it hurt his tired eyes.

'You open letters with it,' said Takahashi, lowering his head into Sam's eyeline and nodding.

Sam inserted the little katana back into its sheath and closed the box. Nothing seemed real.

'It's wonderful,' he said.

He noticed Okamatsu and Takahashi exchange curt nods and the sunshine of realisation blew away the fog.

Nothing was as it seemed. They weren't, as Mr Okamatsu had told Mr Takahashi, going to one of their Chinese plants after the visit to HQ.

Instead, they took a train out to the suburbs, where Mr Okamatsu wanted Sam to meet his family. As the train bumped over the tracks, Sam fell asleep and was woken up by his boss when they reached their stop. It was much quieter here. They wheeled their suitcases up and down some narrow, hilly streets, past houses with all sorts of strange protrusions. The gardens were neatly kept, with evergreen bushes manicured into orbs and curlicues. The thick telephone wires were like scribbles on the grey sky.

Okamatsu's house was set back off the long, deserted street, at the summit of several steep, heavily vegetated terraces, only the windows of the top floor and the curved tile roof were visible. The stone steps were lined with long grasses that shimmered like spirits in the low breeze. The house was wide, with a low, generous wooden porch area; lanterns hanging from the eaves of the roof. Large plated windows looked out over the terraces to the prefecture below. It reminded Sam of a giant toad lying in wait.

A woman came out on to the porch and waved. She was tall and thin and neat, with short, black hair combed into a side parting and a small, pointed nose. Mr Okamatsu nodded to her and kissed her on the cheek, an unshowy display of affection. He said something in Japanese and she nodded and turned to Sam, and when she smiled her efficient face lit up.

'This is my wife, Miho,' said Mr Okamatsu.

Miho curtsied and nodded. Sam smiled and bowed.

The house was clinically clean, which instantly put Sam at ease. He was shown into a dining room, a plain space with black wooden plank flooring, a simple table and chairs, and some fresh flowers in a vase standing in a stone alcove, giving the room a burst of colour. Sam could see the kitchen next door, with the smell of spices and the heat of pans boiling. There was some thumping from upstairs and two children came running down. They were young – younger than ten – a boy and a girl. They threw their arms around Mr Okamatsu, and Sam watched his shoulders relax and, just discernible through the light-sensitive glasses, his eyes close in a serenity that sent a shudder through Sam.

After getting cleaned up they sat at the table and Miho brought out the dishes: a bowl of sticky white rice, a steaming bowl of vegetables, some miso soup and a plate of shredded pickled ginger. The food was simple but delicious. Nobody spoke English, apart from Mr Okamatsu, and when they tried to include Sam in the conversation it was to explain to him how to pronounce the names of certain foods, and the kids loved it when he got it wrong. The family chatted quickly and loudly in Japanese and Sam didn't have a clue what they were saying, though it didn't matter. This was the first family meal he'd been involved in for a long time, the unguarded nature of the unit. He should have felt like an interloper, joining Mr Okamatsu on his first visit home in almost a year, but they didn't allow him to.

After dinner they went out to the garden at the back of the house. It was a large space, a fortunate accident of how the other houses built around it were positioned. A tall wooden fence hemmed the garden, with bamboo trees and cherry blossoms, and a small wooden teahouse on the left-hand side. A stream meandered over round pebbles, with two little red bridges for crossing over and crossing back. Stone lanterns led the way around a path and they walked together, Mr Okamatsu with his hands behind his back.

'Be careful you don't slip,' he said. 'We design the path to be bumpy.'

'Why?'

'Because you need to look down all the time. Then, when you look up, the garden has changed and you are looking at a new scene.' He nodded at a patch of white sand, raked neatly, with a few sharp rocks sticking up. 'It is the world. The sand is the oceans and the rocks are the land.'

Part of the path was moss with stepping stones embedded in it. At one point they came to a stone washbasin that had started freezing over. It was distractingly beautiful. Islands of shrubs were dotted here and there and it was hard to comprehend how lonely Mr Okamatsu must feel, stuck in his flat in the UK.

'Mr Okamatsu, what's happening with the air invoices?'

'It is nobody's fault,' he said. 'They pay half, we pay half. This is fair, no? The cost always has to land somewhere.'

'I'm sorry for what I did.'

'I am sorry too. For being angry.'

And that was that. They crossed the second red bridge that led back up towards the house and they sat on the porch, heated by lamps and blankets, drinking warm sake that Miho had brought out.

'You see that?' said Mr Okamatsu, pointing at a tall stone lantern inscribed down the side with some Japanese characters:

物
の
哀
れ

'It says *mono no aware*. Have you heard this?'

'No,' said Sam.

'We have it in Japan. In Britain you have it, but you don't have a word for it. We worship the cherry blossom here. It is beautiful, but it is sad too. The cherry blossom will not last, and that is what makes it even more beautiful. Do you understand?'

Sam felt numb. 'Everything is transient,' he said to himself.

'Everything must pass.' Mr Okamatsu took a drink of sake and they sat in silence for a moment before Mr Okamatsu said, 'Sam, you have many problems.'

The lights in the lanterns flickered, and Sam said nothing.

'I know about your family, Sam. And I know about the superhero.'

The trees ached in the breeze, and in that moment Sam felt himself open up.

'Is that why you brought me here?'

'You needed to fly, Sam. I knew you would not come unless you thought it was for me. But you need to understand. Everything must pass.'

'I know,' he said.

The red lights on the wing of a passing aeroplane blinked in the distance.

'My father died when I was fifteen. It made me very sad. But I am older than you and I can tell you something you maybe don't know. Your family are still there.' He spoke so kindly – modulating up and down, as he did when talking in detail about a set of technical drawings. 'They are in your heart always. When someone dies you must change. But it is not bad. You change and you grow around that death. Later on, it becomes not sad. It makes you stronger, not weaker.'

Sam dried the corner of his eyes with the sleeve of his coat.

'You are a good man, yes?' Mr Okamatsu's eyes remained steadfast on the garden. 'And it is like the dog, Hachikō. People will always help good people. My father used to say something to me, about people. He used to say, if you look closely, you can see the magic.' He finished his cup of sake and poured himself another. 'You must accept help. It is how you heal.' And after that he said nothing more on the matter.

They sat and drank in silence for a long time and over the course of those moments Sam's emotions flattened, and he started to move past something.

His bedroom was simple and sparse.

He lay down and pulled the cotton sheets over him. He did not need to put on the radio to block out his thoughts, for he had none.

As soon as his head hit the thin pillow, he slept the sleep of ages.

Chapter Thirty-Four

The stool through the middle of his TV had slumped in the few days he'd been away. Shards of glass in the carpet in front of it glowed in the blue twilight. He turned on all the lights. He'd tracked mud right through the house, and it was all over his sheets upstairs. He called a professional carpet cleaner and felt much better with the thought of his carpet being restored to near show-house standard. He pulled the stool out of the TV and put it back under the breakfast bar. He washed his sheets and pillow cases, and returned to the tip, where he deposited his TV, and then went to Tesco to buy a new one. The vivid brightness of the store was a balm for his soul. The sight of all those TVs, of how much happiness they would bring to so many families, made him feel joyous. In the cavernous store he told himself feeling joyous in Tesco was something he had to move away from now.

On his way home he stopped off at his favourite chip shop and bought a chicken and mushroom pie and chips with gravy and a can of Coke, which he ate silently in the kitchen.

This wasn't so bad. He could live like this quite happily for ever.

It was when he was setting up his new TV that he heard voices and footsteps coming up the driveway and a knock at the door. For a moment he thought about ignoring it, but then something spurred him to answer; the will to be normal.

As he opened the door, Blotchy raised his hand.

'Just listen,' he said.

Standing next to him, Tango said, 'Where the hell have you been?'

'Japan.'

They stared at him.

'Bloody hell,' said Tango, putting his hands on his hips and shaking his head dramatically. 'We saw the stool through the TV and . . .'

'I've been on a business trip to Japan,' he said.

Blotchy was being very quiet, and Sam deliberately didn't look at him.

'Well, you're back now,' said Tango. 'And you're coming with us.'

'I can't, I'm busy.'

'Quasar.' Tango opened his eyes wide and stared into Sam's soul.

'I'm not going to Quas—'

'No!' Tango reached forward and curled his fingers around Sam's wrist. 'Quasar.'

Down a dark corridor Sam raised his laser gun. Futuristic neon lights flashing on and off illuminated the shoulder of somebody crouching behind a barrier. He moved towards the target in the same way FBI swat teams do it on TV, side on, legs crossing legs. His back vibrated, and he swung around as a little kid punched the air and scampered into the darkness.

'Dammit,' he said, dropping his gun at his side.

'Sam.'

It was a hushed call. He turned and saw Blotchy and Tango hiding in an alcove.

'Get over here.'

All three of them were bunched tight.

'Tell him,' said Tango.

'Sam,' he said. 'I don't know why you went crazy on me in the community centre.'

'Can we not talk about this now?'

A noxious plume of smoke billowed out from a pump and they all held their breath and closed their eyes.

'I want you to know that I didn't tell anybody about your superhero thing. I know I'm a bit of a prick but I wouldn't do that.'

'Well how else would they know?'

Blotchy's face was all different colours in the dark.

'No idea.'

Sam spotted the little kid again, open and unaware that he was being watched. Sam's laser gun was active again after being hit and he raised it up and fired off a laser beam. It found its mark and the little kid fell to his knees, as if he'd actually been shot, bowing his head.

'Nice shot, Sam,' said Tango, patting his shoulder enthusiastically.

'Cheers.'

'But listen,' said Blotchy. 'Now I don't want you to get mad. That's why we've come to Quasar. I've been to see Sarah.'

'You what?'

'We didn't know where you were, and I didn't know you'd split up. Though I guessed you had. I was trying to help.'

Sam shook his head and thought.

'What did she say?'

'Well here's the thing. There was this guy outside her flat shouting all kinds of shit. She was there, and opened the window and told him to piss off.'

'Was he Scottish?'

'Probably, I don't know.'

'What happened?'

'Eventually, he went away.'

Blotchy took a knee and Sam joined him, leaving Tango to defend.

'I went to visit her after he left, to check she was OK.'

Blotchy half smiled. It wasn't like him to be brave or concerned.

'She was fine, a little shaken up. She said you and her had broken up. I'm sorry, man.' He put a manly hand on Sam's shoulder, which felt forced and weird. 'But she also said you were still friends.'

His heart sprang up.

'I just wanted you to know. So that you didn't think I was going behind your back. I promise you though, on my mum's life, I didn't tell anyone about the Phantasm.'

'Guys,' said Tango. 'We can make a break. Don't think. Just follow.'

He barged past them and ran down the corridor. A man in his forties turned to them but it was too late. Tango had zapped him. The three of them charged past, Blotchy's footsteps incredibly loud as they ascended a wooden ramp painted black, swung round a corner between black netting, where they dived behind a low barrier. The opposition's base was in sight. There were two guards, well protected by a waist-high wall.

Blotchy grabbed Tango's arm.

'Fucking brilliant work, Tango.'

They fist-pumped.

'Sam, listen,' said Blotchy. He put his hand on his shoulder, and this time it felt natural. And Tango put his arm around him too.

'I know you don't see our friendship in the same way but, to us, it's very special.' Blotchy's face shifted colours with the lights. 'We're going to be better at being there, just like you're always there for us.'

Somewhere off in the distance they heard a skirmish.

'We never thought you'd take the leap you've taken but you did it, and it's awesome that you did. We know what it took. So. Friends?'

Nothing happened for a second. The lights stopped flashing and the sounds died down.

He did take the leap. He had done all those wonderful things with her. His eyes flicked between Tango and Blotchy in the stillness. Everything they'd been through zipped across his mind.

If you look closely, Mr Okamatsu had said, *you can see the magic.*

He smiled, his friends staring back at him, their heads close together, and gave a quick nod.

'Friends,' he said.

'Now let's stop being a bunch of fannies. This is a war situation,' said Tango, bouncing on his hams, readying himself. 'Let's do this!'

And he leapt up, the others following, and they charged for the base. The two sentinels were caught off guard. They raised their guns but it was too late. Blotchy, Tango and Sam were firing wildly at them, whooping with joy as the vests of their enemies lit up like Christmas trees.

ⓟ

The Phantasm #013

Bait and Switch

A misty night in a bad part of town. Candles in the apartment window flicker but to him they appear as half-formed suns in the gathering dust of a new galaxy, for tonight there is a thick mist.

Perfect.

When cars roll past their headlights are like the beams of a lighthouse. He waits. Been a busy few days. A deep cleansing has taken place and the horizon stretches out before him, a glorious new day. Except it is night-time.

Acceptance is the final turn of the key. Some find it easier to achieve than others. Some people need a helping hand. A hand of justice.

The target emerges from the dark maw of the block and goes out into the misty night.

Once upon a time a girl got herself mixed up with a bad person. One day she managed to escape but the bad person came after her. Fortunately, a black gladiator was on hand and one misty night he sent the bad person back to the dark lands in the north from whence he came. Scotland.

Like a phantom he glides through the atoms of the universe in pursuit. He knows these roads now like the back of his hand. But the target has switched it up. He's not using the alleyway to deal his poisons any longer. There's a canal now. One of the street lamps is out, and in the mist it is near blackness – the ultimate environment for dark dealings. Three steps lead down to the path alongside the murky waters, and the target descends, as if into the Underworld.

Nerves? Yes. Fear? Some. But fear is there for one reason: to be overcome.

He jumps down all three steps and lands like a cat on the path.

'Citizen!'

The target doesn't jump with shock as our hero hoped. Instead he stops, pins his ears back, and turns slowly. Not so the other figure, who is young and panics at the prospect of authority. He makes quick his escape down the canal path in the opposite direction. Hope you don't fall off the track and into the canal, the crusader for justice calls in his mind, his eyes narrowing. Though you have already strayed far from the path of righteousness.

The champion growls, 'I have a file of photographic evidence, which clearly shows you selling drugs.'

The target is just a figure.

'And you have just come from prison for the exact same offence. But let us on this night broker a deal. Leave town. Leave this place.'

'I know it's you, Sam,' says the target. 'Who do you think told the papers about you?'

The words stun the Phantasm. His mind falters. At the beginning of the sentence this man was just another hood. At the end of it he has changed. Anger burns through the vigilante like hot quicksilver. The hood is now an arch nemesis, and the anger is laced with panic.

'You're not as good as you think you are, wee man.'

They both stand, feet planted, ten yards from each other.

'You think I don't know when someone's following me? You think I've nae been doing this for years? I knew you were there, and I followed you home. And then I told the papers so that she'd dump you.' The figure shrugs. 'You'd do the same. Look what you're doing now.'

'I'm doing this for her, not me. We're over. I can accept it. Why can't you? Just leave her alone. She doesn't need me in her life and she definitely doesn't need you.'

'You're out of your depth, man. You don't tell me where I can and can't live. How fucking dare you? And just remember, you send any photos anywhere, I know where you live. And I know where she lives. I don't want anything bad to happen but if you think I'm nae gonna defend myself you're tripping.'

The waters of the canal ripple. So this is how kryptonite feels. He needs to regroup and think. Quick as a flash he takes a smoke bomb from his utility belt.

'Hark my words,' he says, sensing the sudden lack of power in his voice.

The dark figure of the target remains perfectly still.

The smoke rises from the path and when it clears, the nemesis will find nothing but fresh air.

Chapter Thirty-Five

Only when the mask came off did the fear flood in. But it was fear for Sarah. How could he have been so stupid? So naive. He thought of school and the old sensation of being powerless. Why did he bother doing anything? He simply wasn't strong enough for the world – in a true, physical sense – not big enough to make a mark.

He got showered and thought about getting some extra security latches for his front and back doors. Anger was creeping into him again, about the newspapers. How was it fair that someone who dealt drugs, which ruined people's lives, had the right to ruin Sam's? Because that's what he'd done.

Letting the water rush over his head and down his face, he realised at last the consequences of never again being anonymous in the one place he loved. Whenever he went to the café for his breakfasts or the pub for his lunches, or out with his friends, or to his favourite takeaways, or when he went out running, or when he went to the shops. And it was all because of Zac.

And Sam didn't even have any photos. He'd been bluffing. After a crisis of conscience he'd deleted them from his camera, and there was no way of getting them back. He looked out the bedroom window into his back garden. The street light in the alleyway behind his house was blurred by the mist. He wished he hadn't thrown out his comics. He wished he could climb up into the attic and curl up and go to sleep.

'You're being pathetic,' he said aloud.

In the garden the fluffy ginger cat and his smaller black-and-white friend had got over the fence, and had been joined by a second black-and-white one. They were all staring at him.

The text from Sarah came through mid-morning the next day, asking if she could come over. It was Saturday and the mist from the night before hadn't lifted. Sam sat in his living room, watching the news, with the phone held limply in his hand. Lifting it up, he replied that of course she could come over.

He ran upstairs and got ready. His heart pumped hard, partly with excitement, partly with fear. Thinking back on those words about how he would be happier without her, he hated the cruelty of them, and that he'd said them, when she had done nothing wrong.

She looked exhausted when she arrived. There were bags under her eyes and her shoulders were slumped; she didn't look well.

'Come in,' he said. 'I've got the kettle on.'

They went through to the kitchen and it was Sarah who spoke first.

'Did you go to see him?'

Sam put the bottle of milk down.

'Yes, but—'

'Dressed as the superhero?'

'Yes.'

'Sam.' The exasperation in her voice made him feel like a stupid child.

'Listen,' he said. 'He's bad news, Sarah. I've accepted what's happened between us and I'm fine with it, but Zac is going to wreck your life.'

'You don't get it.'

'You know it was him who told the papers I'm the . . . the thing I do.'

Her eyes flicked up to him.

'He's not a good person, Sarah. And he's dealing again.'

'He's changed,' she said. 'This person who's come here . . . it's not him. It's a different person. He's meaner.'

'He's off his face on drugs all the time. This is what happens in the end.'

She started crying, standing there in the middle of the kitchen. Her shoulders lost their tension and she stood there, head lowered, her chest heaving.

He didn't know what to do. He didn't know if it was OK to give her a hug. Then he went to her and put his arms around her whole body.

'Hey, hey, come on,' he said. 'Everything's going to be fine.'

'It's not.'

'Yeah, it is. We'll make it OK.'

He felt her shake her head.

'What is it?' he said.

'He's going to ruin my life.'

'We'll talk to him. I'll talk to him.'

'You can't.' She waited. 'He's got a video.'

The words snagged, and Sam realised he'd held his breath.

'What do you mean?'

Her voice drifted up quietly.

'There's so much you don't know about me that I should have told you.'

His arms still around her, the embrace became lax. The kettle boiled and there was a click as it switched itself off. Slowly the pieces in the puzzle moved into place.

'Sarah, tell me what's happened.'

He held her close to stop her shaking but she peeled away and sat at the kitchen table.

'My family, we've always been dysfunctional. When I was

in school I couldn't wait to move out and get away. And when I met Zac, I thought . . . things seemed so much better.'

She put her head in her hands.

'I was such an idiot. I was high for so long I couldn't see what was happening. I can't believe . . . how badly . . . I've fucked up,' she said. 'Things had been bad for a while, like he didn't care about anything, and one night we were . . . together, and he had his phone . . .'

His heart broke for what she was saying.

'I hate myself because I let him do it. I was so high, it just happened . . . and in the morning . . . it made me feel so disgusting. I told him to delete it but he was just laughing at me and I flipped out and I just . . . left.'

She broke off, the weight of the words making her stop. She was trembling.

'My parents hated Zac and I always stuck up for him. God, I was so stupid. I couldn't call them. I'd spent years telling them I didn't need them, and by the end they never called me and so, you know, and Zac never came after me. After all that time we'd been together and he didn't even try calling me. He just . . . didn't care and all of my friends were his friends really, and then . . .'

'What?' said Sam. 'It's okay. You can tell me.'

Sarah didn't look at him. Her shouders rounded in resignation. He heard her take a breath.

'I had no money and nowhere to go . . . I ended up on the streets.'

Sam took a seat next to her.

'You were homeless?'

'You think there's support but there's not. There's nothing.'

Sam suddenly remembered the day he'd first met Sarah, when he'd bought a meal for Gloria. Something clicked into place.

'What happened?'

'Kabe happened. I knew him, sort of. But he found me,

and he and Kristen took me in. Got me back on my feet, helped me get out of Edinburgh. And now Zac's back I feel . . .' her voice shook, 'like I'm back at square one.' She took a huge breath. 'He keeps telling me he still loves me and can't live without me, and then he always brings it back round to the video and if I don't . . . he'll . . . I'm a terrible person, I guess I deserve this.'

He was too stunned to think straight.

'This is why you agreed to meet with him,' he said. He thought of Zac's flat, the candlelight flickering on the walls through the window, the man sitting behind that wall. 'Sarah, this is blackmail,' he said. 'I mean, what sort of person lets . . .' He stopped.

She cried some more and Sam shifted his chair across to her and put his arms around her again until she was exhausted.

'Come on,' he said. 'Let's make the tea.'

And they did, in silence, Sam sliding the cups over to her when it was time for the milk to go in. He tried to block out the images that were spiralling into his head, of her, being put through that, and the person Sarah must have been then. They took their cups and went through to the conservatory, away from the world.

'Do your parents know about any of this?' he said.

Sarah shook her head. Her eyes were red, she was all cried out, but Sam was glad she was here, that the house was warm and she could feel safe.

'You really can't call them?'

She shook her head.

'I really thought I was out the other end. When I met you.' She hadn't looked at him the whole time but now she lifted her head and met his eyes. 'You're such an amazing person. You have no idea how *good* you are.'

There was silence as these words held.

'You're a good person,' he said. He watched the tiny nuances on her face, small defensive things; a near-imperceptible narrowing of the eyelids, a tightening of the flesh over her cheeks as she closed her mouth, a nervous swallow. 'I hate that you think you're not. You've been so good to me.'

'Because I love you,' she said, without thinking.

All the air was sucked out for a second.

'My dad used to say to me, people don't change, they only change the way they act.'

'That's cool,' she said.

'So you must've always been a good person. We all do stupid things. Look at me . . . But we're going to sort this out, you know that? All of it.'

'He's going to post the video on my Facebook,' she said.

'He won't do that,' he said, knowing that Zac would do exactly that. 'He can't blackmail you. You can just delete your Facebook. He can't ruin your life.'

Sarah looked over the top of her cup at him, the steam rising between them.

Sam tried to smile, but through the ache he found it hard.

'Do you want to stay with me today? We can do something.'

She shook her head.

'I can't. I've taken an extra shift at the library. It'll take my mind off things I guess.' Her energy had flatlined. 'I'd better go,' she said, setting her tea down. 'I'm gonna be late otherwise.'

'Can I call you later? And you know, if you want to stay over here, to get away . . . the spare room's made up.'

She smiled with a heartbreaking sadness and stood up. Hooking her bag over her shoulder, she made for the hallway. Sam sat there for a second, his mind churning. Then he stood up too.

'Sarah,' he said.

She stopped in the doorway.

'About what I said, in your flat.' He made a decision. 'I lied. I can't be happier without you. You've turned me inside out with how amazing you are.'

The silence in the room had its own gravity.

'You *are* a good person. And you should know this.'

She turned to him. He had to tell her.

'Whatever happens, you've made me want to live again.'

It was misty enough to go out without being spotted. Everything felt unreal. He passed the video shop he'd worked in as a kid, and which had closed down years ago.

Having Zac ruin his life was one thing, but what he was doing to Sarah was so much worse. He tried to imagine the circumstances in which he'd got her to do what she did. It just wasn't Sarah. He had deliberately turned her into that person with his poison over however many years. What kind of man would even want to film someone he was supposed to care about doing that? And then let her just end up on the streets. It was so much information that it seemed almost impossible, like it could never have happened.

As ever, when he was in trouble, he gravitated towards the old housing estate. He turned off the main street and went down the hill until he came at last, inevitably, to his parents' house. In the mist churned a deep nostalgia for the old days, when the world was still wonderful.

He walked for a long time around the estate, down the intersecting alleys he'd cycled as a nine-year-old, around the square patches of communal lawn. On one of the lawns there were three mature chestnut trees. Back in the day, this had all been farmland and between two of the farmhouses had been a tree-lined carriageway. These chestnuts were the remnants of that path, a straight line with the smallest of holloways running alongside – you could see it if you looked closely; the dent of history never really goes away, the past never completely disappears.

What would the Sam of his childhood have made of this Sam now? What would his parents think of him? Constantly hiding behind the force field of his childhood memories. He looked up into the canopy of one of the old chestnut trees and watched an orange leaf snap from a branch and spin away. He knew exactly what they'd think.

But there was a solution to this. He needed to get the phone that had the video on it. Then she could get on with her life.

All he needed was the courage.

ⓟ

The Phantasm #014

Candles in the Dark

Only in darkness can a hero be born. What happens when good men do nothing? The world burns. He pulls the armour down over his chest, the gloves over his hands, the elbow guards, straps on his pack and utility belt. In the mirror he pulls on the mask and descends through the house.

Strip lights flicker and hum. It gleams. The Black Phantom, his trusty steed, gleams in the sterile white lights. Engines fire, gas is revved, remote-control garage door button is depressed. And he is out, away, into the night.

Nothing matters any more. He knows that he is going to do this and runs through the plan once more in his mind. A knock on the door. If there's a peephole, stand to one side. When the door is opened he will mace the target in the eyes with the UK-legal pepperspray alternative he bought from eBay. It's a tough line, but if he doesn't hit hard he will get hit back and the plan will fail. Act on the agent. He doesn't care. This hood has pushed too far, and at this point the well of mercy has dried up. Mace in the eyes so he's disabled, then call the number. When the phone rings, grab it, make quick his getaway, delete every file from Google Photos, cancel account, remove SIM card, smash phone and SIM card into pieces with hammer, burn phone and SIM card separately. Simple enough. He will reimburse money for the phone at a later date, when the waters have settled – he is not a criminal.

Lights out, he rolls to a silent stop and peers up at the apartment window, on the top floor of the block. The familiar flicker of candlelight. Can't be safe for someone like him to own so many candles. He pictures him, the target, beyond the wall. Soon the hero will be in there, doing right – and be damned with the consequences. He cares not. In the mask he is invincible. He is immortal.

Out the car. He jogs to the building, light and nimble on his feet as he navigates the splashes of light from the street lamps. Into the cavernous maw and on to the urine-stench stairs. He trots lightly, his physical fitness supreme. It is as if gravity does not exist for the first few floors. The next few floors and it's trickier. By the time he reaches the eighth, the top, he is breathless.

A quick toke on his asthma pump.

There is one final flight of steps that leads up to a rooftop fire exit, where he can regain his breath in secret. He ascends these steps, disappearing into the shadows, and lets himself out into the night and on to a surprisingly pretty community garden, with benches and potted plants and garden gnomes and, out of place, a stone statue of a deer. He briefly considers the oxygen mask in his pack. No.

Overhead, the stars shine bright – the mist has gone.

His door is the penultimate one on the corridor. Two weak lights illuminate the dingy passageway, one of which flickers and hums. Slowly he pads down the length of the corridor, making no sound. And then he is at the door. He stands there a moment, and looses the mace from his utility belt. In his other hand is a smoke bomb, just in case.

Beyond the door he hears voices. A fracas. Zac's voice, deep and indecipherable. And then a second voice. But this one he recognises. It is shot through with anger. He pauses and a million thoughts crash through his mind. It is her. His shoulders slump, and he leans his brow against the wooden door. Slowly, his hand reaches up. It is time. Finally, he knows it is time. He takes his mask in his fist and, without hesitating for a second, pulls it off his face.

Chapter Thirty-Six

Hold steady your course, his father used to say. Every breath was hard. He was so scared of what he was doing. Doing as himself. But through it all he saw his fist rise up in front of him and thump the door.

The arguing stopped.

'Sarah? It's Sam.'

There were a few seconds of silence and then he heard Zac's voice.

'Do not touch that fucking door. I'm serious.'

It swung open.

Tiny droplets of moisture had formed on the lower half of the inside of her glasses where she'd been crying. Her face changed when she saw him standing there in his costume, with his mask off. He stepped inside and pushed the door shut behind him. There were five thick slide locks screwed into the jamb and he thought, imagine living like this.

'Oh fucking hell, here he is,' said Zac, a smirk spreading across his face, 'come to save the world. Will you fucking take a look at yourself?'

The wind outside was getting up and rattled the windows. They were single-glazed in aluminium frames and some air crept through and blew the candle flames sideways for a second.

'Look at the state of him, Sar. Have you seriously fucked him?' he scoffed.

'He's ten times the man you are,' she snapped, wiping the smile off his face.

Zac shook his head violently, like a dog pulling meat off a bone, and Sam realised he was high as a kite.

'Zac, it's over,' said Sam. 'Give her the phone and leave her alone.'

As Zac bobbed from foot to foot, danger flooded the air. Sam glanced across to Sarah.

'You shouldn't have come,' she whispered.

'I had to.'

Zac skipped across the room and Sam hated himself for flinching. But Zac went straight past him and pulled the door open.

'I'm going to tell you once. Get out.'

'I can't,' Sam mouthed, but the words were lost somewhere in his throat.

Zac shook his head in dismay. His pupils were huge.

'You're a stubborn little fucker eh.'

'What's the fuck's the matter with you?' Her voice was shrill. They both turned to her, her fists clenched at her side.

'I'm moving on, Zac. I'm not that person any more.'

Sam turned slowly back to Zac, who was propping himself up on the door handle.

'Don't say this,' he said. 'I love you.'

'You've ruined my life. You want me to come back to you? And you threaten me with some stupid mistake I made. Don't you get it? I hate you, Zac.'

He came back into the room, pacing like an animal in a zoo, holding his head, and Sam didn't know what to do. He'd never been in a situation anywhere near as volatile as this. Part of him just wanted to go but that part of him, the coward, was shrinking.

'You can do the right thing,' he said.

Zac's head snapped up to him, his puffy eyes wild.

He rushed Sam before he could react, raised his fist, and slammed it with so much force into the side of Sam's face that he felt his own cheekbone give. All sensation dropped from his legs and he stumbled backwards, some far-off realisation that he was falling, back out into the hallway, the sound of a scream, and then nothing.

When he came to, the door was shut. The pain in his head was extraordinary, not like anything he'd ever felt, both sharp and numb at the same time. He still had his mask in his hands. He banged the door with the flat of his bad fist. Pain shot up his arm.

'Sam, go,' he heard Sarah call.

But how could he? He went for his Phantfone to call the police and closed his eyes in dismay when he remembered it had smashed when he jumped off the truck. He put his hands over his eyes and pain lightning-bolted across his face. He remembered how powerless and small he was, how powerless he'd felt all his life, in school, in work, at all times.

He'd never stood up for himself. And even when he had, he still failed.

The wind was strong down on the street, litter blowing along in front of a row of graffitied shop shutters.

He went to the boot of his car and fetched his own phone to call the police when he noticed people gathering in small groups. They were animated by something. It seemed like slow motion as he realised they were pointing upwards, towards the tower block.

His mind stopped, just for a second, reaching, calculating. The air fell out of his body and he was completely weightless.

Zac's window. His mind somersaulted The building was on fire.

Chapter Thirty-Seven

The people gathered in their groups turned away from the fire and towards Sam, in his costume, and slowly directed their phones away from the blaze and on to him, on to the costume.

One of them had called 999 and was giving the address.

He flew up the stairs, rounding the last corner, shoulder into the wall, and on to the top floor. Smoke was coming out from under Zac's door and he could hardly see. People were banging on the door. Sam pushed past them and they stared at him.

There were two little kids in pyjamas, a boy and a girl.

'Get everyone out,' he said to the father. 'I've got this.'

'Dad, is that the Phantasm?' he heard the boy whisper.

'Come on,' their mother said, and she put her hand on Sam's shoulder.

He looked down at the hand, a tattoo just showing under her sleeve, of a green lizard with a red stripe running up its back. And then she was gone.

He slammed the door with his fists.

'Zac!' he shouted. Discordance in his voice.

He pounded again but nothing happened. Taking a step back, he thrust his weight into the heavy door but it didn't budge. The deadbolts. He used his legs to kick off the wall opposite, throwing everything he could into it, but the door didn't give an inch.

His mind tripped, refusing to accept it. This couldn't be happening. It wasn't possible. This wasn't possible.

The devil is a code that runs through us all.

He pounded on the door. 'Zac! Don't do this. Please.'

God, how long had they been in there? The panic leaked everywhere inside him. He barged the door, again and again, but nothing happened, and nothing would happen. His brain wasn't working right. He thought he was going to collapse.

'Sarah!'

His voice split. He kicked the door hard with the sole of his boot but it didn't even shake. Every second lost was a nightmare. Oh God, he was too late. It was happening all over again. He put his back to the door, slid down to the ground and closed his eyes. His mind swirled with chaos, he was losing control as the passageway filled with more smoke.

There had to be something.

Then, through the darkness, he remembered something he'd been told once. Not by his father this time, but by his mother. He saw her, saw her sitting at the table in the back garden in the sun. She was smiling: *You can do anything you want, Sam, anything at all.*

Eyes open. He pulled on his mask.

More people were coming up the stairs but it wasn't the fire crew, it was more neighbours in their pyjamas with their phones. He pushed past them, telling them to get out, and leapt up the steps to the fire exit. He shouldered through the door and across the little garden to the edge of the building, where he looked over the neck-high wall at the orange glow coming from the window.

There was a heavy wooden bench that he dragged over.

'Help me,' he called to the people who'd followed him up.

Two tall youths came to him, pushing the bench across the gravel and at right-angles to the wall. Sam took his length of rope from his pack and tied two knots, one to the leg and one to the armrest. He tried the rope. It held.

A weird sense drove him on; the chaos you feel when the edge of a cliff calls you closer. He thought: what if I'd never played that song on the jukebox? His mother's favourite song, her final gift.

He hopped on to the bench again and looked over the wall, checking distances. It was a long way down to the people with their phones tilted up at the burning building. He wrapped the other end of the rope around his gloves, praying the length was right. This had to work. He could have done nothing for his family; it was just an accident. This was different.

He felt electric, invincible, so much more than a frightened man; like he really could do anything. The wind whipped and made the sky a madness. He took a deep breath and checked his grip, his fingers tapping the rope. He thought of Sarah. He stood on the far end of the bench.

'Mate, you should wait for the firemen,' he heard someone say.

'Nah, go for it, mate, you legend,' the other youth said.

The costume would protect him. He thought of Sarah again and briefly closed his eyes.

Images of his life flashed before him, just like they say they do, images as on a deck of cards being fanned, a new image on each card. His office desk with the bonsai tree, Sally sitting at a small table in his bedroom as he revised for exams, the swimming pool next door with the brilliant-blue sky, the climb up to his old Batcave, Sarah drinking Guinness reading her book, Sarah sleeping on her back with her face turned towards him, Sarah's face when they'd been running to get out of the rain and the way her glasses were dappled with rain-drops, his friends sitting in the fire glow of the pub, Mr Okamatsu sitting on his porch with his Japanese garden before him, his mum and dad at the kitchen table checking bills, sitting there talking, Steve and Sally lying on a blanket on the living-room floor just after they'd been born, Sarah eating salad, Sarah reading a book, watching TV, dancing, singing, smiling, and then, finally, his mum and dad at the edge of the magical pool on the side of the mountain, standing there in the sunbeam. All of this happened in a nanosecond.

When he opened his eyes he could see for miles. Far away on the horizon a thundercloud wall was moving in, deep grey and so charged you could almost see the electricity dance. A crack of blue lightning cut down through the sky and the wind whipped.

The future can be as good as the past.

All sound fell away, the audience of his life held their breath . . .

Be brave.

Sam ran for the wall, along the length of the bench, and launched himself over the edge, head first, horizontal, flying. He opened his eyes and saw the ground hundreds of feet below him, tiny matchstick men, people in stasis. Gravity reached out and brought him down, he braced for the rope jolt, and when it came he felt the muscles tear in his arms and across his chest, and pain flashed from his hand across his body, but he held on. His trajectory was torn from its vector and he was heading now back to the building, swinging in, feet first, towards the direct centre of the single-glazed shitty window of the high-rise. He hit it hard, turned his face away and closed his eyes as the window gave. His body kept going, sliding through the shattered glass, the pads and guards of his costume and mask taking the brunt.

And then, he was in.

Landing hard on his hip, he took in the room with a sense of despair as a tongue of flame flew out the smashed window above him.

The flat was thick with smoke, which followed the fire out the window. There was fire everywhere. The heat was crazy.

There were two bodies lying on the floor, Zac in the centre of the room, face down, and then Sarah, his Sarah, slumped against the wall near the radiator. Alone. There was a shudder in his heart. Her head lolled to one side, her glasses halfway down her nose. The shock of sadness amplified inside him. He was on his feet and over to her, by her side, sliding on his knees, resting her head on his shoulder. He tried to stir her but she was already gone.

'No, no, no, no, no, no, no, no.'

A craziness in his mind almost made him sit next to her so they could drift away together but his other half told him about the oxygen mask in his pack. He tried it on himself, taking two plentiful breaths.

He sat Sarah up and put the mask over her.

The heat was immense but there was a clear path to the door between the flames. He was across the room before he knew it, stopping at Zac and fishing the phone out of his pocket, then sliding the locks across, opening the door. The flames, galvanised by the new oxygen, whooshed across the open space.

'Get him out,' he called to the people outside the door, pointing at Zac.

There were now flames between him and Sarah but he ran through them, covering his face. There was the taste of blood in his mouth and when he put his hand to his face it came away red. He put her jaw into the palm of his hand.

'Come back,' he said.

But she couldn't hear him. She was dead. Everyone was dead again.

He hugged her tight and he started to cry, no numbness, no protection, he started to cry. Great waves flowed out of him and he felt his body grow light, and then he stopped and breathed and watched the movement in the room, the flames dancing, something wonderful in the way they moved, the way the curtains being blown by the wind were like rainbows of thick magma.

Without effort he picked her up and powered through the wall of fire that he was sure he felt move aside as he passed, and he went out into the passageway just as the fire crew pushed past him, and he took her up to the little roof garden, where he laid her on the gravel.

'You have to come back.' He spoke low, almost inaudibly, his voice thick with tears. 'Please,' he said, into her ear. 'Come back.'

The world was motion and force. CPR. He needed to do CPR. All the faces of the people stared at him with so much sorrow, he thought he would melt. And then he watched their faces change, and felt the stirring in his arms.

Look at Sarah, said a higher Sam.

And Sarah was looking back at him. His chest fell into his gut and he pulled her so tight he thought he might snap her.

She pulled the oxygen mask off her face. He felt her shake and there were tears in her eyes when she saw him. He helped her up and somebody wrapped a blanket around her. Then, just hard enough to make itself known, there was a little quake in his heart.

She was alive. At last he could see it now, the arrow of the future. Others still encircled them on the little rooftop garden and her warmth flowed right through him.

Every past was once a future.

He held her tight, as the world went crazy all around them.

Whatever Happened to the Dark Defender?

He lies in wait. It is not night but a bright day in late August, the kind of long summer day that seems like it'll never end. Being out in daylight is alien, but needs must. He watches the back garden from the bushes. There is not a hint of breeze and in the costume he is stifling. A paddling pool is in the centre of a messy lawn, a tricycle is turned sideways. The patio doors at the back of the house are open, and yet the place appears deserted.

It is time to move.

Slowly, he emerges from the bushes. Over to the patio doors. A kitchen lies beyond. Not as neat as he'd like to see, but kitchens become this way when true life is being lived. His ears prick up. There is a rustling in the hallway. Quiet voices chatter, a flash of movement. Immediately he gives chase. His costume, honed over many years, is light and mobility is easy.

Out in the hallway he sees a trailing leg disappear into the living room. But he knows the layout of this house. Next to the kitchen, through a set of double doors, is a dining room. The house is a loop and he can cut them off coming the other way.

It all happens so fast.

'Baaaa!' he shouts.

The evil twins scream, turn, and run the other way. No need to give chase. Notorious trouble-makers, the twins, but not the brightest. He waits behind the double doors and, soon enough, they run in. And just as they do, he pounces, tackling them both to the ground.

'Got you!'

They scream and thrash but it is no good. They cannot escape his superhuman strength. Because they are only four.

'Get off, Dad!' calls the boy, though he is laughing.

'This is no laughing matter. I'm taking you both to jail.'

'No!' the girl squeals. 'Please, Phantasm.'

'Jail. For first-degree ice cream theft.'

'But you gave us the ice cream.'

'The law says you may not eat ice cream until after your dinner.'

'It's not fair,' they say in unison, something that happens a lot.

'I was testing you. And you failed.'

They all stop. The sound of a car pulling into the driveway.

'Let's hide and jump out on her!'

It is a great plan from the boy.

'Let's hide in the garden and throw her in the pool,' says the girl.

Funny. These kids are funny. His pride swells. The key is in the latch. The paddling pool idea will have to wait. They all scurry into the living room and each twin grabs one of their father's legs, and he can feel their body warmth. The front door opens and in the mirror at the end of the hallway he watches her come into the house, carrying a shopping bag in one hand, pushing her glasses up her nose with the other. Her hair falls across her face and she blows it away.

He calls her his sidekick. But she says it's the other way round.

She sees him in the mirror and stops. He puts his finger to

his lips, and she smiles. When she does this, the door swings wider and a thick sunbeam falls across her; he feels it burn hard into his memory and, for some reason, today, thoughts of the intervening years stream through his mind in one mass, the good times and the bad, the tough and the not so tough, all the peaks and troughs a life through the world must take, the highs and lows and ebbs and flows. He loves so much the way her skin crinkles at the corner of her eyes when she smiles now, each crease a disappointment, every line a joy. Slowly she moves down the hallway.

He's patrolling tonight but it's his turn to cook. Sausage, beans and chips. The kids love it (and so does he). She'll tell him about her day, he'll tell her about his. Mr Okamatsu is over from Japan and he's coming to the twins' fifth birthday party on Saturday. Probably Denny was late for his shift at the library today, she'll say, meaning Sarah had to go on lunch late again. As she tells him this, there will be a moment, just a small moment, when her words fall away and he will see her for all that she is, this incredible force of life that puts an excitement in him every day, because he is lucky, in a way, gifted a unique perspective where he is able to perceive how good life is. Then the moment will fall away again, her words will come back in, and she'll tell him to be careful tonight and come home safe.

The Phantasm looks down at the twins, who look back up at him. He holds up three fingers.

A countdown.

Three.

He folds down one finger.

Two.

They stifle laughter, and it's like a friendly ghost passing through him when he sees their faces illuminated like this. A little quake of the heart. It is such a beautiful day today.

One . . .

Acknowledgements

Thanks so much to everyone at Wildfire for your extraordinary help: Alex Clarke, Ella Gordon, Nathaniel Alcaraz-Stapleton, Jason Bartholomew, Shan Morley Jones, Siobhan Hooper for the beautiful cover, Mary Chamberlain, and everyone else involved with the production of this book. And especially to my truly superb editor, Kate Stephenson; I quite literally couldn't have done this without you. Thanks for being so talented.

Thanks to my early readers: Ian Worgan, Richard Jones, Chyrelle Anstee, Margaret Pearce. Thanks to Nick Bush for all your help. And thanks as ever to my wonderful parents, my two brothers, one sister-in-law and three nephews. And to my sister, Anna: the bravest person I know, and my hero.

Thank you to my agent and friend, Laura Morris. I don't need to tell you how much you mean to me but I will anyway: a lot!

Finally, and most importantly, thank you to Amy, the love of my life.

If you enjoyed reading

The
Unlikely ✈
Heroics
of Sam
Holloway

read on for some great discussion
questions and topics . . .

Reading Group Questions

What were your first impressions of the Phantasm? What were your first impressions of Sam?

In what ways does Sam deal with confrontation (both as Sam, and as the Phantasm)? How has this changed throughout his life?

The first line of the book is, 'Only in darkness can a hero be born.' Without the trauma in Sam's past, do you think he still would have become The Phantasm?

Sam has a lot of people in his life who care for him, but it's not until Sarah appears that he begins to heal. Do you think that Sam would have eventually moved past his trauma without Sarah, or would he have stayed the same forever?

Sarah, too, has dealt with hardship in her life. What do you think it is that draws her to someone like Sam?

In many ways, it could be said that Sam is quite childlike. Do you agree? Why, or why not?